I0748436

The Mystic Awakening

The Beginning of Prince Alexander's Journey

By
Johnny O. Hillmon Jr.

"The Mystic Awakening: The Beginning of Prince Alexander's Journey"

ISBN: 978-0-9834152-1-3

I'd like to thank all my family and friends for supporting me and for being fans of the story before it was even published. I couldn't have done it without all of your motivation!

Look me up on DeviantArt: johnnychaosz.deviantart.com

Episode 1
Prominence Town Squabble

My name is Alexander, the first and only son to be born to the Valsoria royal family. Our family rules over Central Kingdom from the capital city, Valsoria. Throughout most of my life, Valsoria and its citizens have enjoyed a tranquil life with only minor conflicts, but that all changed about a week ago. Recently, a group calling themselves Organization Shadow Crystal has surfaced throughout our territory, and the lands of other nearby nations and have been performing suspicious and dangerous activity involving elemental crystals of our world. At first I thought their threat was minimal because they initially came across as a low tier terrorist group, but one night I had a terrible nightmare that involved a dark shadow trying to take control of six powerful elemental crystals known as Soul Crystals. When I scared myself awake, I was sweating as if I had broken a fever. The family heirloom that I wore around my neck, known as the Twilight Star, was pulsating with light as fast as my heart was beating. If it hadn't been for that, I would have shrugged it off as nothing more than a bad dream. My grandmother told me stories about the Twilight Star being able to send its carrier a message through his or her dreams. I had experienced a small glimpse of its power a few years ago, but I was skeptical of the story until now. My mind was running wild after that nightmare, and it was difficult getting back to sleep. I thought back to years ago when my mother first allowed me to wear the Twilight Star. I have no affinity of my own, yet my grandmother insisted I was able to connect with it just like my mother and grandfather, and she was right. I finally drifted back to sleep for the rest of the night.

After what felt like one of the longest nights of my life, I woke up just as the black night sky was beginning to fade into dark shades of blue. I didn't waste any time as I got myself dressed. With a sword strapped to my side and a cloak over my body to help conceal my identity, I quietly retrieved my horse from his stable and rode out through the south gate. I topped a hill just as the sun became much more visible on the eastern horizon. My home was still in view as I took one last look at it. I didn't have any idea of how long I would be gone, but I knew I would be back someday. I set out for the Soul Crystal closest to my kingdom; the Phoenix Soul Crystal. According to what I've been taught, the Phoenix Soul Crystal resides in the Phoenix Volcano which is located near a small town just outside of Central Kingdom's territory. Stories also tell that the Phoenix Soul Crystal is what keeps the volcano dormant. It's said that if the crystal were to ever be removed from the volcano, it would return to life and bring forth a catastrophic eruption. I didn't know how true the story was, but I didn't want to take any chances. It was about noon when I stopped near a brook to let my horse rest while I sat under a tree and ate some energy rations that I had brought with me.

"What will I do once I get there?" I said to myself.

My hand gripped the Twilight Star under my cloak as if I were being urged by it to continue on. Before I knew it, I had fallen asleep under the tree for about an hour. I was awoken when my horse gave me a nudge with his nose.

"Huh?" I was momentarily confused when I found myself waking up.

He gave me another nudge as if he was urging me to get up and continue onward.

"Ready to go my friend?" I asked him as I brushed the bridge of his nose.

I grew a little nervous the farther I rode. While I was expecting to encounter something at the Phoenix Volcano, part of me was hoping that it would turn out to be nothing. As we neared my destination, the volcano was in clear view in the distance. My first stop before making it to the volcano was the town at its base known as Prominence Town. To avoid attracting attention to myself, I thought it would be best for me to make the rest of the trip on foot. I decided to send my horse back to Central Kingdom with a note attached to his saddle that explained why I left. Hopefully everyone would understand and it wouldn't cause a stir. A few hours later, I made it to Prominence town without incident. It's a pretty small, but well build village for its size. None of the streets were paved with stone, which gave me the impression that there wasn't much here. I didn't know much about where anything was in this town, but it didn't take long for me to come across some action. I soon came across a small crowd of guys and girl around my age who were watching two of their friends spar in the dirt road.

"I gotcha this time Vikki!" the boy with mahogany spiky hair stood with his guard up.

He seemed confident that he would win his duel with the dark red headed girl he was up against. Perhaps he was a bit too confident. I didn't realize it, but in the midst of their duel, he caught sight of me and was momentarily distracted.

"You're wide open V.J!" Vikki landed a jump kick to his chest that knocked him into a collection of trash cans.

"Wow," I thought to myself, "That was amazing!"

"Well V.J., you almost had me, but it looks like I'm still the best in town!" she ran her fingers through her hair, and then helped him out of the garbage.

"Damn Vikki, can't we have a do-over or something?" he got up complaining, "Some new guy showed up and distracted me!"

"New guy?" she smiled with suspicion in her eyes, "Yeah right. What new guy?"

"That guy over there!" he pointed at me, "Who the hell are you?!"

I quickly grew nervous as I suddenly became the center of attention. I did my best to keep a calm look upon me as I held my cloak to conceal my identity. The last thing I wanted to do at this point was to reveal my identity to a group of strangers who suddenly were looking hostile towards me.

"H-hi, uh, don't mind me. I was just passing through-" I said nervously as I began to back away.

As I stepped back, a long part of my cloak was caught under my boot. I tried to recover my balance, but gravity took control and caused me to fall backwards onto my back.

"Ow. That was embarrassing," I brushed the dirt off my clothing which made me realize that much of my royal attire was in full view from my cloak slipping off, "Oh no…"

"Check out those clothes!" I heard one of the guys say.

"He's got a sword too!" another girl said.

"Wait a minute!" Vikki got a good look at me, "You're a blue blood, aren't you?!"

"Blue blood?" I stood up, "Well…I am from royalty if that's what you're asking, but-"

“Looks like we got another blue blood to tangle with!” I heard a guy shout as they all surrounded me.

“First that Cornelius guy and now this?!” shouted another.

“Cornelius was here?” I tried asking, but no one was listening.

“It doesn’t matter,” V.J. cracked his knuckles before charging me, “We'll run you out of town all the same!”

“Wait! Stop!” I shouted to stop him, but he was determined to fight.

I parried a fast right jab from him and gave him a left punch to the stomach in the same place Vikki struck him earlier. I finished with a hard right uppercut that sent him stumbling back into the same collection of garbage cans that he fell in before.

“Woah! He just threw Vincent aside!” one of the other female fighters shouted.

“You’ll pay for that!” some of them shouted, “Rush him!”

Before I knew it, I was in a street brawl with seven other fighters, excluding Vikki. Despite being outnumbered, there was no reason to draw my sword as they were unarmed. Its not like they were intimidated by it anyway. The largest of them was the easiest to get by. I merely dived at him with a rolling trip which caused him to fall on top of a fighter that was coming at me from behind. The other five were a little harder to take down. As I ducked some punches, I immediately had to jump over sweeping kicks. As I landed, I managed to grapple a punch and knock a fighter to the ground. I sidestepped two others coming at me, so I used their momentum against them by grabbing their heads and slamming them against each other which knocked them both out. I stopped the remaining two by punching the both in the stomach. Somehow I managed to beat them all until they were lying on the ground in pain.

“Can we please not fight?” I was slightly out of breath, “I'm not here to cause any trouble.”

“I don’t know what’s more impressive,” Vikki eyed me with her arms crossed, “That you were able to fight them all off, or the fact that you can fight at all.”

“What’s that suppose to mean?” I replied, “That’s a harsh assumption. Why wouldn’t I know how to fight?”

“Well…because blue bloods always have someone fighting for them like that Cornelius guy did,” Vikki replied, “At the very least, I expected you to try something cheap like using your sword against us.”

“I don’t know why he was down here,” I said, “But I’m nothing like him. Comparing the two of us is like comparing oil and water.”

“Is that right?” Vikki raised her eye brow in suspicion, “Then why are YOU here?”

“I’m here to look out for suspicious activity,” I said, “The Phoenix Soul Crystal may be in danger.”

“What?” she sounded almost as if she didn’t believe me, “The Phoenix Soul Crystal is what keeps the volcano here dormant. Why would it be in danger?”

“It’s a long story but it might be a target of-”

“Hey Vikki!” I was cut off by the voice of another girl calling from down the road.

Her hair was long and an unusual sky blue color that made me believe I was seeing things at first. As she got closer, it turned out to be her real hair color that matched her eyes perfectly.

"Sup, Selena?" Vikki asked her.

"I just came looking for Vincent to tell him that supper is ready. Um…where is he?" Selena looked around.

"I'm right here sis," he stumbled out of the garbage.

"What happened to you? Vikki did you throw him in the trash again?" she turned to Vikki.

"I did earlier. He's only in there now because his ass just got handed to him by, get this, a blue blood!" she started laughing.

"Ew, did that Cornelius come back?" Selena asked.

"Nonononono" Vikki corrected her, "We've got a new blue blood in town," she turned to me.

"Selena is it?" I asked for her attention.

"Yeah?" she turned and got a look at me, "Oh wow," she thought to herself.

"Sorry about throwing your brother into the garbage," I apologized to Selena, "He kinda attacked me, and so I ended up throwing him."

"Um, ok..." Selena raised an eyebrow at me, "You're apologizing?"

"Now I think I've seen everything," Vikki said.

"Since my cover is blown, I may as well introduce myself," I bowed to both of them, "My name is Alexander Valsoria, prince of Valsoria and Central Kingdom. I'm sorry I had to rough up your friends."

"Well…ah, forget about it," Vikki said, "We're use to a little squabble."

"I say it's a trick!" Vincent said once he got all the garbage off of him, "He's only pretending to be nice so he can catch us off guard later!"

“Like he caught you off guard when you bull rushed him?” Vikki asked.

“Ooooh, you got told!” one of the other street fighters said to Vincent.

“Shut up! You got beat too!” Vincent yelled at him.

“I’m not the one that fell into the trash twice,” he laughed.

“It's nice to meet you all,” I said to bring the attention back to me for a moment, “But I better get going on my way,” the sudden growl from my stomach froze me in my tracks.

"Wow, your stomach is almost as loud as V.J.'s before dinner," Vikki said to me.

“I was so focused on my thoughts that I forgot that I haven’t had anything to eat since this afternoon,” I smacked my forehead, “I should’ve packed more rations. There wouldn’t happen to be an inn here where I could get some food and possibly stay for the night, would there?”

“Nah, sorry,” Vikki said, “This town doesn’t get enough people coming through it to need one.”

“Well that’s unfortunate…” I scratched my head.

“Heh,” Vincent laughed, “Sucks to be you now, eh?”

“Do you want to come with me and Vincent for dinner?” Selena asked, “Even with the size of our family, we always seem to have leftovers afterwards.”

“What the hell Selena?!” Vincent almost flew into a rage, “Don’t invite him to our house!”

“Come on Vincent! Be nice!” Selena yelled at him.

“But he's a blue blood!” Vincent protested.

“Oh suck it up!” Vikki suddenly yelled in a way that caught me off guard.

“Well I suppose I could,” my stomach suddenly assured me that I would take Selena on her invitation.

“You're invited too Vikki! We've got plenty,” Selena said to her.

“Awesome! I love your mom’s cooking!” Vikki said.

“I don’t believe this!” Vincent turned his head in anger.

Vincent, who realized he was outnumbered in the decision, remained silent but still had the look of disapproval on his face. I let out a sigh of relief that all hostility was gone for now. The rest of the kids had dispersed, probably to their own homes for supper, and I would soon have my stomach full before continuing on to Phoenix Volcano.

Episode 2
Organization Shadow Crystal Appears

Joining Selena and Vincent for dinner was the best idea I had all day, although I was a little nervous to show up completely unannounced. Their father, the local blacksmith, and their mother, a craftswoman, were very friendly people once I had the chance to introduce myself. One taste of her food told me that she was also a great cook. Aside from Vincent and Selena, they have 5 other kids; three boys and two girls who were all younger than them. Vincent remained silent throughout all of supper as if silently protesting my very presence. Much of the talk at the table consisted of questions from the younger children about me and what life is like for me.

"What's it like ordering people around all day??" asked the 3rd youngest boy who looked like an eight year old Vincent.

"Whas woyal food like Awex?" asked the youngest girl who looked about three.

"You gots it easy don't ya?" asked the youngest boy who was about five.

"How big is your castle?" asked eleven year old girl almost immediately.

"Well I…I don't-" I was getting a bit overwhelmed.

"One at a time kids," their mother stepped in.

"Whew. Thank you ma'am," I took a breath before answering everything "Well I don't just order people around. I'm mostly out helping people," I said to the mini-Vincent before turning to the three year old girl, "The food I have isn't that much different from what regular people eat, but if you don't get out a lot, you don't get to try a lot of different things," then I turned to the youngest boy, "And being a prince isn't easy like some people say it is. There are rules, rules, and just when you think you're in the clear, there are more rules and formal customs thrown in your face. You're lucky if the only thing you have to do well is keep your room clean," I patted him on the shoulder.

Their dad let out a hearty laugh, "See son? Don't I tell you that all the time?" His youngest son was too embarrassed to look me or his father in the eye.

Then I turned to the eleven year old to tell her about my castle, "And my castle is so huge I actually got lost inside it a few times when I was younger."

"How do you get lost in your own home?" Selena asked.

"There are more rooms and hallways than we sometimes know what to do with," I answered, "Some rooms are only used for royal gathering and other events. Some are fun, but others are kind of boring."

"I'm done," Vincent suddenly stood up and left the room, "Thanks for dinner mom."

"Vincent?" his mom sounded concerned.

"…did I say something wrong?" I asked.

"No…" Vikki put her hand on my shoulder, "I'll go talk to him."

The rest of us continued to hold a conversation after Vincent and Vikki left the house. Vincent was in the back yard leaning against the house in a sulking matter when Vikki found him.

"I can't believe they're all buying his act in there," Vincent said.

"Maybe it's not an act," Vikki replied.

"Oh don't tell me you trust this guy too," Vincent couldn't believe Vikki's simple comment.

"Don't get carried away. I'm not saying I trust him," she defended herself, "I'm just saying that he hasn't really done anything wrong."

"You're not the one that got showed up in front of everyone," Vincent reminded her.

"That was your fault," Vikki stiffed a laugh, "And it was kinda funny."

"No it ain't!" Vincent snapped back, "That was just plain embarrassing."

"Aw, you don't get mad when I show you up in front of everyone," Vikki teased him.

"That's different," Vincent defended himself, "I respect you as a fighter. He's just a blueblood, and yet he fights almost as hard as-"

"One of us?" Vikki cut him off.

"Well I wasn't going to say that, but…I dunno, I'm not buying his cool act," He said, "He claims the Phoenix Soul Crystal is in danger, yet he didn't bring a single guard or knight with him? What kind of royal travels alone? He's got to be up to something, and I'll be keeping my eye on him."

"Don't strain yourself," Vikki made a witty comment.

I was invited to rest at their house for the night. I got a little sleep on the couch until I woke up in the middle of the night as if someone were calling my name. I assumed I was dreaming because my mind was still on my previous nightmare. Before I had a chance to fall back to sleep, I heard voices from outside. I peeked through the window and saw three men disguised in black clothing.

"I thought we would never get here," the first spoke.

"Everyone should be asleep by now. That'll make it a lot easier to get the crystal for the bosses," the second one said.

"It's OSC!" I thought to myself.

"You guys hear something?" the third asked as he looked to my direction.

I quickly ducked below the window to stay from sight. Luckily they didn't discover me.

"Probably a stray cat," the first man spoke, "Let's hurry and get that crystal and get the hell out of here."

"Yeah, we don't wanna be around when that volcano blows," the second said.

I waited until they were almost out of sight before I got back up. I held onto my sword to keep it from making noise as I tiptoed my way to the door. That's when a voice stopped me and nearly stopped my heart from shock.

"Prince Alex?" Selena called me from behind quietly.

"Selena," I whispered, "Did I wake you?"

"No, you didn"t," she said, "Who were those men outside?"

"Those men are from a group called Organization Shadow Crystal. They want to take the Phoenix Soul Crystal from the volcano," I answered her.

"What?? If they take it, the volcano could erupt and destroy our town," Selena sounded terrified.

"I know," I said, "That's why I'm going to catch up with them before its too late and stop them."

"By yourself? It's too dangerous," Selena tried to stop me.

“I'll be fine. I can handle those three,” I assured her, “If I don’t get a chance to come back, please give your family my regards for their hospitality. It was nice to meet you all,” I ended with a bow and ran out the door.

I could faintly see the three dark figures in front of me as I pursued them while keeping myself hidden from their sight, but as I followed those three, two other dark figures were following me.

I lost track of the three men somewhere along the volcano side. I carefully made my way up a path on the volcano’s side and came across an entranceway. As I wandered my way inside, it felt almost as if I was walking through parts of a temple. The only lighting inside was from the burning torches on the wall that seemed as if they had been burning forever. I felt as if I had gotten lost for a moment. The turns and corridors didn’t seem to end. As I was about to round a corner, I immediately pulled back and hid myself low behind the corner when I caught a glimpse of a shadowy figure run by. Time seemed to have frozen for fear that I may have been spotted way too soon. After a few tense moments, I slowly peeked around the corner to check if the way was clear. No one was there, so I cautiously continued my way through. It started to get warmer the farther I went through. It was a lot warmer than I thought a dormant volcano would be. I kept my hand on the hilt of my sword in case I needed to quickly unsheathe it and fight. Up ahead in a lighted room I heard voices and my entire body froze instantly. I stayed motionless as to not blow my cover and to try to hear what they were saying but I couldn’t quite make it out. I made my way slowly and peeked around the corner and I was almost blinded by a red glow. The intruders were staring at the very object I came to check on; the Phoenix Soul Crystal.

"Wow," said one of the intruders, "So that's it eh?"

"It's so powerful, it's hard just to look at directly," said the second.

"It's exactly what we need," said the third, "Let's grab it and go already!"

"Freeze all of you!!" I made my presence known as I held my sword out.

"Damn it, who the hell are you?!" yelled the first intruder.

"I am Prince Alexander of the Central Kingdom! What do you want with the Phoenix Soul Crystal?!" I demanded to know.

"It's none of your concern blue blood," answered the second intruder.

"You're a long way from home boy," commented the third intruder.

"Prince or not, you're no threat by yourself. You're outnumbered and there's no one here who can help you. Now get out of our way before we throw you into the lava pit below us!" said the second one.

As soon as he said that I realized that we were standing on a bridge like structure that was right over a dark red lava pit. I looked back at the intruders and I could tell by the look of their eye that they thought I was going to back down and run. Instead I stood my ground and stared them down as if I was daring them to get past me.

"You're not leaving with that Crystal!" I announced, "I'll defeat all three of you scumbags here and now!"

"Fine Blue blood!" the first grunt charged me, "You asked for it!"

The first found himself falling victim to a parry that was similar to the one I used on Vincent. The second and third quickly learned from the first's mistake and decided to gang up on me with blades that were forged with fire crystals. I battled with them for a few minutes and held my own pretty well, however as I was distracted by the two battling with me, the one I sent to the floor equipped a gauntlet forged with a red fire crystal. By focusing his own power through the crystal, he shot a searing hot blast straight to my face! I barely dodged it, but it threw me off balance, and the two I was fighting took complete advantage of my loss of concentration and gave me a right hook punch which sent my spiraling off the bridge! I barely managed to get a grip on the side to keep from falling to my death, but dropped my sword when I grabbed onto the bridge's edge. It began to glow a bright red with heat before it even hit the magma and melted. One of the grunts grabbed the Phoenix Soul Crystal as the other two laughed and stomped on my hands trying to make me lose my grip. I fought with all my strength to hold on. That's when I saw a flash of fire before my eyes. I don't know what happened, but I ultimately lost my grip completely, so all that was left for me to do was prepare for the hottest and last bath of my life…

Episode 3
Volcano-side Battle!

With my eyes shut, I found myself coming to an abrupt stop before I had a chance to fall more than two feet. I opened my eyes just in time to see one of the OSC grunts fall to his doom into the magma pit below. I got a chance to see his body consumed in fire just before it made contact to the lava. I was then yanked up by the person who saved me.

"Are all you royal types this reckless??" Vincent asked with a smirk as if approving my bravery in coming here alone.

"Vincent!" he was the last person I expected to rescued me, "What are you doing here?!"

"We should be asking YOU that!" Vikki unleashed a flaming round-house kick which sent the second OSC grunt crashing and sliding down the inner wall of the volcano.

"Where'd you two come from?!" asked the remaining OSC grunt.

"We've been here a while watching you three battle with Prince Alex." She said, "For a royal, you handle yourself pretty well."

"Screw this! I got what I came for, so there's no need to stick around here!" he ran off with the Phoenix Soul Crystal.

"After him!" I bolted after him with Vikki and Vincent right behind me.

As we ran through the corridors of the volcano to catch the OSC grunt before he got away, we were completely thrown off balance by a harsh rumbling all around us. I knew instantly what was happening, and so did Vikki and Vincent.

Back in town, everyone else had awoken to the sudden rumbling in the area. Within minutes, the entire town was awake and looking up to Phoenix Volcano which seemed to be coming to life. Several vents in the volcano side began to glow with orange light from the activity inside. Everyone began to panic as they feared that the once sleeping volcano could explode in any minute. The second oldest son of the town's master blacksmith was the first to notice a few people that were missing.

"Mom! Dad! I can't find Vincent!" he said.

"He's not in his room??" asked his father.

"No!" he answered, "And that blue blood is gone too!

"Prince Alex went to the volcano earlier!" Selena told them, "Vincent must've followed him!"

"Why the hell would either of them be out so late?!" her father asked.

"Prince Alex saw some shady looking men on their way to the volcano. He said that they want to take the Phoenix Soul Crystal," she explained.

"But look what's happening! Does that mean that they weren't able to stop them?" her mother asked.

"I'm going after them! Everyone stay here!" Selena's father said before he realized that Selena had already taken off.

"I'll go dad! I can run faster than you!" Selena shouted.

"Wait, Selena, stop!" her father shouted before he was knocked off balance by another tremor.

The OSC grunt raced out of an opening on the side of the volcano with Vikki, Vincent, and I slowly catching up to him. Vincent suddenly lit up a fireball and shot it down towards him to slow him down.

"You ain't leaving with that crystal alive!" shouted Vincent.

The explosion from the impact blew him off balance so bad that he dropped the bag containing the Phoenix Soul Crystal and tumbled down the volcano side. Vikki was quick to pick up the bag and hurled it back to me before it fell any further.

"Great save Vikki!" I shouted.

"Great catch Alex!" She shouted back with a smirk.

I pulled the Phoenix Soul Crystal from the bag to find it completely unharmed. I looked back up to Vincent and held it over my head to show him that it was ok.

"We win!" Vincent held his fist in the air.

Then I looked down to find that the OSC grunt was recovering from his fall just as Selena got to the base of the volcano.

"Oh no! What's Selena doing here?!" I shouted.

At the base, the OSC goon pulled out a slim blade from his overcoat and set his sites on Selena.

"Nice timing woman. I can trade you for the Phoenix Soul Crystal," he said with an evil grin.

"Watch out Selena!" Vincent shouted.

"Vincent, catch!!" I hurled the Phoenix Soul Crystal to him.

"Wow, nice throw," Vikki was impressed.

"Take the crystal back into the volcano! I'll go rescue Selena!" I make a mad sprint down the volcano side.

"Hey hold on a minute!!" Vincent tried to stop me.

"Hurry and get that thing back in the volcano V.J.!!" Vikki commanded him, "If you don't then we're all as good as dead! I'll go help Selena too!"

"Okay!!" Vincent shouted and ran back inside the way we came.

Down below, Selena was struggling to fend off the grunt. When he grabbed a hold of her arm, she was able to break free by grabbing his arm with her free hand and numbing him with a chilling flash of ice aura. He was quick to recover by using the fire crystal's energy from his blade to loosen up his arm. Before he had a chance to grab her again, I was able to put some distance between them with a swift kick.

"Selena, are you hurt?" I kept my eyes on him.

"Alex!" she sounded shocked, "How did you get down here so fast? Where's Vincent and Vikki?"

"Vincent's taking the crystal back into the volcano, and Vikki is on her way down too," I said, "Stand back and I'll fight this guy."

"With what blue blood?" he laughed, "You lost your sword in the volcano! You can't beat me unarmed!"

"Sure about that?" I motioned a challenging gesture with my hand, "Unless you really want to know what I can do, then you should turn tail and run now."

"You arrogant fool! You have nothing on me!" he charged me.

"Except this!" a flash of light shot from the sacred crystal around my neck and blinded him temporarily.

"What are you doing?" Selena shielded her eyes with her arm.

"Watch this," I said looking back with a smirk.

I pulled the Twilight Star from around my neck and held it out in front of me as I began to concentrate my will power into it. As the crystal grew brighter, it reacted with the special alloy forged around it and began to transform. The mass of metal and crystal transformed itself according to my will into my own personal sword. The four-pointed star shaped crystal that rested in the middle of the medallion had split into four crystals. One was at the base of the blade, two were on each end of the hand guard, and the last one was in the middle of the sword's top end. I stood ready to battle with the grunt who just recovered from his blindness.

"En Garde!" the wind began to blow my cape.

Back in the tunnels of the volcano, rocks and dust were falling as Vincent made his way back to the altar for the Phoenix Soul Crystal. Vincent bolted across the bridge as towers of fire shot upward around him. A bright red glow shot from the crystal and seemed to be shielding him from the intense heat as he made his way across the bridge. Before he got to the altar, part of the bridge collapsed in front of him and almost caused him to fall.

"Damn! I'm gonna have to jump it!" he backed up and prepared to leap across the gap.

As Vincent leaped with all his strength, pillars of fire shot upward on both sides of him. Vincent's foot landed right at the edge which caused him to slip. He managed to grab the edge with his free hand to keep from falling but the edge that he grabbed began to crack up.

Outside at the volcano base, I was matching the grunt move for move. There were times where I could avoid his blade with ease, but I couldn't avoid getting singed from the fire that burned with each slash. Our swords came to a clash and we were locked in a temporary stalemate.

"How's a royal whelp like you have so much skill?!" he sounded amazed.

"It's not so much that I'm extremely skilled. I'm just fighting someone with no skill at all!" I began to push him back.

I took to the offensive until he was completely forced to use what he had left just to defend. I leaped up and as he held his sword up to block my strike, I brought my sword down with enough force to shatter his blade completely. When I landed, I rose quickly and held the point of my sword to his neck to keep him from trying anything. After being terrified out of his mind, he pulled a 180 degree turn and bolted. He didn't go far though. He ran right into Vikki's fist and knocked himself out.

"You should watch where you're going. You can hurt yourself if you're not careful," Vikki laughing.

With the battle over, I let out a sigh of relief and rematerialized my sword into the medallion it once was.

"Okay," I held my singed arm, "NOW we won. I'm glad that's over."

"Alex that was amazing," Selena said.

"I gotta say, I think you just earned my respect," Vikki said.

"Thanks. I hope I earned your friendships too," I smiled.

"Sure," Vikki crossed her arms and smiled, "Why not."

"Hey! The volcano stopped erupting," I suddenly noticed.

"Vincent must've made it!" Selena shouted.

"I guess we really did win!" Vikki shouted.

Without thinking about it, we all gave each other a high five in celebration of our victory and a newly forged friendship. I winced in pain after accidentally using my burned arm to high five the girls.

"What's wrong?" Vikki asked, "Did I hit your royal hand too hard?"

"Nah," I laughed slightly, "My arm is just a little burned from the fight earlier."

"Lemme see," Selena quickly grabbed my arm.

"Ow! What are you doing?" I asked.

"Just watch this," she said.

I felt an icy sensation flow through my entire body that completely overtook my senses. A light blue aura around Selena traveled up my arm that sent a chill throughout my body and healed all my burns. It wasn't just my injuries that was affected by her powers. It felt like my whole body was relieved from any soreness and aches I was feeling.

"Wow," I said, "How'd you do that?"

"Burns aren't anything new to me," she said, "I do this all the time for Vikki and Vincent."

"You're looking at the only person to be born with an ice affinity within the region of the Phoenix," Vikki said, "Without her, Vincent and I wouldn't be able to play as rough as we do."

"That's playing?" I recalled the fight from yesterday.

"Whew! What a rush!" Vincent stretched his arms upward as he emerged from an opening on the volcano slope.

"Hey! Hurry and get down here V.J.!" Vikki commanded him.

The sun was rising by the time the four of us got back to town. Vincent was dragging the unconscious grunt behind him with a rope. As we topped a hill, we were greeted by a massive cheer from the townspeople. I was specifically confronted by Vincent and Selena's siblings who must have assumed I saved everyone.

"You saved the town!" shouted the second oldest boy.

"You're a hero!" shouted the second oldest girl.

"Look at him taking all the credit," Vincent thought to himself with his arms crossed, "That's just like a blueblood."

"Hang on a second," I raised my arms to calm them down, "I only helped out. Vincent is the hero you should be thanking. He's the one that saved us all."

"You did??" they all turned to Vincent.

"I did?" Vincent's eyes widened in shock from my statement, "I did!" he quickly covered up his earlier question, "Those punks were nothing!"

I told them all the story of what happened in there; from the battle over the lava pits, to the sword fight at the base of the volcano. Later that morning after a little rest, I got ready to leave Prominence town with much of the town coming to see me off.

"Thanks again for the extra rations," I received a bag from Vincent and Selena's mom.

"It's the least we could do after you helped save our town," she said.

"Where are you going now?" Selena asked.

"Probably back home," I said, "Given the circumstances, I should try to get back there in one piece before going anywhere else."

"You gonna be alright by yourself?" Vikki asked.

"I should be," I said, "Even with OSC agents around, I was taught how to survive. Plus as long as I have this," I held up the crystal around my neck, "I know I'll be able to make it."

"After what I've seen, I believe it," Selena said, "Still be careful."

"Thanks," I said, "You all be careful too incase more agents come after the crystal."

"We will," Vikki said, "Remember that you're not a stranger anymore in Prominence Town. Feel free to come back again."

"I will," I said, "Maybe we can fight sometime."

"Me fight you??" Vikki laughed, "You sure about that? You saw what I did to Vincent, right?"

"I promise I won't even use my sword," I smirked.

"Ha! We'll see," Vikki laughed.

"Well then," I wrapped my cloak around myself and covered my head, "Here I go! Take care everyone! I hope to see you all again someday!"

The small crowd gave me one final farewell cheer as I turned to leave the town. When I got to the top of a hill on the outskirt of town, I gave one final wave before running down the other side. I felt really good after meeting the people of Prominence town-especially Vikki, Selena, and Vincent. I hope I get to see them again soon.

"Hey Vincent," Selena turned to her brother, "Why didn't you say anything?"

"You really gotta get over the blueblood thing with him," Vikki said, "He's a good guy."

"It's not that," Vincent said.

"Well what is it?" Selena asked.

"This royal leaves his kingdom, with no guards-completely on his own, shows up here, makes nice with everyone, owns face, and then leaves like it's just another day," Vincent tried to explain his thoughts, "We don't even know this guy. Hell, we're not even in his ruling territory and he shows up to help us."

"Like I said," Vikki reiterated herself, "He's a good guy."

"Yea, but we still had to save his butt in there," he pointed to the volcano, "And he thinks he'll be alright on his own with nothing but a cloak and that weird crystal?"

"If you're so worried about him, then you should go with him," Vikki stretched her arms upward, "Either way I need some sleep. I need to get home before grandma starts to worry. Later you two," she waved before heading home.

"We better get home too," Selena turned to go home.

"Yea," Vincent hesitated to turn before following Selena.

After a couple of steps Vincent stopped as if zoning out. Selena noticed that he had stopped and was now looking at the volcano, and then back in the direction where I had left. Selena began looking off in the same direction as Vincent turned his whole body in the direction I had left as if deciding what to do.

Episode 4
An Evil Plot Unfolds

With the help of Vikki and Vincent, I took a very close victory, but unknown to me, we were being watched by someone else that works within Organization Shadow Crystal. After witnessing all the events that took place, he quickly returned to an unknown underground location that served as their base of operations.

"M'lord, I have the latest report regarding the status of the Phoenix Soul Crystal," spoke the OSC spy to a shadowy figure sitting on a throne-like chair.

"Go on…" the shadow spoke in a calm but deep voice.

"Yes sir," the spy continued, "The three men you sent to retrieve the crystal from Phoenix Volcano were defeated sir. They were confronted by Central Kingdom's Prince Alexander and-"

"Prince Alexander?!" the dark shadow cut him off quickly, "Of Valsoria??"

"Y-y-yes sir," the spy began cowering, "He arrived alone, but received help from the local town. Two of the men you sent were killed inside the volcano. The third managed to get outside with the crystal in his possession, but he was defeated in single combat by Valsoria's prince."

"Well that's interesting," the dark shadow said.

"If those soldiers let a blue blood get the best of them, then good riddance," a strongly built man with black hair and purple eyes walked up from behind the spy, "Any soldier that can't handle a blue blood needs to be weeded out right now."

“I wouldn’t be surprised if that turned out to be a fifth of our current troops at least,” a taller swordsman with blonde hair and green eyes walked out from the other side of the spy.

“You gotta be kidding me Lancer,” the black haired man said, “He can’t be that good.”

“Much of our forces are just grunts and common bandits,” he ran his fingers through his hair, “The prince possesses a rough fighting talent, so the common soldiers would be wise to not underestimate him. He’s still no threat to the four of us, so there is no need to worry yourself Alfonso.”

“Who said I was worried,” he crossed his arms, “Francis is the one who came back running.”

“I wasn’t running,” he said, “I came back to report as ordered. Anyway,” he turned back to the leader, “It was an interesting duel to watch. Even though the prince lost his sword in the volcano, he brought forth a new one by using something around his neck.”

“Something around his neck you say?” the leader grew curious, “Did you get a good look at it?”

“I can’t describe it in detail, but it looked to be some sort of medallion about the size of my palm. It shined with a bright flash, and when I could see again, he was holding a crystal embedded sword,” Francis said.

“What the hell kind of ability is that?” Alfonso asked.

“It must be the Twilight Star!” Lancer spoke up, “It has to be!”

"So the prince had it with him the whole time," the leader said, "That makes sense. It would explain Valsoria's sudden change in behavior with their guard. What else was he able to do with it?"

"That was all, sir," Francis said, "Using the Twilight Star, he was able to match, and eventually overwhelm the remaining soldier."

"It sounds like anything he was able to do was only because of the Twilight Star," Lancer said.

"In other words," the leader rubbed his chin, "He is powerless without it. The Twilight Star has the power we need to realize our goals. Once we have it, Valsoria will fall effortlessly, and the rest of the kingdoms will soon follow. Send a small force to intercept the prince before he makes it back to Valsoria. Order them to retrieve the Twilight Star and dispose of the prince however they like."

"Yes sir," Francis stood and left the room.

"Alfonso," the leader turned to him, "Dispose of our experiments in the desert. We need to keep Rac' Sagadam too occupied to even think about what may be going on with Valsoria."

"At once, sir," Alfonso left the room.

"As for you Lancer," the leader turned to him, "Set up a plan to get what we need from Zylphan in one swift strike. Zylphan is a powerful nation, so the last thing we need is to blunder up on a mission there."

"As you say," Lancer bowed before leaving.

It was about an hour before noon when I stopped to rest on a large stone several yards off the road. The occasional breeze felt great as I sat and planned my next move.

Just from the encounter I had at Phoenix Volcano, I felt that I had information important enough to share with my kingdom's allies. Rac' Sagadam, a kingdom in the desert, was only about a full day's walk from where I was, but it's practically suicide to travel by myself-especially in the day. Either way, I had a long walk ahead of me since I had sent my horse back home with a note to my mom.

"Maybe that wasn't such a good idea," I said to myself, "I kept a low profile by not taking him to the town, but now I've lost some serious traveling speed."

Suddenly I noticed two men dressed in ragged clothing with a blade and axe walking to my right. I pretended not to notice them until three more rough looking men with weapons began to approach me from my left. I stood up on top of the rock I was resting on and gripped the Twilight Star under my cloak. I knew I was in trouble, and it was too late for me to make a run for it.

"You guys need something?" I firmly asked and they all stopped in their tracks.

A bit further back down the path, twin siblings were making their way up the road. They were traveling light and scanning the area as if looking for something or someone.

"I hope we catch up to him soon," the boy with the headband shielded his eyes from the sun.

"Vincent, are you sure you want to do this?" asked the light blue haired girl, "Just yesterday you couldn't stand him, and now you want to help him?"

"It's not so much that I'm worried about him," Vincent said, "But Selena, last night was the first time I got to fight like that. Sure I have fun roughing it up with Vikki and the others, but that guy's got me curious now. I want to be able to fight like that again, and see how far I can go. If the rest of the guys we come across are anything like from last night, they won't stand a chance!"

"You just hate that you got shown up by a royal," Selena crossed her arms, "Right?"

"Well that too…" Vincent rolled his eyes, "It's not too late for you to turn back ya know. I know you're decent in hand to hand combat when you have to be, but I think I can handle myself."

"I'll be fine," she said, "Lets just both make it back in one piece. Vikki will be mad enough once she wakes up and realizes we left without her, but if something happens to either of us she'll-"

"Get down," Vincent suddenly pulled Selena behind a large stone, "Is that him?"

"I think so," Selena whispered, "He's been surrounded by bandits."

"I knew it," Vincent said, "He's barely left town and he's already in trouble."

"Maybe you can help us stranger," one of the men to my right spoke up, "We're looking for Prince Alexander of Valsoria. We heard that he came through these parts. Ya seen him?"

"F'raid not," I faked an accent, "Whatcha need him for?"

"It's a private matter," the second man to my right said.

"Sorry. Can't help ya." I turned to walk away when a third man blocked my path.

"You sure you haven't seen anyone suspicious?" he said, "Maybe someone posing as a common traveler?"

I gripped the Twilight Star tighter as they surrounded me. I wasn't about to take them all head on, but I had to escape somehow.

"Does he have black hair at about ear's length and green eyes?" I casually asked.

"So you've seen him?" the first man asked.

"There he is!" I suddenly pointed out with my left hand.

"Where?!" all five of them turned their attention to the direction I pointed.

As soon as their attention was off me, I wasted no time in taking advantage of the moment. In a flash of light from the Twilight Star, I slid in front of one of the bandits and struck him with a rising slash and hit another one with a downward strike. The others saw their comrades fall just as I took off running.

"Get him! Don't let him escape!" the three remaining bandits pursued me.

"Damn," Vincent darted after us from behind the stone.

"Here we go," Selena gave chase as well.

As soon as one of the bandits caught up with me, I parried the swing of his blade and struck him hard in the torso. I continued running when he went down, but suddenly an axe swung from behind a tree directly at my face. I slid to dodge it, but ended up falling on my back. Before he could swing his axe downward, I threw dirt in his eyes and stabbed him through his gut before he could recover. One of the bandits threw some rope tied to two stones at my legs which locked me from running. I lost my balance and dropped the Twilight Star as I fell. It returned to its original form upon hitting the ground.

"Got it!" one of the bandits scooped it up, "Now finish him!"

"Gladly," one of the bandits raised his blade.

"Damn!" I tried to move out of the way.

The bandit that was about to end my life was suddenly rushed from behind by an explosive force that sent him flying. He crashed into a boulder and fell motionlessly to the ground.

"The hell?" I looked to see where the attack came from.

"That's twice I've saved you," Vincent stood over me, "You alright?"

"Look out!" I warned him of one of the injured bandits coming up from behind him.

"You're dead kid," he raised his axe before being struck from behind by a chilling blast that made him drop it, "The hell was-"

The bandit turned around to get a rising knee to the face by Selena. Vincent finished him with an explosive blow to his back.

"Nice hit," Vincent said to Selena.

"Thanks," she said, "But there's one more."

"Return that to me now!" I finally freed myself from the ropes.

"No way!" he took of running towards a low cliff.

"Please!" I took off while calling to Vincent and Selena, "Help me catch him!"

The three of us chased him down to the base of a cliff he was heading to. He had gotten a head start in climbing the rocky hillside just as we got to the base. As soon as I lost sight of him over a ledge, he suddenly screamed. It was cut short by the sound of punches in rapid succession and ended with him flying off the edge of the ledge. I noticed he didn't have the Twilight Star, so I climbed up to the ledge from where he fell to see what happened.

"Missing something?" a man with long blonde hair and blue eyes dressed in light clothing and armed with a katana said.

"Keith?" I couldn't believe my eyes, "Keith!"

"And Lan too!" a shorter boy with short red hair and dressed in a light robe poked his head from behind Keith.

"Hey Lan!" Keith pulled me up onto the ledge, "What are you two doing down here?"

"Looking for you," Keith handed me the Twilight Star, "How come you're not home?"

"Well-" I started to answer his question.

"Hey!" Vincent called from the base of the cliff, "What's going on up there?"

"Everything's fine!" I held up the Twilight star to show him and Selena.

"Who are those two?" Keith peeked over the ledge.

"Some new friends I made in Prominence Town," I said.

"They're traveling with you now?" Keith asked.

"Well they weren't, but they saved my life earlier. C'mon and I'll introduce you," I began to hop back down the ledge.

"Here he comes," Selena said, "With some of his friends apparently."

"Hey you two," I landed in front of them, "I can't thank you enough for your help back there. I owe you both big time."

"Damn right you do," Vincent said, "You were barely out of town, and the two of us come out to find you waist deep in-"

“Anyway,” Selena suddenly covered Vincent’s mouth with a chilled hand, “Were those more of OSC’s soldiers?”

“They looked like common bandits,” I said, “But I suppose it’s possible. Either way, they were hell bent on stealing the Twilight Star from me.”

“That thing around your neck?” Vincent pulled Selena’s hand off his mouth.

“That’s what you used to make that sword from before, right?” Selena asked.

“Yes,” I said, “I can never lose this.”

“Good thing he’s got me to bail him out of trouble huh?” Keith landed beside me.

“And you are?” Vincent asked.

“Keith Ishikawa of Jentake,” he introduced himself.

“And I’m Lan!” he grinned from behind Keith.

“This is Vincent and Selena of Prominence Town,” I introduced them.

“Hey,” Vincent nodded

“Hi,” Selena waved.

“So why did you follow me all this way anyway?” I asked Selena.

“Technically,” Selena crossed her arms, “I was following him,” she pointed to Vincent.

“I was trying to catch up to you before you got too far away,” he said, “If you’re gonna be fighting more of these OSC guys, then I want to get in on the action.”

“Are you sure?” I asked, “I’d love the help, but fighting them won’t be like fighting common bandits.”

“Who was the one that got jumped by bandits and had to be rescued?” Selena raised her eye brow.

"Oh right," I lowered my head in shame.

"Ouch," Keith grinned, "That's cold."

"In that case, it will be great to have you two come with me," I said

"Then it's settled," Vincent punched his fist into his palm, "Those guys are gonna pay for trying to mess up my town."

"Then let's all rest at our campsite," Keith said, "We can plan our next move, and you can tell me all about what's up with this OSC."

"Oh right," I said, "I need to tell you everything that has happened thus far."

Episode 5
The Crossing of Mirage Desert

We had settled into Keith's campsite just a few minutes after meeting up. Lan was finishing up a small stew that he made using some wild vegetables and herbs they had found. As we ate, I informed them of what had been recently going on around Valsoria, and the events at Prominence Town.

"So do you know exactly what they're trying to do yet?" Keith asked.

"Not really," I said, "But at the very least, I made a good decision to come down here."

"To think if you had just waited a little while longer before leaving home, we could've took on those guys at the volcano together," Keith said.

"There may not have been anyone to take on by the time we got there," Lan said.

"I guess you got a point," Keith finished his share of the stew.

"So where do we go from here?" Lan asked.

"Yeah," Vincent cut in, "We're not getting anywhere just sitting here!"

"I've been thinking about that," I said, "We need to get some help along the way, but I have a duty to inform my kingdom's allies of what I know before it's too late."

"So we're heading for Valsoria, right?" Selena asked.

"We were," I corrected her, "But if those bandits we fought were sent by OSC, then they're likely expecting me to get to Valsoria as quickly as I can. All things considered, I think its best we try to head to Rac' Sagadam first."

"Where is that?" she asked.

"Rac' Sagadam lies within a desert beyond those rocks," I pointed, "If you've heard of Mirage Desert, then that's where it is."

"Hang on a sec," Vincent interrupted, "Are you nuts?! That place is too dangerous for us to try and cross!"

"It's only dangerous for inexperienced travelers," I said, "We'll be fine."

"How do you know?" Selena asked, "Do you have a map?"

"No," I said, "But I was taught how to navigate through the desert by Prince Jabari. Since we're headed there instead of leaving, it's best for us to travel by night."

"Alright, so how long are we going to be walking through this desert?" Vincent asked.

"If we leave at sunset today and keep a steady pace," I took a moment to think, "We should make it there by sunrise."

"Then we should all get some rest now," Lan said.

"Yes," Selena yawned, "I didn't exactly sleep last night."

"You three go ahead and take a nap then," Keith said, "I'll keep watch till we're ready to head out."

"Thanks Keith," I went to relax under a tree, "Wake me up if anything happens."

Thankfully sunset took its sweet time getting here. By the time the sun was completely gone, we were running on the fast cooling desert soil. The dry soil began turning into sand, and we were past several sand dunes before I knew it. Along with the occasional stops for a break, we were making great time. Both of the moons were out and full, so the night lighting was perfect. The desert sand glimmered like silver in the moonlight. We took another break well past midnight so Keith and I could regain our bearings. The last thing we needed was to be lost when the sun came up.

"Ok there's the North Star," Keith pointed.

"Right," I found where he was pointing, "The Phoenix Constellation is there, so I'm guesstimating a straight shot to Rac' Sagadam in that direction."

"That's what I was thinking," Keith said, "Although I figured we would've been able to see lights in the distance by now."

"Hey Alex," Selena got my attention, "We're not lost are we?"

"Nah," I said, "We can't see lighting from the city yet, but we're definitely on the right track."

"I still say a map would be better," Vincent said, "We're really just suppose to trust the stars? Sounds stupid to me."

"It's not stupid," I said, "It's one of the oldest forms of navigation, and it still works today."

"So what do you do when the clouds roll in?" Vincent pointed upward.

Sure enough, a large patch of clouds began to cover parts of the starry sky. We heard rumbles of thunder, but no rain began to fall.

"This…might be a problem," I stared at the darkening sky.

"Might be a problem?" Vincent questioned me, "I think getting caught in a thunderstorm in the middle of the damn desert IS a problem!"

"It's not humid enough for it to suddenly rain," Lan said, "It's just a false storm. We're not in any danger."

"Not from the storm at least," Keith's pointy ears began to twitch, "Something's coming, but I can't tell from where."

"Stand together everyone," I transformed the Twilight Star into a sword, "Give us some extra light Vincent!"

"Right," he lit a torch on fire and held it up.

"Over there!" Selena pointed to a pair of hounds approaching us.

"I see them," I got into position beside Keith as he unsheathed his katana.

They approached us slowly, but their gleaming eyes seemed to be fixed on me. As soon as I raised my blade, I felt it pulsate with energy. At the same time, the jackals suddenly stopped and started shaking their heads violently.

"What in the world?" I was curious to why the Twilight Star was suddenly emitting energy.

"Hey Alex," Keith pointed to the hounds, "There's something on their foreheads. It looks like a crystal."

"Crystals? Really?" I focused my eyesight on their heads to confirm what he saw.

"This doesn't look right at all," Lan said, "Someone put those on them somehow."

"They look like they're in pain," Selena said.

"I don't know what those crystals are or how they got on those jackals' foreheads," the gems in my sword suddenly began to glow brighter, "But it's causing the Twilight Star to react."

The Twilight Star suddenly let out one final pulse that caused the crystals on the jackals' foreheads to shatter. After shaking the remains of the crystals off their heads, they suddenly calmed down and were looking confused.

“They shattered!” Selena was shocked, “Crystals don’t just shatter like that on their own, do they?”

“No,” I said, “I don’t think those were normal. Those jackals were behaving too oddly. I think the energy from the Twilight Star may have caused them to shatter.”

“It’s a good thing too,” Lan said, “We may have been in trouble if they didn’t.”

All of a sudden, the jackals’ ears stood straight up, and they took off running away from us.

“We’re still in trouble!” Keith suddenly shouted, “Those jackals weren’t what I sensed coming!”

“What?!” I looked around frantically, “Then where-!”

“Something’s below us!” Lan fixed his eyes on the sand.

“Move!!” Keith shouted.

We all took off running together in the same direction just as the sand behind us erupted. At that point, Selena let out an ear piercing scream while looking up behind me. The rest of us whirled around to find that a sand monster has emerged from one of the sand dunes. Its body was a much darker shade of the sand, and its four tentacles hung long like whiskers from its mouth. This monster was like a scorpion the size of a small boat. Its large tail finally pierced from the sand and the foot long poisonous sting at the tip of its tail shined at the tip from the flashes of lightning from the sky.

“What the hell is that thing?!?!” Selena screamed.

“An oversized scorpion?!?!” I screamed as we tried to back away from it.

“Why the hell is it so big?!?!” Lan screamed.

“Who cares?! Run!!” Vincent shouted.

"Run where?!" I stopped him, "We're in the middle of the desert!"

"You're the one that brought us out here!" Vincent yelled, "What the hell do we do then?!"

"We have to kill it!" I held my sword up as I faced the beast.

"You're crazy!" Selena yelled, "How do we fight something like that?!"

"Using everything we got," I narrowed my eyes at the monster as it slowly pursued us, "Anyone got any ideas?"

"Well looking at its exoskeleton, I'm wondering if we can even hurt it," Lan said.

"It may be big, but it's still a bug. I have a few arrows that I know can penetrate it, but unless I can land a solid killing blow," Keith stopped to look at the sky, "Buy me at least a minutes worth of time, and I can strike it down!"

"Are you sure?!" Vincent looked at Keith.

"Trust me!" he gripped one of his steel tipped arrows in his hand and gave it a static charge.

"Alright," I paused for a moment before rushing the monster, "Don't waste a second I give you!"

Selena, Vincent, and Lan were briefly frozen in shock when I ran towards the monster.

"You gotta be kidding me," Selena was wide eyed with her hands over her mouth.

The monster's eyes stayed fixed on me as I ran towards its left. It quickly lunged its poisonous tail at me, which I immediately side stepped. I jumped on top of one of its large pincer that reached out to me and sliced off one of its whiskers as I darted by its head. It hissed loudly with pain as I jumped to its backside and tried to cut off its tail. My slash made a decent gash on its tail, but it wasn't enough to cut all the way through.

"What's wrong Vincent?" I jumped away from a snap of its pincers, "You're not afraid of bugs are you?"

"Oh that's it," Vincent was infuriated at my taunt, "Look out!"

I continued to duck and dodge the snapping pincers and its deadly tail while dealing damage of my own whenever I saw an opening. Vincent finally joined the fray by jumping onto its back and punching it in the back of the head as hard as he could. Lan gave us some support by blasting trails of sand toward the beast's eyes to keep it disoriented. While it was focused on the three of us, Selena was able to focus her powers long enough to shoot stunning waves of ice energy towards it, however they did little to effectively slow it down. Meanwhile, I could hear sounds of thunder as if it were suddenly getting closer and closer. Out of the corner of my eye, I noticed Keith was suddenly surging with static energy.

"Hasn't it been a minute yet?!" I called out, "We can't keep this up!"

Suddenly Vincent was knocked off its back and slapped away with one of its large pincers that sent him headfirst into the sand. As I ran to help him, the monster cut me off by sticking its right pincer into the sand. It immediately knocked Lan and Selena away with its left pincer as they came to help both of us, and then it stuck its pincer into the sand to keep me locked down. It suddenly stood higher on its legs while hissing loudly. Its tail was fully extended into the air as it took aim at me.

"Alex! Get out of there!!" Selena screamed.

"Run!!" Lan screamed.

"Mmmhnmm!" Vincent finally pulled his head out of the sand, "No-!"

"Now! Thunder Sniper!!" Keith shouted as he released the electrified arrow from his bow.

With the speed and flash of a lightning bolt, Keith's arrow found its mark at the tip of the beast's tail. Immediately I heard the sound of lightning charging above me, so I jumped away as hard as I could. A large lightning bolt fell straight from the sky into the beast's tail! All of its limbs violently locked outward from his body and shook violently as the beast shrieked in pain. It was hit with a second strike of lightning that finally brought its life to an end. It collapsed with a loud thud with its limbs stretched outward and its mouth leaking with blood. I had to take a moment to catch my breath before I could even think of what to say, let alone speak at all!

"Woah," I fell to my knees.

"Hey Alex! You alright?" Keith landed beside me, "Sorry that took so long."

"What… the hell was that?" Selena asked.

"It's my brand new signature move," Keith posed, "Thunder Sniper! I've been working on it for about a year now. That's the fastest I've ever been able to prepare it."

"Wow," Vincent was impressed, "You owned him with that shot!"

"Just barely," Keith said, "I think the second strike of lightning was what finished it."

"I wonder…" I finally stood up.

"Wonder what?" Lan asked.

"I wonder if what happened to those jackals happened to this thing," I walked over to the carcass.

I knelt over the head of the carcass and held the Twilight Star just above its head. As I thought would happen, the Twilight Star suddenly began pulsating, and I noticed something sticking out of the head. I was able to pry out a black colored crystal that shattered in my hand just as I was getting a good look at it.

"Just like those hounds," I stood up, "This thing had one of those crystals in its head too."

"Is OSC doing this?" Vincent asked.

"It has to be them," I said, "It makes sense at least. These dark crystals… Organization Shadow Crystal… Something about those dark crystals must've been warping those creatures' minds. This one actually mutated and grew beyond its normal size."

"In the end, it was just a victim of someone's sick experiment," Lan said.

"That's so horrible…" Selena said with remorse.

"I wonder if Rac' Sagadam has been encountering this sort of thing," I looked off towards the clearing sky, "In any case, we should try to press on as quickly as we can. I just hope we don't run into anymore trouble before we get there. I think that's the direction we need to head," I pointed.

Vincent set the carcass on fire before we continued on. At some point, we were walking mostly on dry soil instead of pure sand. The night sky began to lighten the further we walked. A sudden breeze hit us all in the face when I caught the scent of something.

"Does anyone else smell that?" I asked.

Keith quickly pointed to Vincent and said, "He did it."

“What?!” Vincent was confused.

“Gross,” I said with disgust.

Selena took a whiff of the incoming wind as it blew through her hair and said, “I smell it too. Is it water?”

“I think it IS water,” I took off running.

I stopped at the top of a large mount of dirt just as the stars were fading and the sun was peering over the horizon behind me. I welcomed the site of a palace and its city build around a triple oasis, otherwise known as a Triasis.

“It’s the Triasis! We made it to Rac’ Sagadam!”

Selena and Keith were the first to join me atop the mound with Lan and Vincent closely behind them. We all took a moment to celebrate amongst ourselves out of relief that we made it all the way through the night.

“And just in time for sunrise,” I looked behind us.

“Let’s get to the city before the sun gets too high,” Lan suggested.

“Keith, I’ll race you!” I bolted to our destination to give myself a head start.

“Hey that’s not fair!” he dashed onward to close the gap between us.

“Wait for us!” Selena, Vincent, and Lan ran after us.

As the sky grew brighter and the moons faded into the light, we ran onward on nothing but excitement and adrenaline. Nothing else was on our minds except resting and getting out fill of food in the desert city known as Rac’ Sagadam.

Episode 6
Enter Jabari: Prince of Rac' Sagadam

It's been six years since I've set foot in Rac' Sagadam, but it was just as I remembered. I could still read the hieroglyphics that were written at the entrances of buildings and on street signs with ease. The marketplace was filled with activity with venders selling their merchandise and children playing in the streets. Everyone just looked happy to be alive. The people of Rac' Sagadam wore light clothing to help against the heat of the desert. The three oases that support life in this city come from natural underground springs. The main spring flowed from a fountain in the shape of a small pyramid in the palace garden. The remaining two were on the east and west side of the city. They provided clean water for the entire city. One of the guards greeted us at the southern gate. After informing him of my identity, he immediately sent word of my arrival through a messenger to the palace which is where I planned for us to get some rest.

"Is everyone holding up ok?" I asked everyone.

"As good as anyone can be after last night," Keith said.

"I'm exhausted," Selena sat against a tree.

"I'm so hungry…" Vincent's stomach kept growling.

"That's nothing new. You're always hungry." Selena pointed out.

"If that's the case, then he's going to enjoy breakfast at the palace," I laughed, "We should be just in time."

"Sweet," Vincent said, "It's about time we get a little royal treatment."

"Are you sure they're not going to mind all of us showing up?" Lan asked.

“It’ll be fine,” I said, “Pharaoh Meti and Queen Aaliyah are very gracious people. If you give them a chance,” I spoke to Vincent, “You’ll see that they’re anything but the type of royals you think about.”

“We’ll see,” Vincent said.

“Then this means I’ll get the chance to meet Princess Nanu right?” Keith asked.

“Yes, why?” I asked.

“Is what I hear about her true? Is her beauty really from a legendary descent??” Keith asked.

“What are you talking about?” Selena asked.

“Princess Nanu is ONLY the most beautiful woman in world, and I finally get to meet her!” Keith shouted with excitement.

We all just stood there and stared at Keith until he came out of his daydream of Princess Nanu. When he came back to reality, he realized that we were all staring at him and a sweat drop rolled down the back of his head.

“Keith,” I sighed, “For my sake, try to behave yourself…”

“Prince Alexander?!” a voice called out to me.

I recognized his voice immediately as I turned to where it came from. The prince of Rac’ Sagadam stood in front of us. His black shoulder length hair swayed with the wind as his dark eyes stared at me with a surprised look on his face from my sudden appearance to his city.

“Prince Jabari!” I called out to him.

“That’s the prince of Rac’ Sagadam? He looks tougher than I thought he would,” Vincent held his arms crossed.

“Shush, Vincent, or you might get us in trouble,” Selena whispered to him.

“This is a surprise!” Jabari ran up with two of his guards beside him, “I was not expecting you to come and visit. Are you well?”

“I’m about as well as anyone crossing the desert at night and fighting off a huge sand monster before sunrise,” I said to him.

“You encountered one of the savage monsters that have suddenly begun appearing? I am glad to see that you are still alive,” Jabari spoke before turning to my friends, “Are these people with you? They do not look like Valsoria Knights.”

“They’re friends of mine,” I said, “This is Lan-”

“Greetings Prince Jabari,” Lan spoke and bowed.

“Keith-”

“Sup?” Keith spoke and nodded his head.

“Selena-”

“Hello,” Selena spoke and bowed her head.

“And Vincent,” I finished.

“Tsk,” Vincent turned his head.

“What is the matter with him?” Jabari asked.

“Don’t take him personally, Jabari,” I began to explain, “He’s not too fond of us royals.”

“So…why is he traveling with you?” Jabari was confused.

“Cause I can.” Vincent spoke up.

“Vincent, don’t get like this,” Selena sighed.

"Right…" a sweat drop rolled down the back of Jabari's head, "Alex, you all must come to the palace! Mother, Father, and Nanu will be very happy to see you, and you all can rest there as my guest."

"That sounds great right about now," I said, "I hope we haven't missed breakfast."

"You are just in time," Jabari laughed, "Come. Breakfast will be served at the palace in a few minutes."

"Breakfast?" Vincent's attention was instantly snagged.

"Sure, NOW you want to pay attention," Selena commented.

"Guard. Please return to the palace and have our servants arrange rooms for our guest," Jabari commanded one of his guards.

"As you command," the guard responded and ran ahead of us.

"Here I come, Princess Nanu!" Keith thought to himself as he grew excited.

We reached the palace gate within a few minutes. The guards at the gate quickly recognized me and allowed us into the palace garden. The yellow bricked path took us between two long stretched bodies of water which streamed from the center fountain before we got to the steps of the palace. I looked up the steps and found the Pharaoh and the Queen greeting us. They were still the same as I remembered six years ago. Pharaoh Meti, with his short black hair, looked as strong as ever. Even as a Pharaoh, he refused to wear a shirt most of the time so that he could show off his physical strength. Queen Aaliyah's beauty was unchanged. The gold she wore with her white desert dress matched well with her blue eyes and her long black hair.

"Prince Alexander of Central Kingdom! This is a splendid surprise!" Pharaoh Meti shouted.

"Pharaoh Meti and Queen Aaliyah, it is great to see you again," I said as I extended my fist out to them in the traditional greeting or Rac' Sagadam.

"You have grown a lot in the past six years. You look just like your father now," Queen Aaliyah spoke to me, "What brings you here so suddenly?"

"It's a long story. I want to speak with you about it privately a little later if that's ok," I responded, "We all ran through the desert since sundown yesterday till sunrise this morning, so we're all exhausted."

"My goodness, It's a blessing that you made it through alive," Queen Aaliyah said.

"How long are they going to keep yakking?" Vincent said to himself as he grew more impatient.

"Shush!" Selena quietly yelled at him and punched him in the stomach.

"Lets get you and your friends cleaned up and then you can all join us for breakfast," Queen Aaliyah snapped her fingers which summoned up her servants to take us in.

"Finally! Now that's what I'm talking about!" Vincent said with excitement.

"Please excuse any of his rudeness," I put my hand over my face.

"Ha-ha! Do not worry about it," the Pharaoh told me.

"He reminds me a bit of Jabari," the Queen said while laughing.

Several minutes later, we had all showered up and getting dressed. One of the servants helped Vincent, Lan, Keith, and I pick out some new clothes to wear from their desert wardrobe. I was dressed in a white and gold outfit that was similar to the royal attire. Unlike the Pharaoh, however, I wore a shirt. Vincent decided to follow the Pharaoh's example and not wear a shirt and to only be dressed in white pants. Lan looked as if he was wrapped in bed sheets as he tried to keep his mage look. Keith changed clothes into what the common people wear. When we were done, we waited at the breakfast table with the Pharaoh, the Queen, and Prince Jabari for Princess Nanu and Selena to join us. Selena was still getting dressed with the princess in another room. She was allowed to wear a dress that was very similar to Princess Nanu's white and golden dress.

"You have such strange hair," Princess Nanu observed one of her attendants brushing Selena's hair, "Just where are you from?"

"I'm from Prominence town," Selena answered, "Its east of here near Phoenix Volcano if you know where that is."

"I do," she said, "I just thought you may have been from the far north. I have never seen anyone with your hair color down here before. It's beautiful."

"Oh thank you," Selena smiled, "I was born the only person with an ice affinity out of my whole family. My loud brother you saw at the gate and everyone else in my family has the fire affinity."

"Oh!" Princess Nanu suddenly clasped her hands together, "I've read about people like you! You're born with an affinity that doesn't match your parents or the region you come from! It's very rare!"

"Wow," Selena was in disbelief, "I thought it was just me."

"Oh no," Princess Nanu said, "In fact, There are some that believe that people born under those conditions have a greater potential than the average person."

"Seriously?" Selena asked.

"Yes. Won't you please show me what you can do?" Princess Nanu asked.

"Okay, but I don't have much practice with using it outside of healing my brother and friends back home," Selena tried to focus her powers between her hands, but suddenly found it difficult to muster the energy, "Uh oh. It's not working."

"You must be too tired to focus properly," Princess Nanu said, "Or it could be our warm climate. Depending on a person's elemental mastery, certain elements can function well anywhere while others work better in different conditions."

"It's probably my elemental mastery," Selena said.

"Well don't worry," Princess Nanu said, "It's still a great gift to have. So why are you traveling with Prince Alexander?"

"Well it started when he first came to Prominence Town," Selena got up.

For several minutes, Selena told the story of our encounters in Prominence Town and in Phoenix Volcano to Princess Nanu. The princess seemed to really enjoy the short story.

"And no one was with him when he showed up?" Princess Nanu asked.

"No. He was by himself," Selena said, "I think that's why I was so shocked when he introduced himself."

"And now you're traveling with him to help fight this OSC?" she asked.

"Yes," Selena said, "It was my brothers idea to go at first, but I decided to come too so I could keep him out of trouble."

"Great!" Princess Nanu said, "When we meet again, you must tell me about everything that happens!"

"Alright then," Selena agreed, "I promise."

"Wonderful! Then it's a promise between friends, so you have to keep it," Princess Nanu said, "Now let's not keep everyone waiting for us."

"Yes Princess Nanu," Selena followed her.

"Just call me Nanu," she said.

Back at the breakfast table, Vincent was leaning his head against the table with his arm. He was growing more impatient by the minute as he listened to me carry on a conversation with Jabari.

"What is it with women and getting dressed? Are they MAKING their clothes every time they change?" Vincent began to grow impatient.

"Sorry for being so late," Princess Nanu spoke as her and Selena entered the dining room.

Keith took one look at Princess Nanu's short back hair, crystal blue eyes, and pink dress and almost fell out of his chair. His fantasies about her beauty were brought to life right before his eyes. Lan just watched as Keith continued to space out until Princess Nanu sat down across the table from Keith. I was stunned from looking at Selena as she sat down.

"Wow Selena. Y-you look great," I commented while trying to keep from stammering.

Selena couldn't hold back her smile as she looked at herself and then back to me, "R-Really?"

"Watch this," Princess Nanu whispered to Selena before turning to me, "Alexander, how do I look??" Princess Nanu asked me in a teasing manner.

"You look-" I was cut off when Keith put his hand in my face and pushed me back.

"Gorgeous! Just like a princess should look from head to toe," Keith interjected, "Not even the nights of two full moons can compare to you."

"Um, thank you?" Princess Nanu was stunned at Keith's abruptness.

"So…can we eat now?" Vincent pushed Keith back from Princess Nanu the same way I was pushed back.

I simply put my hand over my face from embarrassment, "Could you be any ruder?"

"Yes! Let us, how you say Prince Alexander, dig in!" the Pharaoh spoke almost commandingly.

"Yeah! Finally!" Vincent said as he wasted no time stuffing his face.

"But I never said that…" I thought to myself.

A few minutes had passed and all of us were done feasting except Vincent. He ate as though his stomach were a bottomless pit. I lost count of how many times the servants refilled his plate with food.

"Selena," Princess Nanu spoke, "Your brother eats as much as five desert horses. How does he do it?"

"That's been a mystery since we were born. If you could list all the wonders of the world, Vincent would be in the top ten," Selena commented.

"I'm not complaining or anything, but why do your servants keep refilling my plate?" Vincent asked.

"It is the way of our dining," the Pharaoh began, "Unless a person leaves a little bit of food on his or her plate, our servants will continue to refill their plate until they cannot eat anymore."

"So…it's like all you can eat?? Sweet!! I love this place!!" Vincent said while holding a rib up in the air with his right hand.

This time, Selena put her hand over her face from embarrassment, "Nanu. Forget what I said earlier about him being in the top ten. He would be in the top FIVE."

I sat on the steps of the courtyard several minutes after breakfast. I was enjoying the downtime so much that I began nodding off from fatigue. It took the sound of two blades scraping against each other to snap me out of it.

"Alex," Jabari called me from behind, "You are not too tired are you? I was hoping we could have an after-breakfast sparring match."

"Hey Jabari," I stood up and stretched, "I should probably take a nap before we spar. If we fought now, I'm afraid that I couldn't give you much of a challenge."

"What?" Jabari sounded disappointed, "How am I suppose to burn off this food?"

"I'll probably be at full strength later today or tomorrow," I said, "I know it's been a while since we sparred, but surely it can wait a little longer."

"Hey," Vincent walked up from out of nowhere, "If you want to fight that bad, I'll take you on."

"Y…you?" Jabari almost didn't take him seriously.

"Yeah, me!" Vincent slammed his fists together, "Let's see what you got!"

"That's not a good idea," I warned Vincent, "You don't know how strong Jabari is."

"You do not even have any weapons," Jabari said.

"These are my weapons," Vincent held up his fists, "And I'm gonna show you what they can do."

"Very well," Jabari sighed, "If you wish to fight that badly, then we will fight."

"Oh man," I was a little worried for Vincent as they walked to the middle of the courtyard, "Take it easy on him Jabari!"

"Hey! Who was the one that got rescued twice by me?" Vincent reminded me.

"He's being too arrogant…" I said to myself.

Jabari and Vincent stood five feet from each other as they prepared to duel. Jabari stared unflinching as Vincent stretched his arms and legs.

"I hope you will not hold it against me if you get hurt," Jabari stuck his blades into the ground behind him.

"Don't worry about me," Vincent said, "I'm use to a little roughhousing."

"Then bring it on," Jabari stood with his fists down to his side.

"You got it!" Vincent suddenly lunged.

Vincent attacked Jabari straight on with a hard left jab. Jabari suddenly blocked it with his right palm and pushed Vincent back so hard that he almost fell.

"Do not insult me," Jabari suddenly sounded irritated.

"What?" Vincent was confused.

"If you are not going to fight me seriously, then this is a waste of my time," Jabari sternly said.

"So it's like that huh?" Vincent was furious, "Ok then! You're gonna feel this one tomorrow morning!"

Vincent suddenly unleashed a fierce assault against Jabari who was quickly forced onto the defensive. While Jabari was unable to attack, Vincent hadn't landed a clean blow for what seemed like several minutes. Jabari was parrying and blocking all of Vincent's attacks with seemingly minimal effort.

"Hey what's going on?" Keith asked as him and Lan walked up.

"Long story short," I said, "I was too tired to duel Jabari, so Vincent decided he wanted to duel him."

"Oh no," Selena walked up with Princess Nanu, "Did Vincent do something stupid to anger Prince Jabari?"

"He didn't anger him," I said, "But challenging Jabari counts as doing something stupid in his case."

"Oh dear," Princess Nanu put her hand to her face, "I hope he takes it easy on your brother."

"Does he even stand a chance?" Lan asked.

"Well…" I turned back to watch the fight.

Suddenly Vincent was able to land a left cross to Jabari's jaw that pushed him back a step.

"Gotcha!" Vincent was feeling a surge of confidence.

Suddenly Jabari countered with a hard left punch to Vincent's chest that knocked the wind out of him. Jabari ended the duel with a hard right cross that sent Vincent flipping backwards until he hit his head against a stone wall and fell to the ground unconscious.

"That would be a no…" I finished my sentence.

"Vincent!" Selena ran to her unconscious brother, "Are you alright?!"

"He will be fine after some rest," Jabari said, "All I did was knock him out."

"Wow!" Keith was shocked at how strong Jabari was, "That's some serious strength."

"No kidding," Lan was in agreement.

"Guards," Jabari called, "Please take him to his room so that he may rest and recover."

"At once your highness," two of the guards picked up Vincent and took him inside.

"Thanks for taking it easy on him," I said to Jabari.

"You are welcome," Jabari picked up his blades from the ground, "Come find me when you are ready to duel. I do not like to hold back."

As we all rested, the rest of the day went without incident. We continued to socialize for much of the day. Vincent was still snoozing when nightfall came. As I drifted back to sleep at night, I could only hope that tomorrow would be a smooth day as well.

Episode 7
Vincent's Realization

The next day was a warm and breezy one with partly cloudy skies that provided occasional patches of shade over the city. The Pharaoh and Queen were standing together on the steps of the courtyard as they watched the duel between me and Jabari. While half their attention was on the two of us honing our fighting skills, the other half was on the details that I had given them regarding my encounters up until now.

"Before our conference with Alexander, I was originally beginning to think that the rise of these attacks were due to the dark powers that our sealed in the ancient tombs," the pharaoh said, "I feel better knowing that is not the case, but I am highly concerned nonetheless."

"I am too," the queen agreed, "For Alexander and his friends to have gotten here safely is nothing short of the Twilight Star protecting them."

"He mentioned a dark shadow in his premonition," the pharaoh said, "Even if it is not from the pyramid, dark powers are definitely at work. These dark crystals he mentioned can be proof of that."

"And the sudden outbreak of attacks on travelers and our citizens," the queen cut in, "It ties in almost perfectly with what Alexander mentioned had been happening around Valsoria. What should we do?"

"At the very moment there is not a lot we can do," the pharaoh crossed his arms, "We cannot predict when these infected beasts will attack, and we do not know the location of OSC. For the moment, all we can do is keep everyone on guard and be ready for anything."

"And what about Alexander?" the queen asked, "After I mentioned that the king of Gravadale may know the location of the Golem Soul Crystal, he decided that they would leave today at sunset. Traveling at night with these monsters is dangerous, but trying to get through the desert during the day is equally as perilous."

"The best I can do is to send some of our best warriors to escort them out of the desert," the pharaoh said, "However they would have to return immediately upon seeing them out safely."

"Very well," the queen said, "I suppose all we can do now is watch the duel now and pray for his safety."

"His safety against the monsters, or his safety against our son's strength?" the pharaoh asked.

"Now that you mention it," the queen thought for a moment, "I suppose both."

The duel between Jabari and I had gotten so intense that it drew the attention of some of the palace's guards and servants. Jabari stood with his left blade held low in front of him and his right blade above his head behind him. I stood with my sword held slightly angled horizontally in front of me as I waited to see what he was going to do next.

"You have gotten better," Jabari said, "I cannot seem to knock you down this time."

"Thanks," I said, "Your style seems more solid now."

"I have been practicing for quite a while now," Jabari began to step to his right as I began to do the same, "And it is paying off well."

"I see," I said, "I guess that means you're not ready to quit?"

"No way," Jabari said, "This is just getting fun!"

"They both have gotten better," Princess Nanu watched us resume our duel.

"How many times have they fought each other?" Selena asked.

"I believe," Princess Nanu looked up and put her finger to her lips, "I believe this makes their seventh duel. Jabari has won most of them, but Alexander beat him senseless on their fourth and fifth duel."

"Really?" Selena asked, "I would think that Alex would be at a disadvantage against Jabari since he dual wields."

"Anyone else would be," Princess Nanu said, "But Alexander is different. Even though Jabari is physically stronger and fights with two blades, Alexander fights with an unpredictable fighting style that always seems to catch Jabari off guard. When they duel, they each bring something new and unique to the fight, so it benefits the both of them."

"I never thought of it like that," Selena said, "It reminds me of my brother and a friend of mine back home."

"Speaking of your brother," Princess Nanu looked around, "Where is he?"

"I think he's up on the balcony with Keith," Selena answered.

After taking a hit from Jabari's assault, I slid backwards on my feet and stopped a few feet from hitting a wall. I quickly rose up and deflected his right blade with a rising slash of my sword. As he tried to strike me with his left blade, I spun and parried it with a roundhouse kick that spun Jabari backwards. As I went to strike him, he reached his blades over his head to block the attack, and that's when I kicked him in the back to put some distance between us.

"That was close," I said to myself.

"Lan! Vincent!" Keith yelled, "Are you watching this?! This is getting epic!"

Lan was observing the fight with wide eyes as we fought toe to toe. Vincent was watching the fight with his arms crossed, but with a different look on his face.

"What's wrong with you?" Keith asked Vincent, "Not epic enough for ya?"

"Nah," Vincent said calmly, "Nothing's wrong."

"You're not still mad about yesterday are you?" Keith asked, "So what if he beat you? Look at him! I'd think twice about fighting him head on like you did."

"He didn't just beat me…" Vincent kept watching the fight, "He owned me. He brushed off the first attack I threw at him like it was nothing, and then knocked me out with two hits. This blue-…this guy was way stronger than I thought he would be."

"Way stronger you thought a royal could ever be?" Keith asked.

"…yeah…" Vincent admitted, "I barely even got a hit in…"

The sound of a sudden boom and screams brought our duel to an immediate halt. We all rushed up the stairs of the wall to see what happened. Outside, near the city gates, a large monster had destroyed part of the north gate. While we couldn't quite tell what it was, it didn't appear to have a stinger like the one from the other night.

"Just when it was getting good," Jabari went to get his real blades.

"Wait up!" I transformed the Twilight Star, "I'm coming with you!"

"Oh yeah!" Keith ran after us, "Time to own!"

By the time we got to the battle site, several of Rac' Sagadam's guards had already engaged it in battle, but were being pushed back. Several soldiers that were injured during the surprise attack had to be carried to a safe distance. This monster was so terribly warped to the point that I couldn't tell what it may have been. The only thing that I could see clearly, aside from the dark aura around it, were its fangs sticking out from its mouth, and its large bony tail whipping behind it as it stood on all fours and attacked everything in sight.

"Is this what you fought in the desert?" Jabari asked.

"It's about the same size," I said, "But it was different. It didn't have that dark aura from what I remember."

"Can we beat this one?" Keith asked, "I can't charge up a Thunder Sniper this time."

"We will defeat it," Jabari raised his blades, "We must defeat it! Are you ready?"

"Let's end it fast!" I stood ready to charge, "Strike it at the forehead! That's where its power is coming from!"

"Warriors of Rac' Sagadam!" Jabari called out, "Lend me your strength! Unleash your fighting spirit and attack!!"

Jabari and his soldiers let out a war cry that sounded like the howling of jackals. The monster was quickly surrounded and assaulted with spears and axes. When soldiers would be knocked down, they would be quickly replaced with more as the assault continued. Keith threw several kunai that pierced the monster on its back while I went for one of its legs to throw it off balance. Jabari went straight for the head and blocked its jaws with both of his blades. Jabari landed a vicious strike on the underside of its jaw as it lifted its head up and thrashed about to throw everyone away.

"Keep up the attack!" one of the soldiers yelled, "Do not let it advance any further!"

Suddenly the Pharaoh rushed into the battle and struck it under its jaw with a mighty left uppercut. The impact was so powerful, the monster was briefly stunned and it collapsed to the ground.

"Finish it before it can recover!" I ran to the right side of its neck.

Keith and I struck the beast on each side of its neck with our swords and ripped them through its flesh with all our might. Jabari finished it with an X strike to its forehead that left a deep X shaped scar on top of its head. The last bit of life left it after its long bony tail finally came to a halt and fell flat to the ground with a loud thud. After waiting a moment to assure its demise, the air was filled with cheering at our victory.

"They won!" Princess Nanu and Selena yelled from a safe distance of the battle.

Vincent observed the battle from a higher point from where Selena and Princess Nanu stood. He appeared to be frozen in place from awe.

"That…was incredible…" Vincent said silently to himself.

I observed the spot where Jabari's blades had crossed on the head of the monster. It was there that I saw another dark crystal embedded inside its head.

"Just like the others," I said.

"Is that it?" Jabari stood to my left.

"That's it," I said.

"Do you think there are more out there?" Keith asked.

"There's no way of knowing," I said, "Let's just hope we don't run into any more before we get to Gravadale."

"Are you sure you will not reconsider?" the pharaoh asked me.

"Yes," I said, "There can't be that many more out there. There aren't a whole lot of animals that live in the desert."

"That's true," the pharaoh said, "Then, at the very least, I will send several of my finest warriors to escort you out of the desert. They will be ready to leave when you are."

"Thank you Pharaoh Meti," I said, "We'll definitely make it through with your help.

"Anything to help you succeed against these criminals," he said.

The carcass was later dragged away and burned outside the city where many of the citizens celebrated the victory. It continued to burn into the late evening when the sun began going down. While most of us were making preparations to leave, Vincent was watching the fire from the city gate. He stood motionless as if he were in deep thought.

"Vincent," Jabari called him from behind.

"Huh?" Vincent almost sounded startled.

"Alexander is almost ready to leave," he said, "Should you be making preparations?"

"I've got everything ready. Thanks though," Vincent looked toward the western sky for a moment, "Hold on a sec Prince Jabari."

"Yes?" Jabari was about to leave before Vincent called him.

"One day…if I get the chance," Vincent paused for a moment, "I want to challenge you to a duel again."

"Really?" Jabari almost didn't believe him.

"Really," Vincent confirmed, "It won't be like last time. The next time we get to fight, I'm gonna to be a lot stronger."

“I train myself almost all the time,” Jabari said, “Are you sure you will be strong enough for another duel?”

“Definitely,” Vincent held his head low with his eyes shut, “I’m going to improve so much, I’ll give you a challenge like you’ve never had. That’s a promise.”

“Very well then,” Jabari smiled.

“Huh?” Vincent opened his eyes to find that Jabari had his hand held out to him.

“We will make it a promise between friends,” Jabari said, “So now you have to keep your promise.”

“…alright,” Vincent firmly gripped his hand, “Definitely! I’ll definitely keep that promise!”

We all gathered at the gate with eight of Pharaoh Meti’s hand picked warriors a few minutes later where we said our final goodbyes to the royal family and Rac’ Sagadam.

“Bye Selena!” Princess Nanu waved, “Do not forget your promise!”

“I won’t!” Selena waved back.

The city was barely in sight by the time nightfall came. Our journey across the rest of the desert was a very secure one with the pharaoh’s escort. With all the occasional breaks in between, the trip was surprisingly quiet and uneventful. Eventually, as the night sky was beginning to lighten, much of the sand was gone, and we were back onto harder soil. The escort bid us farewell as they returned to the desert while we continued onward Gravadale.

Episode 8
Sudden Crisis

"Based on the failed experiments," Francis spoke to his leader, "It doesn't look like we can use the dark crystals to control creatures. At the very least, our soldiers can bend the dark energies to their will to a certain extent."

"I see," the leader said, "And what of Prince Alexander?"

"The men we sent to kill him and retrieve the Twilight Star were found dead. Most of them had sword wounds, so I conclude that he was able to defeat them somehow and escape. As for his location, I'm afraid I don't have that information, but at the very least, we know he didn't return to Valsoria."

"I see," the leader said, "Do we have any idea where he may be?"

"Not…really," Francis hesitated to admit, "It's not likely that he would stay at that town near Phoenix Volcano, but there aren't a lot of places for him to go. It would be suicide for him to travel through the desert to Rac' Sagadam on his own, so it's highly unlikely he went that route. Even if he did, the monsters we let loose there would have finished him off. He has to return to Valsoria at some point."

"I see," the leader thought for a moment, "And what is the situation at Gravadale and the location of the Golem Soul Crystal?"

"Gravadale's king and many of his knights have yet to return," he said, "We have yet to find the crystal, but we believe it lies in the forest not too far from Gravadale."

"I believe it's time that we prepare to set another part of our plan into motion," the leader suddenly stood up, "Call forth that scientist we captured!"

"Yes sir!" Francis quickly stood up and ran.

Deep down a dark hallway, Francis entered a large room filled with metal, supplies, and other various junk. Papers were scattered along the floor, but mostly around a large solitary table. Francis walked over to what looked like an oversized suit of armor where a young man sat with his head and arms resting inside the torso piece as he slept.

"Zaalek!" Francis yelled.

"What?" he woke up so suddenly that he bumped his head, "Ow! What is it?"

"The boss wants to see you right now!" he shouted.

"Oh great, alright," he shut the hatch on the armor, "It never fails. As soon as I really get into what I'm working on, I get called away."

"Hurry up before you put him in a bad mood," Francis warned him.

"I'm going!" he ran down the hallway to see the boss, "Hey, uh…somebody said you wanted to see me?" he peeked around the door to the boss.

"Get in here," the boss demanded.

"Right sir," he walked in while smiling nervously as a sweat drop went down the side of his face.

"How goes the progress on the Iron Soldier?" the leader asked, "Is it ready yet?"

"Well, yes and no sir," Zaalek answered, "It looks as if it is going to work and all but it's still a prototype, and I haven't been able to test it yet."

"Have it ready by late tonight," the boss commanded.

"Yes sir. Will I send it with the soldiers to aid in the search for the Golem Soul Crystal?" Zaalek asked.

"That was the original plan, but I'm starting to see a window of opportunity here," the boss said with a grin, "Gravadale's defenses are currently weak due to the king and several of his knights being away. Tonight my soldiers will launch a preemptive strike on Gravadale. It will serve as an example of our growing might, and your little Iron Soldier will be our secret weapon. Have it ready by sundown so that my men can move out!" the boss commanded.

"Yes sir!" Zaalek answered and ran back to finish work on the Iron Soldier.

"The fall of Gravadale will be just the beginning. When Valsoria sees what we can do, they will be forced to submit to us. And Prince Alexander, wherever you are, you can't hide forever. Your fate will be sealed soon enough! …heh heh heh… HAHAHAHAHA!!" the boss's laugh echoed throughout their base.

I wasn't paying attention all too well to the grassy plains we were crossing. My mind was on too many things at once. I was thinking about the dark crystals I found from fighting the monsters in the desert and the dark shadow I keep seeing in my nightmare. I've handled myself through dangerous things in the past, but I'm growing more and more concerned to what me and my friends will run into. I was constantly spaced out even as we stopped to rest on some rocks in the plains.

"Ow!" Selena exclaimed from a sharp pain in her hand, "I didn't see those thorns on the side of the rock there."

"I wonder if Robert will be in Gravadale when we get there," Lan was looking off into the distance, "It's been a while since I've seen him."

"Who's that?" Vincent asked, "A friend of yours?"

“Yes,” Lan said, “We met back when I was still living in the orphanage here. At some point, we both enlisted to become squires with the hope that we’d both become knights. He was accepted, but I wasn’t.”

“Why not?” Vincent asked.

“I’m far from being very physically strong,” Lan said, “The armor was so heavy, I would collapse from exhaustion every time we marched, I would keep dropping my sword during practice, and I just couldn’t keep up. They later decided that I would be too much of a liability on the battlefield, so they discharged me from the group.”

“That must have sucked,” Vincent casually said.

“Yes,” Lan said, “But I’ve gotten over it during the past few years.”

“What made you,” Selena put her hand to her forehead, “Want to become a knight in the first place?”

“Basically,” Lan said, “I just wanted to be stronger so I would be accepted as someone.”

“You ok sis?” Vincent asked from noticing the look on Selena’s face.

“Yeah, I’m fine Vincent,” she said, “I think I’m just tired.

“Alright,” Vincent turned to me, “So how far till we get to Gravadale?”

“I can see it in the distance,” I said, “It’s a long walk, but we should make it there sometime after noon.”

“Good,” Vincent stood up on the rock where Selena was sitting, “Selena is getting tired, and I’m getting hungry.”

“And dizzy,” Selena’s eyes were beginning to look like they were struggling to focus on anything.

"Dizzy? You must be tired," Keith turned around and noticed a little blood on Selena's hand, "Hey when did you cut yourself?"

"I pricked my hand on a thorny vine by the rocks," she said.

"A thorny…oh no," Lan said as if he just got a dark feeling in his gut.

"What's wrong??" I asked.

"This is bad," Lan said after he got a look at the vine at the rock, "Selena, you pricked your hand on Poison Snake Vine."

"Is it dangerous??" Vincent and Selena asked.

"It can be," Lan said, "We need to get you some antidote as soon as we can. I'm sure a pharmacist in Gravadale will have some."

"Then we need to make haste!" I said.

"Can you still walk sis?" Vincent asked.

"I think so," she struggled to hold her balance.

"She doesn't need to move very much if she can help it," Lan said, "If she moves too much, the poison spreads faster."

"Hey Alex!" Keith looked upwards toward Gravadale, "There's some knights heading our way!"

"Then we may be in luck!" I looked up.

The first knight that reached us rode in on a brown stallion. He was covered from neck to toe in Gravadale style armor. His neat cut green hair was clear to see without his helmet on.

"Travelers," he called us, "Just who are you?"

"Robert??" Lan did a double take.

"Lan??" the knight quickly turned his attention to him, "Is that really you??"

"Robert!!" a second knight called him from behind.

She rode up beside Robert on a darker colored stallion. Her red hair was tied in a ponytail that came down to her shoulders. She wore a red cape with Gravadale's Coat of Arms which symbolized that she was of commanding authority.

"Why did you suddenly leave the flank?!" she demanded to know.

"I was checking these travelers to make sure that they weren't up to anything suspicious," he said.

"If they were, they would have overwhelmed you," she said, "There's five of them. Think before you act!"

"Hey!" I interrupted her, "Are you the commanding officer?"

"Yes," she said, "I am third lieutenant Joanna of the Gravadale Knights. Just who are you?"

"Prince Alexander of Valsoria," I said.

"S-seriously?!" she almost didn't believe me.

"We have an emergency!" I said, "Our friend cut her hand on Poison Snake Vine!"

"Uh oh," she said, "How long ago?"

"Just a few minutes ago," Selena said.

"Can you help us get her to a doctor?" I asked.

"Yes," Joanna said, "The king's doctor should have the antidote you need. Do you have the strength to hang onto me on horseback?"

"Y-yes, I think so," Selena answered.

"Good. We can't have you moving too much on your own right now. It'll make the poison spread faster. Someone help her up!" Commander Joannah ordered us.

Vincent and I helped her get behind Joannah on her horse so she could be ridden into town faster than we could carry her on our own. The rest of us were going to hurry as fast as we could on foot. With no way of knowing how damaging this poison could be, we were all in a hustle to get to Gravadale. Birds flew overhead as if they were escorting us to the city. Joannah had informed the guards that I was on my way, so we were able to run right through the gate and straight to the castle. I expected good news when we got there, but what I heard nearly made my heart drop and Vincent exploded.

"What do you MEAN you're out of the antidote?! You're a freakin' doctor! You have to have that kind of medicine when it's needed!" Vincent pinned one of the doctors to the wall outside the room Selena was in.

"P-please sir! C-c-calm yourself! I-" the doctor was struggling to breath from Vincent's grip on his neck.

"My sister needs medicine now and you're telling me you can't give it to her?!" Vincent yelled with rage. He was about to lose it.

"Let him go Vincent!" I yelled, "This isn't helping!"

Vincent dropped the doctor and turned his attention to me. "Alex, they don't even have the medicine! What are we suppose to do?!"

"Sir, if you would have only let me finish," the doctor got our attention after he recovered his breath, "We don't have any antidote made, but I can make one really quick."

"You can??" I asked.

"Well why didn't you say that in the beginning??" Vincent asked.

"You were choking me!" the doctor defended himself, "Anyway, I have most of the ingredients, but I lack the active ingredient, Blue Sage Herb."

"Blue Sage Herb?" Lan asked, "I can find that for you. It grows in abundance in the forest near here."

"Are you sure you can get the herb in time?" I asked him.

"I know the forest pretty well," Lan assured us, "I know my plants pretty well to, so I'll be fine."

"I'll go with you," Keith spoke up, "Let's hurry though. Sundown is in a few hours."

"Ok. Vincent, Alex, you can count on us!" Lan assured us before he and Keith ran off.

"Be careful guys," I said, "And gather as much as you can if you're able!"

"We're counting on you," Vincent said, "Especially Selena!"

"We'll get it and be back in no time," Keith said, "Lead the way Lan!"

"Right!" They both took off from the castle.

Lan and Keith quickly found their way to the forest. Somewhere in there grew the Blue Sage Herb they needed to find to cure Selena of the poison. The doctor was able to give her a tonic to help dilute the poison in her system, but she still needed the antidote for her health to be in the clear. All I could do at this point was to hope that nothing would hinder Lan and Keith's search.

"Pardon me Prince Alexander," Joanna walked up to me.

"Yes?" I asked.

"If you don't mind me asking," she began, "What are you doing all the way here? I ask because you don't have a proper escort or guard with you, nor was there any word that you would be coming."

"I'll be glad to tell you," I said, "But I'd like to be able to tell Sir Rupert at the same time."

"I'm afraid he's not here," she informed me, "He and the king have been in Miliga for quite a while, and won't be due back until tomorrow."

"I see," I said, "Are you in charge of guard while he is away?"

"I am," she said.

"In that case, I should begin telling you of what's been happening lately," I said.

Episode 9
Race Against Time! A New Disaster is Discovered!

After explaining to Commander Joanna the situation involving OSC, she immediately notified the other knights to be on a tighter watch than normal. She even went as far as to announce a curfew for the citizens under a certain age. I didn't want her to put the people into a panic, but I understood her situation. She had only been recently promoted to third lieutenant and was given the task of keeping the city safe while the king and Sir Rupert were away. It's understandably a lot of pressure. I returned to the room Selena was resting in inside the castle. She was doing better, but she was still a little dizzy.

"Is everything alright?" Selena asked me.

"Yeah," I answered, "I informed Commander Joanna of what's been happening, so she's got everyone on high alert for any suspicious activity."

"And anyway," Vincent cut in, "If OSC does attack, we'll handle it. You just concentrate on getting better."

"I must say," the doctor started speaking, "You're handling the poison better than most people have. I'm surprise you're able to sit up and hold a conversation."

"Thanks," Selena said, "I just wish I never touched that stupid vine in the first place."

"It's not your fault," I said "So don't worry about it too much. I'm going to go look around a bit and look out for Keith and Lan to come back."

As soon as I stepped out of the room, I almost ran into Robert. He looked as shocked as I was when I noticed him.

"Oh!" he stopped himself from running into me, "Sorry Prince Alexander! I should have been paying attention to where I was going."

"It's alright," I said, "Is something wrong?"

"Well no," he said, "I just thought I'd come by and check on you all. How is your friend doing?"

"She's conscious enough to talk with us normally," I said, "So she's fine for the moment."

"I understand. I didn't get to properly introduce myself earlier. I am Robert Greenwood, Knight of Gravadale.

"Nice to meet you," I shook his hand, "I'm just glad you showed up when you did."

"Glad to be of service," he answered back politely.

"Your commander is very strict, but she doesn't look much older than you," I said.

"She isn't that much older than me, and she wasn't always like that. It started when she was appointed to the position of lieutenant by Sir Rupert II. She takes the position very seriously," Robert looked around to see if Joanna was around, "Sometimes too seriously in my opinion."

"It's probably a lot of pressure for her," I said, "It's rare for someone to reach that high of a rank that young."

"Well in her defense," Rocky said, "She has worked really hard since she was a squire. She's very diligent and devoted to her duties, but there are times where I feel she's too serious."

"I can see she takes her duties very seriously," I said, "But it must be hard to work under pressure when it's that tense."

"I can handle it," Robert said, "But it's troubling to see her not relax when she's on break."

"It's not my place to say what she's doing is right or wrong," I said, "But there is such a thing as being too serious. When you get that tense in battle, you can sometimes find yourself unable to fight like you normally would, and in some cases, play right into the enemies hands. Your mind has to be free enough to improvise to a changing situation in the blink of an eye."

"Hmm, that sounds like something Sir Rupert II would say," Rocky commented.

"It's something I paraphrased from General Isaac," I said.

"Oh! I almost forgot," Robert slapped his hand on his forehead, "I was ordered to make sure you and your friends had comfortable rooms to stay in. I'll show you to your rooms when you're ready."

"Thank you," I said, "But I honestly couldn't rest at the moment if I wanted too. I'm just still waiting for Lan and Keith to get back with the herbs."

"My buddy Lan really knows his plants. Try not to worry too much. He is a very reliable guy," Robert assured me.

"Hey, I'm hungry. Got anything to eat round here?" Vincent walked out of the room Selena was in.

"Excuse me?" Robert was caught off guard by Vincent's sudden appearance.

"And my sis says she's thirsty. I need to bring her something to drink," Vincent finished.

"Oh, well I think some of the other knights are in the dining room at the bottom of the stairs on the right," Rocky told him.

"Cool, I'll be right back. Want me to bring you back something Alex?" Vincent asked.

"Sure, it doesn't matter what," I told him.

"Ok, I'll be right back," he ran down the stairs.

My mind began to wonder about Lan and Keith's progress. Since they were simply going out to gather an herb I figured that nothing could go wrong.

"Hey Lan, are you sure you're going the right way?" Keith was trying to fight from getting tangled in the overgrown shrubs and overhanging branches.

"Yeah," Lan answered, "There's a small patch around here that the Blue Sage Herb grows in. Finding it shouldn't be a problem, but I just hope we can get out of this dense forest in time."

"Well when you find it, just give it to me," Keith reached into his vest and pulled out what looked like a small wrist guard with small lightning crystals embedded on the underside, "I can use this to get back to Gravadale in no time."

"Your Ninja Drive? I forgot you had that thing with you," Lan said.

"I wasn't using it earlier so all of you could keep up with me," Keith was trying to sound cool.

"It would only be for five minutes," Lan poked fun at Keith, "Then you would collapse from loss of energy and we all would be running past you."

"Dammit Lan," Keith felt stupid from Lan's remark, "Just find the damn herb so we can-"

Keith cut himself off when a small bird snatched up his Ninja Drive and flew it up to a girl with short green hair and wearing a brown shirt and skirt of a unique design.

"Hey, who the heck are you?!" Keith demanded to know, "Give that back now!"

The forest girl simply put on Keith's Ninja Drive as if she didn't hear him. She then motioned to him with her finger as if daring him to come up and get it.

"Grr! I don't have time for games!" Keith yelled.

Keith leaped upwards into the tree, but missed the girl as she leaped backwards to another branch. She began leaping from branch to branch as if she were hoping on stepping stones in a pond.

"Get back here!" Keith pursued her through the treetops.

"Oh great," Lan tried to follow them on the ground.

Keith and the forest girl ran through the tops of the trees as if they were running on solid ground. Keith's abilities as a ninja allowed him to maneuver through the branches without too much difficulty. The young girl moved as if there were no risk of falling to the ground. Keith finally got directly behind her and lunged forward to take her down, but she made a sudden turn by swinging on the trunk of the tree and darted off in another direction. At the very last second, Keith grabbed onto a branch to keep from falling. He swung himself to get back up into the trees, but the branch broke in mid swing and he fell to the ground and landed on his face. He propped himself up with his arms to look around to find the girl that eluded him. He saw her disappear into the denseness of the forest just ahead of him when he got up and began to continue pursuing her.

Back in Gravadale, Joanna was making her rounds on horseback throughout the small town to make sure everything was running smoothly. The mood in the town seemed calm and still all throughout the evening. Robert was just leaving the castle when Joanna rode up to him.

"Is everything well with Prince Alexander and his group?" she asked.

"Yes commander," Robert stood up straight, "The Prince and his companions have been notified of the rooms they are to rest in. They have been offered all the essentials including food and water as well."

"Very good," she said, "Remain here to carry out the rest of your shift."

"Yes commander," he nodded, "Are you about done with your shift?"

"No," she said, "I'll be working late tonight."

"With all due respect commander," Robert stopped her from leaving, "I think you've earned a break. Sir Rupert and the King will be back tomorrow morning so-"

"I'll rest when they return, and no later," Joanna cut him off, "Is that clear?"

"Y-yes commander," he reluctantly gave in.

In an OSC campsite, not far from Gravadale, OSC soldiers were making preparations for the assault on Gravadale. Final tests were being made on the Iron Soldier that was constructed, and everyone was eager to get the attack started.

"Is the Iron Soldier ready to go?" Francis asked Zaalek.

"Y-yes," he answered, "I've got it moving to the best of its ability, but please remember, it's just a prototype."

"We'll judge how well it does in battle," Francis said.

"Where," he started to ask, "Should I have it approach Gravadale?"

"It will approach from the east, but you won't be controlling it this time," he said, "Give that thing you made to control it to me, and I'll give it to one of the soldiers who has worked with it during your testing."

"So what am I going to do?" he asked.

"You will be returned to the base," he answered, "There you will immediately begin work on more Iron Soldiers. Also, you shall construct me a weapon that will help increase my own powers based on your research."

"I see," he sighed.

"Take him back to the base," Francis ordered one of his men.

"Yes sir," he grabbed Zaalek on the shoulder.

Using a forged gauntlet with shadow crystals embedded in them, he focused his will and a small dark cloud of energy formed in front of them. He then ordered Zaalek into the darkness and followed after him where they both disappeared before the dark energy mass faded.

"When do we attack sir?" one of the lead solders asked.

"Your orders are to wait several hours after nightfall," Francis said, "For the most part, I don't care how you go about the attack, but focus your main forces to the north side. That will draw almost all the knights they currently have and the Iron Soldier will be used from the east. That is all."

"Yes sir!" the lead soldier saluted.

The forest girl that took Keith's Ninja Drive stood at the edge of a cliff in a clearing in the forest to oversee the events occurring in the trees below her. Keith somehow found his way to her and was ready to jump her, but he paused when he noticed that she didn't seem to care that he had caught up with her.

"Are you…giving up?" Keith asked confused.

She glanced back at Keith for only a moment, and then turned her attention back to the chaos below her as if asking Keith to watch it with her. Keith cautiously approached her to where he could see the depressed expression on her face. After seeing what she saw, disbelief overtook Keith's facial expression. In the distance, soldiers were destroying the forest and slowly moving deeper into it. There were patches where the forest was still burning from the chaos.

"What in the name of…" Keith was completely stunned by the site of destruction in the forest.

"They seek the heart of the forest…" she finally spoke softly.

"The heart of the forest?" Keith asked, "What's that?"

"It's the embodiment of the earth's energy," she said, "The crystallized essence of the ancient earth guardian."

"I see," Keith continued to watch, "So it's the Golem Soul Crystal they're after."

Just then a small hawk flew down to her and landed on her outreached arm. She brought her forehead to his and leaned onto it gently. The green crystals in her earrings and on her necklace gave a faint glow as she held her eyes shut for a while as if communicating with the hawk telepathically. Keith stood there watching her dumbfounded until she stopped and let the hawk fly on. She then took Keith's arm and put his Ninja Drive on for him. Then she reached into a small bag tied to her waist and handed Keith a bundle of blue herbs.

"I believe you're looking for this?" she spoke again.

"Hey! This is the Blue Sage Herb! But how did you know I needed this?" Keith was confused.

"I can see what he sees form the sky. They will attack your friends tonight," she spoke.

"Tonight?" Keith instantly noticed the setting sun, "Crap! I gotta go!" Keith was about to bolt until she grabbed his arm

"Please try to hurry back as soon as you can," she pleaded with him, "My people are doing their best, but we need help."

"Yeah, I'll come back! I'll bring help too!" Keith assured her.

"Thank you…" she let go of his arm.

The girl then jumped quickly off the cliff before Keith had any time to react to stop her. When Keith ran to where she was she rose up on the back of an enormous hawk. Its beating wings nearly blew Keith off balance as it carried her towards where OSC was cutting through the forest.

"Whoa…" Keith watched them fly off into the distance

"Keith! Are you ok?" Lan emerged into the clearing.

"Lan! I got the herbs! Now we gotta get back to Gravadale fast!" Keith quickly told Lan, "OSC is going to launch an attack there tonight!"

"What?? How do you know?" Lan asked.

"That girl just told me," Keith said.

"And you just believed her?" Lan asked.

"Take a look down there," Keith pointed.

"What?" Lan looked off to see fire burning in the distance, "What happened?"

"The Golem Soul Crystal is here," Keith said, "And these guys are willing to burn down an entire forest to find it! Once we save Gravadale, we have to come back and save this place too!"

Keith and Lan bolted back into the forest as the sky faded into darkness. With a new reason to hustle back to Gravadale, they gave everything they had to get back there as fast as they could to help Selena and warn the knights of the pending threat to befall them. If only finding their way back through the forest in the night sky was that easy...

Episode 10
Under Attack! Organization Shadow Crystal Strikes!

It was well past nightfall and Keith and Lan still hadn't returned. Vincent and I left the castle to see if we could try and find them. I was trying not to panic, but with each passing minute, I was beginning to fear the worst.

"They shouldn't be taking this long!" I ran with Vincent towards the west gate.

"They picked the worst time to get lost," Vincent said.

"Even with both moons out," I looked up to the night sky, "They're going to have a hard time finding their way back."

"Prince Alexander!" Robert stopped us at the gate, "What's wrong?"

"Keith and Lan aren't back yet," Vincent spoke, "That's what's wrong!"

"It's well past nightfall," I said, "They're taking way too long to get back. We need to see if we can find them."

"I've been growing concerned ever since sunset as well," Robert said, "But I don't think it would be wise for you to try and search for them. You would only get lost as well."

"What's going on?" Joanna rode up to the three of us.

"Keith and Lan haven't returned from the forest yet," I said.

Suddenly the Twilight Star began to glow on its own. The energy I felt from it was slightly different than what I had felt before when using it. The way it suddenly surged through my body felt like a rush of energy I would get during a fight.

"Alex!" Vincent saw my reaction, "What's going on?"

"I'm not sure," I gripped the Twilight Star with my right hand, "But something must be wrong for it to react this way."

"Alex!!!" I heard a familiar and welcomed voice coming from outside the west gate.

"Keith!" I saw him and Lan running full force towards us.

"It's about damn time!" Vincent shouted as they skidded to a halt in front of us, "What took so long?!"

"Can't…explain…" Keith was out of breath.

"Attack…" Lan started speaking, "Get ready…"

"Attack who?" Robert asked.

"Get ready for what?" Vincent asked.

Suddenly a loud horn could be heard blowing from the north gate. Even though it was the first time most of us had heard it, I could feel the urgency in its call, and we all knew what it meant.

"Oh no…" Joanna was almost immobilized with shock, "We're under attack!"

"It's OSC!" Keith finally caught his breath, "I learned from someone in the forest that they were planning to attack tonight!"

"F-from who?!" Joanna was almost frantic, "How?!"

"Never mind that now!" I shouted, "We need to deal with the situation at hand! You need to get to the north gate as fast as you can. Your knights are going to need you to lead and organize them for battle!"

“Alright,” Joanna paused for a moment after taking a deep breath, “Seal off this gate! If this OSC wants a fight, then we will answer!”

“Yes commander!” several knights proceeded to close the west gate.

“Ready your lance Robert!” she held up her halberd, “For the King, for Gravadale, we will fight with everything we’ve got!”

“Yes commander!” Robert jumped onto his stallion.

“Did you get the herbs?” I asked Lan.

“We sure did,” Lan answered.

“Great,” I said, “Get them to the doctor as fast as you can. I’m going to help deal with OSC.”

“Me too,” Vincent said.

“Alright,” Keith said, “We’ll join up with you as soon as we can!”

“Can you give us a ride?” I asked Joanna.

“Of course,” she let me onto her stallion, “I’ll greatly appreciate the help!”

“Hang on Vincent,” Robert pulled him up onto his stallion.

The stallions we were riding didn’t seem to lose any speed with the extra weight they were carrying. We were met by another knight just as we were about to turn at the center of the city.

“Commander Joanna,” he called out, “To the east!”

“Enemy soldiers are coming from the east too?!” she asked.

“No commander!” he corrected her, “Something else! Something I’ve never seen before! What ever it is, it isn’t human!”

“You think it’s another monster like we faced in the desert?” Vincent asked me.

"It could be," I hopped down from Joanna's stallion, "Vincent and I will take care of whatever's coming from the east. You focus on the soldiers coming from the north."

"Are you sure?" she asked.

"Yeah," Vincent jumped down from Robert's stallion, "It's not the first time we've been up against something like this. We'll handle it."

"Then be careful," she said, "May victory shine upon you!"

"Thank you," I said, "May victory shine upon all of us!"

"Let's go Robert!" she kicked her stallion to gallop full speed to the north gate.

"Right!" he quickly followed.

Upon reaching the north gate, Gravadale's forces had gathered and were ready to face the enemy. At the top of the hill, the enemy could be seen descending the hill in the moonlight. The exact number of soldiers couldn't be determined, but it was clear that they had an advantage over Gravadale in terms of numbers.

"Alright guys," the commander of the OSC group called out, "Give em' hell! Gravadale will belong to us by the time its all said and done!"

"It looks like they outnumber us, but I can't tell by how much," Joanna gripped her halberd tighter.

"Well we certainly can't go out there and fight them like this," Robert stretched his lance arm out.

"We don't have a choice!" she yelled at him, "Can't you see that they're bringing the fight to us?!"

"That's not what I mean," Robert said, "If we rush out there and let them surround us with the numbers we have compared to them, then we're done. Our best bet is to form a defensive front and let them come to us."

"You think that can work?" Joanna asked.

"It has to work," he said, "Our numbers limit our options for attack as it is."

"Alright," Joanna agreed to his plan, "How many archers are stationed atop the city walls?"

"Just seven," he said.

"That's better than none," she said, "It would be nice to have a mage right about now."

"Here they come!" a Gravadale foot soldier yelled out.

"Alright!" Joanna held her halberd up as the earth crystal embedded in its head began to shine, "Form up together and create a defensive front! Don't let the enemy through, no matter what! All archers are to focus your fire 50 yards out to thin their numbers! For the king and for Gravadale, victory will shine upon us!"

The knights let out a furious battle cry as the first wave of arrows took flight. Several arrows were burning as they shot through the air like shooting stars. All of the enemy soldiers that weren't brought down by the arrows soon found themselves in close combat with Gravadale's Knights.

As the Gravadale Knights battled with the solders, Vincent and I prepared to fight with the threat that approached from the east. We weren't completely sure what we were looking at, but it walked on two legs as if it were human. Along its body, I could make out a faint glow of energy, which gave it a more ominous appearance.

"What the hell is that thing?" Vincent stood ready to fight.

"I don't know," I stood with my sword at the ready, "It looks strong though."

"Any ideas on how to take it down?" Vincent asked.

"Nothing in particular comes to mind," I said, "But we can't let that stop us. The knights are fighting OSC at the north gate, so we have to take care of this threat. This could be something they sent as well."

With each large step it took, I could feel the vibration through the ground get stronger as it got closer. Unseen by the both of us, however, was a person hiding in the shadows that controlled the large titan.

"I don't believe it," the OSC soldier thought to himself, "That's Prince Alexander! How did he get all the way out here?! Oh well, this will be great! If I take him out, I'll get promoted for sure!"

"Show me whatcha got!" Vincent bull rushed the titan.

The monster raised its massive right arm to swing down at Vincent. Vincent was able to intercept it with both hands, but the force was so strong he had to kneel to absorb the full impact. The titan then used its left arm to swat Vincent off to the side.

"I'll get him!" I shouted as I ran to its left side.

"Alex, hang on!" Vincent shouted to stop me.

I ducked the back hand swing of its left arm and avoided a direct hit. I flipped over its head and struck it in the back at full force. That's when a moment of fear struck me. Instead of slashing through flesh, my sword scraped against metal!

"It's metal!" I shouted the moment I realized.

"That's what I was trying to tell you!" Vincent said as he staggered up.

"Uh oh," I said right before getting back handed by its right arm.

"Ok! Time for round two!" Vincent got up and charged again.

The metal monster did a back hand swing with its left arm at Vincent, but this time he was able to side step it. Vincent then side stepped a massive right hand punch which made a large hole in the ground. Vincent then struck it under the joint of its arm as hard as he could with a flaming fist that was strong enough to send the iron titan stepping back to regain balance.

"Yeah!" Vincent yelled, "Take that!"

After pausing for a moment, the iron titan suddenly lunged forward and sucker punched Vincent in the face and sent him reeling back several yards. He was too dazed and stunned to move, let alone get up. I struggled to get to my feet as the iron titan began its march towards Vincent.

"Hang on Vincent!" I charged the metal monster once more.

Meanwhile, during all the chaos and mayhem, the doctor had finished brewing up the necessary tonic to purge the poison out of Selena's body. Selena quickly drunk it, and began to feel the effects of the antidote right away.

"Well?" Keith, Lan, and the doctor asked.

"I feel it working already," Selena finished off the rest of the tonic.

"Phew," everyone let out a sigh of relief.

"It kinda tastes familiar though," Selena put down the cup.

"Familiar?" Lan asked, "Familiar how?"

"It has a taste that reminds me of the blue tea my mom would make," Selena said.

“Blue Tea is actually made from Blue Sage Herb,” the doctor said, “So that’s probably why you taste a similarity.”

“My mom would make it every chance she got,” Selena said, “It’s a favorite in our house.”

“Hmm,” the doctor put his hand up to his chin, “Well that explains it.”

“Explains what?” Selena, Keith, and Lan asked.

“It explains why you had such a high tolerance to the poison from the beginning,” the doctor explained, “Those years of drinking blue tea must have strengthened your natural immune system to fight off the toxins. Heck, I wouldn’t be surprised if it turned out that you didn’t need the antidote after all.”

“You mean after all that,” Lan stepped up, “She would have been fine???”

“It seems that way,” the doctor said.

“Keith…” Lan paused, “We just got owned…”

“Yeah,” Keith stepped onto the window ledge, “Well now it’s time to own some OSC! You ready? Alex and Vincent are probably already dealing with them at the north gate.”

“Actually I saw them head to the east gate while Joanna and Robert went to fight at the north gate,” Selena said.

“Just them?” Keith asked, “No knights went with them?”

“Not from what I could see,” Selena said, “Whatever’s over there, they must’ve been sure they could take it on their own.”

“That doesn’t sound good,” Keith looked out the window and gripped his katana, “Alright Lan. Let’s do this!”

Keith leaped from the two story window with Lan right behind him. As they made their way towards the center of the town, Keith suddenly stopped and Lan almost ran into him.

"Hey why did you stop?" Lan asked.

"I was just thinking," Keith said, "Why don't you go give those knights a hand? I'm sure they could really use your help right about now."

"You think I can?" Lan asked.

"You bet," Keith gave him a thumb's up, "Show them what they missed out on by not recruiting you."

"Okay," Lan ran towards the north gate.

"Hang on Alex," Keith glanced towards the southern gate, "I'll be there as soon as I'm done with these guys."

It was a night of pure chaos. The knights of Gravadale fought hard against the OSC solders while Vincent and I did our best to hold our own against the metal titan, and apparently Keith found a new threat looming at the south gate. Amidst it all, the Twilight Star was giving off the same pulses of energy that I felt right before the attack. The energy was helping me fight harder than I have before, but I still had no idea what was happening.

Episode 11
Fight for Survival! Alexander's Hidden Power!

Just as the Gravadale Knights were getting the best of the invading soldiers, a second wave suddenly appeared and began to swarm the knights all at once. The exhausted knights found themselves fighting back-to-back in a desperate attempt just to survive.

"Damn it!" Joanna held her halberd up against one of the soldiers, "It feels like we've been fighting all night! Where are they coming from?!"

"I don't know!" Robert stood behind her with his shield protecting himself from a soldier's attack, "I can't even tell if we're getting anywhere!"

Both of them suddenly turned about face and changed opponents. Joanna ended the soldier Robert was fighting with an inward thrust to the torso and an outward slash. Robert caught the other one in the face and finished him with a stab to the chest.

"What I wouldn't give… for some reinforcements right about now," Joanna tried to catch her breath.

Suddenly a ground shattering blast was seen just outside of the range where the Gravadale Knights were making their final stand. The sudden shock caused both sides to suddenly stop fighting.

"What the hell was that?!" several of the OSC soldiers yelled.

"What the hell was that?!" several of the knights yelled.

"They've got a mage too?!" Joanna was even more worried.

"No!" Robert looked back towards the city walls, "That came from our side!"

"Who's up there?!" Joanna looked towards the walls, "I can't see who it is."

Atop the walls, both sides on the ground could make out a bright green glow of an earth crystal emitting from a wooden staff. The crystal suddenly let out another burst of green energy that shot straight toward the enemy soldiers which caused another explosion from their feet. The impact from both attacks was strong enough to put a noticeable dent in the enemy's numbers.

"Watch out men!" one of the commanding OSC officers yelled, "They've got a mage!"

"That's gotta be Lan up there!" Robert said.

"I made it not a moment too soon," Lan got a good look at the battlefield, "We're still outnumbered, but maybe we can turn it around as long as more soldiers don't show up."

Lan slid down a vine against the wall as he launched another attack to his right. Upon landing, he immediately met up with Joanna and Robert.

"I knew it was you!" Robert said.

"After we made the antidote for Selena, I thought I would come give you all a hand," Lan said.

"You may be just what we need to give us an edge," Joanna said, "Will you help us?"

"Of course!" Lan held his staff up.

He released another small pulse of energy from the earth crystal in his staff, but instead of attacking, the wave of energy healed most of Robert and Joanna's injuries and restored vigor to them and the other Gravadale Knights closest to them.

"Wow," Joanna felt a new wave of energy flowing through her, "I feel like I could take on 100 enemy soldiers!"

"Then what do you say we get back in the fight?" Robert looked back towards the front lines.

"Alright," she raised her halberd, "We will provide Lan with cover while he softens their numbers! Let's win this fight!"

With a new resolve to fight, Joanna and the Gravadale Knights pressed onward against the OSC soldiers. While Lan continued his assault from a distance, Robert threw his shield attached to a chain to knock out enemy soldiers as they closed in from a distance, and Joanna rushed through with her halberd flashing in the moonlight. Thanks to Lan's help, the Gravadale Knights were able to effectively hold their position.

Back in town, Keith confronted twenty soldiers that had snuck their way past Gravadale's defenses.

"Who the hell are you?" One of the soldiers asked as if Keith was no threat to them.

"I'm Keith Ishikawa," he answered, "And I'm about to kick your asses!"

The soldiers laughed as if Keith was making a joke and then surrounded Keith so that he couldn't try to escape.

"You against all of us?" a second soldier laughed, "Just who are you trying to fool?"

"I would run right now if I were you," Keith shook his head.

"Think you're funny, eh big talker? Then bring it you pointy-eared freak!" one of the soldiers taunted.

"No one calls me a pointy-eared freak and gets away with it," Keith attached the Ninja Drive to his forearm.

The Ninja Drive began to glow as it emitted an electric blue aura around Keith which made his hair appear to glow a shade of light green. Keith took a fighting stance and set his sights on the soldier that insulted him.

"Now don't blink," Keith held his finger up, "Or you'll miss it."

"What?" the soldier blinked and noticed Keith was gone, "Hey, where'd he go?" he suddenly felt a tap on his shoulder.

As soon as he turned around, Keith shot him skyward with a swift flip kick. Then, about fifteen feet in the air, Keith appeared above the soldier and hit him with a hammer knuckle fist that sent him crashing into the ground where he remained there stuck and unconscious. Keith landed swiftly on the ground and looked to the remaining nineteen.

"Ok, who's next?" Keith asked while smirking.

"You're dead!" a soldier swung a massive pole axe downward at him.

"You missed," Keith held his arms crossed after swiftly sidestepping the attack.

Keith rushed the axe soldier with a blow to the chest with his elbow. The attack completely knocked the wind out of him as he slid back and fell unconscious.

"What's wrong? You guys too afraid to come at me all at once?" Keith casually leaned against a wall with his hands in his pockets.

Completely enraged by Keith's casual attitude, all but one of the remaining soldiers attemped to take him on at once. Keith pulled out his katana and sliced his way through the charging soldiers so fast that they had all been cut up before they realized it.

Keith stood behind them with his katana held outward for a few seconds before the slain soldiers fell.

"And now for you!" Keith pointed his katana towards the remaining soldier.

The last soldier let out an ear piercing shriek of a woman and ran away at top speed. Unseen by the panicking soldier, Keith ran right past him and tripped him which caused him to roll at top speed. Next Keith got right in front of him and flip kicked him into the air, then he ran up the walls in the area and sent the soldier flying horizontally with a hard right punch, and finally jumped above him and held his katana back as he prepared to strike.

"Strike of the Assassin!" Keith shouted.

The power behind the attack gave a flash of light as if lightning has struck. Keith landed on the ground as smooth as a cat, swung the blood off his katana, and calmly sheathed it mere seconds before the slain soldier's body hit the ground.

"Well that was fun. Now where are you Alex?" Keith looked around.

Keith's attention was turned toward the east as he heard a loud boom. He caught sight of me and Vincent's silhouettes fighting against something much larger than the both of us. We were both thrown to the ground by the metal creation.

"Oh snap! Hang on Alex!!" Keith began to sprint as hard as he could toward the fight.

Five feet into Keith's sprint, the effects of his Ninja Drive suddenly gave out on him and he returned to his normal running speed. His body, however, was still moving very fast which resulted in him tripping because of his feet unable to keep up. Keith struggled to get up, but the effects of the Ninja Drive left him unable to move.

"Damn it!" Keith struggled to get up, "Why now?!"

It seemed like we were fighting for hours. My whole body was exhausted and in pain from dodging blows and getting hit by those I couldn't avoid. The pulsations of light from my sword were in sync with my rapidly beating heart. The sudden turbulent energies of the Twilight Star made it harder to focus as I tried to settle the energy. It felt as if I were fighting against my own body just to move at times.

"We can't… keep this up," I tried to catch my breath, "I'm struggling just to move now, and it's not just from fighting this thing."

"Is the Iron Soldier too much for you?" I heard a voice from behind the monster.

"Who is that?" Vincent was holding his left arm while kneeling.

"I didn't think that I would have the chance to personally finish off Prince Alexander," the OSC soldier laughed, "If you think this is bad, this is only a taste of the power OSC will soon unleash! Valsoria will soon fall under our might!"

"You…" I staggered to my feet, "…you will be stopped. All of you! I won't be defeated by people like you! I'll protect Valsoria with all of my power!"

"How can you expect to protect Valsoria," he soldier held up something in his hand while the Iron Soldier held up its massive arm in unison, "When you can't even protect yourself?!"

The soldier suddenly threw his fist forward, which caused the Iron Soldier to follow in unison. I held my sword up and braced for impact, but I found myself not getting hit at all. Vincent suddenly got in front of me, and was using all the energy he had left to hold it back with both hands.

"Vincent??" I was shocked to see him holding back the attack.

"You didn't forget about me," Vincent spoke to the OSC soldier, "Did you?"

"I would have let you run if you wanted to," the OSC soldier taunted.

"Run from a coward that has to hide behind something to fight," Vincent said, "Yea right. When we're done with this, we're coming for you!"

"If you can even get past it," the soldier motioned the Iron Soldier to put more pressure against Vincent.

"This thing is one tough bastard," Vincent said, "You sure we can beat this thing?"

"We have too," I continued to struggle with focusing the Twilight Star's power, "Everyone's counting on us…"

It continued to feel as if I were fighting against a storm within myself. The energy of the Twilight Star was raging so much that I could barely get a grip on it.

"I can do this," my eyes were shut as I used all my will power to focus on the Twilight Star's energy, "With your power, I can do this…"

The turbulent energies suddenly began to change. All at once, I felt a calm in the Twilight Star's power. Soon after, I felt the energy return, but it felt more like a strong aura burning throughout my body.

"Alex?" Vincent glanced back and noticed a faint aura around me.

"We won't be beaten!" I forced the energy throughout my body and sword, "We will succeed!!"

"What the hell…?" the soldier took a few steps back.

"And you…" I pulled my glowing sword back and jumped.

"I think I better move!" Vincent suddenly jumped to his left as hard as he could.

"You're gone!! Sword..." I descended upon the Iron Soldier with a diagonal slash that tore through its left side, "...of the...," my horizontal slash to the right ripped through half of its right leg and clean through its left which caused the full weight of the Iron Soldier to come falling towards me, "Rising Sun!!"

With both my hands gripped on my blade, I ripped through the body of the Iron Soldier with a rising slash as I leaped into the air. The burst of energy behind the attack blew apart what remained of the Iron Soldier. The blade shined so brightly with energy, that it could be seen throughout the entire area. The sudden illumination of the area caused the Gravadale Knights and OSC soldiers to stop fighting. For a moment, everyone had thought the sun had risen, but then the real sun began to shine its light over the horizon.

Episode 12

Victory! The Return of the Gravadale Knights

"What…" an OSC soldier found himself shaking, "What just happened?"

"The Iron Soldier has been destroyed!" another yelled, "But how??"

"They beat it?" Joanna gazed out towards where I was.

"I'm not sure what it is they beat," Robert said, "But I'm glad they beat it. What was that flash of light?"

"That must have been Prince Alexander's power," Lan said.

"Wow," Joanna said, "HE did that??"

"Prince Alexander??" an OSC officer peered through a pair of binoculars to get a better look, "Oh no! Commander!! I've got visual confirmation! Prince Alexander DID destroy it!"

"No way! You're lying!" the commanding officer snatched the binoculars away from the soldier to see for himself, "But… but how is he even here?! There's no WAY he went through the desert to get here!!"

"No…" the soldier that was controlling the Iron Soldier sat on the ground trembling, "No this can't be…"

"Yeah," I stood with my knees bent, "We did it. Thank the spirit of the Twilight Star we won…"

"Heh. As if we were going to let ourselves get beat anyway," Vincent stood up.

"Thanks for blocking that thing for me earlier," I said, "Are you alright?"

"I'm fine for someone who's running on almost no sleep," he said.

"Alex!!" Keith ran up to us, "That was AWESOME!!"

“How did you do that?!” Selena ran up as well.

“That,” the Twilight Star reverted back to its original form around my neck, “Was the Twilight Star’s doing. It let out a sudden burst of energy, and I was able to cut that thing down.”

“Are you alright sis?” Vincent asked, “How’d you recover so fast?”

“I’ll tell you about it later,” Selena said, “It’s kinda funny too.”

“Funny for you,” Keith crossed his arms, “Not for me and Lan.”

“Huh?” Vincent and I were confused.

“Anyway,” Keith looked towards the northern side of Gravadale, “Those guys are still left. You wanna go help the knights out?”

“Nah,” I looked towards the north, “I think it’s been taken out of our hands anyway.”

“They’re looking this way!” one of the soldiers yelled, “What do we do now??”

“Calm down!” the commander ordered, “They’re tired and we still outnumber them!”

“Uh…sir?” another OSC soldier tried to get his attention.

“We can still win this battle! All soldiers-!”

“Sir!” the soldier cut him off.

“What?!” he looked behind himself to the soldier who was pointing to the top of a hill towards the north, “Oh…”

At the top of the hill, an entire cavalry of knights were suddenly in full view with weapons drawn. The lead knight with dark green hair and blue eyes suddenly appeared from the group on a white stallion with his lance raised as if he were about to order an attack.

"It's Sir Rupert!" Joanna yelled, "They're back!"

"Not a moment too soon!" Robert said.

"All units," Sir Rupert suddenly pointed his lance towards the battlefield, "CHARGE!!"

"RETREAT!!" the commanding officer ran before giving the order.

"SCATTER!!" many of the OSC soldiers screamed.

With the enemy forces retreating, the Gravadale Knights threw their weapons up in celebration. Even Joanna couldn't help but to celebrate with them. The night had been won, and a new day had begun.

"It looks like they're going to let the retreating soldiers run," I said.

"Is that alright?" Vincent asked.

"Yeah," I said, "The knights are obviously tired, so there's no reason to waste energy chasing after someone who would rather run."

"Well then," Vincent picked up the soldier that was still sitting by the collar of his shirt, "What about him?"

"Please don't kill me!" the soldier was almost in tears as he tried to wiggle free, "I didn't mean what I said earlier! I'm sorry! I'm sorry! I'm-"

"Shut up!" Vincent knocked him out with a right cross.

"We'll just turn him over to Sir Rupert," I said, "Maybe they can interrogate him or something."

"Joanna! Robert! Are you alright?" Rupert rode up to them.

“Yes sir!” they both said in unison.

“I’m glad,” Rupert sighed with relief, “I apologize for not getting here before OSC.”

“You already know about them sir?” Joanna asked.

“Yes. I’ll discuss that with you all later. I feared the worst before I got here,” Rupert admitted, “I’m glad I trusted you with protecting Gravadale.”

“Thank you sir!” she saluted him, “But I must admit that it was Robert’s strategy that allowed us to survive, and Valsoria’s Prince helped us as well.”

“Prince Alexander??” Sir Rupert was shocked, “He’s here?? Where??”

“Right here,” I approached them with everyone else with me.

“When did you get here?” Sir Rupert asked.

“It’s a long story,” I said, “There’s a lot I need to tell you.”

“Then let’s go to our conference room where you can recover as well,” Rupert said, “And who is that your friend is dragging?”

“He’s one of the soldiers we captured,” I said, “I thought it might be a good idea to hand him over to you so that your men might be able to get some information out of him.”

“I see,” he said, “Well thank you. My men will take him in. Let us not waste much more time. Joanna, order all the knights that fought with you to stand down and get some rest. The others that were with me will take over from here. Then report to the conference room immediately.”

“Yes Sir!” Joanna replied before riding off to give the order.

“Robert. I want you with us in the conference room as well,” Sir Rupert said.

"Yes Sir!" he replied.

About an hour past before everything in Gravadale had settled down. The Conference Room that Sir Rupert requested our audience in was rather large and housed several plants in holes on the floor. Above the round table we all sat at, there was a golden and green colored chandelier that several green crystals hung from and radiated their energies throughout the room.

"What's this weird feeling I'm getting in here?" I felt an aura within the room.

"This room doubles as a rejuvenation room," Robert told us, "If you spend enough time in here, injuries will be healed completely, and your fatigue will be reduced to almost nothing."

"Oh, it feels wonderful," Selena held her eyes closed as if she was going into a trance, "It almost feels like I'm in a hot spring, except without the water and heat."

"It's great for when you're stuck with night patrol and you can't sleep," Robert commented.

"It's great for when you haven't slept since leaving Rac' Sagadam!" Vincent laughed.

"I'm back, sir!" Joanna ran in.

"Good. Everyone please have a seat," Sir Rupert called us to his attention, "There is much we need to make each other aware of. Prince Alex, I would first like to hear everything you have learned about Organization Shadow Crystal."

"Very well," I said as I began to recall all the events, "Two weeks before I left Valsoria, we received reports of raids on our crystal mines and refineries. OSC ended up forging new weapons from what they stole and a small group sneaked into the kingdom somehow to attack the palace and demand that we hand over the Twilight Star, or else."

"That thing around your neck?" Robert asked.

"Yes," I held it up, "It's been in my family since my grandfather got it before he became Valsoria's new king."

"It's a pretty piece of jewelry, but it hardly looks like its anything worth being attacked by a terrorist group over," Joannah said.

"Remember the bright light you saw just before the Iron Soldier was destroyed?" I asked, "That was because of this. It holds a great power like the different Soul Crystals of our world, but on a different level."

"The Soul Crystals…" Joanna began to understand the situation better.

"Yes. You may think it weird, but the only reason I suddenly left Valsoria was because of a nightmare I had. Basically there was a dark shadow that was after the Soul Crystals, and based on that nightmare, I made my first destination to be Phoenix Volcano where the Phoenix Soul Crystal resides. Not long after getting there, I encountered OSC grunts trying to steal it out of the volcano. Thanks to Vincent, Vikki, and Selena, we were able to stop them and avert a complete disaster."

"If they had gotten away with it," Selena cut in, "The volcano would have began erupting uncontrollably for who knows how long, and our town would have been destroyed."

"Are they trying to get them all?" Sir Rupert asked.

"I doubt it," I said, "Some of them are either unreachable, or their location is completely unknown. I wish I knew exactly what they would do with them, because I don't believe just anyone could even begin to unleash a Soul Crystals power, let alone control it. Speaking of control, we encountered monsters in the desert that had been warped beyond their normal shape. They had dark crystals embedded in their foreheads, which is what I believed caused them to mutate."

"I'm sure that was OSC's doing in a sick attempt to control animals to do their bidding," Keith crossed his arms.

"I think that's about everything as I currently know it," I said, "How did you find out about them?"

"I believe it was well past midnight when I found out about them," Sir Rupert began to explain, "I encountered Volternia's Prince who was traveling with a hired sword. He told me that his bodyguard overheard plans of an attack on Gravadale, so we raced back as fast as we could. If he hadn't have told us, we may not have made it back until close to noon."

"Really?" I almost couldn't believe it, "That was good of him…"

"Alex!" Keith suddenly stood up, "I completely forgot!"

"What??" I asked, "Forget what??"

"OSC soldiers are deep in the forest, and they're tearing it apart!" he said, "The Golem Soul Crystal is somewhere in there!"

"Seriously??" I stood up, "How bad is it??"

"Well any forest on fire is bad," he said, "But it doesn't look too bad. I think we can take whoever is in there."

"Ok, Keith, you lead the way." I said, "Sorry to have to leave so suddenly Sir Rupert, but-"

"Sir Rupert, come quickly!" a knight ran into the room in a panic.

"What's the matter? Are we under attack again?" Sir Rupert asked.

"Actually good news sir," the knight spoke, "It's time, sir."

"Oh!" Sir Rupert got up, "Joanna! Robert!"

"Yes Sir!" they both stood in unison.

"Go with Prince Alex into the forest! And provide him with any aid that he needs," he ordered them.

"Yes Sir!" they said in unison.

"Prince Alexander, I apologize that I can't assist you myself, but I have an urgent event to attend!" Sir Rupert ran out the door with the other knight.

"We're going to change out our armor and weapons. We'll meet you at the west gate." Joannah left the room with Robert to go to the armory.

"Ok, is everyone able to fight?" I asked.

"Yeah! Let's kick some ass!" Vincent stood up, "After resting in this room, I feel great!"

"I'm ready too," Selena said.

"Me too," Lan said, "Let's hurry."

After leaving the conference room, I felt as if last night's battle never even happened. I felt as if I could take on anything OSC had in the forest. If only I knew exactly WHAT they had...

Episode 13
Forest Liberation

Deep within the forest, a village had fallen to a surprise attack by OSC soldiers. Mass chaos and confusion filled the air as everyone there ran for their lives. Unable to fight against their weapons, they were all captured and tied up along with the village elder. The soldiers then forced the elder into leading three of them to the whereabouts of the Golem Soul Crystal while leaving the rest of the soldiers to keep an eye on their hostages. All of the chaos was observed by a small brown bird who quickly took flight to alert his human friend.

Meanwhile, we were making our way through a thicker part of the forest as Keith led the way for us to follow. During the walk, Selena had explained to the rest of us how she was able to recover so quickly from the poison.

"Seriously?" Vincent asked Selena, "The same stuff mom makes??"

"Uh huh," Selena answered, "It's the whole reason I recovered so quickly. I probably wouldn't have needed it at all after a certain point."

"Man," Vincent shook his head and looked at Lan, "So you two did all that work for nothing?"

"Don't remind me," Lan held his head in shame.

"It wasn't for nothing," Joanna said, "Thanks to them, we found out OSC is somewhere in the forest looking for the Golem Soul Crystal."

"Not to mention that there are people somewhere in here that need our help," Robert said, "I didn't even know anyone lived in here."

"About how far in are OSC soldiers?" I asked Keith.

“It shouldn’t be too much farther,” Keith said, “We’re not too far from the area where that girl showed me.”

“How bad did things look from where you could see?” I asked.

“From what I saw, there weren’t any massive fires yet,” Keith said, “But they were somewhat scattered.”

“So I guess they don’t know exactly where it is,” I said, “But I wonder what made them think to look here in the first place.”

“Everyone stop,” Keith’s ears suddenly twitched.

“What is it?” I froze in my tracks.

“Someone’s coming,” Keith looked around, and then to the treetops, “Up there!”

We all heard a lot of rustling in the treetops before we were able to fix on where it was coming from. The same girl Keith had described to us, now wielding a bow with a small pack of arrows, suddenly appeared from the branches, and landed right in front of us with the grace of a cat.

“Thank goodness you came back,” she said.

“Just like I promised,” Keith said to her.

“Selena, check it out,” Vincent whispered, “She’s got pointed ears like Keith.

“Really?” Selena got a look at her ears, “You’re right.”

“How were you able to stop the invading soldiers at Gravadale so quickly?” she asked Keith.

“Well it wasn’t too hard,” Keith tried to sound cool, “Once they realized who I was, they-”

“Wait a second,” she suddenly looked past Keith towards me, “You!”

"Me?" I asked.

"Yes!" she ran right up to me and stared at the Twilight Star so closely that her face reflected off its surface, "Is that…the Twilight Star?"

"Y-yes," I was startled that she knew what it was, "How did you know about it?"

"Then you must be the one my grandmother foretold us about!" she suddenly jumped with happiness, "She had a vision that the Twilight Star's carrier would come to help us!"

"Really?" I asked, "She must be a Seer or something."

"I get it now," she said, "You destroyed that big thing that attacked Gravadale!"

"How did you know about that?" Vincent asked.

"A little birdy told me," she pointed to a small brown bird that suddenly descended from the trees and landed on her shoulder.

"Aww," Selena and Joanna smiled at the small bird.

"You…can talk to animals?" Lan asked.

"Yes," she said, "My powers can let me see what they see. Oh! My name's Aiyana!"

"I'm Prince Alexander," I said, "But from what you've told me, I guess you already knew that."

Before the others had a chance to introduce themselves, the bird suddenly flew in front of Aiyana's face. For a moment, it seemed as if she went into a trance. I figured she must be communicating with it with her special powers. When she snapped out of it, she had a look of terror on her face.

"What's wrong??" I asked.

"It's my grandmother!" she answered, "She and my people were captured!"

"Oh no," I said, "Are they alright?"

"Yes," she said, "From what I saw, it looks like they're just holding them captive."

"They must be using them as hostages to get someone to tell them where the crystal is," Lan said.

"Cowardly," Joanna said, "How will we go about rescuing them?"

"We've got to do this carefully," I said, "Otherwise we'll be putting their lives in danger just by showing up."

"About how many are there?" Keith asked.

"I saw fifteen from his memory," Aiyana said.

"Then leave securing the hostages to me," Keith grabbed the hilt of his katana with his left hand, "Get as close as you can without being seen. I'll get to a position where I can strike without putting Aiyana's people in danger. That will be your signal to attack."

"Sounds like a plan," I said, "Is everyone ready?"

"You must be careful," Aiyana said, "They have something I've never seen before."

"What are you talking about?" I asked.

"Some of them wear something on their backs that they use to blow fire," she said, "You'll know when they're about to use it when you start to smell gas."

"They can blow fire??" I was a little shocked, "Normal fires are hard enough to fight. This will be trouble if they get the chance to use them."

"Then we just don't let them get the chance," Vincent said, "And if they do, just don't get hit."

"That's easy to say," Robert said, "But I wouldn't exactly be able to dodge something like that in this armor."

"C'mon everyone," I said, "Lets move!"

While we followed Aiyana back to her village, the village elder was currently being forced through another area of the forest by three OSC soldiers. The elder walked as slowly as she could as if she were stalling for time, but the soldiers kept pushing her when she wouldn't walk fast enough.

"You people are making a big mistake," she said, "You are angering the spirits of the forest and trying to control powers you cannot understand."

"Pipe down old woman," one of the soldiers said, "If these spirits were so angry at us, they would do something about it."

"Just lead us to the crystal," the second said, "Or we'll lay waste to this forest completely until we find it ourselves."

"He will come to stop you," she suddenly had her eyes closed for a moment, "The Twilight Star's carrier will come to help us and put an end to all of you."

"I'll put an end to YOU if you don't shut up!" the third soldier said, "Hurry and get us what we want or else!"

"Very well," she said before going into her thoughts, "Wherever you are Aiyana, please be safe."

After several minutes of creeping our way to Aiyana's village, we were able to position ourselves in key locations around where her people were being held. There weren't too many of them from what I could see, but men, women, even children were all tied up together. Vincent, Selena, Lan, and I were crouched in a thick collection of brush several feet from one of the soldiers. Way to my right, Joanna and Robert had taken position behind a tree and tall grass. While I waited for Keith's signal, I listened in on a conversation between two soldiers.

"Everyone else has pulled out of the forest and reported back to base," one soldier said, "As soon as we secure the crystal, our orders are to return immediately."

"It's a shame that the others couldn't take Gravadale before the king and his other knights returned," another said.

"Did we not send enough soldiers?" the first soldier asked.

"I thought we did," the second answered, "They shouldn't have had a problem. Not only did we send the Iron Soldier, but I hear the person in charge of guarding Gravadale was just a woman."

"Ha," the soldier laughed, "I'd hate to be the commanding officer that has to explain how he lost to a group being lead by a woman."

"I'll show you 'just a woman'," Joanna's grip on her halberd grew tighter.

"Calm yourself commander," Robert whispered, "Wait till the signal."

"It doesn't sound like they know I'm even in the area," I whispered to Lan.

"They're probably a group of the lower grunts," Lan said, "So they may not get as much information as someone else in their group."

"Hey what's that?" a third soldier heard something rustling through leaves.

At first I thought our cover had been blown, but then I noticed a pair or squirrels rushing through the treetops.

"It's just some damn squirrels," the first soldier said.

"You evil men will pay dearly for what you have done," one of the forest captives suddenly spoke up.

"What was that?" one of the soldiers got angry, "Pipe down before we actually hurt ya."

"Help will come to us," a woman said, "Our seer has foreseen the carrier of the Twilight Star will appear to help us."

"Seer?" one of the soldiers asked, "If she was such a seer, then how come you were all captured? The only things I 'see' are a couple of captives that'll be burned alive if you don't shut up!"

"You shut up!" two kids suddenly said and almost made me laugh.

"Looks like I need to make an example out of you," One of the soldiers walked to the tied up villagers.

"Leave them alone!" another villager said, "They're just kids!"

"Now who wants to be first?" he asked.

"First victim of my katana says what?" a voice came from nowhere.

"What?" the soldier turned around.

The soldier was suddenly struck with a sharp downward force so hard that it ripped right through his light armor. As quickly as the first strike connected, a second upward strike ripped through his chest and neck faster than he could react. By the time his fellow soldiers realized something was going on, he collapsed to his knees before completely falling over. Upon looking up, Keith was standing behind where the soldier once stood with a static aura glowing around him that soon faded as the soldiers and villagers gasped to what they had just witnessed.

"Fourteen…" he looked around, "That's how many of you are left…"

"By the spirits…" one of the captured women spoke.

"Wha-what the hell?!" all soldiers suddenly had weapons pointed towards Keith, "Where the hell did you come from?"

"Damn," another one of the soldiers spoke, "We must've missed one!"

"You're right," Keith said, "But it wasn't me you missed."

"Aiyana!" two of the children suddenly yelled, "She got help!"

"Ha!" one of the soldiers laughed, "If you call one guy help!"

"Then what do you call two guys?!" Vincent sucker punched one of the soldiers in the back of the head.

"Or three?!" Robert threw his shield straight to one of the soldier's face and knocked him out cold.

"Now…" Joanna swiftly knocked over a solder with her halberd and had him subdued on the ground, "What was that about being 'just a woman?'"

"Are you all okay?" Aiyana descended from the trees in front of her people.

"Aiyana!" the two children screamed with excitement.

"You're ok!" a woman from the group said.

"Yes!" she said as the rest of us continued to fight, "And I got help! He's here!"

"'He' who?" a man asked.

"Wait…you don't mean…?" a woman started to ask.

“OSC,” I stood with my sword at the ready, “We’re freeing these people, and taking you down!”

Episode 14
Rescue Aiyana's Grandmother

Our surprise attack proved to be more than successful. Not only were we able to put ourselves between the OSC soldiers and Aiyana's people, but we managed to take out four of the soldiers that were standing guard at the village. The remaining eight regrouped together before preparing to fight again.

"Who the hell are you?!" one of the soldiers asked.

"Prince Alexander of Valsoria!" I pointed my sword at them, "Leave this place immediately or we will bring you down."

"Better yet," Keith stepped up, "Just stay and let us bring you down anyway."

"Sounds good to me," Vincent also stepped up.

"Aiyana," her mother began to ask, "Is that him?"

"Is he the one the elder said would come?" one of the children asked.

"Yes. Just like she said he would," Aiyana looked around for her grandmother, "W-where is she?"

"Some of those men forced her into leading them straight to the Heart of the Forest," one of the women said.

"What?! Which way did they go?!" she asked.

"I'm afraid I don't know," she said.

"None aside your grandmother knows its whereabouts," an older man said.

"No!" Aiyana screamed, "Prince Alexander! Some of those men have my grandmother and she's taking them to the crystal!"

"Damn," I said, "Where did your men take her?"

"Ha! Like I'd tell you blueblood," one of the soldiers said, "You won't live long enough to look for her anyway!"

"So much for trying to do this the easy way," I held my sword in front of me.

"Now we can do this the fun way," Keith brought up his katana.

"Hey sis," Vincent called Selena, "You and Aiyana help get her people free and out of the area. We'll handle these guys."

"Alright," Selena said.

"You go with them too Lan," Keith said.

"Gotcha," Lan said.

"You kids really think the five of you can stop us?" one of the soldiers asked us.

"These 'kids' just took out four of your soldiers," I said, "And you're all next."

"Then bring it on!" one of his comrades jumped towards me with a large blade.

Gripping my sword with both hands, I met the soldier's attack with equal force and quickly pushed it away with more force than he was expecting. I seized the opening with a rising jump slash to his face that I followed up and finished with a downward strike.

As we engaged the remaining soldiers at the site, the village's leader and three of the OSC soldiers were exploring the dark hallways of a stone construction hidden deeper into the forest. The only thing lighting the way for them through the darkness were bursts of flames that came from the weapon Aiyana described to us.

"Damn!" one of the soldiers cut away some roots growing in the hallways, "You better not be leading us into a trap old woman!"

"Why are there so many roots and vines in the way?" the second soldier asked.

"The energy from the Golem's Soul Crystal gives everything here a strong life force," the elder explained, "Animals and plants alike thrive here much better than they would elsewhere. Please I must ask you again to reconsider what you people are doing."

"I couldn't care less what happens to this place," the third soldier wielding that fire blowing weapon said, "The only thing we're concerned with is our conquest! Once we have everything we need, it's likely this place will burn to the ground as everything else! Now hurry and find the damn crystal! I'm losing my patience!"

"It…should be just down this hall…" the old woman said.

"It better be," the second said, "I don't even remember how many turns we've taken down here."

After a brief struggle with the OSC soldiers, we had brought them all down and had regrouped in a small clearing not far from the battle site. Lan meditated an aura of energy through his staff to heal up the small injuries we took in the fight.

"Is everyone alright?" I asked.

"Yeah," Keith sheathed his katana, "Those guys were crap."

"Nothing like the soldiers we fought last night," Joanna rested her pole axe on her shoulder.

"They must've been some weaker grunts assigned on an easier mission," Lan said.

"Well now that we've dealt with them, now we've got to find Aiyana's grandmother," I looked around for any possible indication of where they might have gone.

"How are we going to find her?" Aiyana said, "She never told me where the heart of the forest is!"

"Well then it should be in the middle of the forest right?" Vincent asked.

"Not necessarily," I said, "Even if it was, there's no telling how far we have to go or how much of this forest we have to search through. It's not like I can sense where the crystal is."

"Wait a minute…" Lan said, "Maybe through the Twilight Star you can!"

"What do you mean?" I asked.

"Can't you use its power to feel the energy through the forest?" he asked.

"I…" I looked around to everyone who had hopeful expressions on their faces, "I'm not sure I know how. I mean it's possible I guess-"

"Please Prince Alex," Aiyana had her hands griped together up to her face, "She needs your help now! We all do!"

I was almost overwhelmed with pressure. The villagers were all focused on me. Aiyana was on the brink of tears, and I knew we were running out of time. I had to try something.

"I hope this works," I placed my hand over the Twilight Star.

I let myself fall into a meditative focus while drawing up energy from the Twilight Star. It felt much like before when I was battling the Iron Soldier, but it felt much calmer. The waves of energy I felt flowing throughout my body felt like a gentle whirlwind that flowed around my body. As it expanded, I began to see everyone around me. I couldn't literally see them, but I could feel their presence with the Twilight Star's power. I let loose a gentle pulse of energy from around me to reach as deeply as I could throughout the forest. At first, I couldn't feel anything unusual, but then felt a power so overwhelming, that I was shocked out of my trance.

"What?!" Keith feared the shock on my face, "WHAT?!"

"I think I found it!" I pointed towards the northwest of our position.

"Really?!" Aiyana was in tears of joy.

"We gotta hurry!" I started running towards the direction, "It's moving!"

"Oh no," Lan said, "They must've found it!"

"If we hurry," I said, "We may just catch them!"

"Wait Prince Alex!" Aiyana caught up to me, "I can get us there faster! Follow me!"

Aiyana and I had gotten a head start in front of everyone. We rushed through a sudden thicket of branches and leaves until we finally ran into another short clearing with a cliff. Waiting for us was the largest hawk that I had ever seen! I skidded to a stop from shock at the tremendous bird. It looked large enough to carry people on its back!

"Come on!" Aiyana jumped onto its back, "This will be faster!"

"Are you serious??" I asked.

"Yes!" she answered.

"Alright!" I jumped on with her.

"Hang on tight!" she said as the hawk began to take flight.

"Don't worry about that," I said, "Tell him to fly in that direction!"

"Alex!" Keith and the others caught up to our location just as we went airborne.

"We'll be fine!" I said, "Just try to meet up with us as quick as you can!"

As we soared above the treetops, I got a look at just how massive this forest is. I saw several bodies of water in scattered locations, but mostly there was just dense forest. There's no way we could've just wandered our way through without help.

"How close are we?" Aiyana asked me.

"Very close," I gripped the Twilight Star, "You said your little bird saw fifteen soldiers right?"

"Yes?" Aiyana responded.

"Then that means there should be three with your grandmother," I said, "None of the others had that thing you described earlier, so I assume one of them may have it."

"You're right!" Aiyana said, "I had forgotten!"

"Hang back when I engage them," I said, "I don't know how well I can defend myself against something like that. Let alone defend someone else."

"Can you beat them?" she asked.

"I'm going to use all of my power to save your grandmother," I looked to her with a smile, "That's a promise."

"And you'll have what power I can lend you too," she said.

"Sounds like a plan," I looked down below and observed what looked like ruins covered in vines and moss, "Circle those ruins. It's there."

The ruins we came across were so old that moss and vines were covering much of the stone structure. There was even a tree growing out of its left side. There weren't any openings aside the entrance and a few places where parts of the ceilings caved in. As we made a second pass, we saw four people emerge from the front entrance. One of them wielded the weapon Aiyana had described to me, the second held the elder bound by a rope, and the third had a large crystal that was glowing with enough energy to be visible from the air.

"That's them alright," I gazed downward, "This will be a little tricky. If we just go down there, they'll have the advantage of hiding behind your grandmother to get away."

"What do we do then?" Aiyana asked.

"Somehow we have to separate them just long enough where we can put a little distance between them and her," I said, "Once I get in between them, it's just a matter of fighting them off. I'm still not sure how I'm going to fight against that weapon, but I think I may have a way of protecting myself now."

"Then you need a diversion?" Aiyana asked.

"Yes," I said, "But how can we make one without being discovered?"

"*We* won't," Aiyana winked, "The forest will help us out. Hang on."

Aiyana guided us down behind the tree that was growing on the side of the ruins where we could keep a good view of the soldiers and stay hidden.

"Alright," Aiyana put her hands together, "Just wait for your chance."

Aiyana suddenly went into a meditative trance like I did earlier. Before I could even ask what she was doing, I suddenly began hearing sounds throughout the forest. Birds suddenly began screeching, wolves began howling, and the whole forest suddenly felt as if it were in an uproar.

"W-what??" The soldier that held Aiyana's grandmother looked around, "What the hell is going on?!"

"What's up with this place?!" the soldier holding the Golem Soul Crystal began shaking.

"Did you do something old woman?!" The soldier wielding the fire weapon turned to her.

"I didn't do anything," she said, "You have disturbed the harmony that exists in this forest by taking the crystal."

"Yea right," he said, "If the forest wants this crystal so bad, it should just try and take it back!"

As soon as he said that, a cloud of birds suddenly burst from the treetops and filled the sky with screeches and cries as they began circling above the soldiers like vultures to a carcass. The howling of wolves got so close, the soldiers didn't know what to focus their attention on. Throughout the chaos, the soldiers grouped together without realizing that they let go of the elder that was tied up.

"Hey boss!" one of the soldiers said, "Maybe there's something to what that old woman said!"

"Nonsense!" the soldier with the fire weapon said, "Even if there's the slightest truth in what she said, nothing here can fight against fire!"

"Maybe they can't…" I said behind them.

"Who the-?" the soldier wielding the Golem Soul Crystal turned around, "B-boss! Look!!"

"Crud!!" the soldier that held the elder captive said.

"Sh… sh…!!" the last soldier was stunned at the site he saw.

Aside from Aiyana, myself, and the village elder, several of the animals that inhabit this forest were seen standing amongst each other on top of and around the stone ruins. Wolves were bearing their razor sharp teeth and snarling as they waited for their chance to strike. Hawks and other birds of prey were circling the area stretching their long sharp talons out as they shrieked downward towards the soldiers in anger. The eyes of the wolves and hawks made direct eye contact with the soldiers and froze them with fear.

"But I can!" I pointed my sword at the leader of the trio.

Episode 15
The Life of the Forest

"OSC soldiers," I raised my blade, "Return the crystal and leave at once, or you will suffer the consequences. That's my only warning to you."

"Aiyana," the elder spoke, "That's him isn't it? He's the one I saw in my vision!"

"Yes grandma," she said, "He and his friends helped me save everyone too!"

"Oh thank the divine spirits," the elder said, "That gives me a lot less to worry about."

"Boss?!" the soldier holding the crystal asked, "What are we gonna do?!"

"Everything that old woman was saying was true!" the second said.

"J-just hold on a sec!" the soldier commanded, "Just who are you?!"

"I'm Prince Alexander of Valsoria," I answered.

"Damn it all!" he yelled, "You really think we're just gonna surrender this crystal to you?!"

"Well it'd be nice if you did," I said, "We're going to get it back either way."

"No! You'll burn before we hand it over!!" the leader raised his weapon.

I caught the smell of gas just as he pointed the nozzle towards our direction. A red crystal at the tip shined brightly with light before shooting a burst of fire directly at us. With the power of the Twilight Star surging through me, I raised my hands up and let loose a wall of its energy outward in front of us. The energy spread outward and formed a barrier unseen to the soldiers assumed we were being consumed by the flames.

"Nice shot boss!" the soldier holding the crystal said.

"I told you there was nothing to worry about," he said, "Even these beasts are hesitating to attack now."

"Well let's get out of here before they change their minds," the third soldier said.

"They haven't changed their minds," I spoke from behind the flames.

"W…what?" all three soldiers turned toward the fire.

I let loose a quick pulse of energy outwards from me that quickly smothered the flames around us. The smoke soon cleared to reveal Aiyana, her grandmother, and I completely unharmed.

"And neither have I," I raised my blade.

"No…no no no no no NO NO!!!!!" the solder holding the crystal took off running through the woods.

"Hey! Get back here!!" the boss commanded.

"Screw this!" the second soldier ran off in a different direction, "I quit!!

As if waiting for a signal, the large flock of hawks in the sky suddenly took chase of the soldiers from the air while the wolves took chase on the ground which left the soldier with the flamethrower standing alone against me.

"Damn…" the soldier was frozen for a moment before raising his weapon in a panic, "DAMN!!!!"

"Look out!" I quickly formed a barrier to defend Aiyana and her grandmother.

In a desperate attempt to kill us, the remaining soldier unleashed fire over the entire area. While I was able to protect the three of us with the Twilight Star's power, it was hard for me to get in close enough to take him out.

While I did battle against him, the two soldiers who ran were being relentlessly pursued by the wolves and hawks of the forest. It wasn't long before they were caught. Their ear piercing screams echoed throughout the forest before going silent.

Aiyana and her grandmother had taken cover behind the large stones of the ruins while I tried to get in close enough to finish the remaining soldier before the whole forest went up in flames.

"You're gonna burn down the entire area at this rate!" I yelled.

"If taking you out means burning down this whole forest then so be it!!" he continued to spray fire everywhere I tried to run.

I did my best to keep fire from spreading too much, but as I defended myself, some of the flames scattered in different directions. One fireball landed near Aiyana and her grandmother which forced them to jump back.

"Grandma we have to help him somehow!" Aiyana said.

"Without my staff, my powers won't reach far enough," the elder said, "It got left behind back at the village."

"There must be some way we can get through," Aiyana peered over the stone, but then suddenly turned her attention to the fireball that landed near them, "Wait a minute. I know how!"

"Aiyana," the elder watched her pull together some dry roots and straw on the ground, "What are you doing?"

"I think we can use his own fire against him!" she tied the dry material to the tip of one of her arrows and set it on fire before the small flames near them burned out, "Wait here grandma!"

“Wait Aiyana!” she tried, but failed to stop her, “Oh please be careful!”

Aiyana quickly ran along the outside of the area while the soldier was distracted by me to get a clear shot at him. She then suddenly slid to a halt as she raised her bow and drew the arrow back to aim at the soldier’s backside.

“What the,” I noticed her just behind the soldier, “What’s she-”

“This is for attacking my people!” she released the burning arrow.

The arrow flared brightly as it took flight toward its target. It found its mark on the large pack on his back that contained the gas that fueled his weapon.

“The hell was that?!” the soldier noticed that the flaming arrow had pierced his gas pack.

“Oh-!” I threw up a barrier up around myself as fast as I could.

“What the fu-!!!”

The gas pack exploded with enough force to knock me off my feet, even from behind the barrier. The shockwave threw Aiyana for a loop several yards backwards and she fell into a thick collection of bushes. The fight was over, but there had been a lot of damage done to the area.

“Damn that was close!” I got up and looked around, “Aiyana? Aiyana?!”

“Aiyana!” the elder ran towards the bushes she fell in.

“Oh no,” I ran at full speed to check up on her, “Is she alright?!”

“She knocked herself out when she fell,” the elder began applying healing energies to her head, “She should be fine.”

“That’s good,” I said, “But how are we going to put out these fires?”

Suddenly, one of the wolves that had given chase to the other soldiers walked up to the elder with the Golem Soul Crystal in his jaws.

"I can take care of that now," she grabbed the crystal from the wolf's jaws.

I stood with Aiyana as the elder stood out in the middle of the clearing with the Soul Crystal. As she held it above her head, it began radiating almost as brightly as the sun. The overwhelming aura from the crystal slowly withered down the flames until they were completely smothered away. The charred patches of grass and trees soon regained their natural colors from the healing energies of the soul crystal, and I could feel all the scratches, cuts, and bruises I received from the battle disappear.

"Wow," I said, "That was incredible."

The lone wolf that was standing next to me howled as if he were agreeing with me.

"Now the rest of the forest can begin healing," the elder said, "Prince Alexander, you have my deepest gratitude for all you've done for us."

"Thank you," I bowed my head, "But in the end, I think Aiyana deserves most of the credit."

"She has done a lot to help fight against those invaders," the elder said, "She's earned a good rest."

"I'll take her back," I lifted her up in my arms.

Several hours later, Aiyana woke up in her hut looking straight up at the ceiling trying to make sense of where she was. After she remembered the encounter with the OSC soldiers, she quickly sprang up and ran outside to find that everyone was in celebration of the liberation of the forest.

"I'm back home?" Aiyana looked around to regain her bearings.

"Hey Aiyana's up!" one of the kids yelled.

The villagers went into an uproar of cheers for Aiyana that nearly paralyzed her with shock.

"Thank you Aiyana!" yelled a villager.

"You and the foreseen one saved us!" yelled another.

"You two were amazing!" Aiyana's mother yelled.

"Hey!" Vincent yelled, "What about us?!"

"Who are you again?" asked one of the children.

"Wait!" Aiyana looked around, "Where's the elder?

"I'm right here," she parted her way through the crowd, "Are you feeling ok?"

"Yes ma'am," she responded, "But how long have I been out?"

"About an hour or two," she answered, "Prince Alexander brought you all the way back here."

"H-he did??" Aiyana's face suddenly turned pink.

"Ooohh!" some of the kids started pointing at Aiyana's face, "Aiyana likes the foreseen one!"

"No! It's not like that!" she shook her head.

"Aiyana and the foreseen one, sitting in a tree!" the kids sang in melody.

"Shut up!!" Aiyana continued to fuss with the children.

"Well they all seem happy," Joanna said.

"You would be too if your home was just helped saved by a passing stranger," Selena said, "It's like when he helped saved Prominence Town."

"Even if he only came down our way cause of the Soul Crystal," Vincent said, "It…it was a good thing he showed up when he did."

"Speaking of Alex, where is he" Robert asked.

"He went over to the lakeside after the feast," Keith looked towards the lakeside, "He looked like he had a lot on his mind."

There was a lot on my mind. Since the fight with the Iron Soldier, I had only just begun to grasp the Twilight Star's power like that. First then, then again against the soldier wielding the flamethrower. My mother had allowed me to first wear the Twilight Star when I was 13 under the advice of my grandfather before he passed away a year later. I wasn't suppose to formally receive it till my 18th birthday, but he and my grandmother both thought I might have the potential to wield it with much more power than he and my mother. I'll never forget what he told me about its power so many years ago…

"The Twilight Star has the power to bring great miracles in the right hands and the power to bring epic destruction when in the wrong hands. It has the ability to choose who can wield it and how much power they can naturally draw from it. I was the first person it allowed to wield in hundreds of years for the sake of stopping a great catastrophe from destroying our world. Since then, our family has been chosen to carry the Twilight Star until the time comes when the chosen one would need to use it at its full power to save our world. That is according to the will of the Twilight Star's Spirit. Out of the three in our family that can use it, the Twilight Star seems to show the greatest compatibility with you. I pray that nothing so serious would come in your lifetime, but there may come a time where you will have to draw much power from the Twilight Star in

order to protect the balance that exist in our world. Don't be afraid of its power, but don't take it lightly either. It's like I said earlier; it has the power to bring great miracles in the right hands, and the power to bring epic destruction in the wrong hands."

"Carriers of its power…" I said to myself while watching my reflection in the lake, "Great miracles and epic destruction…"

"Something wrong Alex?" Keith walked up to my right.

"Hey Keith," I greeted him, "Nah not really. I'm just a bit tired."

"Did you lose something in the water?" Aiyana walked up to my left.

"Hey Aiyana," I was surprised to see her up, "How are you feeling?"

"I'm feeling fine, thanks," she smiled.

"That's good," I said, "And no, I didn't lose anything in the water. Your grandmother reminds me a lot of mine."

"Really?" Aiyana asked, "How?"

"It's because although she's really powerful," I started, "You wouldn't know it just by looking at her. Also, when she does have to use her powers, she does it with no fear."

"Being able to use that much power without flinching probably comes with experience," Keith said.

"They've seen and been through a lot more than we could even imagine right now," Aiyana said, "And grandma wasn't always that powerful. She once told me that everyone's elemental mastery grows at different rates. Some grow slow while some grow really fast."

"I was shocked when I first learned of my nature element," Keith said, "No pun intended by the way. Once I got to using it though, it was just like another part of me and it felt natural."

"I guess that makes sense," I said, "If it's been with you that long, it should feel natural. I guess I was just taken how well your grandmother wielded the Golem Soul Crystal to smother the flames."

"It must take real talent to control that much power," Keith said.

"Yeah," Aiyana said, "But it's different than using a normal crystal. Normal elemental crystals only serve to channel a person's own natural power. A crystal like the Golem Soul Crystal is its own source of power. Anyone of the earth affinity can use it to some degree, but it takes a lot of skill and talent to greatly channel its energies."

"You know the Twilight Star doesn't seem so different when you look at it like that," Keith said.

"Really?" I asked.

"It's like Aiyana said," Keith said, "It takes a lot of skill and talent to channel power like that. You seem to have it on lockdown."

"Lockdown?" I was confused at what he was trying to say.

"I thought you'd be use to my occasional slang by now," he said, "I mean you've got it under control really well."

"Oh!" I realized what he meant, "Then thanks. That means a lot to me."

"No problem," Keith said, "So what's the plan now?"

"We'll get some rest at Gravadale before heading out again," I said, "I don't think I have enough strength to do much else today."

"You're all leaving?!" Aiyana asked.

"Yeah," I said, "We've stopped OSC here, but they're far from finished. I have to keep going till they've been brought down for good."

"Can't you all stay a little longer?" she asked.

"I suppose we can stay for a little longer," I said, "It's a really nice place to relax here."

"Great!" Keith ran back to the cookout site, "Then I'm gonna get some more of that stew before Vincent slurps it all up! Want me to save you some?"

"Yeah!" I said, "I'll be there in a second!"

With that little conversation, I felt better about everything that has happened. Most of all, I felt better about what has happening with me and the Twilight Star. I felt I had a better understanding of its power, and what my grandfather told me several years ago. If you can hear me granddad, I think I have a better grip of its power. I think...I've got it on lockdown.

Episode 16
A New Day; Old Rivals Appear

It was close to noon the next day when a pair of travelers stopped to rest at the top of a short cliff to the northeast of Gravadale. One was a rough looking mercenary with spiky blue hair. He wore a chain mail and light plated armor that covered his left shoulder, his upper chest, and upper back area. The dark blue jacket he wore came all the way down to just below his knees. His companion couldn't be more different. His dark blond hair was cut clean and well groomed. The white stallion he rode in on, along with his hand tailored uniform, indicated that he was of noble birth.

"At last, we have made it to Gravadale," spoke the prince, "And you're certain that he is in the area?"

"I am," spoke the mercenary, "I'm good at gathering intelligence. My sources say that Valsoria's prince was here when Gravadale was attacked the other night."

"Just what is that sorry excuse of a royal doing prancing around the land?" the prince asked himself out loud.

"There's been word spreading about this Organization Shadow Crystal raising hell and-" the mercenary started to explain.

"I wasn't asking you. I was thinking to myself," the prince cut him off, "But go on."

"Well," the mercenary sounded annoyed, "To make a long story short, it seems Prince Alexander has been doing battle with their soldiers and grunts ever since leaving Valsoria."

"Surely you jest!" the prince laughed, "Him trying to take on that terrorist group? The whelp can't even wield a nature element! He's so pathetic! Even that barbaric Prince Jabari can wield a nature element!"

"Well, unlike other people, he doesn't hide behind others," the mercenary commented.

"I'm not paying you for your smart remarks," the prince bucked his stallion to move, "Now let's move, and he better be down there!"

"If I known that I was going to have to put up with this for so long, I would've asked for more than 20,000 shards," the mercenary thought to him self as he followed his employer.

I decided that we would spend the rest of the day in Gravadale while I tried to decide where to proceed to next. The citizens of Gravadale were more than willing to feed us and get us suited up with new clothes and supplies. I was walking by myself when I decided to go find Sir Rupert before speaking with the king of Gravadale.

"Prince Alexander!" Robert called out to me from behind, "Are you looking for Sir Rupert?"

"Yeah," I answered, "I wanted to see why he had to rush off so fast yesterday."

"He's in the Knight's Hall with his wife. He wishes for your audience right now," Robert informed me.

"Alright," I said, "What's going on?"

"It's a surprise," Robert said.

When we arrived at the Knight's Hall, there were a crowd of knights that Robert and I had to squeeze our way through. I finally got through to where Sir Rupert and his wife Michelle were, and I immediately realized what all the commotion was over.

"There you are, Prince Alexander," Sir Rupert spoke.

"Come closer and see out newborn son," his wife said.

"Wow!" I was overtaken by the newborn's cuteness, "I didn't know you were about to become a dad! Congratulations! What's his name?"

"Well we were going to name him after me," he said, "But an endless chain of names gets boring, so we went with Will."

"It fits him," I said, "Did the doctors analyze an affinity with him?"

"Yes," his wife said, "He has the earth affinity like his dad."

"He's so cute," Joanna rubbed her finger gently on top of his head.

"He looks like he'll be a healthy boy," I said as I let him grab my pinkie finger, "And it feels like it too."

"Thank you Prince Alexander," Sir Rupert's wife spoke.

"Thanks you for letting me see your new son," I said, "I'm glad I got to see him before we left."

"You're leaving today??" Sir Rupert asked me.

"Tomorrow," I said, "I want us to be able to rest here for tonight. We'll get an early start tomorrow."

"You and your friends are more than welcome to stay," he said, "But why leave so soon?"

"The thing is," I said, "Judging by the soldiers' reaction, they didn't even know I was here before the other night. The last time I fought with their grunts was across the desert. It might be dangerous, but I think its best we keep moving. I'm hoping to get enough information to report back home so we can figure out what to do."

"I see," he said.

"Honey, I need to get the baby home," Sir Rupert's wife said.

"Alright," he spoke, "I'll meet you home in a few minutes. I need to take care of a few things here."

"I'll walk you home ma'am," I offered his wife.

"Thanks you, Prince Alexander," she said as we left.

"Joanna and Robert, step forward. The rest of you return back to your post." Sir Rupert ordered the knights.

"Yes sir!" they all said in unison.

"I don't think I need to tell you how complicated things are going to be from this day forth," Sir Rupert began, "The sudden attack on Gravadale has put us on high alert, but it's going to be really difficult for me to be on command as much as I was since the birth of my son. Joanna, you have proven yourself to be an effective commander by protecting Gravadale in my absence. Can I count on you to continue to pick up the slack while my duties are divided?" he questioned Joanna seriously.

"You can count on me sir!" Joanna stood at attention, "I won't let you down!"

"Very good," Sir Rupert spoke, "Please continue to prove that my decision to appoint you as commander was the right choice."

"Yes sir!" Joanna replied.

"Now the other thing that has me concerned is Prince Alexander's safety," he started, "It's nothing short of amazing to see how far he's traveled and how much he's done, but I don't think I could live with myself if something happened to him without us even trying to do something to help him."

"Do you have something in mind sir?" Joanna asked.

"Yes," he answered, "Robert Greenwood, as of tomorrow morning, you will be under the command of Prince Alexander."

Joanna's eyes widened from shock, but she remained in an attention stance. Rocky felt just as surprised, but maintained to keep his composure.

"An escort mission sir?" Robert asked.

"Somewhat," Sir Rupert said, "Follow his orders and do everything in your power to see him succeed in defeating OSC. I believe this will be good for the both of you. Do not fail, but most important, come back alive. Do you understand?"

"Yes sir!" Robert said.

"Very good," Sir Rupert grabbed a sheathed sword from the wall, "I want you to give this to Prince Alexander as my gift to him. This sword is newly forged and should prove to hold up very well in battle."

"Yes sir," Robert spoke.

"You two are my most exceptional knights. I'm counting on you," Sir Rupert spoke to both of them.

"We won't let you down, sir!" they both replied in unison.

"Very well," Sir Rupert spoke, "Dismissed."

"Sir!" they both replied at attention before leaving.

"Wow," Robert looked to the sky.

"What is it?" Joanna asked.

"I can't help but feel a little excited," he said, "This will be my first big mission that might go beyond Gravadale borders."

"You're not nervous?" Joanna asked.

"Maybe a little," he answered, "But the fact that Sir Rupert entrusted me with a mission this important, it's empowering. When someone is counting on me like that, it's fills me with enough confidence to the point I believe I can do anything."

"At least *you're* feeling confident," she said.

"You're not?" he asked, "You're a lieutenant commander now! What's wrong??"

"Everything just happened so quickly," she said, "I never expected us to be attacked almost right after getting promoted. I just got shaken up pretty bad I guess."

"You were scared? Hell I sure couldn't tell. I think you handled it pretty well with the limited knights we had," he said, "Your constant diligence is what helped us hold off those soldiers and win. I think you're doing fine."

"Seriously?" she asked.

"Seriously," he said, "Just keep doing what you're doing, and everything will be fine."

"Alright," she took a deep breath, "I think I feel better now."

"So you can handle things here without me?" he asked.

"My shield is leaving," she teased him, "Whatever will I do without him?"

"Wow," he laughed, "The commander just made a joke. I better take a coat with me in case it snows."

"Ha ha," Joanna crossed her arms, "Well you better go find Prince Alex so you can begin preparing."

"Right right," Robert said, "Good luck keeping the kingdom safe while I'm gone."

"And good luck on your mission," she shook his hand, "I'd give you a hug, but I don't want the other knights to get the wrong idea and think I show you favoritism."

"Right," he said, "Loss of morale and everything. Well, see you tomorrow morning."

"Yeah," she said.

As Robert parted with Joanna to find me, I was nearing Sir Rupert's home with his wife and newborn son. We had just reached the door when I heard the king's voice call out to us.

"There you are Prince Alex and Lady Michelle," the young king ran up while being escorted by two of his guards.

"Your Majesty," she was caught off guard by the king's sudden appearance, "Greetings!"

"Hey King Richie!" I gave the young king a high five, "I was just about to come see you."

"I heard what happened! Thanks for helping my knights defend Gravadale!" King Richie said.

"No problem," I looked up to see my friends walking together, "But I'm not the only one that you should thank. Hey! Over here!"

"There he is," Keith ran up with everyone else.

"Where've you been?" Selena asked me.

"Just walking around," I answered, "Everyone I want you to meet King Richie. King Richie, this is Selena, Vincent, Keith, and Lan."

"You're the king?" Vincent tilted his head as he looked down at the young king, "But you're just a kid! How does that work?"

"Its part of the rule of inheritance of a kingdom," I began to explain, "Under normal conditions, should something happen to the current rulers of a specific kingdom, their child automatically inherits the kingdom and assumes rule over it."

"I may only be 12 years old," King Richie started, "But I'm starting to get the hang of things thanks to Sir Rupert and everyone here."

"I get it," Vincent said, "Sorry if I offended you by calling you a kid. You're not a kid if you can take on that kind of responsibility."

"It's ok," King Richie said, "Nice to meet you all!"

"Likewise," Vincent said.

"Also, I'd like you all to meet Lady Michelle," I said, "She's Sir Rupert's wife and this is their newborn son, Will.

"Yeah! I almost forgot to say congratulations!" King Richie spoke up.

"Thank you, young majesty," she said smiling.

"Aw, he's adorable!" Selena got a close look at the baby, "Hi Will."

"Thank you, Selena," she spoke before Will started crying lightly, "I better get him inside. I think he might be getting hungry. It was nice meeting you all."

"Take care," I said.

"Thank you Prince Alex," she said before entering her house.

"I have to go too," King Richie said, "How long will you be staying with us? You know you're welcome to stay as long as you want."

"Thanks Richie," I said, "I plan for us to leave tomorrow after we're all rested up."

"Cool," King Richie said, "I'll see to it that anything you need is prepared for you all. See ya later!" he left with his guards.

"See ya!" I waved.

"Prince Alex!" Robert slid to a halt beside me.

"Hey Robert," I answered, "What's up?"

"Prince Alex," Robert took an attention stance, "Under direct orders of Sir Rupert II, I am now under your command to assist you in any way possible from now until your mission is through!"

"Seriously?!" I was shocked at the sudden news.

"You're coming with us?!" Lan spoke up.

"Yes," Robert answered, "Whatever may happen, I hope that I may be able to serve you well, Prince Alex."

"That's great," I shook his hand, "We're glad to have you with us!"

"Thank you," Robert said, "Sir Rupert also asked me to give you this as a gift from him," he handed me the sword he was carrying.

"Awesome!" I took the sword out of its sheath, "It's a little on the heavy side, but it'll definitely make my sword swings stronger!"

"But you can make a sword with the Twilight Star," Vincent pointed out, "Why would you even need another one?"

"Two reasons," I began to explain, "First, it may get to the point where I'll need to conceal the Twilight Star as much as I can, so it helps to have another weapon I can use, and second, it's always good to have a backup weapon just in case."

"What kind of sword is that?" Selena asked, "I don't remember seeing one like that before."

"That two handed sword is called a Claymore," Robert spoke up, "They're very strong, but they're heavier than the average sword, so it takes more strength to wield."

"I won't have a problem with it," I sheathed the sword on my back, "Not after some practice anyway."

As soon as I sheathed my new sword, we were all alerted by the loud shriek of a hawk. We all looked up to catch the sight of one flying overhead, and when it looped around to prepare for a landing, its passenger leaped off with a long bow across her shoulder.

"It's Aiyana!" Keith yelled.

"Aiyana!" I said, "What are you doing here?"

"Two reasons," she handed me a scroll, "First, grandma wanted me to give you this map."

"Awesome!" I said, "This will really make things easy for us."

"Hey Aiyana," Keith asked, "What's the bow for?"

"That's the second reason I'm her," Aiyana answered, "I'm coming with you!"

"Really?" Keith almost didn't believe his pointy ears, "This is awesome!"

"Glad to have you with us," I said to Aiyana, "It's almost like we have an official unit now."

"Ha!" someone laughed from behind us, "If one could call one knight and these ragged peasants a unit!"

If there was anyone that could kill a mood, it was him. I didn't even have to turn around to know who just spoke. That voice belonged to one of the most spoiled men I could ever know. The richest prince from the rich nation of Volternia, and my biggest nemesis, had just shown up here of all places.

"What a pleasant surprise to see you," I turned to face him, "Prince Cornelius Volternia."

Episode 17
Alex vs. Mark

"It IS a pleasant surprise for you to see me," Cornelius pulled the bangs from over his eyes, "I assume your quaint little kingdom is holding up well?"

"Valsoria is just fine," I plainly said.

"Wait…" Vincent began to recognize him, "You're that blueblood that came to Prominence Town!"

"Yeah," Selena said, "That's him alright."

"Excuse me?" Cornelius tilted his head, "You both seem to know me, but I don't know either of you."

"I can help you remember if you want," I could hear the anger in Vincent's voice.

"Easy Vincent," Keith stepped in front of him, "Let Alex handle this."

"I'm surprised at you Alexander," Cornelius chuckled, "I realize you have a strange taste in friends, but couldn't you have found some better behaved companions? Were the Vanguards too busy to accompany their beloved prince?"

"Why are you here?" I changed the subject.

"More importantly," Keith looked to the blue haired mercenary, "Why are YOU here Mark?"

"What's the matter?" Cornelius crossed his arms, "Even I like to get out of the kingdom every once in a while."

"And I'm here because I'm getting paid good money for my services," Mark plainly answered.

"You couldn't find anyone better?" Keith asked.

“Who better than the prince of Volternia?” Cornelius asked.

“Um,” Keith pretended to think for a moment, “How about anyone?”

“Hmm,” Cornelius decided to ignore Keith’s comment, “How’s your battle against OSC going?”

“What are you talking about?” I pretended not know what was going on.

“Don’t play dumb with me,” Cornelius said directly, “Whenever you do something out of the ordinary, word tends to spread like wildfire amongst these commoners. So what happened here the other night? Word is that you had a hand in holding off invading soldiers until the king returned.”

“I just helped out,” I said, “I didn’t do too much.”

“What about this Iron Soldier I heard about?” Cornelius asked, “Is it true that you were the one to defeat it?”

“Well,” I crossed my arms, “I had help.”

“Of course you did,” Cornelius glared with a grin.

“What’s that supposed to mean?” I asked.

“You possess a rough talent in swordsmanship, but it borders on barbaric,” Cornelius began a rant, “Furthermore, you don’t possess an affinity, so it’s hard to believe you could do anything against anyone with real competence.”

“You might think that,” I said, “But you’d be wrong.”

“He helped save my whole village from destruction!” Selena stepped up from behind me.

“And he helped save my people too,” Aiyana said.

"I find that hard to believe," Cornelius said dully, "Have you forgotten how you struggled against a common mercenary in my special tournament two years ago?"

"I still haven't forgiven you for that," Keith pointed to Cornelius, "Using my sister as a prize was just sick."

"No harm came to her, so what's the problem?" Cornelius raised his hands, "Besides, what better way to search out some of the strongest warriors in the land than by baiting them so?"

"You barely made me break a sweat," Mark said, "You're lucky I found out who you were when I did, otherwise I wouldn't have held back."

"Don't let it go to your head," I said, "A lot of time has passed since then, so don't think I can't kick your ass now."

"You want a reminder just how strong I am?" Mark grabbed his blade from over his shoulder.

"Now Alexander," Cornelius said, "I wouldn't want you to get yourself hurt. There's no shame in backing down."

"Oh don't worry about me Cornelius," I grabbed the hilt of my claymore, "If you can't control your attack dog, then I'll just have to put him in his place."

"You really think you can take me on now," Mark smirked, "Okay then, let's go outside the city and I'll show you just how weak you are against me."

We all met near a small lake outside the city. My friends stood together while Cornelius stood alone to give us room to duel. Mark unsheathed a two handed blade that was larger than the claymore Sir Rupert gave to me. A large blue crystal was forged into the middle of his sword that extended from the guard to the middle of the blade which allowed him to channel his water affinity more easily through his attacks. On top of that, he has a high mastery level of his element, so I knew I was in for a challenge.

"So is this Mark guy as strong as he claims to be?" Robert asked.

"Yes," Lan said, "Mercenaries are generally stronger than the average soldier or knight simply because they're less bounded by rules and ethic codes of honor."

"Doesn't that mean he's likely to cheat?" Selena asked.

"How's that going to be a fair fight?!" Vincent said.

"It'll be a fair fight because I'm not out there helping Alex," Keith smiled.

"What?" Selena looked past Vincent to Keith, "What do you mean?"

"It's true that Mark pretty much owned the both of us two years ago, but we've both improved a lot since then," Keith watched the battlefield, "Aside from that, there's one key factor here in this duel that wasn't there back then."

"Wait," Selena looked back towards me, "You don't mean…?"

"Here I come!" Mark shouted as he charged me.

I barely had time to unsheathe my claymore before jumping over a horizontal swing from Mark's oversized sword. When I swung downward, he swung upward to block. Upon our blades colliding, droplets of water hit my face. I remembered this was part of his fighting style to break my concentration, so I did my best to ignore the water. We continued to parry each other's swings until we were caught in another deadlock. When our swords broke free, I jumped back to avoid another swing of his blade, but he suddenly stopped it in mid-swing, stepped forward, and swung back. Using the flat side of the claymore and bracing it with my left hand, I blocked his strike, but was thrown back several yards. My feet slid across the ground until I stuck my sword into the ground to slow myself down and finally stop.

"Oh Marcus," Cornelius called him, "Do please try not to hurt him too badly."

"Oh don't worry about me," I stood up, "I don't want him to blame his loss on holding back."

"Alright then," Mark was sounding angry, "In that case, I'll start fighting seriously!"

Mark's blade began to glow with a blue aura. It was a sign that he was preparing for one of his special attacks, and I didn't want to be on the receiving end of them. I ran to close the distance between us just as he was bringing his blade back to attack.

"Take this!" Mark struck his blade on the ground, "Wave Strike!"

A small wave of water about three feet high rose from where he stuck his blade and raced directly at me. Just before it reached me, I flipped over it and completely avoided it. In mid flip, I saw that he stepped forward to attack, so I used my momentum, and met his blade with a downward strike. In sync with the recoil I felt from striking his blade, a sudden rush of water swept my whole body, and I was thrown back several feet as he swung me off his blade. I hit the ground hard, but I was able to get to my feet by leaning against my claymore.

"Damn," I coughed for air, "I don't remember him being able to do that at close range."

"C'mon Alex," Vincent yelled, "Get up!"

"You can do it!" Selena yelled.

"I'm getting bored Marcus," Cornelius yawned, "Hurry and finish this duel so we can move on."

"Fine whatever," Mark said, "I wish he'd stop calling me by my full first name."

Mark's blade radiated a bright blue when he raised it above his head. As he drew it back, water could be seen drawing towards it, and as he swung it, it released a larger and more focused version of his Wave Strike directly at me.

"Get out of the way!" Aiyana yelled.

"It's coming too fast!" Lan yelled.

"Let this be a lesson to you," Mark said, "You'll never defeat someone with real talent!"

Just as his attack got into range, I extended my left hand outward. At that moment, I held my eyes closed as I drew power from the Twilight Star hidden under my cloak. I let loose enough power to create a barrier that protected me from Mark's attack with relative ease.

"Huh?" Mark couldn't tell what just happened, "Wait, what?"

"Sorry Mark," my eyes glowed for a moment, "What was that you said about beating someone with real talent?"

"What in Volternia's name?!" Cornelius's eyes grew wide.

"It's about time," Keith said.

"Go get him Alex!" Selena yelled.

"Kick his ass!" Vincent yelled.

"Now come on," I motioned my hand for him to attack.

"W-Wave Strike!" Mark unleashed several attacks at me.

With each swing of my sword, I let loose enough energy to deflect each of Marks attacks as I ran towards him. As soon as I was in range, we locked into close combat once again. As soon as there was an opening, I jumped forward and feinted a sword strike, but kicked him in his chest instead and knocked him off balance.

"Damn it!" Mark stopped himself from falling with his blade, "Where's that power coming from?!"

"What are you doing?!" Cornelius yelled, "Why are you losing?!"

"Shut up!" Mark yelled, "I'm not losing!"

"Yes you are!" I said.

"No I'm not!!" Mark swung his blade with enough force to knock my sword from my hand.

"Yes..," I jump kicked him in his face and jumped off his shoulders, "…you…," I reached into the folds of my cloak and pulled out the Twilight Star, "Are!"

"Is that…?" Cornelius's eyes grew wide when he saw the Twilight Star.

In a flash of bright light, the Twilight Star took the form of a sword once again and shined with power as I descended down upon Mark.

"Sword of the Rising Sun!" I swung downward as I landed.

With my first swing, I managed cut off some of Mark's spiky hair on his right side. He jumped back to avoid my second horizontal swing, but he got grazed on his chest armor. Getting angry, or perhaps scared, Mark gripped his blade with both hands and swung downward at me with all his might. I met his attack with and upward swing so powerful, it unleashed a burst of light that was almost as bright as the sun. The force of my swing cleaved right through his blade and sent Mark flying and flipping backwards until he hit the city wall.

"Ugh…" Mark tried to move but collapsed from exhaustion.

"Wha…" the piece of Mark's blade that broke off suddenly stuck into the ground where Cornelius stood, "Ahh!"

"I may not have the same talent as you," I let the Twilight Star return to its original form, "But I've got more than enough skill to make up for it."

"Hmph," Keith smirked.

"He… he beat him!" Lan yelled.

"He won!" Selena yelled.

"Yeah!" Vincent looked towards Mark, "Get yo ass whooped!!"

My friends regrouped with me and we celebrated amongst ourselves over my victory. Cornelius stood alone in complete disbelief over what just happened.

"Damn. I don't believe this…" he said, "He had the Twilight Star with him this whole time? And he can use it now??"

"That was great Alex!" Keith put me in a one armed headlock.

"Nice moves with the kick!" Selena said.

"Thanks everyone," I looked towards Mark who was just getting up, "Hey Mark!"

"W-what…?" he reluctantly answered.

"How does it feel to lose to someone with 'real talent'?" I asked.

My friends and I laughed together while Cornelius and Mark just sulked in anger. Mark picked up what was left of his sword and cursed himself over and over for losing.

"Don't worry Mark," Keith said, "I'm sure you'll be able to get a new sword with the money you're earning from Prince Cornelius."

"But if he keeps slacking like this," I started laughing, "He'll probably cut his pay!"

We continued to laugh together as we returned to the city to rest and prepare for our departure tomorrow.

"Curse you Alexander," Cornelius watched us leave the area, "You'll rue the day you made a fool of me!"

Episode 18
The New Team Marches Forward

The next morning, many of the Gravadale knights, including Joanna, Sir Rupert, his wife, and King Richie had all assembled at the north gate to formally see us off. The knights stood at attention on both sides of the gate as we said our final goodbyes to each other.

"Good luck with your battle against OSC," the king shook my hand, "And come back to visit anytime!"

"We will," I said, "You can count on it!"

"All of you be safe," lady Michelle said.

"We're counting on you Robert," Sir Rupert said, "Make us proud!"

"Yes sir," Robert saluted, "You can count on me."

The crowd went into an uproar of cheer and praise as we began our departure from Gravadale. When we reached the top of a hill on the path, we turned around to wave goodbye one final time.

"Hey look!" Selena pointed towards the forest, "Aren't those your people Aiyana?"

"Yes they are!" Aiyana waved to them.

"I guess they came to see us off too," Vincent waved with the rest of us.

"You be careful Aiyana," Aiyana's grandmother thought to herself, "Spirits of the Land, please watch over her. And you Prince Alexander, I pray for your safety as well as your friends also. I don't believe any of you realize yet the difference you all will make in this world."

For most of our walk, we followed alongside the main road from Gravadale. The moderate cloud cover kept the sun from being overbearing. Several hours later we reached a small rocky cliff side where we decided to take a short break.

"Prince Alex," Robert got my attention.

"Huh?" I turned around.

"Where is our first destination?" he asked.

"Yeah," Vincent cut in, "Where ARE we going anyway?"

"Well…" I began to think, "I guess we can figure that out now."

As soon as my friends realized that I didn't have any idea of where we were going, they fell in shock.

"You don't have a clue where we're going, do you?!" Vincent shouted at me.

"Don't worry," I pulled out the map, "I have a pretty good idea where we should go. It's just…"

"What is it?" Keith asked.

"It's this map," I said, "It's written in a language I can't read."

"It's the ancient language of my people," Aiyana scratched her head, "I guess I forgot about that."

"Well," I handed her the map, "You can read it, right?"

"Yes," she held up the map.

"Ok," I looked at the map with her, "Where is Kaydra?"

"Right here," she pointed to one of the symbols on the map, "Its three towns up from where we are now."

"So if we follow this path, we'll get to Deloria," I moved my finger up the map, "Then Einquin, then Kaydra. Then," I ran my finger to the right along a road on the map, "This must be Valsoria."

"Valsoria?" Vincent asked, "Isn't that your kingdom?"

"Yes," I said, "If we head to Kaydra first, then go east along this path, we can have a straight shot there. Either that, or when we get to Kaydra, I can send word to Zephyros and try to meet with him first."

"Who's that?" Vincent asked.

"Zephyros is the crown prince of Zylphan, the kingdom that lies to the north of Valsoria," I said.

"Another royal huh?" Vincent crossed his arms, "Well is he anything like you, Jabari, or Cornelius?"

"Well," I said, "As far as mannerism and appearance, I guess he's like Cornelius, but he's not conceited at all. Between me, him, and Jabari, he's the more traditional royal you would probably picture, and he's a highly skilled fencer."

"Fencer?" Vincent asked.

"It's a style of swordplay that involves using a rapier for quick and precise attacks," I said, "It's not a style I could use with the Twilight Star or any sword other than a rapier."

"Do you know how to fence?" Selena asked.

"I'm ok at it," I said, "But I'm no where near Zephyros's level."

"Do you think he would be willing to help us?" Lan asked.

"I'm sure he would," I said, "I'm just deciding on which way to go first."

"Well if we make our first destination Kaydra," Keith got up and stretched, "We'll have plenty of time to decide a course of action."

"Alright," I said, "Sounds good to me."

"How long would it take us to get to the first town?" Selena asked.

"I think we can be there before noon tomorrow," Aiyana said.

"Looks like we'll be camping at nightfall," Vincent said.

"I don't like the idea of camping outside a city while OSC may still be about," I scanned the area, "But I guess it can't be helped."

"Me either," Keith said, "But if we take turns keeping watch, we should be ok."

"We won't have to," Aiyana said smiling, "I have an idea."

"Really?" I asked, "What is it?"

"You'll see," she said with an innocent smile.

Elsewhere, while we were planning on where we were going to sleep and what we were going to eat, the leaders of OSC were discussing the failures at Gravadale and looking towards a new course of action.

"The boss really didn't take that news well," Alfonso had his large arms crossed.

"Oh really?" Lancer asked sarcastically, "Was the dark aura of lightning your first clue?"

"Haha," Alfonso said, "Well then genius, what are we going to do about this?"

"Our soldiers failed to take Gravadale," Lance thought out loud, "And they failed to retrieve the Golem Soul Crystal because Prince Alexander, somehow, managed to make his way across the desert to Gravadale."

"Not to add more bad news," Francis ran up to Lancer and Alfonso, "But all of the beast we released in the desert near Rac' Sagadam have either died from the effects of the experiments, or have been killed off by their warriors."

"Have they begun to make a move?" Lancer asked.

"Not yet," Francis informed him, "But there's nothing keeping them preoccupied now."

"Well it's not like they have any way of finding us," Alfonso said, "We're too far north."

"Still," Lancer said, "We can't afford anymore mistakes now. I've already done my part to lure out the Soul Crystal of Roc. Now it's just a waiting game for me. The real question is getting rid of Prince Alexander before he makes it back to Valsoria. If he manages to get help from Valsoria's Vanguards, getting to him will become that much more difficult."

"Not to mention that we still need a little more time for the Iron Soldiers and Iron Sentinel to be completed," Alfonso said.

"Sentinel?" a woman's voice was heard down the hall.

From the shadows, Lancer, Alfonso, and Francis were approached by a woman heavily disguised in dark tight fitting clothing and light armor. A black cloth covered her mouth and her forehead which gave her the appearance of a ninja. Metal plates were attached to the forearms and shins of her outfit. Her hair was tied in a tight ponytail and covered mostly with black ribbon to cover as much of her blond hair as possible.

"That must be that large thing I saw that dwarfs the other iron Soldiers," she said.

"It's about time you got back," Lancer said.

“My assignment took a little longer than expected,” she said, “But I got the job done.”

“Very well,” he said, “That’s all that matters. At least someone can get things done right.”

“That’s not fair Lancer,” Francis said, “All the soldiers and bandits I get can’t seem to do a competent job.”

“I’m starting to wonder why the boss put you third in command over the girl,” Alfonso said.

“It’s alright,” she said, “I’m fine with what I’m doing.”

“Keep it up and you may take Francis’s spot,” Lancer said.

“N-no! She can’t!” Francis said, “Besides, I have a plan to get rid of Valsoria’s prince and anyone that may be with him.”

“Oh really?” Lancer asked.

“Yeah really,” Francis said, “I’ll assemble a small group of soldiers and bandits together to take on his companions. As for him, I’ll take him on myself.”

“Will you now?” Alfonso smirked, “Feeling brave all of a sudden?”

“I don’t fear him,” Francis said, “But he will fear me and my power once I’m through with him. Just you wait,” Francis turned to walk down the hall.

“Where are you going?” Lancer asked.

“I’m going to pay our little friend a visit,” he said, “He’s got something for me.”

At the very end of the dim lighted hallway, they entered a room that was littered with paper, metal pieces, crystal shards, and other piles of scrap that have been used in the creation of their weapons. In the middle of the room, there was a large table where a young man with brown short hair sat with his head down on the table. It wasn't until Francis and the ninja girl were standing beside where he sat when they realized that he was sleeping.

"Hey!" Francis slammed his hand on the table, "Wake up!"

"Huh?!" Zaalek's glasses almost flew of his face when he raised his head, "I didn't do it! I…oh. Y-you're one of the leaders here?"

"It's Francis," he said, "You'd best show some respect and try to remember it."

"Sorry," he straightened his glassed with his middle finger, "I'm just so tired, and I hardly get a break."

"Yeah whatever," Francis said, "Where's that device I asked for?"

"This thing here?" he reached for a cloth that was covering something.

When he pulled back the cloth, it revealed what appeared to be a left handed gauntlet that would cover the entire forearm. It was build with a large hexagon cut wind crystal attacked to the back hand of the gauntlet. From the crystal, metal strips that were made with crystal dust ran down to the end of the gauntlet where wires began to stretch to a shoulder guard that contained another large cut wind crystal build into it.

"It looks impressive," Francis put on the device, "Not bad Zaalek. Is it ready?"

"Y-yes sir," he said, "But please don't try it out in here. I'll lose track of everything that I've been asked to work on."

"Oh don't worry about that," he said, "I've already got someone in mind to try it on."

"Who?" Zaalek asked.

“Prince Alexander or course,” he began to leave the room, “It’s time I put a stop to his little ‘adventure’ once and for all.”

After Francis left, Zaalek let out a huge sigh of relief that he wasn’t harassed like any other time a high ranked OSC official would come to see him. The ninja girl sat up on the table and began looking through some of the papers that Zaalek had written lots of numbers and drawn designs on.

“They sure have you busy,” she said.

“Yes,” he said, “I’ve spent the last few days cranking out ideas and designs for their weapons. I’m just thankful that I’m not the one actually building the Iron Soldiers.”

“There’s one that’s humongous,” she said, “Is that the Iron Sentinel they mentioned earlier?”

“Yes,” he said, “They want that to be their strongest weapon against Valsoria. They really don’t like the Valsorian royal family I guess. You know, you’re quite friendly for someone to be working in OSC.”

“I get to do a lot of running,” she said, “So I’m almost always in a good mood.”

“Yea, but it’s like you’re completely out of place here,” he said, “Where did you come from anyway?”

“Don’t worry about that,” she said, “Just worry about staying alive and not getting hurt.”

“Oh sorry,” he began looking through his papers again.

“Don’t get so nervous,” she said, “I don’t mean you any harm.”

“Oh alright,” he said, “Um…just between you and me, I hope Prince Alexander can handle that guy.”

“I’m sure he can,” she said.

“Really?” he asked.

“Yea,” she said, “Just don’t tell anyone. By the way, do you have those fire gloves I asked for?”

“Oh yes,” he opened a drawer at the table and pulled out a pair of lightly plated fingerless gloves with a red fire crystal built into the back hand of each glove, “These have to be the easiest thing I’ve been asked to make. I didn’t know you had the fire affinity.”

“I don’t,” she took the pair, “But they will be useful.”

“If you say so,” he said.

“I better leave you to your work,” she got off the table, “I don’t want any trouble getting started…just yet.”

“Alright then,” he said, “But, could you at least tell me your name? I might be able to remember yours.”

“I guess I can tell you that much,” she stopped at the door and looked back, “Its Lyn Ishikawa. Just remember that I’m not your enemy, and everything will be fine…I hope.”

Episode 19
A Looming Threat

It was late in the evening when we had settled on a spot to camp for the night. It was under a large umbrella tree that sat on a hill several yards off the road we were following. Its long branches were thickly covered with leaves to provide a great amount of shade, as well as keep us dry in case of rain. I sat with Lan, Selena, and Aiyana while Vincent worked on putting together a camp fire. Robert had gone to fill our water canteens at a nearby spring while Keith had gone hunting for food.

"This is a nice spot you picked out, Aiyana," Selena reclined on one of the large roots of the tree.

"Thank you," she said, "I thought it was a beautiful spot to rest for the night."

"I agree," Lan poked at a flower.

"How's the fire coming, Vincent?" Selena suddenly sat up.

"Almost ready," he stacked several pieces of wood and straw inside a circle of stones, "Keith better get back here soon. I'm hungry."

"Me too," Selena said, "Why is the fire taking so long?"

"Cause I'm trying to focus on making a small starting flame," he said.

"You never had a problem with using fire during all the times we were fighting," I said, "What's different this time?"

"What's different is the fact we're NOT fighting," he said, "It's easier to use while I'm fighting. When I'm not, it's sometimes hard to control the way I need to. The best I've been able to do is those burst of fireballs you've seen, but that'll burn up our kindle too fast."

"At least you CAN use your affinity freely like that," Selena said, "The most I've been able to develop on my own is the healing I can do. I can't attack as well as you can with mine."

"I've never seen you really try," he said.

"What am I suppose to do? Throw snowballs?!" she raised her hands in frustration, "I don't have it as easy as you! Everyone in Prominence town that has an affinity is fire with maybe one or two people that can use earth. How am I suppose to learn how to use something that no one else I know can do??"

"It sounds like both of you don't have a strong element mastery level," Lan said, "If you had equipment with the right elemental crystals built into them, you would both have an easier time controlling and training with your affinity."

"It's more complicated in Selena's case than that," I stood up.

"Why?" Vincent asked, "Cause she doesn't have anyone to teach her?"

"No," I began to explain, "You know how there are six nature affinities: earth, fire, wind, water, lightning, and ice?"

"Yeah?" Selena and Vincent said.

"Well, even though some people have an easier time mastering their element than others, some of those affinities are naturally harder to master than others. Ice is one of the hardest elements to master. It's second only to lightning."

"So, how am I suppose to master it?" she asked me.

"Well having some ice crystals would help," I put my hand to my mouth to think for a moment, "But what would really help you is to get a teacher."

"Do you know anyone that can use ice?" she asked.

“Yes,” I said, “Three actually, but only one of them would be able to really help you in my opinion. The only problem is that she’s turned down everyone that has sought her out so far. My grandmother keeps saying that she only wants to teach someone she thinks is worthy.”

“Do you think I’m worthy?” she suddenly got up, “Please tell me you can get her to teach me!”

“I’d like to, but it’s not up to me,” I raised my hands in defense, “She would have to decide for herself, but I could at least get her to meet you.”

“Alright,” she sighed with relief, “I’ll do my best to prove myself to her and you. Thanks Alex.”

“No problem.” I said.

“I’m back!” Robert walked up the hill, “Did I miss anything?”

“Nah,” I said, “We were just talking.”

“Keith hasn’t returned yet?” he asked.

“No,” Vincent finally got a small fire going, “And it’s getting on my nerves. He should’ve been back by now. I’m starving!”

“What’s he hunting for anyway?” Selena asked.

“He’s going after turkey,” Lan said.

“Turkey?” she asked, “What’s that?”

“It’s a wild fowl that lives in this part of the land,” Lan answered.

“You never had turkey before?” Aiyana asked.

“No,” she said, “I’ve never heard of it before now.”

"I tried some when a traveling merchant group stopped in Valsoria to sell some of their goods," I said, "It's very lean, and really tasty."

"They aren't rare in this part of the province, but they can be tricky to catch. Keith must be finding that out the hard way. I better go find him and see if he needs help," Aiyana grabbed her long bow.

Aiyana's suspicions were right. Keith was currently trying to catch three turkeys to bring back, but they proved to be more elusive than he originally thought. He finally tracked down one of the turkeys whose tail feathers were sticking out of a bush.

"Damn bird," Keith stalked the hidden turkey from behind a tree, "I've got you now!"

Keith sprang from behind a tree like an animal attacking its prey. When Keith hit the bush, he quickly discovered that the feathers he saw in the bush were simply stuck there as he grabbed an armful of leaves. As he got up from the decoy, he heard the gobbling in the distance as if they were laughing at him.

"Son of a-" Keith suddenly heard the sound of turkeys squawking.

The painful gobbling he heard quickly subsided. Keith ran to where he last heard the turkeys to find all three of them lying dead with a wooden arrow stuck into them.

"Arrows," Keith looked to the direction the arrows had to come from, "Who…?"

"Here's the deal. I killed them, so you clean them," Aiyana giggled as she set her long bow back over her shoulder.

"What?" Aw, damn it," he hung his head low.

It was about an hour after sunset before the turkeys were cleaned and roasted over the camp fire. Lan was still helping Keith recover from nausea. The slimy feel and horrible stench of gutting the birds had nearly made him throw up.

"They smell delicious," Selena smelled the aroma of food.

"The herbs I ground up on them should really bring out the flavor too," Lan was making a small tonic for Keith.

"Why did you get three?" Rocky asked, "They're not small at all."

"Have you seen Vincent eat?" Keith looked back with a queasy look.

"He could probably eat one and a half of them by himself," Selena commented.

"Two," Vincent corrected her.

"Speaking of eating," I cut the two legs off of one of the roasted birds with my knife I had concealed, "It looks like they're done."

"Sweet! I call the biggest one!" Vincent snatched the largest bird from its stake and began tearing at it like an animal, "Hot! Hot! Mmmm, good!"

"Wow," Rocky was stunned at Vincent's manners, "I-I've never seen such savage behavior."

"That's cause…mmm…all you knights and royals gotta be all proper and crap," Vincent's words were muffled by the food still in his mouth.

"Still," Selena cut in, "Would it kill you to eat like a person?"

"I can't help it if I'm hungry!" Vincent looked to his sister and then resumed his meal.

"Oh geeze…" Selena face palmed herself.

"Here Selena," I handed Selena one of the legs, "It's still a little hot, so be careful."

"Oh! Thanks Alex," Selena took a bite out of it, "It IS good!"

"Those herbs were a great touch Lan," Aiyana bit into half a breast.

"I agree," Robert bit down on a short thigh.

"Its even better with Kykriano sauce," Keith poured some on half a breast.

"Can I try that?" Vincent held the half eaten turkey towards Keith.

"Yea, but be careful," Keith poured a few drops on it, "It starts out sweet, but gets spicy really quick."

"Mmm," Vincent kept eating, "I love it!"

After a few moments, Vincent's face suddenly turned red with heat. He then suddenly spat fire from his mouth due to the intense spice of the sauce which stunned us with disbelief.

"Woah," Robert and Lan stopped munching on their wings.

"Anyone else want some?" Keith asked.

The rest of us looked at each other and said back to Keith, "We'll pass."

Nothing except the bones of our meal remained a few minutes later. With our stomachs filled, we all laid and reclined under the umbrella tree to prepare to sleep.

"Hang on," I sat back up, "You said that we wouldn't have to take turns keeping watch. What did you mean?"

"Oh that's right," Aiyana remembered, "Everyone listen for a moment."

"I don't hear anything but crickets," Vincent said.

"Exactly," Aiyana said, "The crickets are out chirping because everything is so still."

"Oh!" I said, "I know what you're talking about."

"Mind clueing me in?" Vincent asked.

"It's one of the basic survival techniques when you're out in the wilderness," Keith said, "Back in training, I learned that when ninjas were out on long missions and had to spend the night outside, they would listen out for the crickets to warn them of any possible danger."

"If anything was moving around, the crickets within the area would stop chirping all at once," I said, "That way, we'll know if something's near us."

"How do YOU know that?" Vincent asked me.

"It was a technique my dad used when he was out camping," I said.

"For a royal, you're sure good at surviving in the wild," Vincent said.

"I learned a lot from my dad and other knights in my kingdom," I leaned back to the tree, "Well I'm too tired to stay up much longer. Good night everyone."

"Me too," Vincent plopped down to the ground, "G'night."

We all managed to sleep soundly for most of the night. The fire had withered down to glowing coals by the very early hours of the morning. The sky was still dark when the crickets suddenly stopped chirping in one direction. Aiyana was the first to wake up from the sudden silence.

"Wake up everyone!" Aiyana whispered loudly.

"What is it?" I was feeling a bit groggy.

"Something's coming," she pointed towards the road.

"I hear it too," Keith's ears twitched from hearing the rustling of grass.

"I can't see anything," I said.

"Hang on," Keith said as everyone else was finally waking up.

Keith put his hands close together and began to focus some static currents through his hands to illuminate the immediate area. As he focused his hands outward to cast the light forward, we could make out the silhouette of a cloaked person who appeared to be limping.

"It's a person," Aiyana said.

"He looks injured," I said, "We better check this out."

"Let's be careful," Keith said.

"What's going on?" Selena sat up.

"Someone's here," I said, "He looks injured, but we're going down to make sure. Wait here."

"Alright," she turned to Vincent, "Vincent. Vincent, wake up."

Vincent turned out to be a very hard sleeper. Realizing that she couldn't wake him by normal means, she focused her ice energy into her right hand until it was ice cold. Then she stuck her hand down the back of his shirt to finally wake him.

"Sele-!" Vincent gasps briefly before Selena covered his mouth.

"Someone's here," she said.

"Oh snap," Vincent got up to look where Aiyana, Keith, and I went to check on the person we found, "Is it OSC?"

"No, I don't think so," she answered, "But he looks like he might be hurt."

"Oh," Vincent tried to rub out the blurriness of his vision, "Well they can take care of it. Besides…"

"Besides what?" Selena asked.

"I gotta go take care of some business," he said as he held his stomach, I'll be right back!"

"Ew," Selena lowered her eye brows with disgust, "Just don't get lost out there."

We got the cloaked man to sit down at the base of the hill. He sounded almost completely out of breath as his bloody right hand held his cloak tightly around him.

"What happened to you? How badly hurt are you?" I reached to move the cloak out of his face.

"No, never mind me," the man weakly gasps to catch his breath, "My friend needs more help than I do right now."

"Where is he?" Keith asked.

"He's further down the path," he pointed, "Just a little ways over the hill. We were jumped by two bandits that beat us and took all our money. He was too injured to walk, so I hid him and went for help."

"Shameless men looking to make some easy shards," Keith said, "Where exactly up there did you hide him?"

"When you see a big rock on the side of the path, dart right a couple of yards into the trees and look for a huge umbrella tree. He's under there. You can't miss it," he said.

"Alex," Keith got my attention, "I'll run up ahead and try to find the guy."

"By yourself?" I asked, "I think it would be safer if we all went. You might run into a larger group of bandits."

"I can take them," he said confidently, "Don't forget I'm a ninja. Bandits are too clumsy to catch me. Be back in a flash!" he ran off at top speed before I could stop him.

"Is Keith really that good?" Aiyana asked me.

"Keith's is stealthy enough to get past some of my royal guards without being detected, so I shouldn't be worried," I said.

"Alex," Aiyana got my attention after about three minutes of Keith leaving.

"Something wrong?" I asked.

"I've been listening in the direction Keith ran to try and hear anything, and I'm getting a little worried," she answered me.

"Do you hear something?" I asked.

"No, but that's exactly why I'm getting worried. Even with Keith and the other man up there somewhere, the crickets are way too quiet in that direction," she said as the man slowly reached into his cloak while we weren't paying attention.

"Is there something else out there that's making them stay quiet?" I asked.

"I don't know, but it shouldn't be *that* quiet," she answered.

"Now you've gotten me worried. We should have all went together. I'm getting a really bad feeling about this…"

Episode 20
Midnight Assault

After several minutes of Vincent being gone, Selena left the campsite in search of him. With one moon on its last quarter and the second moon completely out of sight, it was difficult for Selena to see clearly beyond a few yards. It was then that she realized that she had lost sight of the campsite.

"Oh no," a chill ran down her spine, "Please tell me I haven't gotten lost."

Selena began slowly pacing backwards as she became increasingly nervous. She couldn't see anything, but she could feel that she was being watched somehow by something or someone. Seconds felt like minutes as fear threatened to overwhelm her. As if to validate her fears, a rough-feeling hand grabbed her left shoulder from behind. As she spun around to confront the person who grabbed her, a second hand silenced her mouth before she even had time to scream.

"Aiyana, we should get everyone," I said, "We need to go after Keith. He's taking too long."

"I agree," she looked back towards the camp, "Wait…where is everyone?"

"Probably dead by now," the cloaked man suddenly spoke in a sinister voice.

"What did you just say?!" an ominous feeling gripped my heart as I turned to face the now standing man.

Instinct took over my body's actions as I gripped the hilt of my new sword and unsheathed it from over my shoulder. Aiyana and I both spun around to confront the man, but we weren't fast enough. We both were caught directly in the path of a focused wind gust that sent us flying over twenty yards.

"Heh," the standing man threw of his cloak, "So that geek CAN make something useful after all," he eyed the device strapped to his right wrist.

"Oh no," I staggered to my feet, "Aiyana, are you ok?"

"My arm…!" she held her bleeding right arm in pain.

"She's not the only one you should be concerned with, Prince Alexander!" the man shouted at me, "As we speak, my men are dealing with the rest of your little band of vigilantes!"

"Who are you?!" I demanded an answer, "How do you know me?!"

"You've given our soldiers quite the trouble as of late," he pointed at me, "So now I am here to deal with you personally. I am third in command of OSC, Commander Francis"

"Third in command??" I almost couldn't believe what I heard, "This is bad! We walked right into a trap!"

"Alex, what are we going to do?" Aiyana stood behind me.

"I commend your efforts, but there is nothing you can do now," Francis raised his right arm, "Even with the help of your friends, you don't stand a chance against me. This is the end for you!"

"They're stronger than you think," I readied myself, "They won't fall to the likes of your group, and neither will I!"

"You sure have a lot of confidence in them. It's a shame it's all in vain. If you really think you can stop me, then now's your chance. Just try me-I dare you! I want to test the full extent of my new toy!" Francis challenged me.

"You're going down!" I raised my sword and charged him.

"Let's see how you handle this!" Francis shouted.

I was forced to stop dead in my tracks as he quickly brought forth an intense whirlwind around himself that felt like a tornado. The violent whirlwind suddenly disappeared as quickly as it came.

"Damn that was powerful!" I had my arms up in defense.

"Alex look above you!!" Aiyana warned me.

An intensely focused gale force wind dropped from the sky and slammed me into the ground with enough force to knock the breath out of me. I almost couldn't catch my breath after the impact.

"Not bad," Francis eyed his device with great admiration, "Oh this will do nicely!"

"Da…damn," I struggled stand against the wind, "What is…that thing??"

"How do you like the Gale Force Amplifier?" Francis taunted, "Surely it's not too much for you."

The raging whirlwind suddenly stopped and I was able to fully stand upright. He then unleashed a gust of wind directly at me. Quickly drawing power from the Twilight Star, I was able to defend myself against the wind, but I struggled to maintain the barrier's strength. He huddenly stopped the attack, and then pulled an updraft from behind me that spun me in the air until I was as high as the umbrella tree we were sleeping under. I felt as if I was spinning in every direction possible as he forced me to the ground. Bleeding from my head, I looked up with blurred vision as he stood there laughing maniacally and prepared to attack once again.

By this time, Keith had made his way to the area that Francis had described. He calmly walked around and observed his surroundings with an odd look of curiosity on his face.

"Way out here," Keith said under his breath as his ears twitched from sounds he picked up in the immediate area, "That's pretty typical. This would have been risky either way, but I just hope I can handle all that may show up," he thought to himself as he readied his Ninja Drive.

"Keith!" Lan called out to him from behind.

"What?! Lan! Robert!" Keith was shocked by their sudden appearance, "What are you two doing here??"

"We thought you may need some help in case you were to get ambushed," Rocky replied.

"You don't understand!" Keith didn't realize that he was yelling, "I was EXPECTING to get ambushed! It's a trap!!"

"Surround them!" A voice commanded from the shadows.

Twenty-one OSC soldiers quickly formed up in a circle around Keith, Rocky, and Lan. Their weapons ranged from various blades and axes, to gauntlets fitted with elemental crystals.

"Oh no!" Lan raised his staff in defense as he, Robert, and Keith stood back to back, "If you knew this was a trap, why did you go ahead alone???"

"I can handle a few goons," Keith unsheathed his katana, "It's the camp I'm worried about! I thought if anything, OSC would send a stronger group to the camp sight!"

"Gotta give you credit for figuring that one out, pointy ears," one of the OSC soldiers commented, "Commander Francis, is probably half-way done with Prince Alexander and the rest of your friends."

"We had to get some of you separated," another soldier spoke up, "The bosses want you all gone and quick."

"Divide and conquer," Robert held up his shield and sword, "Classic battle tactic…"

"Listen to me guys," Keith said, "Somehow, we have to fight our way back. If he's up against one of their elite, he's going to need help."

"Good luck getting past all of us!" a third soldier taunted, "Even if you make it past us, all that will be waiting for you are a couple of corpses! We'll be sure that all three of you join their pile!"

"Kill them!" the first soldier ordered the attack.

"Now Lan!" Keith shouted.

"Gaia Explosion!" Lan shouted.

Lan channeled his powers through his staff to let loose an explosion under some of the charging soldiers. The blast was enough to kill five of the soldiers instantly while sending the rest flying in different directions.

"Run for it!" Keith signaled for them to run.

As soon as thye bolted for the campsite, the surviving soldiers gave chase. The faster soldiers that were catching up to them were cut down when Keith suddenly stopped and slashed them up in rapid succession. Robert threw his shield and knocked out several soldiers as he swung it around and pulled it back. Lan proceeded to attack again when a soldier leaped from behind a large boulder.

"No you don't!" he raised his blade to attack Lan.

"Watch out!" Robert intercepted the blade with his shield and finished him with a stab to the gut.

After shoving the soldier off his sword, he thrust his sword into the ground and unleashed a quake of his own. While it didn't cause an explosion like Lan's attack, it was enough to shake most of the soldiers off balance again. Taking advantage of the situation, Keith quickly ended the lives of three of the soldiers before the rest of them could recover. Robert was forced to lock blades against two incoming attacks from two soldiers while Lan did his best to defend himself by raising spikes from the ground and defending with his staff. Keith quickly activated his Ninja Drive to come to Lan and Robert's aid. Once Robert was free from a few of OSC's attacks, he swung his sword upward and call forth a flurry of sharp stones to shoot upward from the ground. Several soldiers were caught by the attack, but the rest retaliated with skills of their own. Two of them combined their strengths to unleash a fiery explosion that knocked Lan, Keith, and Rocky off their feet. In a terrible stroke of luck, Keith's Ninja Drive hit a rock as they fell and broke it to the point where it was unusable. More soldiers appeared from the shadows as the trio rose to their feet again and stood back to back.

"We can't get through!" Lan shouted.

"We have to!" Robert looked for a way out, "Somehow we have to!"

"We're surrounded by goons and my Ninja Drive picks NOW of all times to break!" Keith stood in a defensive stance with his katana.

“Give up!” the leader of the group ordered the trio, “You won’t survive against all of us for much longer!”

“We’re not giving up!” Keith shouted.

“Alright then,” the leader said, “I hope you all had a good life. Finish them!”

Episode 21
Blazing Counterattack!

Selena's fear was quickly consumed with relief as she made eye contact with the young man who had snuck up on her. She took a moment to catch her breath and recover from the shock as the young man released his hand from her mouth.

"Sorry sis," Vincent apologized, "I just didn't want you to scream."

"Don't scare me like that!" Selena was angry, yet relieved at the same time, "I was worried that something had happened to you!"

"Like what? OSC? Their soldiers aren't anything we can't handle," he said.

"You sure about that?" a voice spoke from behind them.

Selena and Vincent spun around to meet a heavily disguised female figure who kept a distance of about ten yards from them. The black garb that wrapped around most of her face along with the metal plates attached to her arms gave her the look of an assassin. Her arms remained crossed as she calmly faced the twin siblings.

"Who are you?!" Vincent stood ready to fight.

"I'm currently with OSC," she replied, "but I'm no one you should be worried about right now."

"If you're with OSC, then why should we care about anything you say?!" Selena demanded to know.

"Alex needs your help right now," she said.

Selena and Vincent's blood suddenly ran cold from what they just heard.

"W-what do you mean?! What's going on?!" Vincent asked out of anger and fear.

"Francis, OSC's third in command, is fighting against him right now," she said.

"Third in command?!" Selena and Vincent were shocked.

"Listen to me," she continued, "The guy he's fighting uses a special gear created by us to amplify his own powers. He uses the wind element, so it will be hard for you to get close to him."

"So how can we fight him?" Selena asked

"You can use fire right?" she looked to Vincent.

"Y-yeah," he took a step back, "How'd you know?"

"Don't worry about that now," she tossed a pair of lightly armored, fingerless gloves with a fire crystal build into the back hands to Vincent, "Use these."

"These are…" Vincent held the pair of gloves in each hand, "Seriously?"

"They should give you better control of your affinity," she said, "As well as give your attacks more power. Just don't get the idea that they alone will guarantee you a victory."

"Why are you helping us?" Selena asked.

"I've got my reasons," she turned to walk into the darkness, "Just hurry and go help Alex. Keith and the other will need your help too. Do your best and survive."

"Wait!" Selena called out, "Do you know Alex?"

"We'll meet again soon," her voice projected softly as she disappeared into the mist.

"She's gone," Selena looked around.

"C'mon sis," Vincent ran towards the campsite, "We gotta hurry! It's time to own face!"

I was out of options before I realized it. Francis continued to take advantage of his amplified powers and I couldn't get close enough to do anything. All the energy I had left was used to defend Aiyana and myself, but his last attack left me unable to stand any longer. Aiyana proceeded to draw an arrow, despite her injuries, but Francis forced her to the ground with me before she could pull back the string.

"Is this all you can do?" Francis approached me as I lay face down on the ground, "Surely the wielder of the Twilight Star is capable of more than this!"

I felt too exhausted to respond. I was in pain from all the cuts and bruises I suffered. My vision was so blurred that everything seemed to spin.

"I'm done here," he rubbed his short hair back, "I'll be taking the Twilight Star now."

"Take THIS!!" Vincent suddenly rushed him with a blazing sucker punch that sent him reeling over 20 yards!

"Alex! Aiyana!" Selena screamed, "Speak to me!"

We both let out a weak painful groan to let Selena and Vincent know we were still alive.

"Hang in there buddy!" Vincent proceeded to rush Francis into close combat, "I'll take it from here!"

"Hold still Alex," Selena advised, "I'll patch you up."

"Get…Aiyana first," I weakly said.

"You-" Francis got up, "Who the-"

"Take this!" Vincent slammed his burning hands on the ground.

Vincent unleashed a fiery assault beyond what I've ever seen him able to do! He unleashed a blast of fire that trailed along the ground and erupted at Francis's feet. After being thrown for a loop, he was forced to defend himself from Vincent's fire with a whirlwind he conjured with the help of his Gale Force Amplifier. In the middle of an explosion of fire caused by their two attacks colliding, Vincent leaped from the fire and caught Francis with a punch so hot, it burned his face.

"Ahhh!!" Francis fell back in pain.

"What's he wearing?" I noticed a pair of gloves on Vincent's fists, "When did he get those?"

"Wow," Selena said, "It's amazing!"

"Incredible," Vincent thought to himself while eyeing his fists, "I've never been able to do this before!"

"You…" Francis began to push the Gale Force Amplifier to its limit, "Insolent little pest!"

"Pest?" he glared at Francis while bringing his hands together to his side, "This pest is about to kick your ass for messing with my friends!"

Through Vincent's concentration, a fireball began to spin between his hands to the point where it began glowing brighter and hotter with each passing second. Francis was conjuring up another whirlwind around himself in preparation for another attack, but the Gale Force Amplifier began sparking, and it was making it harder for him to concentrate. Before he could gain control, Vincent shot forth an inferno so hot, the ground below it began to glow orange with heat! The result of the two attacks created an explosion so violent that fire was set to the immediate area!

"Vincent!" I shielded myself, Selena, and Aiyana with the Twilight Star's power.

"Gah!" Francis jumped back from the flames, "Where did that arrogant punk get to?"

"Gotcha bastard!" Vincent jumped threw the fire and hit him square in the face.

Francis reeled backwards and bounced along the ground for several yards. His face was partially scorched, his nose was broken, and he lost a tooth in the process.

"AAHHHH!!!" Francis's screams were muffled by his own hands as he rolled in pain, "You son of a-AHH!!"

"You just got a Prominence Town Beat Down!" Vincent wiped his nose with his right thumb.

"Please don't say that again," Selena face palmed herself.

"I'll kill you all!" one hand was still over his face when he raised the Gale Force Amplifier that soon began sparking, "What the hell?? Work you piece of junk!"

"You can come finish him off if you want too Alex," Vincent said.

"This can't happen," Francis rose to the air, "This can't happen!"

"He can fly?!" Selena was shocked.

"Get back down here!" Vincent ran under him.

"This isn't over!" Francis shouted, "This isn't over by a long shot! You'll see me again soon! Count on it!!" he disappeared into the darkness of the night sky.

"Yea you better fly!" Vincent shouted.

"Wow Vincent!" I ran up to him, "Way to kick his ass!"

"Heh," he smiled, "That's how me and Vikki run things back home."

"That was one of OSC's top guys," I said, "Even though you fought him off, it looks like they're getting serious."

"Let's worry about that later," Vincent looked down the road, "We gotta go help Keith and the others!"

"C'mon," we all ran down the path together.

Somewhere in the distant darkness far away from the battlefield, Francis was forced to land due to being so fatigued and injured from battle. His face felt like it was on fire after taking a direct hit from Vincent's punch. As he cursed himself and tried to fly again, the same assassin that appeared before Selena and Vincent appeared before him.

"Y-you…!" he called her, "Help me get…back to base… I've must…get this thing fixed…"

"I'm afraid I can't do that," she calmly said.

"W-what?" Francis sounded confused, "What are you talking about?"

"It won't be getting fixed," she unsheathed a pair of katanas held at her side, "And you won't be going anywhere."

"N-no-!" his voice was filled with horror when he realized what was about to happen, "You're a-!"

"Goodbye," she finished the conversation in two smooth strokes of her katanas.

The four of us ran as fast as we could to assist them. Keith, Robert, and Lan were completely on a running defensive as they tried to survive the assault of the numerous soldiers that ambushed them. Lan's earth attacks proved valuable to allow them to gain a little distance, but it did little to deter the remaining soldiers. Robert defended with his sword and shield as best as he could, but even he was being forced to retreat to keep from getting surrounded again, and Keith's Ninja Drive was so damaged it was useless. Even he was beginning to run low on stamina as he fought hard for his life.

"Strike of the Assassin!" Keith finished a soldier and continued to retreat back, "We can't keep this up! Run faster!"

"You try running in all this armor!" Robert parried enemy blades from himself, "I'm usually on horseback anyway!"

"Fight them," Lan continued to use his earth spells, "Not each other!"

"Gotcha shorty," a soldier back-handed Lan to the ground and raised his large knife.

"Lan NO!!!" Keith was stuck in combat with two other soldiers.

"Roll away!!" Robert was pinned down.

A wooden arrow suddenly pierced the throat of the soldier that was about to strike Lan down and brought him down with a loud thud. Before the other soldiers could react to the first attack, a trail of fire shot through the crowd which distracted them long enough for Rocky and Keith to pull away and get to Lan's side.

"An arrow!" Keith observed the projectile.

"Fire?!" Robert looked back to the source of the flames.

At the top of the hill, Aiyana stood tall beside Selena with another arrow already ready to fire. Vincent stood ready with his fist enflamed once again as I unsheathed my claymore. My Twilight Star began to shine brightly as Vincent and I charged down the hill.

"Well it's about time!" Keith shouted as he turned his attention to another soldier and sliced his throat.

"GO!!!" Vincent and I shouted as we entered combat.

Episode 22
Enter the Super-Mart Caravan

"Did you see anything ahead," Aiyana spoke to a small bird landing on her shoulder.

Morning just couldn't come fast enough, but we were greeted with overcast skies instead of the usual sunrise. It was nothing short of a miracle that we all survived the chaos from last night. It was well into the morning as we rested far off the road. Lan was exhausted, but still found the energy to radiate healing energy from his staff. Robert and I sat back to back as his necklace radiated a small amount of energy to assist in the healing process. Although Selena was able to heal the majority of our surface wounds, it took the energy from earth power to heal our more serious injuries.

"Wow," Selena said, "I can't believe we survived all that."

"Fifteen…twenty-three," Vincent counted out loud, "How many of those guys did we put away?"

"All of them. That's how many we put away," I weakly lifted my head.

"Honestly how did we survive?" Lan continued to cast his healing, "There were so many."

"Yeah," Keith fiddled with his broken Ninja Drive, "But those guys were only grunts. Alex and Vincent had the tougher fight with that third in command of OSC."

"Aiyana," I called out, "Did he see anything ahead?"

"Yes!" she smiled brightly, "Deloria is just ahead. There are also people dressed similar to Robert."

"Deloria doubles as an outpost for Gravadale," he said, "We'll be safe to rest there."

"We need to hurry," Aiyana said, "It's going to rain soon."

"How soon?" I slowly stood up.

"Soon," she looked towards the west where clouds were getting darker, "Judging by the wind, I'm not sure if we can beat the rain to Deloria."

"How's your leg Vincent?" I asked.

"I think its fine to walk on now," he slowly stood up, "It's still a little sore."

"I can't tell how fast those rain clouds are coming," I observed the horizon, "It's hard to guess how fast we need to move."

"Hey look," Selena pointed down to the road, "There's a group of carts that look like they're going to Deloria."

"They must be a small merchant convoy," Robert observed, "I think it would be a good idea to try and get a ride. I don't think we can get to town before the rain starts."

"I agree," I said, "But I'd rather not get a ride by letting them know who I am. I think it's best I conceal my identity for a little while."

"How are you going to do that?" Robert asked.

"Well no one outside the royal families and a few other people even know what I look like out here, so I just need to take on an alias for a while," I began to explain, "I think to make this work, we need to take on a group alias."

"So what's the plan this time?" Vincent crossed his arms.

“I got it,” I said after thinking for a few moments, “We’ll pretend to be a group of traveling mercenaries. We’ll be able to move about freely among the common people. As for my personal alias, I want you all to call me Raymond from now on.”

“Mercenaries?” Selena questioned me, “Where did you get that idea?”

“Before my grandfather became king of Valsoria, he was a mercenary himself,” I said, “There’s a long story behind that. I’ll tell you about that later.”

“That’s actually a good idea,” Keith said, “But how are you going to explain a knight of Gravadale traveling with us?”

“We’ll tell the merchants that we just happened to be going the same way,” I said, “We might have to think of something later.”

“Well we need to do something now,” Selena said, “Look! They’re under attack!”

“OSC?” Keith asked.

“No,” I said, “They look like common bandits.”

“We’re going to help them, right?” Vincent asked.

“Unless they’re paid in advance, most mercenaries wouldn’t waste their time with common bandits,” I said, “But mercenaries will sometimes put a potential client in their debt. I feel bad about going at it like this, but we’re going to save them and ask for a ride in exchange.”

“Ready when you are, Al-Raymond,” Vincent almost slipped up.

“Alright guys,” I unsheathed my claymore, “Attack!”

Compared to fighting OSC grunts, kicking the ass of some desperate thugs was mere child’s play. The merchants in the convoy were more than happy to give us a lift in their wagons. The rain began as soon as we loaded up into their carts. I was able to find room in the first cart of the caravan where I was getting to know the man in charge, his wife, and son. Their clothes were simple, but well tailored.

"I sure am mighty thankful you mercenaries showed up when ya did," the black haired merchant said, "I thought you all looked a little young to be mercenaries, but your combat skills proved otherwise."

"We get that a lot," I said, "We appreciate the ride Mr.…"

"Byson," he said, "Byson Tassel, but call me Byson. I'm the leader of the Super-Mart Caravan."

"My name is Sheryll," the brunette woman said, "And this is our son, Byson Jr. We specialize in common household items and clothing. We can even tailor to a person's needs."

"Hello," he quietly said.

"Nice to meet you all," I said, "My name is Raymond. I'm the leader of our small group."

In the second cart, Selena and Vincent were getting to know the couple and their daughter that resides in that cart. The red headed man wore a white shirt with rugged looking pants, his wife wore a green dress, and their daughter was in a normal shirt and skirt.

"So you're a blacksmith?" Vincent asked the man.

"Yup," he spoke with a piece of straw in his mouth, "Jack Lumber; traveling blacksmith at your service! Need a weapon tempered or an armor piece crafted? I'm your guy! If it ain't from me, it ain't worth jack!"

"Save that energy for when we get to town dear," his violet haired wife said, "I'm Cathrynne. I sell medicines for nearly any ache or illness you may get."

"That's great news," Selena said, "How long have you been merchants?"

"We've been merchants for most of our lives," she said, "We started the Caravan a year before Jack and I got married. Our paths usually take us through Gravadale, and other towns within the territories of Zylphan, Volternia, Rac' Sagadam, and Central Kingdom."

"And one time we actually WENT into Valsoria!" an excited young blonde girl in a ponytail spoke up, "Did you know I'm the same age as Princess Alyssa?"

"Central Kingdom has a princess??" Vincent and Selena asked.

"Uh huh!" she nodded, "She has an older brother too! Mama says he's really cool!"

"He's the type of person you wouldn't even know was royalty if you just randomly met him on the street," Cathrynne said.

"Maybe you'll be able to meet him one day," Selena smiled to the girl.

"Oh I hope so!" the little girl got excited, "Daddy, when are we going back to Valsoria??"

"It's gonna be a while Nina," Jack said, "We got several stops to make before we circle that way again. Besides, I heard that Prince Alexander isn't even there right now. Rumor has it that he's out fightin' some terrorist group."

"Oh! Then maybe we'll run into him!" Nina said with optimism.

"You just might one day," Vincent gave a smirk look to Selena.

In the third cart, Aiyana and Keith were getting to know the two men who were in charge of that one. They were twin brothers; one with dark blue hair, and the other with brown hair.

"I'm Tom," said the older twin.

"And I'm Jerry," said the younger twin.

"Hey Tom and Jerry," Keith said, "Something smells delicious."

"That's cause you're in the grocery cart," they both said in unison.

"I handle fruits, vegetables, and lot of desserts," said Tom.

"And I handle meats, breads, and the best spices," Jerry said.

"Here," Tom handed Aiyana an apple to sample, "I only sell the best! Try it!"

"It's delicious," Aiyana continued to eat at the apple, "It's very juicy and sweet."

"Try a sample of my jerky," Jerry handed Keith a piece.

"MMMHH!!" Keith enjoyed his snack, "This is GREAT!!"

"There's plenty more good food where that came from!" they said in unison, "Once we get to town, we'll cook you all up something delicious!"

"Oh I can't wait!" Keith and Aiyana said in unison.

Lan and Robert rode in the final cart with a beautiful blonde woman who seemed more interested in getting to know Robert than anything.

"How do you do? My name is Stacey."

"I'm Lan," he smiled.

"And I'm Robert," he bowed.

"You're mighty handsome is what you are," she flirted with him.

“T-thank you,” he held his composure, “That’s very kind of you. You are a pretty woman yourself.”

“We’ve only just met. Let’s get to know each other first,” she teased, “What’s a strong handsome knight like you doing with a group of mercenaries?”

“We just happened to be traveling the same way, so I thought it would be nice to stick with them and help them out,” Robert said.

“Oh how noble of you,” she gave a seducing smile, “Don’t you sound like the perfect ‘knight in shining armor’.”

“Do you sell crystals of all types?” Lan tried to save Robert by changing the subject.

“Oh,” she turned her attention to Lan, “I do, but certain ones are hard to come by-even for a jewelry merchant. I mostly sell common pieces of jewelry like earrings, bracelets, necklaces, and things like that.”

“Your inventory looks great,” Robert said, “It’s no wonder you’re so successful.”

“Oh my,” she blushed, “You sure know how to sweet talk a girl.”

“So where are you all heading after Deloria,” I asked Byson as the town came into view.

“After we rest here, we plan to head to Kaydra,” he said, “Its one of the best cities to set up shop at. We always get good business there this time of year.”

“Would you like some protection getting there?” I asked, “My team is currently looking for work, and we happen to be going to Kaydra anyway.”

“We could use the protection,” Sheryll said, “With that terrorist group running around, I’d feel safer to have someone watching our backs.”

"I'm not sure," Byson said, "How much would this cost us?"

"It depends to be honest," I was unsure of an exact price to ask, "Usually my previous clients and I can work out a deal that benefits the both of us."

"Sheryll and I will talk to Jack and the others about it," he said, "Until then, you're welcome to hang around with us till tomorrow. Once we settle in a good spot, Tom and Jerry will make us all lunch. You're welcome to join us."

"Thank you so much Byron," I shook his hand.

The members of the Super-Mart Caravan were very hospitable. The lunch Tom and Jerry made was nothing short of exquisite. The rain stopped sometime in the late afternoon, but clouds were still overcastting the sky. Out of all the merchants, this seemed to be a great town for Jack, Tom, and Jerry to sell their goods to the residents and knights that occupy the town.

"So Al-Raymond," Vincent almost slipped up again, "Did they decide to hire us?"

"Not yet," I said, "They haven't come to tell me anything yet."

"If they do, then we'll have to walk a lot less," Robert said.

"We'll have good food to eat the entire way," Aiyana munched on another of Tom's apples.

"Not to mention we could have access to new and fresh clothes," Selena said.

"And crystals," Lan said, "They would really enhance our abilities."

"Yes," I said, "If we can get access to some crystal embedded gear, it would really help us out. Well, it would help you all out anyway."

"Wait that's right," Vincent said, "You don't have a nature element to use. How are you going to fight without using the Twilight Star?"

"You'll expose your identity if you do," Selena said.

"I've still got my swordsmanship," I said, "I'll just have to do my best without it."

"Hey Raymond!" Byson called me.

"Yes?" I replied.

"C'mere," he said, "Let's talk about that proposal of yours!"

"Okay!" I said to him, "Wish me luck guys."

"Good luck!" Selena called out.

After several minutes of discussion and negotiating payment and price plans, we finally came to an agreement.

"Well?" Vincent asked.

"Well guys," I had my head down, "…we are officially hired!"

"Yeah!" everyone else cheered in unison.

"So how's it gonna work?" Vincent asked.

"For every day we make it through, they're going to pay us a thousand shards each. In addition, Tom and Jerry will provide us with free meals, and we'll get a ten percent discount on their other goods," I explained, "The only other thing we'll have to pay for are rooms at an inn if we stay at one."

"Way to go boss," Keith gave me a high five.

"Kaydra, here we come!" Vincent shouted.

"They're gonna protect us from the bandits?" Byson Jr. asked his mom.

"They sure are," Sheryll assured him, "You won't have to worry with them around."

"That means I'll have that handsome knight to protect me," Stacey brightly smiled, "This really is our lucky day!"

"They sure are an interesting bunch," Cathrynne said.

"They probably think the same of us," Tom and Jerry said in unison.

"Especially the way you two act," Jack held his axe over his shoulder.

"What do you mean?" they both asked in unison.

The entire caravan couldn't help but laugh. The sun even managed to peep through the clouds. I was sure by their bright spirits that we would enjoy traveling with the Super-Mart Caravan. Now it's time to get to work. It's time to some first hand experience of the life of a mercenary.

Episode 23

Stolen! Recover the Stolen Goods!

We got an early start by leaving Deloria before daybreak the following day. Byson Jr and Nina were still asleep for much of the ride. During a brief rest, the caravan was targeted by a group of seven bandits wielding knives and axes. Vincent, Keith, Robert, and I made quick work of them before anyone could get hurt, and then we continued on without too much trouble. It was about 1:00 in the afternoon with mostly cloudy skies when we arrived in the next town known as Einquin. Byson decided on resting the horses and vending for a few hours before continuing on. Einquin is a small town, so he didn't expect to get much business here.

"We'll leave for Kaydra later in the evening," Byson said, "We're making good time thanks to you and your mercenary crew."

"It's no problem for us," I said, "We're thankful for the job. And thanks for the discount on the jacket and shoulder piece."

"No problem Raymond," he said, "Though I am curious as to why a swordsman would need bombs."

"I like to be prepared for anything," I said.

"Well make good use of them," he said, "Those are new and hard to make-even for Jack."

"I will. If you don't mind, I want to take a walk around town and check the place out," I told him.

"Go ahead," he said, "You got time."

"I'll come with ya," Vincent was now wearing a chain mail under his black and red sleeveless shirt, "I wanna stretch my legs."

"Me too," Selena was now wearing a blue and white tunic.

"Something on ya mind boss?" Vincent had his hands in his pocket as we walked through the town streets.

"I almost can't believe it's been a little over a week since I left home," I said, "A heck of a lot has happened in such a short time."

"That's all that's passed? Are you serious??" Selena was shocked.

"Uh huh," I said, "I wonder how everyone's doing back home. I'm sure OSC is no match for Central Kingdom's forces, but I know everyone's probably worried sick about me. I wouldn't be surprised if we started seeing Valsorian knights on the lookout for me soon."

"Ya know, I've been wondering something," Selena started, "A lot of things really."

"What's that?" I asked.

"Well, what made you decide to train in swordsmanship?" she asked, "I never could picture a royal in combat like you've been lately."

"Well part of it was due to traditional teachings we go through," I said, "The academy I attended as part of my education had fencing as one of its classes."

"Yea, but you don't fence at all," Selena said, "Your style is…I don't even know how to describe it."

"Yeah. It's kinda cool how you fight. You're better than some of the knights I've seen, and so is Jabari," Vincent added, "Where did you learn to fight like that?"

“A little bit from a lot,” I said, “I learned the basics by watching and sparring with knights while they trained. I couldn’t quite get fencing down like everyone else, so my grandfather and everyone else taught me to break away from traditional swordplay, and I ended up developing a style of my own that’s anything but formal.”

“Ya think?” Vincent laughed, “I’m no expert at swordsmanship, but I don’t think kicking someone in the chest and jumping off their shoulders is traditional swordplay.”

“It got results didn’t it?” I laughed, “I’m always trying to adapt my style when I can.”

“What about Jabari?” he asked, “Do yall use the same style?”

“Oh hell no,” I said, “Don’t you remember our sparring match? The way he fights offensively with dual blades is second nature to him. He can overwhelm someone with offense and raw strength a lot better than I can. Matching his strength is something I could never do, so I have to play more evasively against him.”

“Well that’s cool,” Vincent leaned up against a fence, “So what’s up with you and that blonde jackass back at Gravadale? Prince Cornelius?”

“He’s a very spoiled and prejudice person,” I said, “It’s not just him though. Most of everyone in the Volternia royal family has this superiority complex that everyone is beneath them. He’s always had it out for me since we were young, especially when it came time to attend the academy. Despite his prestigious attitude, he’s quite a good fencer. Oh and when he found out that I didn’t have an affinity of my own, he and his friends really began giving me a hard time.”

“What about the Twilight Star?” Selena asked.

"Well I didn't have it with me back then," I said, "Plus I didn't know how to use it then anyway. If it weren't for Zephyros keeping the peace and the other friends I made, I don't know how I would've made it through."

"It sounds like you had it rougher than I thought anyone like you would," Vincent said.

"Yeah," I said, "Oh Jabari got him good one day when we were kids. He insulted a dish that some of Jabari's cooks brought to one of our gatherings and said something like 'Not even a dog would eat this garbage'," I said mocking his voice, "So Jabari took a piece of meat and snuck it in Cornelius's back pants pocket. I've never seen anyone run so fast from dogs trying to take a bite out of his ass."

"AH HAHAHAHA!!" they both laughed out loud.

"'I guess even dogs will eat it too' is what Jabari said while they chased him across the courtyard," I let out a laugh from remembering the scene.

"Oh man I wish I could've SEEN that!" Vincent was still laughing.

"Even if I need help to do it, I always got the last laugh against Cornelius," I said.

"Raymond!!" Aiyana ran up to us, "Big trouble!!"

"What happened?" I asked, "Is it OSC?"

"No!" she said, "We've been robbed! Stacey's wagon got robbed of some of her crystals and jewelry."

"How did they get past everyone??" Selena, Vincent, and I ran back to the caravan with Aiyana.

"I don't know," Aiyana said, "I was in Tom and Jerry's wagon when it happened. Keith is already tracking them down now."

"Raymond I apologize," Robert said as soon as I got there, "Bandits should have never gotten past my guard."

"It's hardly making us look good," I said, "But maybe we can still get her stuff back. Can you tell me what they looked like?"

"Well there were only two," Stacey said, "I didn't see their faces, but they seemed very specific in what they took. They took a bag of my largest uncut crystals and a small blue chest containing something I was suppose to deliver to a customer in Kaydra."

"What what's in it?" I asked.

"They are a pair of white silk gloves Mrs. Tassel and I crafted. They're trimmed with golden beads and have an ice crystal fitted onto the hands. If you can't get the bag of crystals back, you must get those gloves back!"

"Ice crystals…" Selena quietly said to herself.

"Alright then," I said, "On my honor, we'll get your merchandise back. In the meantime, I want you to get everyone ready to leave as soon as we get back."

"Alright," she took Robert's hand, "I'll go find Byson and Jack right now!"

"Woah! Hang on a second!" he almost stumbled with Stacey.

"Vincent, I want you and Lan to remain here with the caravan as well," I said.

"Hold up! Why?!" Vincent protested.

"Because if other bandits show up, some of us need to be here to protect the merchants," I said, "I want you to come with me Aiyana."

"Okay," she agreed.

"I need your help too Selena," I said.

"What do you need me to do?" she asked.

"You just might be the deciding factor whether or not this works," I said, "If I can get a hold of those gloves, you may be able to use them and give us the edge we need."

"Okay," Selena agreed.

"Listen," I directed Vincent, "The gloves might get back before I do. If that's the case, give me 10 minutes. If I'm not back by then, tell Byson to head out for Kaydra. I'll catch up."

"Alright man," Vincent ran back to the Caravan, "You all better get back in one piece!"

"Okay," I turned to Selena and Aiyana, "Let's move!"

"Right boss!" they said in unison.

Keith had already tracked the two bandits to a gang of about 12 others when we finally caught up to him. We all lied on our stomachs on a high rise from their little base camp.

"Where's everyone else?" Keith whispered.

"Guarding the caravan," I quietly replied, "Is he ready Aiyana?"

"Yes," she replied, "He's ready as soon as you need him."

"You got a plan already?" Keith asked.

"Yeah," I said, "I hope it works."

"Hey look," Selena whispered, "Someone's approaching them."

From the shadows, the same woman Selena and Vincent encountered the other night approached the bandit leader with what looked like a bag of shards.

"It's that woman from the other night," Selena whispered.

"The same one you said gave Vincent those Heat Knuckles?" I asked.

“Yeah,” she responded, “What’s she doing here?”

“Can you hear what they’re saying, Keith?” I asked.

“Yeah,” he began to listen, “Hang on.”

“It’s an ok haul,” she said to the leader, “I was hoping to present the bosses with more. This is hardly enough to finish the project.”

“Hey if you keep paying us like you are, then there’s no end to the amount of crystals we can get you,” the leader said.

“My boss is bound to promote me soon,” she said, “Especially now that Francis is out of the way. Hey what’s the blue chest for?”

“Oh that’s nothing,” the leader said, “That’s our own little souvenir from the heist.”

“You’re not holding out on me are you?” she grabbed one of her blades attached to her waist.

“N-no! Never!” the leader threw his hands up in defense, “I may be a thief, but I’m an honest thief. You pay us to steal something for ya, we get it!”

“Hmph,” she glanced in our direction for a split second without us realizing, “I guess I’ll take you at your word for it. I’ve got to get back. Nice doing business with you,” she ran off.

“Heh. I don’t give a damn what that organization does with those crystals, any day is a good day when these amounts of shards are involved,” the leader said.

“She’s getting away with the crystals,” Keith said, “Should we go after her?”

“Well,” I thought for a moment, “If nothing else, we need to get those gloves back. As for the OSC agent, we can use her to our advantage.”

"What are you talking about?" Selena asked.

"If she's heading back to OSC, then she'll lead us right to them," I explained, "Do you think it's too late to catch her, Keith?"

"Do you forget who you're talking to?" Keith boasted, "I'm the best ninja Jentake has to offer. I'll catch up to her and find OSC's base of operations in no time."

"Alright," I said, "Go for it, and be careful."

"No problem," Keith grinned and sped off in an alternate path to avoid bandit detection.

"Time for us to prove our worth," I slowly got back up on my feet.

"Be careful," Selena and Aiyana whispered in unison.

I snuck down the backside of the cliff and into the woods to get a better starting point for my attack. The bandits were so busy celebrating, I don't think they would've heard me if I was making noise.

"We're gonna be set for life if this keeps up!" the leader chugged down a beverage.

"How much did we get this time boss? Double? Triple?" one bandit asked.

"Even more!" the leader replied, "We did good today boys, and our second prize is gonna make us a pretty shard too! We're eatin' good tonight!"

"Try this out for an appetizer then," I reached into my jacket.

I pulled from my jacket one of the small spheres constructed by Jack. It was a small bomb filled with red crystal dust that would unleash a small explosion of fire when set off. Using a piece of flint attached to the bomb, I lit the wick and rolled it towards the bandit group as hard as I could.

"Huh?" the bomb tapped his foot and suddenly began shining with a bright red light, "What the fu-!!" BOOM went the bomb and bandits were scattered from the force of the blast!

"Now!" I made a B-line for the chest while they were disoriented.

"Ow!" one bandit sat up, "What the hell was-H-HEY! Stop that guy! He's got the chest!!"

"Who the hell are you?!" the leader raised his axe.

"Just a sell sword earning his keep in this rough world!" I drew my sword, "I've got a job to do, now get out of my way or you might get hurt!"

"You against all of us?! That's a laugh! Ah ha ha ha ha!! Get him boys!" the leader ordered.

As soon as they made their charge at me, I pulled out another bomb and threw it right at my feet. This one was a dense smoke bomb that instantly filled the immediate area with smoke and disoriented the bandits rather effectively. It reached all the way to the bottom of the high rise we were spying from. I picked up the blue chest and held it up to be picked up by a pair of large talons flying by.

"Where is he?!" the boss yelled, "I can't see!"

"Hey man! Back off it's me!" one bandit bumped into another.

"Wow," Selena said, "I can't believe this is working."

"Selena," Aiyana pointed to the sky, "Here it comes!"

The large hawk Aiyana used to get around in the forest flew overhead and released the chest from his talons where it landed safely in Aiyana's hands. Selena opened the chest, and was startled at how well the gloves were made.

“Wow,” she lifted them out, “They’re beautiful!”

“Hurry and put them on!” Aiyana said, “The smoke is clearing!”

“Alright!” she put them on and began concentrating.

“Where’d that bastard go?!” the leader readied his axe as he looked around for me.

“There boss!” all of them were grouped together.

“What the hell did you do with our loot?!” the leader pointed his axe at me.

“Here goes,” Selena clenched her fists.

“All of you just chill out,” I pointed to Selena.

Selena’s power began to surge through her to the point her hair began swaying back and forth as if the wind were blowing. With her hands radiating strongly with an icy aura, she reared back and let loose an intensely cold blast of ice energy towards the bandit group in a similar fashion Vincent attacked Francis the other night. Feeling the temperature drop behind them, they turned around to see what was happening, but they were too late. I had just enough time to shield myself with the Twilight Star’s energy as I ducked for cover. Even from behind the barrier, it felt as if a blizzard had suddenly blown in! When things got quiet, I got up to find that the entire area was covered in ice! All of the bandits were on the ground and shivering with ice flakes covering their cold blue bodies.

“Um…damn?!” I looked around the icy area.

“Wow…” Selena looked to her hands, “I did that!?”

“You’re just full of surprises,” I smiled to Selena, “Nice work!”

“T-thanks,” she almost sounded nervous, “I didn’t expect to do…THAT!”

"Boss look out!!" Aiyana screamed.

I ducked just in time to avoid a horizontal swing from a large axe and counter attack with a rising slash from my claymore. I looked around to see that seven more bandits had shown up to help their frozen comrades.

"We're coming boss!" Selena screamed.

"No!" I raised my hand, "Get those gloves back! I'll cover your retreat! Ride out as soon as you get back!"

"We can't leave you here!" she screamed.

"C'mon!" Aiyana grabbed Selena's arm, "He'll be ok!" she threw a smoke bomb down near her feet.

"You w-w-wretches get b-b-back here w-w-with our l-l-loot!" one of the frozen bandits said.

"You won't catch them. You'll be too busy with me!" I reached in my jacket and threw another bomb.

Selena and Aiyana ran down the path as fast as their legs would carry them. They were beginning to feel like they were in the clear until Aiyana's ears began to twitch. Hearing a projectile approaching from behind her, she quickly pushed Selena to the side.

"Get down!" Aiyana barely had time to dodge the arrow herself.

"Give it up!" a lone bandit with a crossbow said, "You ain't getting away!"

"Stay out…" Selena spun around with her pointer finger shining an icy aura, "…of our way!"

Upon pointing, Selena shot loose an intensely focused beam of ice that went into the bandit's torso and froze into a large ice arrow upon contact! He was send rolling back several yards and screaming in agony.

"Wow," Aiyana looked back, "Nice shot."

"Thanks," Selena grabbed Aiyana's arm, "Let's hurry!"

Back in town, the caravan was lined up and ready to ride as soon as they got the signal.

"They're taking too long," Vincent said, "I should've gone with them."

"Hey! I see someone!" Nina jumped onto Vincent's shoulders.

"It's Aiyana and Selena!" Lan held his hand over his eyes to block the light of the setting sun.

"Where's Raymond and Keith?!" Robert noticed their absence.

"We have to go now!" Aiyana handed off the blue chest to Stacey.

"Wait! What about Keith and the boss?" Vincent said.

"They're gonna catch up with us!" Selena said.

"How the hell are they going to do that?!" Vincent asked.

"I don't know," Selena said, "We just have to trust them!"

"Damn," Vincent thought for a moment, "Alright, let's get out of here!" he and Selena boarded Jack's wagon.

I was left with nothing to do but throw bombs and run to stay alive as the rest of the unfrozen bandits ran me down. Before I knew it, I suddenly found myself cornered on another cliff. This one was too high to jump, and I only had one bomb left.

"End of the road, sell sword!" one of the bandits said.

“Got any last words before we gut ya and feed ya to the wolves and crows?!” another licked his own knife.

After looking around, looking over the cliff, and above, I looked back to the bandits and sheathed my sword. I leaped as hard as I could away from the group of bandits as I threw my last bomb at them. The explosion threw them to the ground and blew me off the edge. I twisted my body around with my arms stretched outward as I dove for the ground. Seconds before impact, my arms were gripped by a pair of large talons that saved me from death and lifted me upward into the sky.

“That was close,” I said looking down at the disoriented bandits, “We cut it close, but we made it. Let’s head back. Everyone’s waiting on us my friend.”

The large hawk let out a shriek that echoed throughout the area as if he understood me. By the time the sun was setting, the caravan was already out of sight of the town.

“Where is he?” Aiyana looked around outside the window of Tom and Jerry’s wagon.

“C’mon,” Selena looked out the window of Jack’s wagon.

“What’s that in the sky?” Catherynne saw a figure in the sky.

“It’s a bird!” Tom pointed.

“It IS a bird!!” Jerry confirmed.

“It’s the boss!” Aiyana screamed, “He made it!”

“He made it!” Selena and Vincent said in unison.

“Thanks for the ride,” I landed on top of Tom and Jerry’s wagon and rubbed the hawk’s neck out of gratitude before he lifted off into the sky.

"And look!" Lan pointed ahead from the last wagon, "There's Keith!"

"It looks like he got the crystals back as well," Sheryll said.

"Going my way?" Keith pretended to be trying to hitch a ride as Vincent pulled him up into Jack's wagon.

"Everyone made it back," Byson said to his wife, "These guys really are good at what they do."

"Hey boss," Aiyana climbed on top of the wagon, "You were really cool today."

"Aw thanks," I couldn't help but grin, "I think Selena was the coolest today."

"Thanks boss," her cheeks turned red with happiness.

"Thanks again for the setup Aiyana," I said.

"You're welcome boss," Aiyana took a bite of an apple.

Episode 24
Valuable Information

The sun hadn't completely disappeared on the western horizon as one of the moons became visible in the eastern sky. I continued to rest on top of Tom and Jerry's wagon to look out for any bandits that might be tailing us. Aiyana and Keith kept me company for much of the ride.

"So you ended up using all of the bombs you bought?" Keith asked.

"Yeah," I said, "More bandits showed up after I sent Aiyana and Selena back to the caravan."

"If that OSC agent wasn't so fast, I might have been able to make it back to help you out," Keith said.

"It all worked out in the end," I said, "So what did you find out?"

"Well, long story short," Keith crossed his arms, "I think she's a double agent."

I listened closely as Keith began to explain his encounter from earlier today. The idea that a double agent had made her way into OSC was interesting.

"…why did you stop?" Keith cautiously stepped from behind a tree.

"Because I wanted you to catch me," she disguised her voice.

"If you don't want to die here, then you're going to tell me what I need to know about OSC," Keith said.

"That hot headed loudmouth didn't do too badly against Francis," she suddenly changed the subject.

"What the-" Keith was caught off guard, "Hold on a second. You were there that night?"

“If it weren’t for me, you would’ve faced more numbers than you did. That hothead and that blue haired girl would have been killed if I hadn’t intervened.”

“What’s going on? Just who are you?! Are you with OSC or not?!” Keith was growing impatient.

“I hope you realize it only gets worse from here. That Iron Soldier you faced at Gravadale? That’s only a taste of what OSC is planning to unleash on Central Kingdom.”

“They’re making more of those things?!” Keith was shocked.

“They’re nothing like what Alex faced in Gravadale. They’re much bigger, and there’s one in particular they’re working on that scares me. Even if you somehow beat the others, that one might be unstoppable,” she looked to the sky, “None of you will even see them if you can’t get past the other two commanding officers. They will most likely use a strange technology like Francis had.”

“How are they even making these things?”

“They’re using the work of an innocent man to create weapons like no one has ever seen. Things like the Iron Soldier you fought at Gravadale and the Flamethrower used in the forest,” she suddenly dropped the bag of crystals she was carrying.

“What are you doing?” Keith asked her.

“This was just bait to lure you out here,” she said, “I was hoping you all would follow me, but when I saw that they had stolen something else, it nearly messed things up for me. Besides, OSC nearly has everything they need.”

“How can those-” Keith got cut off.

“Zylphan,” she called out the capital city of the Zylphan Province, “You and Alex have to get there before it’s too late. You don’t have much time left. OSC has already dealt Zylphan’s royal house a serious blow.”

“Dealt a serious blow how?!” Keith asked.

“I have to go,” she said, “We’ll meet again.”

“And then she ran off too fast for me to stop her,” Keith broke from his flashback.

“A serious blow to Zylphan’s royal house…” dread could be felt from my voice.

“What does that mean?” Aiyana asked me.

“It’s…” I hesitated to tell her what came across my mind, “Listen; I’m afraid this is quickly turning into a worse case scenario. The kingdom of Zylphan is not so easily targeted by its enemies. If OSC has managed to do some damage to them, then we have to head for Valsoria ASAP.”

“What about what she said for us to get to Zylphan before it’s too late?” Keith asked.

“By the sounds of it, it seems that their primary strength is somewhere near Zylphan,” I said, “So we’re going to need some extra help. If I can talk to General Isaac or one of the other Vanguards, we can put together a small army to fight against OSC and whatever weapons they have.”

“Do you think we can make it all the way there safely?” Aiyana asked.

“I don’t know to be honest,” I said, “If the caravan isn’t headed that way, we’ll have to part ways for their own safety.”

“Aw. I’ll miss them if we have to leave,” Aiyana said.

“I think you’ll miss those apples more,” Keith said.

“They’re GOOD!” Aiyana protested.

“Hmph,” I managed to crack a smile, “Looks like we’re pulling over for the night.”

“Alright,” Keith hopped down from the cart roof, “I’ll take the first watch.”

“I’ll watch with you,” I hopped down, “I’ve got a lot to think about. Aiyana, you get some sleep. I’ll have Lan and Rocky take the next watch.”

“Okay,” she reached into her leather bag and threw us each an apple, “Catch you two!”

“Thanks Aiyana,” I said before taking a bite, “These ARE good!”

Deep within the Zylphan Province, the OSC agent had made her way to a secret underground base. Bringing with her needed supplies for the completion of the Iron Soldiers, she made her way down to the armory where Zaalek was working on pieces of a new armor suit.

“So what do they have you slaving on now?” she asked.

“A new type of armor,” Zaalek replied.

“Why? What's wrong with their traditional armor?” She asked.

“Nothing really, but they wanted me to design an armor that would be impervious to the elements,” he said.

“Is that even possible?” she asked.

“Anything’s possible. I just need to figure out how,” he laughed.

“If you say so,” she raised an eyebrow, “How’s it coming?”

“Eh, it’s so so,” he began looking at some papers, “I’m having trouble calibrating the crystal matrix interface with the armor.”

“Which one of the elites ordered you to make that?” she asked.

“To be honest, I can't remember which one, but I think it was the..... um that first elite-whatever his name is.” He began unscrewing some parts to replace.

“Uh oh...” Lyn thought to herself with a worried look, “That sounds like Lancer. He's suppose to be OSC's top swordsman.”

Zaalek stared at her with a raised eyebrow for a moment, “But yea, I guess that’s the guy I’m making this armor for. Unfortunately, with the deadline, I'll only be able to get the armor to be impervious to just one element. Anything more I need time to research.”

“What’s the deadline?” she asked.

“Ummmmm,” he looked up as if to help his memory, “I was given the task about Monday last week, so I think about 3 days from now.”

“That's not much time,” she said, “You said you would only get it strong enough to absorb one element right?”

“Right,” he said, “I would need a lot more time to figure out how to make it resist all elements.”

“That reminds me,” she looked around to make sure no one was listening in, “Why did the Gale Force Amplifier short out so quickly?”

“It might have gotten overloaded when that other elite went up against someone from Alex's group.”

“Huh. I guess some technology can't beat natural raw power.” Lyn smiled with confidence.

“Hehe, yea I suppose,” he nervously scratched his head.

“It'll be a lot different for Lancer though. He’s actually very skilled.” she crossed her arms, “Honestly that guy scares me.”

“Nearly everyone here scares me,” Zaalek laughed.

“That's understandable considering who you're working for,” she said.

“I just wish they weren’t as strict. It’s kinda hard to focus with the elites breathing down my neck,” he stopped to stretch for a moment, “Yep, these guys are stifling my genius.”

“Just how did they find you anyway?” she turned curious.

“Well, I figured they found me because of a paper I tried to publish a year ago.”

“What's all that about? What did you come up with?” she asked.

“You know the Crystal Matrix Interface I’m always working with?”

“Yea?” she sat on the table.

“It was the research paper on that device. I had tried to publish in Volternia, but I had no idea they would react the way they did,” Zaalek face palmed himself.

“What did they do?” she tilted her head out of curiosity.

“They confiscated my paper and stored it into their archives to never see the light of day,” he said, “They said that the world wasn’t ready for such things, but in reality, they didn’t want power to be given to the average person. With my ideas, people without an affinity could use an element.”

“Sounds like them. They enjoy being the continent's most powerful Kingdom-rivaled only by Zylphan. But that doesn't explain how you ended up here,” she looked around the room.

"About a month or so ago, not really sure anymore, I was doing research on growing crystals and someone busted into my house, hit me on the head, and I woke up here. One of the soldiers shoved the paper I wrote on the Crystal Matrix Interface and commanded me to build it. Somehow, someone in OSC must've gotten into Volternia's archives and found my paper," he explained.

"They must think a lot of your work if they believe it can help them conquer all of Central Kingdom," she said.

"You want to know the worst part of this whole thing is?" he looked up.

"Wha…what is it?" she asked.

"As bad as they are, the Volternian royals were right to censor my paper… Look at how much damage it's caused. I honestly can't sleep at night sometimes because of what I've created, but my desire for innovation keeps me working. I really have a love hate relationship with science," Zaalek tried to smile.

"Hmm," she thought to herself for a moment, "I really don't have much an opinion whether it should've been censored or not. Maybe some of these thing you come up with can be useful in a positive way," she began browsing through a mess of papers on the table, "I wonder what Alex would think about this technology..." she accidentally said under her breath.

"What was that last sentence?" Zaalek thought he heard something at the end.

"Oh nothing. I was just thinking outloud," she looked around to make sure no one else heard her.

“Yeah. I suppose you’re right though-about it being able to be used in a positive way. I’m just forced to see all the negatives ways,” Zaalek began to drift off in thought a little bit.

“You’ll get your chance to try one day,” she got off the table.

“But not today,” he laughed, “Stupid calibrations,” he continued with fiddling with the CMI.

“Before I go, what can you tell me about those Iron Soldiers? And that other one-the Iron Sentinel? How far are they in development?”

“Well... since the Iron Soldier prototype performed better than anticipated, the refined version of Iron Soldiers are stronger, larger, and perform much better. The Sentinel, on the other hand, is a bit of a problem. We’re having some energy to weight ratio problems, but when it’s done, it’ll make the other Iron Soldiers look like miniature poodles. As far as development goes, the refined Iron Soldier is coming along quickly. I wouldn’t be surprised if they were ready for mass production by the end of the month. The Sentinel on the other hand is taking the longest. Not sure when it'll be ready.”

“I think I feel a little better now...” she said.

“Are they getting on to you to about my deadlines?” he asked.

“Oh no. Nothing like that,” she turned her head, “Maybe I have a little more time then.”

“A little more time for what?” Zaalek was curious now.

“Does it surprise you at all that Alex beat your prototype?” she asked.

“To be honest, I’m not surprised at all,” he said, “Anyone who has studied the origins of the crystals a little bit can tell you that the Twilight Star is capable of enormous power. Stories even say civilizations of antiquity have crumbled from the misuse of its power. If anything, I might be more afraid of Alex than OSC."

"You wouldn't be if you got to know him," she said.

"You sound like you've met the guy before," he tilted his head.

"Listen I have to go. I think someone's coming. Try to stay alive to see all this through," she left out the door.

Zaalek watched her leave as he reclined in his chair and rested his feet up on the table. With a pencil in his mouth, he began drifting off into thought.

"So she is one of the good guys..... Maybe I can tell her about the flaw....."

It was an hour before noon when the caravan started packing up to finish the trip to Kaydra. Robert and I were just wrapping up a round of sparring.

"Ok, that's enough for now," I stood back up after resting, "Lets not burn up all our energy in case of an attack."

"Well…" Robert was flat on his back, "You definitely fight like a mercenary."

"To be fair," I helped him get on his feet, "I did warn you I might fight dirty."

"They don't teach us much about fighting dirty," Robert said, "Besides I'm better with a lance anyway."

"Hey boss," Vincent ran up to us, "They say they're ready to head out as soon as you're ready."

"Alright everyone," I sheathed my sword, "Lets move out."

Episode 25

Kaydra Confrentation: A Mysterious Woman Arrives

Kaydra is one of the largest cities in the land that isn't a capital city. Much of its streets and buildings are built with marble stone. While it lies within Central Kingdom territory, four major roads branch from it. The road that branches to the east leads to Valsoria, the road to the north leads to Zylphan, the road to the south leads back to Gravadale, and the road to the west leads to the distant territories of Jentake. It makes for a great market city, and its marble construction makes for a great place to live and for travelers to rest. Through the streets of Kaydra, a swordswoman from Zylphan with purple armor that covered her shoulders, hips, and breasts paced the streets with her rapier unsheathed. Her long dark purple hair flowed in the eastbound wind as she walked westward towards the center of town. Her mere presence sent an ominous chill down the spines of some of the citizens as her dark blue eyes shot daggers at everyone she observed.

"Everything seems normal on my end," another lightly armored female soldier from Zylphan with short crimson hair and red armor approached her.

"Same here," she looked around, "But stay on guard. I don't know what it is, but I sense something powerful coming. If it turns out to be a threat, then we'll have to deal with it before our guests arrive."

"You haven't seen them yet?" the crimson haired girl asked.

"I thought that they would be here by now," she said to her subordinate.

"Do you think they're ok?" she asked.

"I'm sure they're fine. They may already be here and we just haven't crossed paths yet. This is a large city," she said calmly, "Keep patrolling and await further orders."

"Yes Lady Eleanore," she replied.

Several hours later, we arrived in Kaydra. The merchants we protected the entire way were busy setting up their shops in the market plaza. Keith and I had left the group to have a look around the city and talk about a new course of action. Everyone else stayed with the convoy to help them out in their shops.

"So she does have some ice gemmed jewelry for sale?" Vincent asked Selena as they discussed things behind the caravan.

"Yeah, but they're too expensive-even at a discount," Selena had her hands on her hips, "I need something to help me better channel my powers like when I used those gloves we had to recover. You should have seen it. It was like a power tried to wake up inside me, but ever since giving those gloves back, I don't know how to bring it out again."

"What about that one attack I saw you working on this morning?" Vincent asked.

"I've sort of got it down," she said, "I first used it yesterday when I had those glove on, but without them, it takes too long for me to focus the energy. It almost takes as much time to get off a proper shot as it did Keith to use his Thunder Sniper attack. Sometimes I wish I had fire instead of ice. At least then I would've had someone to teach me like Dad taught you."

“Don’t forget about the boss’s grandmother,” Vincent said, “He said he would talk to her about training you.”

“I know,” Selena looked down, “But what if she doesn’t think I’m worthy? He said she’s turned down everyone that’s asked her for training so far, so what am I suppose to do to prove myself?”

“So you must be the customer I was expecting?” they both overheard Stacey talking to a customer.

They both peeked around to see Stacey talking to an elderly looking woman wearing a light brown cloak around her. Right away they sensed something about her that neither of them could quite put their finger on.

“Yes,” she responded to Stacey, “I hope I didn’t keep you waiting for too long.”

“It’s no problem ma’am,” Stacy replied, “If it weren’t for a group of mercenaries, we might not have gotten here ourselves. Here are two of them now,” Stacey pointed Vincent and Selena out.

“Hello ma’am,” Selena waved and smiled.

“Hey,” Vincent motioned a half wave.

“Grandma! Grandma!” a young child, also wearing a light brown cloak around her, ran from behind Selena and Vincent to the old lady.

“And just where did you run off too young lady?” she said with a stern tone in her voice.

“I was just looking at all the stuff here,” she said, “And guess what!”

“What’s that?” she asked her granddaughter.

The young girl got on her tiptoes to whisper into her grandmother's ear. Selena and Vincent were unable to hear what was said, but they noticed the elderly woman's facial expression suddenly change. She feinted a glance at Selena, but quickly averted her eyes back to her granddaughter.

"Are you sure?" she whispered back to her granddaughter.

"Yes grandma," she nodded, "Absolutely."

"I see," the old lady said before turning back to Stacey, "Sorry about that, and thank you for the fine work you've done making these."

"Of course ma'am," Stacey handed over the box and received her payment.

"Wow," Selena whispered to Vincent, "She must be loaded to afford those at full price."

"Yea no kidding," Vincent said.

"Well I guess we're done here," the old lady said to her granddaughter.

"Can't we look around a little more grandma?" the young girl asked.

"Perhaps if we had more time," her grandmother answered, "But you know that we have a very important appointment to meet. Come on now."

"Okay," the girl responded.

"Excuse me," the old lady addressed Selena and Vincent, "Would you two mind escorting an old lady and her granddaughter back to her home? It's just on the other side of town."

"Um," Selena looked to Vincent for a moment and back to the old lady, "Sure ma'am. We don't mind."

“Alright” Vincent stretched, “I’m getting bored just standing around here anyway.”

“I hope you don’t mind me borrowing your hired guards,” the old lady said to Stacey.

“It’s alright,” Stacey said, “I’ve got my knight in shining armor to protect-” she looked around to see that Robert was nowhere in sight, “Robert? Oh Robert, where are you?”

Stacey hadn’t noticed that they had left already. They made their way up a street on the east side of the city while making idle chat. The young granddaughter was hopping around as if she had limitless energy, and for a second, Selena could swear she saw the young girl falling more slowly at times.

“You know I have to be honest,” the old lady spoke, “You two don’t look like the mercenary type.”

“Why not?” Vincent got worried that she may be onto them.

“Well, for the most part, mercenaries aren’t that much different than bandits. They’re mean, rough, rude, wild, and all they care about is getting paid and having a good time. You two are too polite to fit the description of a common mercenary. Does your boss fit the description better than you two do?”

“He ain’t like that,” Vincent defended me, “Raymond actually cares about people.”

“He’s really powerful, but very kind too,” Selena said.

“He’s an honorable guy,” Vincent added.

“R-Raymond?” the old lady suddenly stopped, “That’s what you said, right?”

“W-what?” Vincent stuttered, “What are you talking about?”

“Ya know my late husband was a mercenary when we were both young,” the old lady said, “He once told me that he would sometimes have to adopt an alias to protect his real identity.”

“You married a mercenary?” Selena asked, “What happened to all that stuff about them being rude and selfish?”

“He was different,” the old lady said, “I didn’t think so at first, but he turned out to be an honorable man. He was very powerful, but kind also. He actually cared about people. Those same qualities that described him and your boss also describe my grandson, and if that’s not enough, my late husband’s first name was Raymond, and it got passed on as my grandson’s middle name.”

“Your grandson?” Vincent and Selena both asked, “Who are you?”

“I’m someone you both can trust,” the old lady suddenly turned around, “I am Valsoria’s first queen; Caliandra Valsora.”

The younger subordinate soldier was making one more round down city alleys and streets when the acronym “OSC” suddenly caught her ear. After first looking around as if to determine the source, she flew to the top of a house and crouched down on her stomach to spy on Keith and I having a conversation about the past events.

“Even though the Iron Soldier was defeated, Gravadale still took a significant hit,” I said, “It’s not likely they’ll be able to do anything too far from the capital for a while until things settle down there.”

“Yea,” Keith agreed, “We still shook things up for those guys huh?”

"We sure did," I said, "I actually heard someone talking to someone else about what I did there. I thought that would've died down by now."

"Well it's not everyday that someone can rip through armor like that," Keith laughed, "Well I'm gonna go look around in the market plaza again. We need to get ready if we're heading for Valsoria next."

"Alright," I said, "I'll meet you all later on. Come search for me if there's a problem."

"I can't believe it," she said to herself as she watched Keith run out of the alley and down the street, "OSC soldiers here?! This must be what Lady Eleanore sensed earlier!"

As I turned to walk the other direction, she descended in front of me with her sword unsheathed and her gaze fixed on me. Right away I recognized something familiar about the design of her crimson and gold trimmed armor, but I just couldn't quite place it. The only thing I really sensed at that moment was that I was in trouble.

"Who are you?" I immediately grabbed the handle of my claymore out of defense.

"Those who know of the Zylphan Valkyries," she gave a dark smile as she ran her fingers through her crimson hair, "Know that we never fail to serve justice!"

"A Zylphan Valkyrie?!" My eyes widened with shock.

"I am known as Karen of the Crimson Tempest," she raised her blade to her face as a small whirlwind that circled it suddenly was engulfed in spirals of fire, "Now surrender peacefully OSC scum, and I shall make your end swift!"

"Wait!" I put my hand out, "You've got it all wrong! I'm not with OSC! I'm actually-!"

"Denial will do you no good," she pointed her sword directly at me to attack, "I heard you and your friend talking about what you did in Gravadale. As soon as I'm done with you, I'm hunting him down as well! Blazing Spiral!!"

"AAHHHHH!!!"

From across the city, Eleanore was making her last rounds when she noticed a large pillar of smoke suddenly rise from the distance. After thinking for a moment, she became suspicious of the source.

"Oh no," she face palmed herself, "I really hope that's not who I think it is. What are you getting yourself into now?"

As she took flight, Keith noticed the same smoke cloud from another part of the city and knew that I may be involved with the cause.

"Oh hell," he bolted in its general direction, "That looks too close to where me and Alex were just at! Hang on buddy! I'm on my way!"

I was able to avoid a direct hit and escape the attack pretty much unscathed. I pushed myself through the smoke and escape from the alley. With no other choice, I unsheathed my claymore and ran for the closest opening in the city that I could find. She immediately sprang upward from the smoke and took flight after me. The sudden conflict quickly caught the attention of every citizen within sight of us. This was WAY more attention that I wanted to attract at this point. As I ran past a fountain, I looked back just in time to catch her diving straight at me, and was barely able to avoid the swing of her blade by a quick spin. Although I didn't get cut, my jacket took a large slash to the back. By simple quick reaction, I took hold of her ankles, and by using my momentum and hers,

I was able to spin her off course and send her straight into the crowd that was forming around us.

"Look out!" she screamed to the crowd before slowing herself to a halt in midair, "That scum!" she stared daggers at me, "You won't make a fool out of me!" she raised her sword.

"Can we please talk?!" I tried to stop the fight before it got out of control, "I'm not who you think I am!"

"Dance of the Burning Tornado!" a swing of her sword sent a small cyclone of fire straight at me.

"Good grief!" I set forth a barrier using the Twilight Start that was still hidden under my shirt to protect myself.

"He was able to stop it?" she observed me emerge from the fire unscathed, "Then stop THIS! Crimson-!" she was suddenly caught off guard by a lightning bolt that knocked her off her feet.

"Stopped," Keith was in a fighting pose with his katana before leaping into the air for an aerial strike.

"Wait Keith! She's-" a sudden blur of darkness that suddenly rushed from behind me and into the air caused me to freeze in mid-sentence.

"Strike of the Ass-"

Time seemed to slow down as I saw a Valkyrie in dark armor make contact with Keith in midair. It only took two strokes. One stroke disarmed him, while the other made its diagonal path across his chest. First his katana fell to the street and stuck upright, next his limp body fell into the fountain, and finally the Valkyrie descended to the ground near her subordinate.

"It's not like you to have this much trouble from some common street trash," she helped up her fellow Valkyrie.

"It's them Lady Eleanore!" Karen pointed at me, "They're with OSC! I saw them talking to each other in an alley about their attack on Gravadale!"

"Is that so?" her dark gaze was suddenly fixed on me, "Let me handle this."

"Oh okay," Karen obliged.

I'm not sure what it was about her, but something about her terrified me. Whether it was from how quickly she came or how quickly she put Keith down, I suddenly found myself barely able to move and barely able to breathe. I was struggling to slowly pull my left hand up to my neck. My face became saturated in more sweat with each step she took towards me.

"Those who know that they can never escape their own shadow," the crowd grew quiet as she approached me, "Also know that they can never escape death. I am Eleanore of the Ebon Wind. If you have anything left to say, I would hear it now. Choose your words carefully," the tip of her blade was shining with an ominous power.

"Okay…" I finally took a deep breath, "How's this for careful words," I pulled the Twilight Star from my undershirt, "Eleanore of the Ebon Wind and Karen of the Crimson Tempest… sheathe your blades in the name of Valsoria!"

Episode 26
New Allies and a New Goal

The crowd that had gathered was as silent and motionless as Eleanore and I were. She seemed unflinching to who I revealed myself to be. Either way, I still couldn't muster the strength to move. After a few moments, she slowly withdrew her blade and slowly turned her head to Karen. When her attention was off me, I felt as if some force released its grip on me, and I was able to stand again.

"Come here," I felt a cold vibe from her voice.

"Yes Lady Eleanore?" Karen approached her superior.

"Are you," Eleanore turned to face Karen completely, "Trying to give the Zylphan Valkyries a bad name?!"

"Lady Eleanore I-" Karen tried to speak.

"That's Valsoria's Prince, Alexander!" Eleanore scolded her, "How the HELL do you mistake HIM for an OSC agent?!"

"Lady Eleanore!" Karen tried to explain herself, "You don't understand!"

As Eleanore continued to scold her subordinate, I let out a sigh of relief that I wasn't in danger anymore, but then I remembered that Keith had fallen into the fountain after being attacked.

"Keith!" I ran to the fountain as fast as I could.

"You better pray to the spirit of Roc that I didn't just kill an innocent person," Eleanore said to Karen as she watched the fountain.

As soon as I got to the fountain, a hand stuck out of the water and Keith pulled his head above water. I grabbed him from under his arms and pulled him from the water as carefully as I could so that I wouldn't tear his wound. I checked to see how serious the hit was as he was still coughing up water. I could see blood coming from his chest. The blade had cut clean through his jacket, his undershirt, and part of his...

"C-chain mail?" I noticed that he had been wearing a fitted chain mail shirt under his clothes.

"Never..." he coughed, "Leave home without it..."

"How deep is the cut?" I asked.

"Thanks to the chain mail, not too deep," he said, "But it hurts to move..."

"Prince Alexander," I heard Eleanore's voice behind me.

I quickly spun around with my claymore gripped. I had it halfway out of its sheath when I noticed that both she and Karen were kneeling in front of me.

"We made a terrible mistake attacking you and your friend. Karen sorely misjudged who you were, and as her superior, please accept my humblest apology on both of our behalf," Eleanore apologized.

"Her 'mistake' nearly got us killed," I narrowly eyed Karen.

"I'm so sorry," Karen started crying, "I overheard part of your conversation in the alley and mistook you for OSC agents."

Seeing what looked like a heartfelt apology, I sighed and sheathed my claymore. As I did, I felt a familiar aura from behind me. I looked back to find Keith surrounded by a blue-ish white aura that healed the gash across his chest so well, that there wasn't even a scar left.

"What in Twilight's name?" I was baffled at what just happened.

"Wow," Keith suddenly sprang to his feet, "That light healed me completely!"

"Alex!" Selena ran up to us.

"Selena! Did you do that??" I asked.

"That wasn't me," she said, "It was-"

"ALEX!!!" the small girl that was with her grandmother leaped right out of her cloak and into my arms.

"Alyssa?!" my 9 year old little sister was the last person I expected to see in Kaydra, "Alyssa! Be careful!" I almost fell from the sudden tackle.

"It looks like our guest made it after all," Eleanore rose to her feet.

"Aww," Karen admired Alyssa, "She looks so happy to see her brother!"

"What are you doing here??" I asked her.

"I'm here with Grandma," she hopped to the ground.

"Grandma?!" I turned to the elderly woman covered in a brown cloak.

"Glad to see that you're safe and sound," she pulled her cloak back.

"Grandma!" I gave her a hug.

"Your mother has been very worried about you, but I knew that you would be alright," she said, "You have the protection of the Twilight Star and your grandfather's instincts."

"So then it was you who healed me, Queen Caliandra?" Keith asked.

"Yes," she said, "But I'm no longer the queen. I fully passed down rule to my daughter a little over a year ago."

"Then if I may call you Lady Caliandra," Eleanore kneeled in front of my grandmother with Karen kneeling with her, "My name is Eleanore, and this is my subordinate, Karen. We are here on direct orders of Queen Athena to provide you and

Princess Alyssa further escort to Zylphan. We will depart as soon as you and the princess are ready."

"Very well," grandma nodded, "I'd like the both of you to come with me so we can properly join company with our escort from home."

"As you wish," Eleanore rose to her feet.

"You come with us as well," she told me, "There's something I feel that you need to know."

"Alright," I said, "Should I go get everyone else and-"

"It will have to wait," she cut me off, "Just you and everyone that is here should be fine."

"Oh, alright," I heard the concern in her voice.

"Dude what happened to you?" Vincent asked Keith.

"I don't want to talk about it," he responded.

My grandmother and Alyssa had traveled to Kaydra as secretly as they could. She told me that she brought two of Valsoria's knights with her, and that they were staying in the inn.

"I'm getting worried," a beautiful knight with long pink hair said, "The market isn't THAT crowded at this time."

"I'm sure they're fine," a knight with a lance reassured her, "Princess Alyssa probably wanted to check out the whole market."

"I wish Lady Caliandra would have let me gone with her," she said.

“Yea, but we’re trying to keep a low profile,” he said, “We can’t have too many people knowing what we’re doing. Even at her age, the queen is more than powerful enough to handle any trouble.”

“Wait,” she put her hand up to stop the conversation, “Someone’s coming.”

“Lady Lydia? Sir Damien?” my grandmother spoke through the door.

“We’re in here, Lady Caliandra,” Lydia whispered.

“Lydia!” Alyssa ran in as soon as the door was open.

“Not so loud princess,” Lydia gave Alyssa a hug, “Are you alright?”

“Uh huh,” she nodded, “And look who we found!” she said as soon as I walked in with Selena, Vincent, and Keith.

“By the Twilight Star…” Lady Lydia was almost too shocked for words when I walked in.

“Prince Alexander??” Sir Damien nearly dropped his lance as he and Lady Lydia knelt to the floor

“Your highness, we didn’t expect to see you here,” Lady Lydia spoke.

“I didn’t expect to see ANY of you all here,” I said, “Let alone two of Valsoria’s Vanguards.”

“Vanguards?” Selena asked, “Didn’t you mention them before?”

“Must be a special rank,” Vincent said.

“Not just that,” Keith said, “The Vanguards of Valsoria are considered the best of Valsoria’s military. There are a total of seven of them, and they each have their own nickname.”

"Keith, Vincent, Selena," I got their attention, "Allow me to introduce you to two of our finest; Lady Lydia, The Lilac Knight, and Sir Damien, The Mad Lance."

"Nice to meet you all," Lady Lydia rose to her feet.

"I'm glad to see that you made some new friends along the way," Sir Damien said.

"This actually isn't everyone," I said, "I'll let you meet the others later. You said you had something important to tell me grandma?"

"Yes," she said, "Lady Eleanore, if you could close the door."

"Yes milady," Eleanore peeked out to make sure no one was listening in before shutting the door.

"Alex I'll start with the good news," grandmother got everyone's attention, "Both you and Alyssa were dubbed at birth as not having a nature element of your own. While you still haven't shown any signs of a nature affinity, it appears Alyssa has been showing signs that she indeed does have a nature element. After we did a little testing, it appears that Alyssa has the wind affinity."

"The wind affinity??" I was shocked, "Are you sure??"

"Uh huh. Watch this!" Alyssa jumped and held herself up about a foot above the floor for a few seconds before falling, "Ow…"

"Well…wow! Why didn't they notice it when she was first born?" I asked.

"We're not really sure," grandma said, "But the doctors are calling her a late bloomer. According to them, it's very uncommon for someone to go from showing no signs of an affinity, to suddenly having one."

"Well, do you think that I might be the same way?" I asked.

“At this point I doubt it,” she said, “I’m almost certain that if you were to have a late showing nature element, it would have shown by now.”

“Oh I see,” I crossed my arms.

“And that’s partly why we’re on our way to Zylphan,” Grandma said, “So that Alyssa can learn how to fly and develop her powers.”

“Well that’s great then,” I smiled.

“Yea! You’ll be flying like the Valkyrie’s in no time!” Karen told Alyssa.

“Cool!” she said.

“But now,” grandma paused for a moment, “The bad news.”

“Y-yes?” I was almost afraid to hear what it was.

“We were sent here to meet Lady Caliandra and Princess Alyssa to provide extra security for them,” Eleanore started, “Do you remember Count Marcus of Miliga?”

“Prince Zephyros’s uncle?” I asked, “Did he send you?”

“No,” she responded, “We take our orders from Queen Athena. Count Marcus…has been assassinated.”

“What???” I could have sworn I heard wrong.

“We have strong reason to believe that it was by the same terrorist group that you are fighting,” Eleanore said.

“OSC…” I said.

That’s when I remembered the information Keith had obtained from that OSC agent. “OSC has already dealt Zylphan’s royal house a serious blow.” I didn’t know it was this bad.

"We believe it happened during a failed attempt to steal the Roc Soul Crystal. He was guarding it at the time, but he managed to slip it away before they got to him," Eleanore continued, "The entire province is on high alert for any suspicious activity, so the queen sent Karen and myself to provide Lady Caliandra and Alyssa safe passage."

"If it's that dangerous, then why not just have Alyssa come at another time?" I asked.

"We thought about that," Lady Lydia said, "But we had just gotten to Kaydra when we heard the news. So instead of trying to make a return trip home, we decided to get to Miliga safely and figure out what to do. It would be faster to go there than to turn around for home."

"Hey Alex," Keith got my attention, "Do you remember the information I got from that agent?"

"That's right!" I said.

"What information?" Eleanore asked.

"Lady Eleanore," I started, "Keith and I have reason to believe that OSC's base of operation is located somewhere in Zylphan's borders."

"Really?!" she asked, "Are you certain??"

"It makes sense according to information I was able to obtain from one of their agents," Keith said, "If nothing else, it's the best lead we've got."

"Also ever since I left home, we've been fighting nothing but grunts," I said, "But as soon as we began to turn to the direction of Zylphan, we ran into their third ranked leader."

"What do you think Lady Eleanore?" Karen asked.

"We should definitely report this back to the king and queen," she said, "But we still have our assignment to give Lady Caliandra and Princess Alyssa safe passage. Prince Alexander, will you come with us?"

"Of course we will," I said, "Lets team up and bring OSC down before they can do anymore damage."

"Are you sure about this Alex?" grandma asked me.

"Yes grandma," I said, "They're tough, but they're not invincible. I believe we can do this."

"You'll have my help too," she said, "But you still have to be careful."

"I promise I will be," I assured her.

And with that, we formed a stronger team with the immediate goal of reaching Miliga. We spent the rest of the day preparing for the trip. After a full night rest, there was one last thing I had to do. I managed to find Byron in the market square early in the morning just in time to inform him that we had to depart.

"Are you sure I can't interest you to travel with us?" he asked, "I can pay more if that's what it takes."

"I appreciate the offer," I said, "But it's not about the money. This is a special job we just had to take on."

"Very well," he shook my hand, "If that's your decision. I hope we can do business again together sometime."

"I'm sure that we will," I said, "Thank you for the support you've given my group."

"No," he said, "Thank you."

“Tell everyone I said to be safe for me, ok?” I asked before running off, “Oh, and don’t be a stranger to Valsoria if you’re ever close by!”

By the time he looked back, I was already out of sight. Outside of the north gate of the city, I caught up with the group who were all set to go.

“Are you ready?” Eleanore asked me.

“Yes,” I answered, “Let’s move out.”

Episode 27
Waltz with a Valkyrie

"Queen Adelyne?" a beautiful priestess with long blonde hair and blue eyes ran through the halls of the Valsoria palace, "Where are you, your highness?"

"Out here, Lady Claire," a voice from the outside balcony spoke.

Out on the balcony stood Valsoria's queen. Her shoulder length blend of blond and black hair blew gently in the wind as she stared off to the northern part of the land. Her green eyes shined as she gazed in the direction of Zylphan.

"Is something wrong?" Queen Adelyne asked.

"No your highness," Claire shook her head, "I have a letter for you. It arrived just a few minutes ago by messenger bird."

"It must be from my mom," she turned around smiling, "I hope they rendezvoused with the escort Queen Athena sent without any trouble. She sent me a letter about a day after my mother and Alyssa left saying that she was sending two valkyries to meet them in Kaydra."

"It appears that they have," Claire nodded, "But the letter wasn't written by Lady Caliandra. It was written by Prince Alexander."

"My son?!" she almost couldn't believe her ears.

"Yes your highness," Claire handed Adelyne the letter, "It appears that they met up in Kaydra and are now traveling together to Miliga."

"Dear mother," Adelyne began reading the letter aloud, "It's me, Alex. I hope I haven't worried you too much since I've been gone. I just want you to know that I'm doing fine. I met up with Keith, Lan, and a few new friends along the way. A lot has happened since I left home such as Phoenix Volcano almost erupting, Rac' Sagadam being attacked by monsters, and Gravadale being attacked by OSC. When I get home, I'll tell you all about it in detail, because I don't have enough time to explain it all in a letter. By sheer luck, I met grandma and Alyssa in Kaydra, and we're now traveling together towards Miliga with the help of two of Zylphan's valkyries. I've been fighting OSC at every turn since I left home, but by the Twilight Star, I promise you that they will be brought down. I think I may have found a lead that may lead to their base of operations somewhere near Zylphan, so be on guard in case they launch an attack before we can get to them first. Until then, be careful mom, I love you. Alexander," she finished.

"My goodness," Claire said, "That sounds like quite the adventure."

"Indeed," Adelyne gave a sigh of relief, "At least I know he's alright. It makes me feel better that he's traveling with my mother too."

"Between Lady Caliandra and the Twilight Star, I don't see anything posing them a big threat," Claire said.

"Yeah," Queen Adelyne said, "Be careful son. All of you."

"By your leave your highness," Claire bowed before turning to leave.

"Hang on Claire," Queen Adelyne suddenly had a devious look on her face.

"Uh, yes?" Claire suddenly got nervous.

"Did Sir Damien send you a letter yet?" she teased Claire.

"Ah!" Claire was caught off guard by the sudden question and turned pink in the face, "Your highness!" she began stammering in mid sentence.

"Hah I'm just teasing you," Adelyne laughed, "Allow the queen a little fun."

"Its ok your highness," Clare smiled.

Our group was nearing the bridge that crosses a large river between Kaydra and Miliga. Throughout most of the trip, we had all gotten a chance to introduce ourselves and get to know each other. I spoke with Karen and Eleanore throughout most of the way as we walked ahead of the group. They told me that OSC activity has been fairly active up to the point of the last attempt to steal the Roc Soul Crystal, and I informed them about everything that we've been through ever since I left home.

"And the monster was made of metal?" Karen asked about the Iron Soldier, "How is that possible?"

"I don't know how they did it, but it turned out to be something that wasn't alive," I said, "Think of it as a large suit of armor, but without anyone inside."

"You mentioned that your friend obtained information from one of their agents that they are operating somewhere near Zylphan," Eleanore cut in, "Do we have any way of knowing how accurate that is?"

"Well no," I said, "But I trust Keith's ability to gather information. I don't believe he would have told me about it if it wasn't worth checking out. Either way, it's the only lead we have at this point."

"I understand your point," Eleanore said, "As soon as we get Lady Caliandra and Princess Alyssa secured in Miliga, we should discuss this with the Queen. I'm sure Prince Zephyros will want to hear about this too."

"How will we go about fighting OSC if your information turns out to be true?" Karen asked.

“As directly and quickly as we can,” I said, “Once we find their base, we should find the leaders and bring them to justice.”

“You make it sound easy,” Eleanore said, “Didn’t you mention that you were almost defeated by one of their officers? Their third rank officer at that?”

“That-,” I defended myself, “We were ambushed in the night when we got separated, and he was using something he called a Gale Force Amplifier. It made all of his wind based attacks against me much stronger than they probably would have been without it. If I were just able to get in close, then it would have been different.”

“If we face anyone like that, then you should probably leave them to Lady Eleanore and I,” Karen said, “It sounds like you have a hard time fighting against someone with the wind affinity.”

“It’s more of a range problem than an affinity problem,” I said, “But it would explain why I’ve never on a practice match against Zephyros.”

“Prince Zephyros is in his own league,” Eleanore said.

“Yea,” Karen agreed, “If you couldn’t defeat me, then you wouldn’t stand a chance against him anyway.”

“For the record, I wasn’t even trying to fight you back there,” I pointed out.

“No offense Prince Alexander,” Karen said, “But if you have a hard time against those with a wind affinity anyway, then I don’t see how you could beat me-even with the Twilight Star.”

“Next time we get the chance,” I said, “I’d like the chance to see how that would turn out.”

"Well then," Karen stopped, "How about right now? I've always wondered how I would fair against another royal other than Prince Zephyros."

"Karen," Eleanore turned around to her, "We don't have time for this."

"Please Lady Eleanore," Karen pleaded, "I promise it won't take long."

"Won't take long?" I raised an eyebrow, "Ok now we *have* to fight."

"You can't be serious," Eleanore face palmed herself.

"Its like she said," I quoted Karen, "It won't take long."

"Hey Alex," Vincent ran up, "Why'd you stop?"

"We're gonna take a short break to have a match," I took off the claymore strapped to my back, "Hang onto this."

"Heh, sounds like fun," Vincent took the sword, "Don't you go and lose."

"Just what are you going to fight me with?" Karen asked, "Your fists?"

"This," I took the Twilight Star from my neck and it took the form of a sword, "Now prepare yourself."

"Oh my," my grandmother said, "Be careful Alex!"

"The prince of Valsoria versus a Valkyrie of Zylphan," Sir Damien dismounted from his horse, "This shall truly be an epic match!"

"Here I come!" Karen leaped into the sky with her blade unsheathed.

Karen dove from the sky and clashed her blade against mine with surprising force. After pushing it away, she continued to slash at me in a very fluid motion as if it were a fast waltz. I was able to match her blow for blow surprisingly well. I noticed that my attack speed with the Twilight Star was a lot faster than I remember. It must've been due to fighting with a claymore so much.

"Wow she's fast!" Robert and Aiyana said.

"And Alex is actually keeping up with her?" Keith sounded impressed.

"He's gotten faster since he left home," Damien said.

"It's from all the fighting we've done," Vincent said, "He's good."

"He's gonna win!" Alyssa said, "Isn't he Lydia?"

"Its hard to say," Lydia said, "She is a Zylphan Valkyrie for a reason, so he can't underestimate her."

"Maybe," Selena said, "But Alex has always managed to surprise us in some way. I'm sure he'll do it again today."

"Go Alex go!" Alyssa shouted as we continued to clash blades.

"Gotcha!" I threw her off balance with a parry and went for a sweeping kick.

"Woah!" she jumped off the ground and stayed about three feet in the air to avoid the kick, "Sorry, but that won't work."

"Almost," I brought my sword back up in a defensive position.

Karen pointed her blade directly at me from the air, and then pulled it back into a thrusting position. I could see the small whirlwind of fire forming around the blade from the hilt to the tip, and it made me remember our confrontation from yesterday.

"Blazing…!" she tightened her grip.

"Here it comes," I prepared myself to either defend or dodge.

"Spiral!" she thrust the blade forward which shot a spinning trail of fire straight at me.

At the last second, I rolled to the side and just narrowly avoided getting burned. I leaped up to her before she could get another shot at me and swung my blade downward.

She quickly met my blade with her own which was still hot from her attack, parried herself from me, and roundhouse kicked me in the back. I landed on my feet, and spun around just in time to clash blades with her again.

"Not bad," I said, "That's something I would do!"

"And believe me," Robert said, "He's done it before against me."

"You're pretty good yourself!" Karen said.

"Ya know," Selena spoke to Vincent, "This is almost like watching you and Vikki fight, except with swords."

"Ya think so?" Vincent asked.

"Uh huh," she said, "Its always fun to watch, and this is the first time since we were home that I've really seen Alex go at it. It's amazing!"

"It's not like when he fought Mark," Keith said, "I can tell that Alex actually has to try now."

"It's almost like watching Raymond fight again," my grandma said to herself.

Karen flipped backwards on the ground and put some distance between us and held her sword straight up with her left arm behind her head. She spun once and a whirlwind began to form around her as her blade began to glow hot with fire.

"Dance of the Burning Tornado!" She spun again and a large twister of fire raced straight at me!

"Oh snap!!" Vincent yelled.

"What the hell?" Rocky yelled.

"Alex!" Selena, Alyssa, and my grandmother screamed.

"This is bad!" I held my sword up with the flat side facing forward.

I formed a barrier with the Twilight Star's power and was able to stop the attack in its tracks. However, the attack itself didn't disperse. I suddenly found it pushing me back as the flames seemed to get closer.

"He's learned to defend himself with the Twilight Star's power!" my grandma noticed.

"He can attack with its power too if he could get close enough," Vincent said, "It sucks he doesn't have ranged attacks!"

"Come on Alex!" Alyssa continued to cheer me on, "You can do it!"

"Damn!" I thought to myself as the flames got closer, "I have to find a way to turn this around!"

Episode 28
A New Skill and Learning Experience

Everyone watched in suspense as our powers were caught in a stalemate. I was able to stop myself from sliding, but it was taking all of my focus just to hold the burning whirlwind at bay. Clashing blades is one thing, but fighting against special attacks is what really gives me a hard time!

"At least," I kept my force up against Karen's attack, "This is good training for me! It helps me learn how to focus the Twilight Star's power a lot better!"

And that's exactly what I needed to do. Up until recently, I was doing fine because I was always able to fight at close range. Now I need to find a way to channel the Twilight Star's powers outward offensively instead of defensively with a barrier. That's when I got an idea. I shifted the angle of the barrier that I was using to hold back Karen's attack and the burning tornado rolled off to my left side and away from everyone else before finally dispersing.

"Hmm," I glanced back where the tornado stopped before glancing back at Karen.

"If you want," Karen had her left hand on her hip, "We can stop now. I don't want you to get hurt."

"Don't worry about me," I suddenly had to shield my eyes from the sun rays peering through the clouds, "Let's do it this way: we'll stop when one of us is disarmed."

"Fine by me!" she flew at me.

"When did Alex learn to make a barrier?" my grandmother asked.

"It was when he helped me save my grandmother," Aiyana said, "She's the sage of my villiage in the forest."

“I see,” she said, “I’m glad he’s learning different ways to use its powers.”

“How much can you do with the Twilight Star?” Selena asked.

“Actually I can’t use it,” grandma told her, “When I was young, I was part of a group called The Order of Twilight that watched over it. Our purpose was to keep it safe until the person that it would chose to wield it came forth. Since then, the only ones that have been able to use it were my husband, my daughter, and now my grandson. The Twilight Star is able to choose who wields its power.”

“How can a crystal choose a wielder?” Vincent asked.

“We believe it to have a spirit,” she said, “We think it communicates with its wielder on a subconscious level. It has happened several times before with my husband and daughter.”

“That reminds me of something Alex told me,” Selena said, “When we first met, he said that he had a dream that the Soul Crystals of the world were in danger, and that the Twilight Star was pulsating when he woke up.”

“Then it was definitely the spirit of the Twilight Star communicating with him,” my grandmother said, “It must’ve been warning him of OSC’s plot.”

“It makes sense,” Vincent said, “We fought them at our hometown when they tried to steal the Phoenix Soul Crystal.”

“We fought them when they launched an attack on Gravadale,” Robert said.

“And again in the forest when they held my people hostage to find the Golem Soul Crystal,” Aiyana said.

“My brother saved you all?” Alyssa asked.

“In a weird way he did,” Selena said.

"It sounds like things would have turned out badly if Prince Alexander hadn't shown up where and when he did," Lydia said.

"He seems to have a way of changing the outcome of a situation," Damien said.

"Just watch," Keith said, "He's gonna turn this fight around too."

The last clash between Karen and I sent us sliding back from each other. Eleanore had a slight smile on her face to see her subordinate actually doing well. With each burning cyclone Karen sent at me, I was able to parry away by shifting the angle of the barrier I used to defend myself. Suddenly I was caught in another stalemate where I couldn't effectively shift the barrier either way.

"Damn!" I said, "I can't shift it this time! Maybe I can…" that's when I got an idea that made me smile.

"What are you smiling about?" Karen asked.

Focusing the energy through my sword, I gripped it tighter and brought it above my head. While still focusing on the barrier itself, I swung the sword down as hard as I could and pushed the barrier and the burning tornado forward straight to Karen.

"AHH!" she dove out of the way just in time.

"He pushed it back!" Lan was shocked.

"I told you he would turn this around!" Keith said.

"I didn't think you meant literally," Lan said.

"Yay!" Alyssa cheered.

"That's showing her!" Selena cheered.

"Thanks!" I waved to them before turning back, "I think I'm figuring out how to do this!"

"What do you mean?" Karen stood up, "You just caught me off guard!"

"You're taking me to a new level whether you realize it or not," I said, "Even if I loose, I still consider this a valuable experience."

"What are you saying?" Karen asked, "You really don't care if I beat you?"

"I can't win every fight," I said, "I may have the Twilight Star, but I'm still learning."

"Really?" she asked.

"Yeah," I said, "As are you still learning."

"I've nearly mastered the art of fencing," she said.

"I may not be good at it, but I still know the basics of it," I pointed my sword at her, "That means I know EXACTLY what to expect from you in close combat!"

"W-what?" Karen suddenly looked shocked.

"Mastering a style doesn't do you much good if your opponent knows it too," I pulled my left hand into my long sleeve, "Combat isn't about how well you use a certain style, but how well you can use your skills to improvise and adjust to any situation."

"That's exactly what Raymond said," grandma couldn't help but smile.

"Prepare yourself!" I charged, "Here I come!"

I rushed Karen into close combat again before she had time to summon up another attack. This time, I pressed hard to keep myself on the offensive and her on the defensive. As soon as she raised her blade to defend again, I faked a vertical strike and instead ducked low and swept her off her feet with a low sweeping kick. The sudden change in tactics left her unable to react and she fell flat on her back. I kept the pressure on her by leaping into a sideways rolling heel drop above her. She rolled out of the way and just barely kept her head from getting hit.

"This is just like when he trained against me!" Robert said.

"Hmm?" Eleanore glanced over in curiosity.

"His fighting style," Robert recalled the duel we had before arriving in Kaydra, "I didn't know what to expect when he changed tactics all of a sudden. The way he engages you at one moment and suddenly changes up really threw me for a loop. It's like his style is ever changing."

"Before he was able to use the Twilight Star," my grandmother said, "He would fight randomly like that to keep his opponents guessing. It was his way of making up for not having a nature element of his own."

"Wow," Selena said before watching our fight again, "That's really smart of him."

"Damn!" Karen avoided a horizontal swing of my sword, "Now I've got-ahh!!"

Karen stopped immediately when I pointed my sword straight at her. The tip was barely an inch from her nose. I threw the sword upward as a distraction, and it worked. I took an extra smoke bomb I bought from Jack and threw it right at our feet. Completely disoriented, Karen swung her blade randomly to keep me at bay until she finally blew away the smoke.

"Where is he?!" Karen looked around and suddenly noticed a dark cloth around her waist, "What the-!"

"Gotcha!" I pulled on the jacket I had wrapped around her waist.

I pulled as hard as I could and we began to spin in place. She tried to lift up higher into the air, but I held tight for several more spins before suddenly releasing her. As she spun out of control to the ground, I caught my sword from the air. The four crystals, one at the tip, one at the base of the blade, and the others on each end of the guard, were glowing almost as bright as the sun.

"Solar…" I gripped the sword with both hands and reached backwards.

"Ahh!" Karen finally recovered from her spin, "What kind of fighting is-" she stopped and looked up as soon as she heard me shout 'Solar'.

"Shockwave!!" I swung my sword down as hard as I could.

As I swung my sword downward, a flash of light shot forth. The wave of energy rippled through the air straight for Karen. She brought her blade up against the shockwave, but she was unable to hold it back and was sent sliding several yards backwards into the dust. Everyone's eyes were frozen open from shock. Even Eleanore couldn't help but to react to Karen suddenly getting hit by the new attack.

"Whoooooaaa!!!" Everyone except Eleanore yelled in unison.

"When did he learn to do that??" Selena and Caliandra ask in unison before turning to each other and back to me, "Just now???"

"Wow…" Alyssa was leaning over Lydia's shoulder, "That's so cool!"

"Your brother really is something," Lydia looked to Alyssa.

"Do it again!" Alyssa yelled.

When the dust cleared, Karen was bringing herself up to her feet. She looked stunned and just as worn out as I was feeling. Without saying a word, she raised her blade and summoned up another burning tornado. I responded by lifting my sword overhead and summoned up enough energy for one more attack.

"Looks like it's about to be over," Keith had his arms crossed, "They're both exhausted."

"C'mon Alex," Selena and Vincent looked on in anticipation.

"I can't lose…" Karen's focus was completely on me, "I'm a Valkyrie. Even against you… I can't allow myself to lose, even to you!" a whirlwind whipped around her, "Dance of the…!"

"Solar…!" my sword began to glow with energy as I pulled it back over my head.

"Burning…!" she swung her blade, "Tornado!!"

"Shockwave!" I brought my blade down as hard as I could.

"Uh oh," Eleanore watched the two attack approach, "Take cover!"

The initial forces from both attacks were able to cancel each other out, but the exploding impact blew rocks and debris in all directions. Eleanore took to the sky as the others ducked for cover. Lydia got down with Alyssa behind her shield and Damien spun his lance with enough speed to deflect any flying debris from my grandmother. I slid back several feet with my left arm shielding my face and waited for the smoke to clear. I caught sight of Karen's silhouette just before she flew from the smoke straight at me. I raised my sword to defend myself, but then-

"Karen!" I suddenly yelled, "Watch out!!!"

"Huh?!" She slid to a halt and turned to look behind her, "What?!"

That's when I kicked her blade straight out of her hand. She looked back and I already had the tip of my sword resting on her chest armor when I caught her blade with my free hand.

"Touché!" I smirked, "That's what."

It felt like everyone was stunned for a full ten seconds before anyone could even move. Karen finally realized what just happened when everyone else recovered from shock.

"Wha…bu-but I…you…" Karen was lost for words.

"You've got to be kidding me…" Eleanore watched from above.

"He…won…?" Lan's eyes were wide open.

"He won!" Selena and Alyssa screamed.

"Damn that was awesome!!" Vincent and Keith yelled.

"I-I don't believe it," Karen sunk to her knees in disbelief.

"Phew," I fell to my knees, "That was a close one Karen."

"Alex!" Alyssa ran from the group towards Karen and me.

"I can't believe I allowed myself to be distracted," Karen lowered her head in shame.

"Karen," I put my hand on her shoulder, "Are you ok?"

"Yes," Karen paused for a moment, "I'll be fine, but…why did you trick me like that?"

"I honestly didn't think it would work," I said, "You're such a good swordswoman that I had to find a way to disarm you somehow."

“You’re just saying that,” she turned her head, “I couldn’t figure you out at all, but you seemed to learn me quite well.”

“Not so much you,” I said, “But your fighting style in general. You relied too much on one technique of sword play to the point where I knew exactly how to defend. There is no one perfect style, no matter how well you master it. Learning to read and adapt to your opponent is a big part of swordplay. Once you learn to do that, then it’s just a matter of finding your own style to work with and refine.”

“Such wise words,” she turned back to me.

“Thanks, but they’re my grandfather’s words,” I stood up.

“All the same,” Karen stood up, “Thank you Prince Alexander.”

“Just call me Alex,” I put my hand out, “All my friends do.”

“Alright then,” she shook my hand.

“That was so cool!” Alyssa jumped on my back.

“Ow sis!” I had to keep myself from falling, “That hurts.”

“That was well done Prince Alexander,” Lydia said.

“I expected no less from Valsoria’s Prince,” Damien said.

“Awesome new trick Alex!” Keith said.

“Way to go!” Selena said.

“Thanks everyone,” I took a deep breath, “Now that was a workout. I’m sorry we took so long Eleanore. We can continue on now.”

“It’s fine,” Eleanore said, “But are you even able to walk?”

“Of course not!” Damien cut in, “After an epic duel like that, you mustn’t try to do any walking! I insist that you ride my steed and rest!”

“Very well,” I took a deep breath, “Since you insist.”

“Lady Karen,” Lydia said, “You should rest too. Ride upon my steed with Princess Alyssa.

“Alright,” Karen agreed.

It was about sundown when we finally crossed over the bridge. Eleanore informed me that we would be arriving in Miliga by the next morning if we kept our pace up. We could all use a nice bed to sleep in. Karen and I were still riding on horseback much of the way.

“You know,” Karen got my attention, “You were pretty cool back there. Do you think that we could train together sometime?”

“I don’t mind,” I said, “But don’t think that I’m going to teach you my fighting style. It’s signature to me.”

“Aw,” Karen pouted, “Not even just a little?”

“If I did, then I would never be able to beat you again,” I laughed.

“You’re just afraid that I’ll use it better than you do!” she teased.

“You’re right,” I laughed, “It would be perfect if I could fly.”

Episode 29
A Grim Situation

In the darkness of the night, a lightly armored shadowy figure leaped rooftop to rooftop in Miliga. Upon reaching an abandoned house, she jumped through an open window without making a sound. The dark clothed person snuck her way down into the basement where she rendezvoused with an ally of hers.

"What took you so long?" her ally asked, "You're not normally late."

"Sorry Victor," she said, "It was a little harder to sneak away this time. Have you had any trouble avoiding OSC?"

"Nah," he said, "I'm starting to think that they have stopped looking for me. I just hate that I had to blow up my home."

"You did the right thing," she said, "Even with Felix's power, there wasn't enough time to move everything, and we can't risk anything you made falling into their hands."

"How are those katanas and that armor holding up?" he asked.

"The armor fits great," she looked herself over, "And the katanas are amazingly easy to work with. How did you even get a hold of these things? They're made of Astra Metal, and you know how rare that is."

"A guy owed me a favor," he said.

"Ha," she gave a short laugh, "Nice."

"Now about OSC," he began to ask, "What's new to report?"

"Well the only good news I have to report at the moment is that Francis is dead," she said, "After Alex's group chased him off, I found him injured and finished the job. The bad news is that OSC will be making another attempt to get the Roc Soul Crystal."

"Any clues to where the Roc Soul Crystal was taken after the incident?"

"I failed to find that out," she looked down in shame.

"Well tell me about this Alfonso and Lancer," he began to ask, "What threat do they pose?"

"Alfonso," she started, "Is OSC's second ranked commander. He is skilled with a sword, but what makes him dangerous is a new armor he has that was built for him. Instead of being made of iron or steel, it's made of Astra Metal. Aside from the armor being very strong itself, it somehow has the ability to absorb the energy from an elemental attack."

"Using that guy's design?" he asked, "Zaalek or something?"

"Yes," she said, "It also allows him to harness its absorbed power and turn it back against anyone. I did notice something during the testing of the armor. It looks like it can only absorb one element at a time, and it can only absorb nature elements."

"So the powers of light and dark can still get through?" he asked.

"Yes," she said, "And I assume twilight as well."

"Well at least it has a weakness," he said, "What about Lancer?"

"Lancer," she started, "Is much faster than Alfonso, and insanely good with swordplay. He's no slouch with his wind affinity either. He gives me the chills."

"Do you think Alex or Keith could take him?" he asked.

"I don't know," she said, "It's been a while since I've seen Alex in action, but I honestly don't see how they could."

"Even with Keith's ninja drive?" he asked.

"It's been…damaged somehow," she informed him.

"Well…damn," he said, "With my workshop out of commission, I don't think I could fix it."

"In the long run," she said, "It may turn out to be a good thing for him. It'll force him to focus on making himself more naturally adept to his affinity rather than relying on the drive to manually boost his power."

"That's true," he said, "By the sound of things, I hope that neither of them end up fighting Lancer."

"Me too," she said.

"Now what about these Iron Soldiers and Iron Sentinel?" he asked.

"The Iron Sentinel still isn't functioning yet," she said, "But I don't think we have much time before it becomes a threat. The Iron Soldiers, on the other hand, have gotten to a point where they are producing more of them. After working out the problems with the prototype that was used on Gravadale, these new models are bigger and bulkier. They are able to have a person inside to operate them using that Crystal… Meto… Mater… that thing I told you about. It works similar to the Ninja Drive."

"Are they made of Astra Metal as well?" he asked.

"Thankfully no," she said, "But fighting them would be like fighting a giant suit of armor. I think there are about 15 of them that are operational. If we don't do something soon, we may end up with too many to deal with."

"I just thought of something," he interrupted, "If their target is Valsoria, how are they going to get those things down there unnoticed?"

"It turns out that their leader," she crossed her arms, "Has a similar ability to Felix. Not only that, but he's somehow created manmade crystals with dark powers that allow some of the other soldiers to do the same."

"That's," he paused, "Gonna be trouble. They could practically show up at Valsoria's doorstep whenever they're ready."

"We need to figure out what to do soon," she said.

"I know," he brought his hand up to his chin, "If we had more people, we could launch a surprise raid. I hate to go in without a plan, so we just need to play it safe for the moment."

"Alright," she said.

"So what about this Zaalek guy," he became curious, "I'd like to rescue him now, but I'm afraid of your cover getting blown too soon."

"It's your call boss," she said, "We could take him anytime. That reminds me of something I wanted to ask you though."

"What is it?" he asked.

"Last time I talked to him," she reached into her scarf around her neck and pulled out a piece of paper, "I noticed this weird mark on his neck. This is what it looks like. What does it mean?"

"Hmm," he examined the black design that resembled a claw, "I've seen this before. I can remember this much; it's not good."

"Uh oh," she said.

"Try to keep an eye on what Alfonso and Lancer are up to," he said, "In the meantime, I'll look into this. It's on the tip of my tongue of what it is, but I can't quite remember."

"Alright," she said, "So I'm going back under cover?"

"At least for now," he said, "But be careful. If it looks like it's going to get dicey, you and Felix get out of there."

"Understood," she said and left the room.

"Hmm," he examined the paper one more time, "It's like a bad omen."

We arrived in Miliga about an hour before noon. Miliga isn't a normal city. It's known as a Citadel. The design of the city is like a giant circle. The walls protect the city from outside attack and everything from people's houses to the shops are built inside. The roads themselves are like giant circles from an overhead look, but the main roads all lead to the center clock tower. Miliga has a lot to offer within its walls. It holds an academy I attended when I was younger, and it has a very large library full of stories and knowledge. It's a common place for mages, sages, and sorcerers to come looking to improve their abilities.

"The last time I was here was when I was in the academy," I scoped out the citadel.

"Is that were you learned fencing?" Karen asked.

"Yeah," I said, "Aside from Zephyros, there was one person there in particular that I could never best. I think his name was Lancer. He was insanely good. He would end a match within seconds, and I could never get through his attacks. Even Zephyros struggled with him, but any match between those two was guaranteed to be epic."

"That's the first I've ever heard of Prince Zephyros having trouble with anyone in fencing," Eleanore said.

"I wonder what Lancer is up to," I looked to the sky, "I'd like the chance so see where I stand against him after all this time."

"Well we shouldn't be wasting anymore time," Eleanore said, "Our orders are to take Princess Alyssa to the clock tower."

"We have a surprise for you," Karen knelt to Alyssa's level.

"What is it?!" she asked.

"How is it going to be a surprise if we tell you?" Karen teased her.

"If it won't cause you any trouble," my grandma spoke to Eleanore, "I'd like you to go on ahead without me. There's something I need to do."

"Very well," Eleanore said, "We'll guard Princess Alyssa with our lives."

"I'll go with you as well," Lydia said to Eleanore.

"Alright," Eleanore said.

"We will meet you all at the clock tower," grandma said, "Are you ready Selena?"

"Y-yes ma'am," Selena nodded.

"So your grandma is going to help Selena focus her powers?" Vincent watched them walk down a road with Damien.

"It looks that way," I said, "Grandma told me that she thinks Selena possesses a lot of potential, so she wants to do anything she can to help her."

"I see," Vincent said, "How good is your grandma?"

"I couldn't even begin to explain it to you," I said, "Her abilities are beyond supernatural. The fact that she wants to train Selena really says a lot about her."

“Why’s that?” Vincent asked.

“Grandma has been looking to teach someone, but aside from the fact that people with the ice affinity aren’t all that common, the few that have sought out my grandma weren’t worthy according to her.”

“Wow,” Vincent said, “Does she have an ability to see a person’s potential or something?”

“I dunno,” I said, “Either way I’m glad she found someone to teach. It’ll really make her happy.”

“C’mon Alex!” Alyssa pulled on my arm suddenly, “Let’s go already!”

“Alright,” I said.

As we headed to the clock tower, two men covered in black cloaks met in an abandoned shack several hundred yards to the east of the citadel.

“And you’re certain that they brought it here?” the man with blond bangs covering his left eye asked.

“Most certain,” the man with black hair poking through his hood confirmed, “Being a Citadel, this is the only place that makes sense to try and hide it.”

“Very well,” the blonde said, “I should be able to handle the Valkyries on my own as I try to escape. Are your men prepared for your part of the plan?”

“Yes,” he said, “I have several men and four Iron Soldiers ready to go as part of the distraction. I shall lead the attack myself. With this new armor, I shall be invincible.”

“Very well,” he said, “I will leave the east gate assault to you then. I authorize you to crush anyone that stands in your way without mercy.”

"This shall be fun," Alfonso said.

The man with black hair removed his cloak to reveal his suit of black plated Astra armor. On its chest, shoulders, and hips were clear spheres of crystal that were linked to each other by strips of metal made with particles of crystals that ran across his armor.

"I can't wait to see the look on the faces of anyone that tries an elemental attack against me when I send it right back at them!"

The clock tower seemed much higher from the top floor. I could see the entire citadel and all the surrounding land. The wind was pretty strong too. I had to hang onto the window ledge just to keep my balance as I peered outward. Just then a man with a brown cloak walked through the door.

"Well it looks like our special guest has arrived," the man said, "Excellent work Lady Eleanore."

"Thank you Count Jacques," Eleanore said, "However we had some unexpected help getting here safely," she pointed to the rest of us.

"I say," he pulled his glasses a little closer to his face, "Do my eyes deceive me, or is that Valsoria's Prince??"

"Hello Count Jacques," I said, "It's good to see you again."

"Well met your highness," he bowed, "But where is Lady Caliandra?"

"She and a friend of mine are attending to some business somewhere in the citadel," I said, "She said that she would meet with us when she's done."

"Very well," he said, "I suppose at the very least I can show you why you were brought here."

"Is that the surprise you were talking about?" Alyssa asked Karen.

"Sure is," she said, "Are you ready?"

"Uh huh," she nodded.

"Behold," the count reached into his satchel.

A bright light suddenly filled the room and made me feel like I was standing inside a lighthouse! After shielding our eyes for several moments, the light finally dimmed enough for us to see what he was holding.

"Is that what I think it is?!" I asked.

"It's a Soul Crystal!" Lan said.

"That's the Roc Soul Crystal," Lydia said, "The very essence of a legendary bird known as Roc; the spirit of the wind."

"Roc was said to be so enormous, that it could blow down a city with a simple beat of its wings," the count said, "This crystal is one of Zylphan's most precious treasures, and our beloved Count Marcus gave his life to protect it."

"So I've heard," I glanced off.

"But lets not forget why we're here," he said, "We've decided to perform a special blessing for Princess Alyssa to assist in her affinity's development."

"Really???" Alyssa was shocked to think that she would actually get to touch the crystal.

"That's right," Eleanore said, "Queen Athena authorized it herself."

"Yay!" Alyssa reached for the crystal but suddenly pulled back, "Wait! Can we wait till grandma gets here?"

"If that is your wish your highness," the count said.

"We may have to wait anyway," Vincent was looking out the east window, "Alex we've got a serious problem."

"What is it?" I ran to the window and caught sight of a large crowd of armed men, "Oh no. We're under attack!"

"What?!" everyone else said in unison.

"It's definetly OSC," Vincent said, "If you want proof, look just past the front line of goons."

"This is bad!" I caught sight of four behemoth-like figures in the distance, "Are those Iron Soldiers?"

"They must be," Vincent said, "But they look different."

"It looks like much of the Miliga Guard is already preparing to intercept them!" Keith said.

"They're going to need our help defeating those Iron Soldiers!" I said.

"I'm ready when you are," Vincent said, "Its time for a little payback!"

"AHHHH!!!" I heard a scream from behind me that sent a chill down my spine.

Count Jacques has fallen to the floor with a large gash across his chest. Standing above him was a black cloaked man whose ebon colored rapier was dripping with blood. In his right hand was the Roc Soul Crystal.

"Count Jacques!!!" Eleanore screamed.

"Too easy," the man said.

"Don't you move!" Eleanore quickly had her blade pointed to the man, "In the name of Zylphan, hand over the crystal!"

"You'll have to catch me if you want it so bad!" he flew out the window.

“Stop!!” Eleanore quickly gave chase.

“Count Jacques!” Karen knelt to his side, “Count Jacques speak to me!”

“Ugh…” he let out a weak and painful moan.

“Don’t move Count Jacques!” I said, “Lan can you help him?!”

“I’ll try!” Lan quickly got to work on trying to heal the large slash across the count’s chest.

“What do we do now?!” Karen began to panic.

“Calm down,” I said, “He’s going to be alright! Lydia, can you stay with Alyssa and assist Lan?”

“Right away your highness,” she said, “But what are you going to do?”

“Since Eleanore has gone after that man, we’re going to help the Miliga Guard stop those Iron Soldiers,” I said.

“Please be careful your highness,” she said.

“I will,” I then turned to my crying sister, “Try to calm down Alyssa. Count Jacques is going to be fine. We’re going to get those guys who are responsible for this, so don’t worry.”

“O-ok…” she managed to speak through her crying.

“You stay here as well Aiyana,” I said.

“Alright,” she said.

“I’m going to assist Lady Eleanore,” Karen got up, “Good luck Alex!”

“You too,” I told her, “Lets do this!” I said to Vincent, Keith, and Robert.

The four of us rushed as fast as we could to the east gate. Rushing to the front lines, I managed to find one of the commanders of the Miliga Guard.

“Commander!” I called for his attention.

“V-Valsoria’s Prince Alexander?!” he was shocked to see me, “Your highness please return to the safety of the Citadel!”

“No!” I yelled, “Those things out there are OSC’s Iron Soldiers! You’re going to need our help to destroy them!”

“We’ve fought against one before in Gravadale!” Robert said, “Please allow us to help you!”

“If you can help us get through,” I said, “We’ll take them down for you!”

“Very well,” the commander said, “Solders! Prince Alexander and his company are here to assist us! Deal with as many of the enemy units as you can, and leave the Iron Soldiers to them! Protect the Citadel at all cost! Move out!” the commander and his troops ran forward.

“Now,” Keith, Robert, and Vincent lined up by my side as I transformed the Twilight Star, “Ready guys?”

Keith unsheathed his katana and brought it to his side, “Always.”

Robert brandished his sword and shield, “On your command.”

Vincent clutched his burning fists, “Let’s fight!”

“CHARGE!!!”

Episode 30
Outmatched

The numbers we faced here were much larger than what we faced at Gravadale. Thankfully, the number of Miliga allies present was greater than the number of Gravadale knights present at that time as well. With our combined efforts, the four of us were able to fight our way through the bulk of OSC soldiers. We were still several yards away from the Iron Soldiers, but we could tell that they looked much larger than the one I destroyed in Gravadale. They were scattered, so we targeted the closest two to us and combined our efforts in pairs.

"We'll get this one first!" I ran towards it, "Get ready Keith!"

"Gotcha," Keith cut down an OSC soldier, "Let's get him!"

"Then we got this one." Vincent ran straight for another.

"I'll back you up," Robert followed Vincent.

The Iron Soldier Keith and I faced lifted its large arm into the air and brought it down to the ground with enough force to split open a fissure straight for us. We both jumped in time not to be affected by the sudden quake, and then we proceeded to rush it. Using its hand it had on the ground after attacking, it lifted a large piece of earth and hurled it straight at us. I unleashed a Solar Shockwave to cut right through it and Keith used the opening to jump on top of it.

"Too slow!" Keith jumped behind it.

"What?" a voice could be heard from inside the iron soldier, "Where'd that blonde one go?"

"Hey Alex!" Keith called from behind, "There's someone inside!"

"Seriously?" I ducked to avoid a swing of its large arm, "Too bad for him!"

"Don't make me laugh," the soldier inside the Iron Soldier spoke, "I'll crush the both of you!"

As the two of us fought for an opening, Robert and Vincent were just shaking off a quake attack from the second one. Robert had used a quake attack of his own, but the iron soldier just wouldn't fall over. They could hear laughter coming from inside it, and it was making Vincent burn with anger.

"Damn it!" Vincent prepared another fire attack, "We can't knock it down!"

"We have to do something," Robert shielded them from a piece of earth thrown at them, "We still have more to deal with!"

"It's armored from head to toe," Vincent unleashed a steady stream of fire against it, "But it still has to have a weak point!"

"Give it up!" the voice in the iron soldier said as it slammed its arm to the ground to defend against the fire, "I'm unstoppable!"

When the dust cleared, the iron soldier's emerged forward from the fire. It appeared to be completely unfazed until Vincent noticed a spot near its torso and right side that appeared to be glowing red.

"What the…" Vincent noticed the glowing spot, "Did you see that?"

"See what?" Robert was unsure what he was talking about.

"Watch again," Vincent held his hands together at his side.

After generating some concentrated fire for a moment, Vincent unleashed another intense stream of flames straight into the Iron Soldier. When the fire dispersed, the same spot was glowing a little more clearly.

"There!" Vincent pointed, "There's a weak spot in the metal right there!"

"R-really? How can you tell?" Robert was a bit baffled.

"It's glowing in that spot because the metal hasn't been forged evenly," Vincent said, "The son of a blacksmith is gonna know this stuff!"

"Wow. Then let's go for it!" Robert held his sword behind him as he charged.

"Yeah! Let me get at it once more before you attack!" Vincent charged.

Vincent quickly flipped to the side to avoid a swing of its heavy arm, and then struck the same spot with as much fire as he could. Then Vincent went to distract the controller of the Iron Soldier while Robert moved in to strike his opening. With a heavy swing of his sword, he struck the side of the armor so hard that it tore open a large gash that left enough of an opening to see the leg of the soldier inside.

"Ahh!" the soldier screamed from shock, "They broke it?!"

"Hello," Vincent peeked into the hole, "And goodbye!"

Vincent unleashed an inferno through the large hole in the Iron Soldier's armor that forced the soldier inside to escape from the top. Vincent and Robert were able to jump away seconds before it exploded into pieces.

"Yeah!" Vincent held his fists up in celebration, "One down!"

"Sword of the Rising Sun!" I descended downward with a slash that ripped through the side of the one Keith and I were fighting.

"Damn!!" the soldier piloting it leaped from the wreckage, "I gotta get-"

"Nope," Keith ended his life with three swift slashes of his katana.

"Yes!" I yelled, "Now for the other two!"

"I can't let you do that, Alexander," I heard someone call my name.

"Who said that?" I looked around.

"Over there!" Vincent pointed.

Several yards away, a heavy built man wearing a strange suit of black armor stood with his blade held to his side. His black armor had strange markings that ran across the armor to several points where clear crystals were built into the metal.

"You!" I called out to him, "Are you the commander of this army?"

"I am," he carefully eyed the four of us, "I am Alfonso; second in command of OSC."

"So now the *second* one shows himself," Keith stood ready, "This should be interesting."

"You won't have the advantage Francis had by separating us!" I said.

"Hmph," Alfonso glared at me, "I don't need such tactics to defeat the likes of you. There is nothing your combined powers can do against me."

"In that case," Vincent began charging fire at his side with both hands, "I'll just make you eat those words!"

Eleanore had quickly caught up to the man who attacked Count Jacques and engaged him in speedy and deadly close combat. Matching each other blow for blow, Eleanore just couldn't find an opening to strike him directly. She suddenly found herself on the defensive as he spun around one of her whirlwind attacks and assaulted her.

"I didn't expect I'd have to fight off a Zylphan Valkyrie just to get away," he continued attacking, "This would have been much easier without you here!"

“Those who know that they can never escape their own shadow…” her voice was cold as she locked blades with him, “Also know that they can never escape death. I, Eleanore of the Ebon Wind, shall make you pay for your crimes with your life!”

“Is that right?” his eyes suddenly flashed with a dark aura.

At that moment, he unleashed a sudden gust of wind that was strong enough to break Eleanore’s momentum and take her for a spin. She fought for a moment to regain her bearings in the air and stopped herself from spinning out.

“Damn!” she shielded her eyes, “Is he drawing power from the Roc Soul Crystal?”

“I hope that wasn’t too much for you,” he taunted, “I haven’t even begun to unleash this thing’s power.”

“Blazing Spiral!” Karen struck him from behind with a spinning force of flames.

“Huh…” Eleanore was surprised to see him consumed in a fiery whirlwind, “She actually hit him.”

“Those who know the Zylphan Valkyries know that we never fail to serve justice!” Karen swung the fire from her rapier, “Surrender and make it easier on yourself!”

“Ha!” he laughed from inside the fiery whirlwind.

He suddenly blew the flames and the smoldering remains of his cloak off him with a mighty tornado that nearly sent Eleanore spinning out of control. Karen tried to resist, but was send flailing away until she was able to stop herself from hitting the ground. From the ashes floated a very lightly armored blond man with evil gazing green eyes.

"That wasn't a bad try," he glanced to Karen, "But you valkyries are going to have to do better than that against me!"

"Just who are you?" Eleanore was growing concerned.

Our battle with Alfonso just started and he was already standing in a pillar of fire from when Vincent struck him directly with a blast of flames. Everyone congratulated Vincent on his well aimed attack, but something didn't feel right. Not only was that too easy, but Alfonso didn't even bother to put up a defense.

"Everyone, stop," I told everyone, "Something's wrong."

"What do you mean?" Vincent tried to catch his breath, "I nailed that guy straight on!"

"Yeah you did," I watched the flames, "But something doesn't feel right…"

Suddenly the fire surrounding Alfonso suddenly began growing smaller and smaller until Alfonso was left standing as if nothing happened. Not a hair on his head was singed in the slightest, nor was there a burn on him. His armor didn't show any signs of damage either, but his armor did appear to have an unusual glow of red.

"What…the hell?" I was shocked.

"He's still standing!" Robert yelled.

"No way!" Vincent yelled, "I hit him dead on! I know I did!"

"So…" Keith scratched his head, "What happened?"

"Here," Alfonso pointed his sword at us, "I'll show you!"

Before anything else could be said, he unleashed an intense blast of flames directly at us. I yelled for everyone to get down as I formed a barrier to shield us from the fire, but the explosion it created on the ground in front of us threw us all off our feet and left us stunned.

"Oww…" Vincent grabbed his head in pain, "He just shot an attack stronger than me!"

"He…he's got the fire affinity?!" I stood up, "Was that how he was able to take your attack head on??"

"Ha," Alfonso laughed, "I actually have the water affinity, but that had nothing to do with how I stopped such a weak attack!"

"Weak?!" Vincent stood up.

"You're welcome to try again if you want," he held his arms open, "Here I'll even welcome it with open arms!"

"You son of a…" Vincent began focusing an aura of heat with his hands again.

"Wait Vincent! Don't!!"

I tried to stop him, but it was too late. He unleashed a blast so powerful, I had to shield myself from the heat! It exploded upon colliding with Alfonso, and he disappeared into smoke.

"There…" Vincent was breathing hard, "How's that…for weak?"

"A little better…" Alfonso spoke from the smoke.

"W…wha…" Vincent was completely baffled.

"…but it seems like you're tapped out," Alfonso finished.

"I'm…" Vincent paused before darting straight at him, "Just getting warmed up!"

"No Vincent!" Keith yelled after him.

Vincent had gotten so angry, he couldn't hear us. As soon as he leaped into the air and went for attacking at close combat, Alfonso raised his hand, and the designs on his black armor suddenly began running red as if they were filled with blood. A sudden blast of fire suddenly shot forth from his hand and hit Vincent directly which sent him spiraling back to us. He bounced and rolled on the ground for a moment before stopping unconscious.

"Vincent!" I ran to see if he was still alive.

"Alex, look out!" Robert suddenly shoved me out of the way.

Robert raised his shield to intercept a large fireball coming our way, but was blown away when it exploded on contact! He hit the ground hard and knocked himself out as well.

"Robert!" Keith yelled.

"Damn!" I got between Vincent and Alfonso, "Now what?!"

"If you think you're in a hopeless situation," Alfonso said, "You should see who those valkyries are fighting against."

"I would've guessed he was one of yours," I said.

"Not only is he one of ours," he said, "But he's someone you know."

"Someone I know? What are you talking about?!" I asked.

"I wouldn't worry about it if I were you," he said, "If you can't get past me, then you have no chance against OSC's first in command; Lancer!"

Episode 31
A Double Saving Grace

I couldn't believe what I had just heard. The guy I knew from the academy several years ago...the guy that gave Zephyros a run for his money...that same guy was in OSC, and their leader??? I didn't know whether to be angry or confused!

"No way..." I shook my head, "I don't believe you!"

"What's not to believe?" Alfonso asked, "Are you afraid? How do you think someone was able to get so close to Count Marcus without getting caught? He even got past you to get to Count Jacques without you noticing before it was too late! I'm sure you're familiar with his skills in combat-the way he can strike an opening in an instant."

Everything he was saying made me think back to the duels we would have. Everything he was saying was true, and after so many years, it's likely that he's only gotten much better. If that's really him fighting against Eleanore and Karen, then...then-

"It's your armor!" Keith suddenly interrupted my thoughts, "It's that weird armor that stopped Vincent's attack!"

"So you've figured it out," Alfonso said, "This armor is designed to be immune to any elemental attack you throw at me. If I get hit, the armor will just absorb its energy, and I can turn it right back against you!"

"Damn," I raised my sword, "I knew something was strange about it. That explains why those orbs and markings suddenly turned red."

"Alex," Keith looked to me, "If elemental attacks won't work, then we just have to take the fight to him in close combat. Cover Vincent and Robert for me. I'm going in."

"Wait! Are you sure about this?" I asked.

"For the first time in a while, not really," he admitted, "But we gotta try something. If that Lancer guy is as bad as he says, then those girls might need our help ASAP! Here I go!"

Keith ran at top speed while jumping from side to side to avoid each blazing attack Alfonso sent his way. Throughout all the fire and smoke, Keith found a way to get behind him, and swung at his backside at hard as he could. His attack was suddenly stopped cold when his katana bounced off his armor and was vibrating under intense stress!

"Ahh!" Keith tried to stop it from shaking, "What the hell?!"

"You can't cut me with that thing!" Alfonso grazed Keith with his sword as he jumped back, "On top of being immune to elements, this armor is forged with Astra metal!"

"Astra metal?!" Keith and I yelled in unison, "The rarest and strongest metal there is?!"

"Yes," he laughed, "You don't have a chance of scratching me with normal weapons!"

"In that case," I began focusing power through the Twilight Star, "I'll use a weapon that's not normal!"

Running at him at full speed, I knocked away each small fireball he sent my way until I engaged him in close combat. I quickly found that it was tough to match his strength, even when I was using my sword with two hands. When I went for a jump slash, he quickly knocked me off balance with a parry and hit me with a pulse of water that threw me several yards back! Keith went to seize an opening in his defense as soon as I was blown away. Keith went for a quick thrust to his head, but Alfonso quickly raised his shielded left arm to brush off the attack. At that point, Alfonso swung his blade heavily at Keith who had to leap over his head to avoid getting hit. He then went for a falling slash to his head which was intercepted by Alfonso's shielded right arm which snapped his blade in half! Stunned from shock of his katana breaking, Keith was caught on his side by Alfonso's blade and was sent reeling until he hit the ground hard. His chain mail saved him from a fatal hit, but he was still bleeding from his side as he stood up with his left hand holding his wound.

"Damn!" Keith only had one eye open, "He broke my katana! …and I think a rib…" he suddenly coughed up blood.

"I don't care how agile you are," Alfonso said, "It does no good if you can't hurt me!"

"Solar Shockwave!" I made a direct hit against him with my attack.

"Damn!" he knelt for a moment before standing, "Not bad."

"Thanks," I held my sword back, "Do you want me to do it again?"

"How about I turn that energy back against you?!" Alfonso swung his blade, but nothing happened, "What?"

"Nothing happened?" I was a little shocked, "So I guess that armor can't absorb the Twilight Star's power."

"Hmph. Maybe not, but I still have more than enough firepower to take you both down," he raised his blade to draw forth fire from his armor, but the flames were considerably weaker, "What the…?"

"It looks like your fire's about burnt out," Keith let out a weak laugh.

"I can protect myself against something that weak," I said.

"Maybe YOU can," he turned his attention to Vincent who was just pulling himself up beside Robert, "But what about them?!"

"N-no!!" I yelled for him to stop.

Alfonso unleashed a trail of fire that I didn't have time to run and protect Vincent and Robert against. As it raced towards them, I felt a tremble in the ground getting stronger as it approached them. Vincent was just barely on his feet seconds before he and Robert disappeared into an explosion of earth and smoke! Keith and I stood motionless at what just happened. We couldn't see anything in the smoke, nor could we hear anything. The silence was only broken by Alfonso's laughter.

"You…" I paused before raising my sword to attack, "You son of a-!!"

"It would appear that I have made it just in time," I heard a voice suddenly speak.

"Huh?" I turned towards the smoldering spot where Vincent and Robert were.

"What?" Alfonso stopped laughing.

"Are you all ok?" a figure with gold armor on his chest and forearms became visible.

"Is…that…?" Keith couldn't believe his ears.

"Is that the enemy, Alexander?" he asked.

"Y…you…?" Vincent quickly recognized him.

"Yes!" I said with excitement, "He's second in command of OSC!"

"In that case," the dark skinned warrior stepped forward with his dual blades, "An enemy of yours is an enemy of mine!"

The battle with Eleanore and Lancer had accelerated to the point where it was like trying to fight in a wind storm. Even with both valkyries teaming up on him, they found it hard to land a solid hit against him. Eleanore had just been sent spiraling to the ground where Karen was crouched down holding her injured left arm. She was able to stop herself just before hitting the ground, but when she looked up, Lancer's eyes appeared to have an ominous glow to them as he laughed at them.

"If this is all the Zylphan Valkyries are capable of, then I had nothing to worry about after all!" he laughed.

"Damn it," Eleanore glared at him, "Karen! Can you fly?"

"I think so," she painfully said.

"I see no other option but the Valkyrie's Waltz," she said.

"B-but Lady Eleanore," Karen began to protest, "There's only the two of us here, and I don't know if…"

"We have to do this," Eleanore cut her off, "I'll help you get your momentum going, but then you will have to take over. Understand?"

"Y-yes milady," Karen reluctantly agreed.

"Now!" Eleanore suddenly rose to the sky with Karen right behind her.

"What?" Lancer watched them soar above him, "Now what are you ladies up to?"

Eleanore and Karen suddenly began circling above Lancer like hawks hunting prey. As they began to spin faster and faster, a dark whirlwind slowly became visible as it began to descend downward from them. In the middle of their circling, Eleanore broke off the path and stopped in the middle of the whirlwind. Her body began to give off a dark glow that spread within the whirlwind and created a black tornado. Karen disappeared into the darkness of the wind while Eleanore stayed within the vortex with her blade to her face.

"Damn," Lancer suddenly found himself within the dark vortex, "I can barely see! Now what?"

"Prepare to die," Eleanore's voice echoed within the tornado, "Sword of the Ebon Wind!"

Eleanore suddenly faded into the darkness before Lancer could lock onto her position. As he looked around for the both of them, he was struck several times in an instant across his back and chest. Yelling from pain, he found it difficult to defend against the raging winds of the tornado and Eleanore's assault. Several strikes later, Lancer's left arm was red with blood and his clothes cut up from her attacks. Eleanore went to move in for the final strike, but the black tornado suddenly began to dissipate.

"What?!" Eleanore froze in midair, "No! Karen!"

"I'm sorry milady…!" Karen was slowly falling from above, "I can't…"

"You…BITCH!" Lancer rushed Karen.

In a fit of rage, Lancer thrust his rapier straight for Karen's head. She was barely able to parry the attack, but lost some of her hair in the process. He then quickly back handed her in the jaw and sent her spiraling to the ground where she was knocked out on impact.

"Karen!" Eleanore yelled out.

"You're next!" Lancer dove straight for her.

Lancer suddenly locked Eleanore down to the point where all she could do was defend herself. Drawing more power from the Roc Soul Crystal, he unleashed a terrible wind pulse from the swing of his rapier and sent her spiraling out of control, and then struck her repeatedly before sending her crashing down beside Karen.

"Shit…!" Eleanore slowly rose to her feet, "Karen! Can…you hear me?"

"I…it hurts to move…" she laid there motionless.

"Don't worry," Lancer pointed his rapier towards them, "Soon you won't feel anything at all!"

"No…" Eleanore thought to herself, "Now what? Karen's down, I'm getting exhausted, and he's still got the crystal to draw power from!"

"Milady…" Karen weakly spoke, "I'm sorry…I was too weak…"

"Damn it Karen," Eleanore stood between Karen and Lancer, "We can't…go down like this!"

"How noble of you to defend your fallen comrade to the end," Lancer grinned, "But it hardly makes a difference to me!"

With a swing of his rapier, he unleashed a pulse of wind that generated a violent twister that ripped up the ground along its path. Unable to fly, Eleanore held her arms up in defense and braced for the violent impact. At the last possible moment, a second twister appeared from nowhere and intercepted the first moments before it had a chance to strike Eleanore. Using all the strength she had left, she dug her blade into the ground and held onto Karen to keep from being blown away by the violent winds.

"W-what?" Eleanore looked around, "What just happened?"

"What the hell?" Lancer turned to see where that second twister came from.

"I didn't expect for us to meet like this," a figure from the sky said.

"You…" Lancer glared with a suspicious grin.

"Eleanore!" he called out to her and Karen, "Are you both alright?"

"M-milord…!" Eleanore was nearly speechless.

From the air, a silver haired swordsman fitted in a purple uniform and dark blue cape descended to the ground beside Eleanore and Karen. With him descended a valkyrie with long blue hair and blue armor similar to Karen and Eleanore's. The crystals embedded in the guard of his rapier glimmered with energy as he raised it towards Lancer. The valkyrie wielded a short spear fitted with one large ice crystal and several small wind crystals.

"Thank goodness we made it," the new valkyrie said.

"You…brought the prince with you?" Eleanore asked.

"Actually, it was he who brought me," she said.

"Lancer," the prince began to ask, "Are you the one responsible for all of this?"

"I am," he plainly answered.

"Then nothing more needs to be said," a whirlwind began to brew around him, "In the name of Zylphan, I, Prince Zephyros Zylphan, shall bring you down. Prepare yourself!"

Episode 32
Raw Power of Royalty

I almost couldn't believe our luck! At the very last second, one of the best allies I could hope for just appeared from nowhere and saved Vincent and Robert! His golden Sphinx Armor shinned with glory as he casually walked towards where I stood. Somehow, someway, Prince Jabari had found us, and was ready for battle!

"Jabari!" I yelled with excitement, "Are we glad to see you!"

"Likewise my friend," he said, "Not long after you left, many of the monsters that were appearing suddenly stopped. After that, I brought a few of my best warriors with me to track you down."

"Thanks for the save," Vincent stood up.

"You have not forgotten your promise, have you?" Jabari asked Vincent, "You better not die before our duel."

"Who? Me?" Vincent wiped the blood from his mouth, "No way. I was just taking a short break."

"Really?" he smiled, "It appeared as if you were knocked out cold," he suddenly turned his attention to Alfonso, "You there! What is your name?"

"I'm Alfonso," he replied, "Second in command of OSC!"

"Very well, Alfonso," Jabari raised his blades in a fighting stance, "I am the crown prince of Rac' Sagadam! "I, Jabari Sagadam, shall end your life and bury you with my power! Prepare yourself!"

Jabari wasted no time closing the distance before Alfonso had a chance to prepare an attack. He was quick to block the heavy swing of Jabari's blade with his own, but suffered a tremendous shock upon impact like he never experienced. It was enough to force him to step back and regain his footing before defending against Jabari's second blade with his shielded left arm. With each blow Alfonso intercepted with his blade, he felt his arms getting weaker and weaker. After trying multiple times to counterattack, he quickly found it increasingly difficult to get a clear swing through Jabari's assault. After a momentary deadlock between their blades, Jabari swung free and went right into his Raging Sphinx Strike combo. Even with his Astra armor, he felt the full force of each hit Jabari dealt him. His arm was getting crushed, he felt ribs crack, and he began coughing up blood as Jabari sent him reeling backwards after the last strike.

"Dude!" Vincent watched Jabari give Alfonso a merciless beating, "He's kicking his ass!"

"Not even that Astra Metal armor can protect him from a blow from Jabari," I said, "His blades are made of Damascus Steel. It's just as strong as Astra Metal, but it's much heavier."

"Damn!" Vincent said, "No wonder he's dealing so much damage!"

"Ugh…" Robert slowly sat up, "What…happened? Wait! Where-!"

"Hey," Vincent called him, "You ok?"

"My head hurts," he said, "But I'm otherwise fine…I think."

"You got knocked out after you saved Alex," Keith stood with them holding his wound, "We tried taking Alfonso on, but we couldn't get through. Then, when he tried to take you and Vincent out, Prince Jabari appeared from nowhere and saved you."

"Prince Jabari of Rac' Sagadam?" Robert asked.

"Yup," Vincent said, "And he's kicking Alfonso's-!"

"Excuse me," A Rac' Sagadam Priestess with long braided black hair interrupted him, "My name is Fukayna. I arrived with Prince Jabari. You were with Prince Alexander when he visited Rac' Sagadam."

"Y-yeah," he said, "You remember me?"

"I do," she said, "You were the loud one at the breakfast table."

"Oh yeah…" Vincent looked embarrassed, "Sorry about that…"

"Do not worry," she smiled, "I am here to assist you. Please allow me to tend to your injuries."

"Awesome," Vincent said, "Thanks a lot."

"You're welcome," she began working on Vincent first.

"Da…damn…" Alfonso was kneeling on one knee, "So much power…it's not human. Even my armor is…falling apart. Why did he…have to show up?"

While Jabari continued to battle Alfonso, Zephyros had already engaged Lancer into close combat high in the air. Their blades rang loud and fast as they parried each other's thrusts and slashes. Eleanore and Karen were being treated for their injuries by the new valkyrie that had arrived. Focusing her energy into a light blue sphere of chilled purified air, she was able to mend Eleanore and Karen's minor injuries and bruises as well as give them a second wind.

"Your Aether Sphere," Eleanore paused to enjoy the soothing moment, "Has never felt so good. Thank you, Rachel."

"I love it," Karen spun once in place with her arms stretched outward, "I think this is the first time you've ever used it on me."

"I'm a little surprised I needed to use it so strongly on you two at all," Rachel continued focusing her power, "This Lancer must be tough to give you trouble, Eleanore."

"Well," Eleanore looked away out of shame, "We tried to waltz him with Sword of the Ebon Wind, but…" she suddenly looked to Karen, "That didn't…end to well…"

"I'm sorry milady," Karen said, "I tried to keep the tornado up as long as I could…"

"Don't be too hard on her," Rachel defended Karen, "You know that waltz's like that are meant for at least three of us to perform together."

"I know that," Eleanore held her arms crossed, "But we were running out of options fast."

"Well worry not," Rachel ceased her Aether Sphere, "I'm sure the prince can handle this villain."

"Wait a second," Karen thought for a moment, "Lancer? Ah!"

"What is it?" Rachel asked.

"Prince Alexander mentioned him when we arrived!" Karen said.

"Alexander is here?" Zephyros overheard Karen yelling, "Did he come with Queen Caliandra?"

"He did," Lancer avoided a flurry of thrusts to his head from Zephyros's rapier, "I believe he's still doing battle with OSC soldiers on the other side of the city. That is, unless Alfonso hasn't gotten to him by now."

"I assume he's one of yours?" Zephyros asked him.

“He’s our second in command,” Lancer answered, “Even with the Twilight Star, there’s no way he stands a chance against him.”

“Are you sure about that?” Zephyros locked blades with Lancer, “I’m sure he’s gotten better since you last saw him.”

“Hmph,” Lancer pushed Zephyros away, “The kid never could touch me at the academy. I highly doubt he could be a threat to me-let alone Alfonso.”

“Maybe, but he’s not the one you need to worry about, is he?!” Zephyros suddenly grazed Lancer in the abdomen with a quick forward slash.

“Agh!” Lancer flew back, “Damn!”

“You may have the Roc Soul Crystal,” Zephyros prepared to strike again, “But even you can’t keep this up forever.”

“Grr,” Lancer thought to himself, “Now what to do…”

By the time Vincent and the others had their injuries mended, Alfonso was left with barely enough energy to breathe. The last strike Jabari unleashed on him knocked the wind right out of him.

“Damn it…all,” Alfonso said, “I…might have…to retreat…after all.”

“I will not give you the chance,” Jabari suddenly struck the ground and split open a fissure towards him.

“Ahh!” Alfonso fought to keep his balance.

“Tomb Blade…” Jabari leaped right above Alfonso, “Strike!”

With all his strength, Jabari struck Alfonso so hard, the ground exploded all around him and they disappeared in a cloud of falling dirt and rocks! When everything cleared, Jabari was standing over a pile of rubble where Alfonso was last seen.

"Now sleep," Jabari said over the pile of rubble, "And may your soul be judged with mercy."

"Yeah!" Vincent yelled, "Owned in the face!"

"Take that!" Keith jabbed his fist forward, but suddenly pulled it back from pain, "Ow!"

"Please be careful," Fukayna kept Keith from falling, "You might pull open your wound."

"S-sorry…" Keith laughed.

"Most impressive," Robert said.

"That was great Jabari!" I shook his hand, "I can't thank you enough for showing up when you did."

"You are welcome," he said, "I am happy to fight for my friends."

"That was excellent your highness," Fukayna said to Jabari.

"It was nothing," he said, "Thank you for tending to their injuries."

Just then, we all felt a sudden rumble from where Alfonso was buried. A large spout of water suddenly burst from the rubble, and Alfonso weakly pulled himself from the hole. Blood was all over his face and dripping from his chin as he surrounded himself with a blue aura to try and mend his damage as best he could.

"He's still alive?!" I yelled.

"How?!" Vincent yelled.

"It seems that I did not bury him deep enough," Jabari began to walk towards him.

"I will not…die here," Alfonso pulled out a dark crystal, "Not when…we're so close…" a dark energy suddenly surrounded him, and he was gone when it vanished.

"Damn!" Vincent yelled, "He got away!"

"Cowardly…" Jabari sheathed his blades to his side.

"Well he's gone…" I said, "There's nothing we can do about it now. I'm sure we'll see him again."

"I will not allow him to escape again," Jabari said.

"Well," I looked back towards the battlefield, "Now that he's gone, we still need to help the Miliga knights deal with those Iron Soldiers."

"Those big behemoth things I saw earlier?" Jabari asked.

"Yes," I said, "They're like a suit of armor and…"

"Why'd you stop?" Keith asked.

"Lancer!" I yelled, "I forgot the valkyries are fighting him! They may need my help!"

"Where are they now?" Jabari asked.

"On the other side of the city," I answered, "That's going to be a long run…"

"We can take my chariot," Jabari whistled for the two horses pulling his chariot, "Come! I shall take you there!"

"Ok," I stepped onto his chariot with him, "But we still need to deal with those Iron Soldiers! I can take out one on the way, but the other-"

I was interrupted in mid sentence when the Twilight Star suddenly began to resonate. With its energy flowing through me, I could feel that it was reacting to something, and as I looked around, I noticed a bright blue light emitting from the east gate.

"What the…" I held my hand over my eyes, "That light…"

"What is it?" Robert asked.

"Is that…my grandma?" I asked.

"Someone's with her," Keith caught sight of another figure.

"I think," Vincent got a good look, "That's Selena! What are they doing?"

Episode 33
Caliandra's New Student and a Royal Reunion

"That's it," my grandmother watched Selena meditate, "Just like that. Keep it tightly focused and wait until you feel it's ready to be released."

Selena, surrounded by a bright blue light, stood with my grandmother as she steadily focused a small sphere of ice energy out in front of her with both of her hands. My grandmother observed her closely as she gave her some assistance by emitting an Essence of Ice from herself to give Selena's power a small boost.

"I'm sorry it took so long to build up," Selena said.

"You're doing fine, Selena," my grandmother said, "For someone just getting started, you're doing much better than I expected."

"Thanks you, Lady Caliandra," a confident look appeared on Selena's face, "I think I'm ready!"

"Oh hold on a sec," my grandmother suddenly said.

"Huh?" Selena asked.

"Oh Sir Damien!" my grandmother called him.

"Yes your highness?" he broke from the battle, "Are you alright?"

"I'm fine," she said, "But could you see if you could get the Miliga soldiers to clear a path for her attack? She's just getting started, and I don't want them to get caught in the crossfire."

"At once, your highness!" Sir Damien rode out to the battlefield, "Hear me Miliga allies! Make way for Lady Caliandra and her student as they prepare to attack!"

"Say what?!" Several Miliga soldiers came to a halt, "Lady Caliandra??"

"All units clear an opening NOW!!" the Miliga knight commander ordered.

"Now Selena," my grandmother pointed towards the nearest iron soldier, "Aim carefully and release it forward!"

"Right!" her energy suddenly intensified, "Freeze…Flash!!"

In a sudden flash of light, Selena unleashed forth a large beam of ice energy that flew straight through the crowd of Miliga soldiers and grazed several OSC soldiers as her attack landed perfectly against the Iron Soldier! The explosive shockwave it caused blew several OSC soldiers away and forced us to duck for cover as ice shards flew in all directions! When we looked up, all fighting had ceased and the Iron Soldier was encased in a large stalagmite of ice!

"I-I got it!" Selena began jumping for joy, "I did it! I did it!"

"I have to say that was very excellent for a first shot," my grandmother smiled.

"Woah…!" Keith paused for a moment, "Selena did that?!"

"She DID!" I was struck with awe, "She stopped it cold in its tracks! I didn't know she could do that!"

"*I* didn't know she could do that!!" Vincent yelled, "Your grandma must've taught her that!"

"Yea, but still!" I looked back and forth from the frozen Iron Soldier and Selena, "It looked like my grandmother was barely helping her focus! That was mostly her!"

Suddenly the ice around it shattered. Though it was free, the iron soldier struggled hard to move before finally collapsing to the ground. The soldier controlling it soon slowly emerged from the ice cold metal and was blue in the face from cold.

"She got the third iron soldier!" one of the OSC commanders yelled.

"Do you want to try and get the other?" my grandmother asked.

"Yes!" Selena began focusing her power immediately, "Freeze Flash!"

In half the time of her first attack, Selena fired off another Freeze Flash against the remaining iron soldier. This one was split in two when stalagmites of ice spiked from the ground and nearly impaled the soldier inside.

"Nicely done!" my grandmother approved of her work.

"Yes!" Selena yelled, "Thank you!"

"That was stronger than her first!" I yelled, "It's incredible!"

"Damn!" an OSC commander yelled, "The iron soldiers have fallen and Alfonso has been defeated! All units retreat!"

As the OSC soldiers fell back, a dark mass of energy appeared for them to run into. The Miliga soldiers let out a roar of celebration of victory as they disappeared into the darkness.

"Yeah!" Vincent yelled, "You better run!"

"I am disappointed that I did not get to fight much," Jabari smiled with his arms crossed, "But I am happy for our victory nonetheless."

"Great job Selena!" I said as we met them at the gate, "I didn't know you had it in you!"

"Way to send those soldiers running!" Vincent gave a thumb's up.

"So this means you're really going to take her on as your student?" I asked my grandmother.

"Yes," she said, "I think Selena may just have the talent and abilities I've been looking for."

“Then congratulations Selena,” I stuck my hand out, “I can’t wait to see what else you’ll be able to-!”

“Thank you Alex!” she suddenly gave me and Vincent a hug, “You two don’t know what this means to me!”

“Easy sis, easy!” Vincent was still feeling sore.

“You’re welcome!” I smiled.

“Alex,” Jabari spoke, “I hate to interrupt you, but I believe we still have one foe left to face.”

“Oh you’re right!” I broke away from Selena, “Grandma! Jabari and I are going ahead! For some reason, Lancer is in OSC!”

“Wait for me!” Jabari ran after me.

“Be careful your highness!” Fukayna yelled out to Jabari.

“Lancer?” Selena asked, “Didn’t Alex mention him earlier?”

“That man was in the academy with Alex,” Caliandra said, “I never really liked him, but I never thought he would be responsible for this…”

Lancer and Zephyros had landed on the ground due to exhaustion to continue their fight. Zephyros had sustained a few cuts to his upper body and left arm and Lancer had about an equal amount of injuries.

“Lancer,” Zephyros began to ask, “Why has a man of your talent allied himself to OSC? I’m curious.”

“I’m afraid that’s none of your business, Prince Zephyros,” he said.

“It became my business the moment my uncle was assassinated!” Zephyros yelled, “I’ll get it out of you one way or another!”

"Lancer…!" Alfonso suddenly stepped out from a dark energy swell behind Lancer.

"Wha-" Lancer turned around, "Alfonso! What happened?!"

"He's here…" Alfonso weakly said, "They're coming…"

"He who?" Lancer asked, "They who?"

"Prince Alexander…" Alfonso paused, "…and Prince Jabari…"

"Prince Jabari of Rac' Sagadam?!" Lancer couldn't believe what he was hearing, "How?!"

"I'd like to know that myself," Zephyros thought to himself.

"Lancer!" I yelled out as I stopped beside Zephyros.

"Alex!" Zephyros was caught off guard, "You're all right!"

"Of course he is," Jabari stopped on the other side of Zephyros, "It was I who came to his aid."

"Jabari!" Zephyros yelled.

"The prince of Rac' Sagadam," Eleanore said.

"That's him…?" Karen gazed at Jabari, "He's Prince Jabari?"

"All three of you are here," Lancer took a step back, "Damn…"

"Lancer," Alfonso said, "The iron soldiers have fallen. A retreat has been ordered. We must go. You've got the crystal, so we need to hurry while we can…"

"Very well," Lancer looked back to us, "You may have stopped those iron soldiers, but I still got the Roc Soul Crystal. Next time you see us will be during Valsoria's fall!"

"Oh no you won't!" I stepped forward with my sword raised.

“Stay alive till then…” Lancer stepped into the darkness with Alfonso.

“Solar Shockwave!” my attack missed when they disappeared, “…damn…”

“Lancer…” Zephyros said, “What’s going on…?”

“Zephyros,” I called for his attention, “I didn’t know that you would be here.”

“Alex…Jabari…” he looked to both of us, “Well met, but I wish it were under better circumstances.”

“Milord,” Rachel grabbed him by the shoulders gently, “Let me get you somewhere inside so I can treat your wounds.”

“Yes, thank you,” he said, “Alexander and Jabari, please come with me. There is much we need to discuss.”

“Yeah I know,” I said, “I’m sorry they got away with the crystal.”

“We’ll worry about that later,” he said, “They won’t attack again so soon.”

We had all regrouped in a large room at the base of the clock tower where we had a chance to heal and have a small meal. Due to a request by Zephyros, Jabari, Eleanore, Karen, my grandmother, and I waited in a room separate from everyone else. In the next room, Zephyros, Fukayna, and Rachel were checking on Count Jacques's condition while we waited to hear how he was doing. Although we had attained a victory by warding off the invading soldiers, the mood in the room was uneasy and anxious. While we waited on Zephyros, I took the time to catch Jabari up on the events that happened since leaving Rac' Sagadam. Suddenly, he emerged from the room.

“How is he?” I was almost afraid of the answer.

“He passed out from loss of blood,” Zephyros said, “The doctors think he’ll make it, but it could be a while before he wakes up.”

“Thank goodness,” Eleanore said.

“What a relief,” Karen said.

“Now to the matter at hand,” Zephyros sat down at a table with me and Jabari, “I assume you’re both aware of my late uncle?”

“Yes,” I said, “Eleanore and my grandmother briefed me about it in Kaydra, and I was just telling Jabari.”

“I do not understand how anyone was able to get so close to him,” Jabari said, “Let alone past all of his guardsmen.”

“At first we suspected an underground plot within his territory to overthrow him,” Zephyros said, “But we found no evidence to prove such. We weren’t even sure if OSC were responsible at first. We didn’t expect anyone within their ranks to be capable of getting that close to him, but based on what our agents have been finding out, and on what I’ve seen today, I’ve concluded that they were responsible after all.”

“They must’ve been after the Roc Soul Crystal when they went after him,” I said, “It would make sense. There were times when they went after me after I left home.”

“Except…” Zephyros paused for a moment, “He didn’t have it in his possession.”

“Then why?” Jabari began to ask, “Why was he targeted?”

“The last time I was able to speak with him,” Zephyros began to explain, “He had informed me about OSC. They weren’t an immediate threat to Zylphan, but he said that much of their hostility has been in various places surrounding us and Valsoria. He had put together a small group of his best agents to figure out their motives and find their base of operations so we could take them down as swiftly and quietly as possible. Lancer…was one of those agents.”

"So he turned out to be a double agent?" I asked.

"I don't know if he was with them before or after my uncle assigned the job to him," Zephyros took a deep breath, "But he is apparently the enemy now."

"He must have been close to a breakthrough," Eleanore said, "He must've found out something important, and they needed to keep him from talking."

"He was a brave man," my grandmother said, "And a good friend."

"I made it to his side before he passed on," Zephyros said, "The last thing he said to me was 'Don't be taken in by the shadow of grief. When our world is threatened by evil and chaos, a defender of mankind must step forth…pierce through the blinding light…battle through the darkness…so the rising sun will shine another day…'

"The rising sun…" my grandmother said to herself.

"Alexander," he suddenly stood up.

"Y-yes?" I looked up.

"If your fight is with OSC, then I shall fight with you!" he declared.

"Your highness?" Eleanore looked a bit surprised.

"Let's unite our strengths together to put an end to this!" he said, "As the crown prince of Zylphan, you have my full support!"

"I will fight with you as well!" Jabari stood up, "We shall unite, and fight! They shall regret the day they made an enemy of Rac' Sagadam!"

"Alright!" a surge of confidence got me standing, "Then let this day be known as the beginning of the end for OSC! We'll bring down their ambitions and bring peace back to the land once again!"

"Lady Caliandra," Karen whispered to her, "What's happening?"

"What you're seeing is the birth of an epic alliance," she said, "And possibly…the beginnings of a prophecy…"

"For my uncle and justice…" Zephyros held his rapier over the table.

"For our people…" Jabari held his blade up with Zephyros's rapier.

"For everyone…" I held the Twilight Star with their blades.

"OSC shall fall and we shall triumph!"

Episode 34
Preparations for Battle

Under Zephyros's order, we were all provided rooms at Count Jacques's mansion. We decided to spend the next few days preparing ourselves for battle and discussing the intelligence we had managed to gather thus far. Everyone was finding ways to prepare in their own way through either training, buying items, or other means.

"Of all the rotten luck…" Keith paced down a street, "Now how am I gonna fight? Broken katana…broken Ninja Drive…besides one kunai I have left, I've got nothing to fight with now!"

"What's up?" Vincent caught up with Keith, "Weren't you going to go by the blacksmith?"

"I did," Keith turned around, "But he doesn't have anything I can use. All he's got are axes, broadswords, spears, and other common gear. Can you believe he didn't know what a katana is?"

"I didn't know till I saw yours," Vincent said.

"…well," Keith paused for a moment, "Well anyway he doesn't have one. And I guess now that I think about it, I shouldn't be surprised. Jentake does have a whole different culture after all."

"Could he forge you one? Or at least try to fix yours?" Vincent asked.

"Nah," Keith said, "He said he broke his hand not too long ago, so it'll be a while before he can forge anything."

"Hmm," Vincent thought for a moment, "Well if I can talk to him, I might be able to forge you one myself."

"You can?" Keith suddenly sounded optimistic, "Are you serious??"

"Yeah," Vincent said, "I'm the son of a blacksmith after all. It'll take at least a day for me to make, depending on the material he has for me to work with. C'mon."

"You got it!" Keith was excited.

Several minutes later, Vincent and Keith were inside the blacksmith's workshop with his permission. After getting the furnace going, they began looking at what they had to work with.

"Okay," Vincent pulled out several bricks of metal, "It looks like he mostly has steel alloys. A few of them feel like Damascus Steel."

"Is it going to matter which one you use?" Keith asked.

"Definitely," Vincent said, "Some alloys take longer to get melted down than others, and are harder to work with. Also the heavier the metal, the heavier the blade, and that can be a problem if there's a weight change you can't get use too fast enough."

"So how are we going to pick the right metal to use?" Keith asked.

"I've already separated the best five for something like this," Vincent said, "Now it's just a matter of you checking out which one you want."

"Alright then," Keith began weighing the bricks with his hands, "Hmm…no, not that one. Not this one either. Damn this is hard."

"No pressure or anything," Vincent said, "But if it helps you decide, try picking the one you could most likely trust with your fighting style, as well as your life."

"If he had some Astra Metal, that would be awesome," Keith said, "I'd get a little more speed and I wouldn't have to worry too much about it breaking."

"Well he's got Damascus Steel," Vincent said, "And that's just as strong."

"Yeah, but it's heavier," Keith paused for a moment, "If only…wait a second!"

"What's up?" Vincent asked.

"I got it!" Keith suddenly ran off, "I'll be right back!"

In Count Jacques's mansion, Zephyros, Jabari, and I were in the middle of a discussion about past encounters I've had with OSC. We sat at a table with several pieces of weaponry that were confiscated by the Miliga soldiers.

"And it was after leaving Gravadale when we first encountered one of their top commanders," I said.

"After all of their other strategies got foiled," Zephyros said, "They must've been getting worried that normal grunts and soldiers wouldn't be able to stop you. They got serious and tried to send one of their strongest against you."

"That's what I was thinking. Then we-" I was interrupted when Keith rushed through the door.

"Stop!" a guard suddenly confronted Keith, "This is a private meeting and-!"

"Hey Alex! Did you guys happen to pick up a-" Keith noticed a black piece of metal on the table, "Yes!"

"Keith! What are you-?" I tried to ask him before he picked up the metal.

"Sorry guys! I need this! Bye!" he ran out of the room as quickly as he came in.

"Um…what?" Jabari was baffled with confusion.

Back at the blacksmith workshop, Vincent was studying Keith's broken katana when he finally returned.

"This!" Keith tossed the metal piece to Vincent, "Catch!"

"This is…" Vincent tapped the metal with his finger, "Astra Metal?! Where'd you get this?!"

"It fell off Alfonso's armor after he got beat up by Jabari," Keith said, "Is there enough to make a katana with that?"

"Hmm," Vincent set the metal down, "There just might be! Alright! Help me finish making a mold for the new blade, and we'll get started!"

"You got it!" Keith quickly got to work.

The three Valkyries had gathered together to rest at the clock tower. All three of them sat on the roof top to oversee the city and relax.

"Did Prince Zephyros say when we were going to move out yet?" Eleanore looked up from her book.

"Not yet," Rachel laid back, "He, Prince Jabari, and Prince Alexander are still updating each other and discussing a course of action. It's been a while since they've all been together, so they must be spending some time catching up as well."

"Do we really have time to just sit around?" Eleanore asked.

"I don't know," Rachel said, "But I don't mind the downtime honestly. Besides, it's nice to see the prince in a more talkative mood."

"You've got a point," Eleanore said, "Ever since Count Marcus's passing, he's had a lot of trouble eating and sleeping. He wouldn't even practice his fencing. It was like he lost all of his motivation."

"He took it really hard," Rachel said, "But I think something finally got through to him when he heard that Alex was coming to Miliga with Lady Caliandra."

"What do you mean?" Eleanore asked.

"It was when the queen received Lady Caliandra's letter to her," she said, "He overheard the part where she mentioned Alex had left home to fight against OSC. Something about that must've sparked his spirit because he suddenly picked up his rapier and took off for Miliga. He took off so fast I almost didn't catch him."

"At least he finally stopped feeling sorry for himself and decided to do something," Eleanore bluntly said.

"Eleanore!" Rachel suddenly sat up, "You shouldn't say such things about the prince!"

"Well it's true," Eleanore leaned back, "I understand him being sad about his uncle's passing, but he can't mope around forever."

"Still…" Rachel looked to Karen who appeared to be daydreaming, "Karen? Is something wrong?"

"Huh?" she asked, "What happened?"

"You're unusually quiet," Eleanore raised an eyebrow.

"Oh I'm fine!" Karen held her hands up, "I was just thinking about the upcoming battle!"

"Oh really?" Eleanore sounded suspicious.

"Yes!" she stood up, "I felt so inspired after seeing the three princes unite like that! I can't wait to finally bring OSC to justice!"

"You sound ready," Rachel said.

"I am!" she clenched her fist, "After seeing what Prince Zephyros and Prince Alex can do, I can only imagine what Prince Jabari might be capable of!"

"So that's it," Rachel suddenly smiled.

"What's it?" Karen asked, "Why are you looking like that?"

"Does our little Karen have a crush on Prince Jabari?" Rachel teased her.

"Wha-no! No!" Karen waved her hands, "That's not it!"

"Prince Jabari?" Eleanore looked to Rachel, "I thought she had a crush on Prince Alexander."

"I don't!" Karen's face was turning red.

"Well it wouldn't work," Eleanore went back to her book.

"Why not?" Rachel asked.

"Yeah, why not?" Karen asked.

"So…" Eleanore glanced at Karen, "You DO have a crush on one of them?"

"No! Stop it milady!" Karen was growing frustrated.

Selena, my grandmother, Alyssa, Aiyana, Lady Lydia, and Lan sat at a table in Count Marcus's courtyard. Much of their time spent was discussing each other's abilities.

"The reason you had so much trouble developing your powers was because you were treating it as if it were the same as fire," my grandmother said, "Each of the six nature elements; earth, fire, wind, water, lightning, and ice, all have a different nature to them. Each one takes a different type of focus to harness its power. In our case, a more docile focus is needed just to get our bodies use to wielding its power, but once you get to know how well it can work for you, you'll soon find it much easier to use, and your casting and attacking will be much faster and stronger."

"I had no idea," Selena said, "Back at home, I was just trying to do what my brother did to bring it out. I didn't even notice that when I would use it to heal, it came to me much easier because I was much calmer."

"How did that even happen?" Aiyana asked, "You said that everyone in your family had the fire affinity, right?"

"They call that an Albino Occurrence," my grandmother said, "It happens when someone is born with a nature element that's completely different from their parents, or out of place with the region they're from. In Selena's case, it was both."

"Princess Nanu mentioned that when we were in Rac' Sagadam," Selena said, "She said it's very rare."

"Where we live," my grandmother said, "It's almost as rare as being born with the lightning affinity."

"Aside from standing out more, it doesn't make them any different from anyone else," Lady Lydia said, "They can master their powers and be just as strong as anyone else if not stronger. People with the Albino Occurrence usually have greater potential than the average person."

"Is that why your hair and eyes are pink?" Alyssa asked, "And why you're a Vanguard?"

"Yes princess," she said, "My parents both had the wind affinity, but I wasn't appointed a Vanguard simply for that reason. I had to work hard like everyone else, and it wasn't easy."

"Your healing abilities are amazing," Lan said, "How are you able to fight like a knight and use your affinity like a mage?"

"Well it helps that my equipment is made of Astra Metal," she said, "I mostly play a supportive role when I have to be deployed in battle, and when I'm not, I'm Princess Alyssa's body guard. You know, your abilities are pretty good for someone so young."

"T-thank you milady," Lan's face slightly turned red, "But I didn't do too much."

"Don't sell yourself short," she said, "I don't know if I would have been able to heal Count Jacques fast enough on my own. I'm sure you must've been a big help for Prince Alex."

"I hope I was," Lan looked down, "I don't like being a burden to anyone."

"You're so modest," she got up and took Lan's hand, "I don't know if you realize what you might be capable of. Come with me. I'd like to see what else you can do."

"Wha-really?" Lan struggled to fight against his shy nature.

"Will you be alright here princess?" she asked.

"Mmm hmm," Alyssa said, "I'll stay with Aiyana and watch Selena train."

"It is about time we get back to work," my grandmother said.

"Yes milady," she got up and brushed off her tunic.

"If you're going to be helping my grandson take down OSC once and for all, I want you in as best of shape as I can get you before they head out," she said.

"Yes milady," Selena said, "I won't let you down!"

While Selena and my grandmother resumed training, Sir Damien was already in the middle of sparring with Robert outside the city. Robert had just fallen flat on his back after being swept of his feet by Sir Damien's lance.

"Your form isn't bad for someone who has trained under my rival," he said, "But you could still use some work in keeping up your defenses."

"Well…" Robert leaned up, "How was I suppose to know you would sweep low like that?"

"You weren't!" he pulled him up, "A situation can change in the blink of an eye in battle, and you must react with lightning fast reflexes to adapt and ready yourself. You've seen my wild fighting style yesterday, correct?"

"I caught a glimpse of it after I woke up," Robert scratched his head, "The way you would leap off your horse and use your lance as a jumping pole to fight was incredible."

"I lack an affinity of my own, much like Prince Alexander," he said, "So I have to make up for it by using every resource I have available, and that sometimes means using my fighting talent in unconventional ways. Do you understand?"

"I think so," Robert said.

"Mind games are just a part of combat as the actual combat itself!" he said, "If you learn ways to keep your opponents always guessing, then you'll find yourself at a quick advantage against your enemies-especially against common enemy soldiers! Take your shield with a chain for example. It could possibly be your greatest asset once you learn how to maximize its use!"

"I never thought of it like that," Robert looked at his shield, "I just had it made like that so I could attack with a little range."

"That's good," he said, "But don't stop there! Continue looking for ways to maximize its usage! Alright, let's take a lunch break. My treat."

“Yes sir,” Robert said, “And thank you for training me.”

“You’re welcome,” he said, “I want you in top shape for our battle against OSC!”

Episode 35
Critical Decisions

While we continued to make preparations, my grandmother and I decided that it would be a good idea to send a letter to my mother by messenger bird. I believed we still had time before OSC made another move, but we felt that we should leave nothing to chance and warned my mother to be prepared for an attack at anytime. When she received the letter the following day, she held an emergency meeting with the five Vanguards that were still in Valsoria to explain the situation and plan for a course of action.

"And that is the situation we are in at this moment," she sat down at the table, "They plan to search out and attack their base of operations soon, but there's a chance that OSC may attack us between now and that time."

"At least we know why it's been so quiet," Claire said, "I thought they were slowly dying down, but they've just been preparing for a massive attack?"

"They probably stopped appearing near Valsoria on purpose to lure us into a false sense of security," a man with navy blue hair said.

"You're probably right, Jin," the vanguard with brown hair said, "I'm not so concerned about how many soldiers we may face. It's these things the prince described in his letter. The Iron Soldiers is what he called them?"

"Yes General Isaac," my mother answered, "My son says fighting one is like fighting a giant suit of armor. They haven't faced too many yet, but he says they are powerful and take a greater effort to bring down than the average warrior or knight would be capable of doing."

"Are they larger than me?" a heavily built man with a thick dark blue beard asked.

"I believe so, General Bruce," my mother said.

"Bwa ha ha!" General Bruce laughed, "You need not worry about these 'Iron Soldiers' my queen! I shall wall them with my defense and crush them!"

"You're certainly confident General Bruce," the youngest vanguard with light green hair said.

"Their weapons mean nothing to me, young Tobias!" he laughed, "If they truly wish to challenge Valsoria, then their Iron Soldiers shall meet *The Frozen Sentinel!*"

"Speaking of Sentinel," my mother cut in, "My son mentioned something of an Iron Sentinel that's basically a much larger version of the iron soldiers."

"How much larger?" General Isaac asked.

"I don't know," she said, "He hasn't actually seen it yet, but according to him, it dwarfs the iron soldiers."

"If the prince and his allies were able to defeat some of them, then I'm not too worried about the iron soldiers," General Isaac said, "But the way they can show up from nowhere, on top of these iron soldiers, is the problem. It makes it hard to be ready."

"I hate to put Valsoria in a panic after the past few days have been so calm," my mother said, "But I don't believe we can take any chances at this point."

"I agree," General Isaac said, "How would you have us prepare?"

"I want Valsoria to be on full alert," my mom ordered, "Strengthen the patrol around the city, and make sure all of the outer gates are shut by the time the sun has fully set. I want all knights to be ready to take arms at a moments noticc. OSC must not be allowed to catch us off guard!"

"Very well your highness," General Isaac said, "I shall coordinate our soldiers into taking shifts throughout the morning, day, and night."

"Very good," my mother said, "I will speak with the citizens at the palace circle in one hour. Tobias and Bruce, could you please spread the word as fast as you can? I want as many people possible to attend so I only have to speak directly about this once."

"It shall be done my queen!" Bruce said, "You take the east side Tobias! I'll take the west!"

"Very well sir," Tobias said.

"Agent Jin," my mother said, "How have our 'friends' in Volternia been behaving?"

"Nothing unusual as far as I can tell," he said, "The most I've seen lately was when Volternia's prince left home with an escort."

"I see," she said, "Well we'll worry about them another day. I feel that we may need you here at home, so I'm temporarily relieving you of your assignment until further notice."

"Very well," he nodded, "Your word is my mission."

"Thank you everyone," my mother stood up, "With all of your hard work, we shall continue to protect our kingdom from all who would harm it. I call this meeting to a close. Vanguards, dismissed!"

The five Vanguards stood at attention before breaking up to attend to their assignments. Claire, however, stayed with my mother who suddenly sat down with her head buried in her arms on the table.

"Something the matter your highness?" Claire asked.

“This wouldn’t be happening if my father were still alive,” she said, “I was prepared to rule through most of my life, but I never imagined how difficult it can be when suddenly I’m the one making the tough decisions.”

“I wouldn’t worry about it too much your highness?” Claire said, “I think you’ve been doing a great job so far.”

“You think so?” she asked.

“Of course,” Claire said, “Lady Caliandra wouldn’t have passed rule to you if she didn’t think you were ready. I’m sure the late King Raymond believes in you too. Even now, I believe he smiles down upon Valsoria when he sees how you handle things.”

“Yeah,” she cracked a smile, “I think his passing was just something I never got quite over.”

“He was a great man,” she put her hand on my mother’s shoulder, “And he had a great daughter and grandchildren whom he passed his strength onto. Do you remember what he use to say? ‘To bow to someone in power is to show full faith and trust to their leader. It’s the trust that through good times and bad, their leader will always strive to make the best decisions for his or her people.’ I wasn’t sure if I understood what he meant the first time I heard that, but now I do. Your people trust you with their lives, and they display that trust through bowing. We all trust the job you’re doing, and we will continue to stay with you through good times and bad.”

“Thank you Claire,” my mother stood up, “I think I feel a little better now.”

“Any time your highness,” she said, “If you’re ready, we should prepare for your address to the people.”

“Yes, I am,” she said, “Let’s go.”

Later that day, I had just wrapped up another meeting with Zephyros and Jabari when we left the mansion. Suddenly Zephyros stopped me for another quick word.

"I need to ask you something," he said.

"What is it?" I asked.

"Your companions you brought with you," he thought for a moment, "Do you think it would be a good idea for all of them to assist on the raid against OSC?"

"What do you mean?" I asked, "I'm sure we all can handle it together."

"They're all far more talented than the average person," Zephyros said, "But with the exception of Robert, and perhaps Keith, they don't exactly have any sort of military training."

"Well no," I said.

"I see where Zephyros is going with this," Jabari said, "And I must agree with him. Your friends are good, but they all may not be suited for this."

"You think we should have them stay out of the final fight?" I asked.

"I think it's something you need to consider," Zephyros said, "If we're going to be successful, we can't afford any mistakes, otherwise they could end up getting seriously hurt, or worse. You don't have to give an answer now, but think on it and get back to me later."

"Alright," I said, "I'll do that."

"Is it time for dinner yet?" Jabari asked Zephyros.

"It should be," he said, "Let's go before everyone is waiting on us."

While everyone else was making conversation at the dinner table, I found myself eating more slowly than usual. What Zephyros said had me thinking really hard. I understood his point of view on the matter, but it was hard for me to think of leaving anyone behind after all we've been through.

"Hey!" Vincent got my attention.

"Huh?" I asked.

"You gonna eat that?" he pointed to the steak on my plate.

"Y-yeah," I said.

"Something wrong?" Selena asked.

"Nah, I'm fine," I started eating.

"Hmm," my grandma paused for a moment, "Alex, you should come watch Selena train with me later this evening. I think you'll be amazed at how much she's improved. I think she might give YOU a run for your money."

"R-really?" I asked.

"What?!" Selena was a little stunned, "I don't know about THAT…"

"I'm serious," my grandma said, "You're more capable than you realize."

"I'm with Lady Cali," Vincent said, "It's like you were able to do all that your whole life and just didn't know it."

"Well what about you?" Selena changed the subject, "How's your training coming along?"

"Oh you know I'm not slacking around after everything that's happened," Vincent said, "I've been polishing up my moves as well. I was even able to forge some extra gear with the scrap metal. I'm so ready for this!"

"That new katana we forged is working wonders for me!" Keith said, "My attacks are faster and more precise than ever!"

"I feel well prepared as well," Robert said, "Sir Damien's training is incredible!"

"Well I'm not the Mad Lance for nothing!" Sir Damien said.

"I've learned some new skills from Lady Lydia as well," Lan said, "But I'm still having trouble focusing just the right amount of energy."

"You'll get it with time," Lydia said, "You're already proving to be a promising mage."

"Everyone's been working so hard…" thought to myself, "I don't want them to have done all that for nothing…but…"

"Hey Alex!" Keith called me, "You wanna spar after dinner? It's been a while since we've gone at it."

"Huh?" I looked up, "Say what?"

"Are you sure you're alright?" Keith asked, "You look really out of it."

"Sorry. I'm just feeling a little dizzy. Please excuse me everyone," I stood up and bowed my head before leaving.

"Alex?" Selena broke the brief silence in the room, "I wonder what's wrong…"

"Well," Vincent pulled my plate towards himself, "No use letting good food go to waste."

"How greedy…" Zephyros face palmed himself.

I stood by myself on the high west balcony of the mansion to try and clear my mind enough to make a decision. Even by myself, it was hard to concentrate.

"Ya know," I suddenly heard my grandma behind me, "Your grandfather would do the same thing you're doing now when something was troubling him."

"Grandma!" I jumped, "How long have you been standing there?"

"I think you should tell me what's on your mind," she said.

"Well…" I looked down to the marble floor, "Zephyros thinks we should leave most of my friends out of the final battle."

"Is that so?" she asked, "Did he say why?"

"He did," I answered, "And I understand his concern completely. It's just…"

"I'm listening," she sat at a table on the balcony.

"We've been through a lot since I started this journey, and we've gone through things that even military training can't prepare you for," I sat down, "And everyone's been working so hard to do their part to see this through. I don't want to see them get hurt during the raid, but I don't want all their work to go to waste either."

"So you're stuck between asking them to stay behind and jumping right into the danger?" she asked.

"Exactly," I said, "I didn't think a decision like this could be this hard."

"Just wait till you're the ruler of Central Kingdom," she gave a light laugh, "Then you'll really know hard decisions. It's something your mother still struggles with. She's never been very confident when it comes to political decisions."

"Well," I lifted my head up, "What do you think I should do?"

"Well to be honest," she said, "I'm not the one you should talk to about this."

"Wait, what?" I asked.

"The decision you're going to make will have an effect on a lot of lives, including theirs," she said, "So if you're going to make a life decision involving them, you should at least try and understand their feelings about it."

"You're saying I should hear what they have to say first?" I asked.

"Exactly," she said, "They seem to trust you a lot, and you trust them just as much. You won't have a problem deciding what to do once you talk with them."

"I hope so," I stood up, "I'll give it a shot. Wish me luck in making the right choice?"

"You'll hardly need it," she smiled, "But good luck."

"Thanks grandma," I left to go find everyone.

"He needn't worry," grandma thought to herself, "He's just going through some of the same things you went through Raymond."

It was sunset when I had gathered Selena, Vincent, Keith, Lan, Robert, and Aiyana together in the courtyard. Instead of telling them why I called them altogether, I wanted to talk to them all at once.

"So what's this all about?" Vincent asked, "I was about to get a little more training in before dark."

"Did something happen?" Selena asked.

"No. Nothing's happened," I said, "I just wanted a chance to talk to you all seriously for a moment."

"Oh," Keith asked, "About the raid on OSC?"

"Yeah," I said, "How did you know?"

"I kinda listened in on your conversation with Prince Zephyros and Jabari," he said, "That must've been what was troubling you at dinner today."

"Oh," I blinked, "So then you already know what this is about then."

"Wait, what?" Selena asked, "What's going on?"

"Well we were talking about the raid," I said, "Long story short, Zephyros wanted me to consider having some of you hang back."

"Hang back as in not join the fight?" Lan asked.

"What's up with that?!" Vincent yelled.

"Wait," I held my hand up, "He only suggested it because none of you, aside Robert and Keith, have any official military training. However…" I paused with my eyes closed.

"Yes?" Selena asked.

"He hasn't seen," I opened my eyes with a smile, "What I've seen. I know for a fact that I wouldn't be standing here right now if it wasn't for all of your hard work. Phoenix Volcano, Mirage Desert, the attack on Gravadale, the forest, against Francis, bandits, and even the attack on Miliga. There's not a single doubt in my mind that all of you were the reason I was able to come this far," I bowed my head, "So let me just take this moment to thank you all from the bottom of my heart."

"Dude…" Keith was nearly speechless.

"H-hang on now…" Vincent smiled, "Don't get all sappy on us. It ain't over yet."

"It's not sappy," Selena smiled with a tear in her eye, "I think its sweet…"

"After traveling with you, I can safely say that my assignment from Sir Rupert is no longer the driving motive for me," Robert said, "You are a brave man who is well worthy of leadership and respect."

"Don't worry about me," Aiyana said, "I want to help you see this through!"

"Me too," Lan said, "My power is yours to command as you see fit."

"Well…" I looked around to everyone, "I guess that answers my question. It wouldn't feel right without you all fighting by my side anyway. Still, this is going to be the toughest task we've ever done. I wish I could say we have a concrete plan, but we don't. However, when we do, we're going to have to follow it to the letter. We can't afford any mistakes, understand?"

"Yes sir!" everyone said in unison.

"You all sound ready," A voice spoke from behind a tree.

"What the," Keith recognized the voice, "That sounds like-"

"It is," he stepped from behind the tree.

"Victor!" Keith and Lan said in unison.

"It's good to see you all safe," Victor said, "I wish there was time to catch up, but since it appears you're ready to take on OSC, there's some things I need to let you in on, and not much time to do it. Please gather all who will be coordinating the raid and lend me your ears."

Episode 36

The Final Plan: Rescue and Raid!

We had all gathered in the conference room and listened carefully at Victor's information. He revealed to us that he had been previously targeted by OSC, that he began investigating their activities ever since he escaped them, and probably most importantly, the location of their base of operations.

"You mean it was right under our noses this whole time?" Zephyros asked.

"Yes," Victor said, "They have an underground base dug out at the ridge east here. Here's a map one of my agents sketched of their underground layout."

Victor unrolled a map on the table for all of us to see. Several rooms, including a very large one at the end of the hallways, were labeled and sketched on it.

"So those rooms are where their basic weaponry are built?" Zephyros pointed to two rooms adjacent to each other.

"And these rooms are their soldier's sleeping quarters," Jabari pointed to three larger rooms.

"What's this biggest room for?" I pointed to the one at the end.

"That room," Victor began to explain, "Is where their Iron Soldiers and Iron Sentinel are being constructed. Since my last report, they had 12 Soldiers complete."

"Wait," Vincent stopped Victor, "We gotta fight 12 Iron Soldiers?!"

"If you think that's bad," Victor paused, "The Iron Sentinel they're working on, is roughly as tall, if not taller, than this mansion."

A look of horror hit everyone's face when Victor said that. After trying to picture something that large, I finally broke the silence.

"Bigger than…this mansion?" my voice trembled, "We…we can't fight something like that."

"It will take everything we have just to bring down 12 Iron Soldiers!" Jabari said.

"If you can get to them all and destroy them before someone begins operating them, then there won't be a problem. The problem is, the moment you're discovered there, they'll begin manning them immediately. They may even begin their attack on Valsoria."

"How can they when they are so far away?" Jabari asked.

"Some of the soldiers were granted abilities to create dark vortexes by someone in the group that allows them to 'jump' long distances by walking through. That's how they were able to appear so quickly here and in Gravadale."

"Then they could launch an attack while we're trying to get there and we wouldn't even know it until it was too late," my grandma said.

"Even if we get there in time, how would we even begin to fight this Iron Sentinel?" Zephyros asked.

"There's no way to fight it straight on," Victor said, "It's so large, it requires multiple soldiers to control its movements and attacks. The only hope you have is that my agents are successful in rescuing OSC's captive that's responsible for designing all their weapons. Based on my information, he was targeted when they discovered he was working on advancing technology similar to how I work. If the Iron Sentinel gets going, he's your only hope to stopping it."

"Then we should not even allow them the chance to wield these weapons!" Jabari said, "Time is short! I suggest we prepare an immediate assault them before they have time to react!"

"I like the sound of that," Vincent said.

"We can't simply rush in without a plan," Zephyros said, "I agree time is short, but we won't be helping anyone if we rush in recklessly and get ourselves killed."

"He's right," Keith said to Vincent, "We may know where they are, but they're still going to have the home team advantage."

"We will have the element of surprise on our side!" Jabari protested, "If we hit them from all sides, they will either go down quickly or surrender!"

"And if they escape through those dark vortexes and begin and attack on Valsoria, then what?!" Zephyros countered, "Alex did send a letter to Valsoria to prepare for an attack at any time, but they're not going to know how to stop that Iron Sentinel if it's allowed to escape us!"

"Alex! We must attack now!" Jabari yelled to me.

"Not without a plan we don't!" Zephyros yelled to me.

"What's this long path here?" I pointed to the map.

"Wait, what?" Jabari and Zephyros looked to the map.

"That's an alternate secret passage that they created," Victor said, "From their base, it leads to an abandoned shack several hundred yards east of here. They created it whenever they needed to leave the base in a way that wouldn't give away their location. Their main way of entry is within the ridge."

"Hmm…" I stepped away from the table to think.

"Alex?" Jabari began to asked.

"What are you thinking?" Zephyros finished the question.

For a few moments, I stood silently in deep thought for a plan to come into view. Time was limited just as Jabari said, but we need to have a tactical approach just as Zephyros said. After a few moments, an idea lit up in my mind.

"I've got it," I snapped my fingers, "I think this can work."

"Well what's the idea?" Zephyros and Jabari asked.

"Gather around everyone," I stood to the table, "This plan will bring the best of our abilities and talents together."

This plan took about 10 minutes to fully explain and hammer out the details with everyone. Between Jabari, Zephyros, and I, we discussed and answered questions about the different roles each person would play for this attack. After some reassurance from my grandma, we were all feeling confident about this new strategy, and we were feeling pretty psyched about going through with it.

"I must say I approve of this idea," Zephyros said.

"As do I," Jabari said, "Well done my friend!"

"Thanks," I said, "We're going to need everyone on their toes, so let's all get some rest tonight. We begin the attack early tomorrow morning."

"Awesome!" Vincent said, "I'm so excited, I don't know if I'll be able to sleep now."

"Ha!" I laughed, "Well do your best."

“I shall adjust my plan to coincide with yours,” Victor said, “I’ll have my agents finish their rescue mission to be in time with your operation. Come with me for a moment Keith.”

“Alright,” Keith followed Victor out of the room.

Keith followed him to the abandoned house where Victor had met with one of his agents the other day where they waited on their arrival.

“I’m guessing that Felix is one of your agents?” Keith asked.

“You guessed it,” Victor answered, “He has an ability similar to what OSC uses to get around, so he’s been very effective. You’ve actually met the other one, though I’m surprised that you didn’t figure out who she was.”

“That girl that gave Vincent those fire knuckles and the one I tracked down?” Keith asked.

“Duh,” the female agent said from behind him.

“Woah!” Keith spun around, “Wait…are you kidding me?!”

“For a ninja, you sure had a hard time recognizing your own sister,” she said.

“Lyn?!” Keith was dumbfounded, “It was you this whole time! When did you even-?”

“I trained in secret with Victor and Felix,” she said, “Cause I figured you wouldn’t teach me.”

“That’s why you didn’t tell me?” Keith asked.

“Well part of it was so that no one would accidentally blow my cover,” she said, “But I just wanted to be helpful. I got tired of being the one getting rescued, so now I get to rescue someone.”

“Well…” Keith scratched his head, “You must’ve been doing a good job to get that close to OSC, but I still wish you two trusted me more to tell me at least that she was getting special training.”

“I was going to, but then OSC came after me and…yeah.” Victor said.

“It all worked out,” Felix stepped from the shadows, “So what’s the plan this time?”

“You are to go ahead with the rescue mission,” Victor said, “Prince Alex and his allies will be launching their attack tomorrow, so I want you to get him to safety just before it begins and make sure either Lady Caliandra or Prince Alex can speak with him. I did some research, and it turns out that the mark Lyn showed me is a Reaper Mark.”

“What’s that do?” Keith asked.

“It’s an evil mark that allows whoever placed it on a person to track wherever they go, and if they wish, kill them on the spot,” Victor said.

“Woah,” Keith said, “Is there a way to get rid of it?”

“I’ve read that someone with a divine affinity, either light or dark, can remove it,” Victor said, “It’s possible that Prince Alex could remove it with the Twilight Star’s power. Whatever we do, we gotta make sure it gets removed quickly, otherwise trying to get him to safety will be pointless.”

“Alright,” Lyn said, “You can count on me.”

“I’m counting on you too,” Keith said, “So make sure you two are successful.”

“I will,” Lyn smiled.

“Alex’s mission will start early in the morning,” Victor said, “So make sure you get a little head start on them.”

"Right," Lyn and Felix said.

I had just gotten ready for bed when I took one last look out of the east balcony. I wasn't quite sleepy enough to go to sleep, so I stood alone to meditate to myself.

"Tomorrow," I said to myself, "It all ends tomorrow."

"What a relief that'll be," Vincent leaned up against the balcony rail.

"You can't sleep either?" I asked.

"I can't either," Selena stood to the other side of me.

"They call this the calm before the storm," I said, "It's how the knights describe what it's like the day before a battle."

"Are you nervous?" Selena asked.

"I'd be lying if I said I wasn't," I said, "After everything we've gone through, we can't turn back now."

"I think we can do it," Selena said, "We're a lot stronger than we use to be, and you came up with a great plan earlier."

"Thanks," I said, "I'm glad Jabari and Zephyros both approved of it too. It's not often they agree on how to deal with situations like this."

"At least we know what we're going to do now," Vincent said, "What'll we do after this is all over?"

"Celebrate I'm sure," I said.

"Well yeah, but I mean what will there be left for us to do?" he asked.

"What do you mean?" I asked.

"I know where he's going with this," Selena said, "We all teamed up for the sake of stopping OSC, but once it's all over, there's nothing left to do."

"Are you kidding me?" I asked, "That won't be enough to stop us from hanging out together."

"Really?" Selena asked.

"Of course," I said, "I don't know what else we'll run into, but I'm sure there's a lot more out there for us to explore together."

"Well if things get calm, don't forget about us in Prominence town," Vincent said.

"Don't worry," I said, "You're both too great of friends to forget."

"You are too," Selena said, "Just make sure we win tomorrow."

"You got it," I said.

"I guess I'll try getting some sleep now," Vincent stretched, "See ya bright and early tomorrow."

"Me too," Selena said, "G'night."

"Good night," I said.

It was about an hour before sunrise when Lyn had infiltrated OSC's base and snuck her way down until she got to the room Zaalek was locked in. Without making a sound, she snuck in and found him lying face down on his bed. After shaking him a few time, she finally got him to awaken. Before he had a chance to speak, she immediately covered his mouth with her hand.

"Don't say a word, don't make a sound," she whispered, "We're getting out of here now."

Episode 37
Charge!!

Lyn and Zaalek quickly crept throughout the long and dark hallways in the final hour before day break. The more they tried to keep from making a sound, the longer the escape seemed to take. After reaching a corner at the end of a hallway, they stopped to rest for a brief moment and wait on Felix to arrive.

"Okay," Lyn carefully scanned the hallway they just ran down, "No one seems to have discovered us."

"I thought you were one of the good guys," Zaalek said, "You were working for Prince Alexander after all?"

"Not directly," she whispered, "At least I wasn't originally."

"Then what's going on?" he asked.

"In a few moments," Lyn looked around before finishing, "Alex and his allies will arrive here and begin an assault. We're bringing down OSC, and my orders are to get you out of here so you don't get caught in the crossfire."

"Are…you serious?" he couldn't believe what he was hearing.

"Yes," she said, "We're rendezvousing with a co-agent to escape any minute now."

"Y-you can't," a look of fear overcame him.

"Don't worry," she said, "We won't be caught so easily."

"It's not that," he pulled down the collar of his shirt, "See this mark? It's some type of curse someone put on me. They can find me with it no matter where I go, and if they want, they can kill me with it on the spot."

"I already know about that," she said.

"You do?" he was puzzled, "How?"

"I noticed it on you the last time I checked in on you," she said, "I had my boss check it out, and we know of a way to remove it."

"Then I really will be free…" he was almost speechless.

"Yes," she said, "That's why we must hurry before the one who placed that on you discovered us and-"

"I can't let you do that Lyn," Lancer approached from their destination.

"Oh no," Lyn grabbed the hilts of her katanas.

"Not that I miss the weakling, but I was beginning to get suspicious when Francis didn't return with you," Lancer unsheathed his rapier, "I'll give you a chance to return to your room like a good boy, Zaalek. You Lyn, however, won't escape with your life."

"Don't underestimate me," Lyn stepped between Zaalek and Lancer, "Or you just might regret it."

"Is she seriously going to fight him?" Zaalek thought to himself, "Didn't she say he gave her the creeps?"

"An interesting boast, but your defiance won't change a thing," Lancer lunged at Lyn, "Now perish-!"

Their blades were inches from meeting each other when Lancer suddenly disappeared into a vortex of darkness that vanished as quickly as it appeared.

"Wha…" Zaalek was nearly speechless, "What just happened?"

"Felix cut it too close," Lyn sheathed her katanas, "That's what."

“Sorry,” Felix stepped from the shadow on the wall, “I had to wait until he would literally run straight into it.”

“We have to hurry now,” Lyn said, “It won’t be long before he escapes and warns everyone.”

“Come on,” Felix opened another dark vortex, “They’re on their way right now.”

Just as the sky was beginning to brighten, an owl landed on Aiyana’s extended arm and fell into a trance once she placed her finger on its forehead. After releasing it, a mocking bird landed on her fingers and began communicating with her in the same way as the owl.

“The path to get to their main entrance is clear enough to approach,” Aiyana said, “Once you’re half way up the rocky path, you’ll begin running into guards. As long as you’re not discovered before then, you can get several soldiers into position in time for the attack. The abandoned shack is clear as well.”

“Alright,” I nodded, “Excellent work Aiyana. Jabari and Zephyros, are both of your groups ready?”

“Yes. We all shall get into position as quickly as possible and await the signal. Be safe my friends,” Jabari rode off ahead with his Sagadam warriors and a few Miliga soldiers.

“We’re ready too,” Zephyros said, “Let’s fly Valkyries.”

“Yes sir,” they began to take flight after Zephyros.

“Good luck Alex!” Karen waved before catching up to her group.

“Ok everyone,” I took off running, “Lets move!”

We made it to and inside the shack just before the sun began to peak over the horizon. Vincent, Keith, and Robert began searching through all the junk immediately until they discovered a door on the floor that lead to the underground path.

"Found it," Robert said.

"Yes!" I said.

"I hear someone coming!" Robert said.

"Get ready everyone," We all stood ready to fight.

"We made it," I recognized the voice on the other side of the door.

"It's Lyn!" I watched the door open.

"Alex! We made it," she hugged me immediately.

"To think that was Keith's sister the whole time," Vincent crossed his arms.

"We've brought the scientist," Felix helped Zaalek out of the hole.

"So *you're* the one responsible for all those new weapons and technology," I slowly approached Zaalek.

"Prince Alexander," Zaalek fell to his knees, "My designs…my ideas…I never meant for them to be used like this."

"I was briefed about your situation," I said, "We'll talk about all that later, but you're safe for now."

"Not yet," Lyn said, "There's a Reaper Mark here on his neck. Until it come off, the person who put that on him can find him wherever he goes or kill him on the spot. Can you use the Twilight Star to get it off?"

"A Reaper Mark?" I noticed the claw on his neck, "I've never heard of that before, but maybe I can do something about it. Hold still."

The ominous energy I felt from the Reaper Mark felt similar to the dark crystals I came across in the desert. I focused the Twilight Star's power directly on it and found an unusually powerful force trying to resist it. After giving one more strong pulse of energy to it, the mark suddenly burst into a black flame that quickly disappeared without leaving any burns!

"Ah!" the dark energy stunned me to the point where I fell to my knees, "That was strong…!"

"Are you alright?" Selena helped me up.

"Yeah," I said, "Thanks."

"It's gone?" Zaalek put his hand on his neck.

"All gone," I said.

"Ha…ha ha! I'm free!" Zaalek was in tears, "I can't believe after all this time I'm finally free-"

"Listen I'm really happy for you, and I'll let you finish," Felix cut Zaalek off, "But Prince Alex needs to get going before it's too late!"

"Oh no, that's right!" Lyn suddenly remembered.

"What happened?" Keith asked.

"It's Lancer!" Lyn said, "I don't know how he did it, but he discovered us when we were escaping!"

"No!" I couldn't believe my ears, "This is gonna mess everything up!"

"Not if you hurry," Felix said, "I trapped him within a dark vortex before he got a chance to attack, but I don't know how long it will hold him."

"Alright," I said, "Lyn, I want you and Felix to take Zaalek and meet up with Jabari at the planned rendezvous point. Worst case scenario, we may need to reach him quickly."

"Alright," Lyn said, "Do you have enough energy to get us there Felix?"

"Yeah," he opened up a dark vortex, "C'mon."

"Good luck Alex," Lyn stepped into the vortex after Felix and Zaalek.

"Follow me everyone!" I ran down the stairs of the secret passage.

Vincent and I kept the path lit as we ran at full speed. When the floor suddenly changed from dirt to a smooth surface, we all knew that we had made it to the base. We rounded each corner with caution until we came across what appeared to be the main hallway. I peeked around the corner to see several doors on either side of the main walk way, as well as over a dozen soldiers who looked to be preparing for battle and conversing with each other.

"Ready everyone?" I whispered.

"Let's do this," Keith popped his katana loose with his thumb.

"I'm ready," Robert prepared his sword and shield.

"Let's go," the crystals on Vincent's gauntlets began to shine.

"Ready when you are Alex," Selena began focusing her power.

"We've got your back," Lan raised his staff.

"Go for it," Aiyana set an arrow into her bow.

"Go!" I rushed around the corner, "Solar Shockwave!!"

My surprise attack quickly felled three soldiers and stunned several others as the rest began arming themselves to come my way. Keith and Robert quickly formed up beside me to form a wall while Aiyana and Lan supported us from behind with arrows and earth based skills. While we were in combat with the incoming soldiers, Selena and Vincent were each on one side of the hallway to enter each door we pushed passed and destroy everything in the room.

"W-what the-?!" three soldiers were caught off guard by Vincent's appearance.

"EAT IT!!!" Vincent lit the entire room up with fire, "That's one room down!"

The room Selena opened was stocked with unfamiliar weapons as well as some of the things we face before such as the flamethrower. She quickly filled the room with ice pillars that crushed and destroyed everything in the room.

"Sound the alarm!!" one OSC soldier yelled.

"It's too late for that!" Keith continued to carve his way through the incoming soldiers.

"Push them back!" I unleashed another Solar Shockwave and cut a hole in their offense, "We have to get all the way through!"

"You got it!" Robert threw his chain shield into the oncoming soldiers.

"We're all through with our part," Selena joined up with us.

"Then I'll give the signal," Aiyana began to concentrate her telepathic powers towards the outside.

"Let me take care of this," Vincent stepped towards the front, "Infernal Flash!"

Most of the soldiers left were consumed in the sudden burst of flames Vincent shot forth. The few that escaped began to fall back and scream for reinforcements as we began to pursue them deeper into the base.

Outside, above the base, an eagle was heard screeching loudly overhead. Jabari noticed that it was flying in an unusual way before ceasing its cry and flying off.

"Is that the signal Aiyana described?" Fukayna asked Jabari.

"Yes," Jabari smiled, "They made it through. Soldiers, prepare for battle!"

"Sir!" the Sagadam and Miliga soldiers followed Jabari's lead to a rocky clearing.

"They're moving into position," Zephyros watched from overhead, "Get ready!"

"At once, your highness!" the Valkyries flew over the soldiers to prepare a Valkyrie Waltz.

We pursued the fleeing soldiers down several corridors until we all ran into a very large room where over 60 OSC soldiers were waiting for us. We immediately stopped in our tracks and stood together to keep ourselves from getting surrounded at the door. I noticed a second level in the room where more soldiers stood on extended platforms from the walls with weapons at the ready.

"Hey…uh…how's it going guys?" Keith asked sarcastically.

"I uh…I hope we aren't interrupting anything," I carefully scanned the entire room of enemy soldiers.

"Oh no," one soldier said, "You're just in time for the party!"

"I love parties!" Vincent said, "Especially parties that involve people getting their ass whooped!"

"Then you're about to have a great time!" the soldiers began laughing, "Show no mercy boys!"

A sudden tremor interrupted our confrontation. Several more shocks shook the room until the ceiling began to warp and crack until it collapsed completely. Most of the soldiers were able to avoid the falling debris, but some were crushed by the falling rocks. Atop the hole, Jabari and several of the Sagadam and Miliga soldiers stood with weapons drawn and ready to attack.

"What the hell is going on?!" an OSC soldier asked.

"Soldiers of OSC," Jabari pointed his blade downward, "It is time for you to pay for your crimes! With your burial, your terror shall end! Prepare yourself!"

Episode 38
Disaster! A Fear Becomes Reality

Jabari was the first to descend from the ceiling with Zephyros and the Valkyries following after him in a black whirlwind. Jabari struck the floor with both of his blades that sent two fissures towards the soldiers on both sides of the room. As Eleanore, Karen, and Zephyros began to do battle with the soldiers on the second floor, Rachel created a large ice ramp for the other soldiers to slide down and join the battle. Throughout the chaos, Jabari and Zephyros were able to meet up with me after fighting their way through.

"We weren't late, were we?" Zephyros asked.

"Right on time," I said, "We're about to head deeper to find the Iron Soldiers."

"Valkyries!" Zephyros called out, "I'm going ahead! Continue assisting the troops to secure the base!"

"Very well," Eleanore ran her blade through one soldier and then another, "Be careful your highness!"

"We'll find you as soon as we're done!" Rachel casted Aether Sphere to heal the wounded allies.

I led my group deeper into the base and ran into a little resistance as we searched of the Iron Soldiers. Upon reaching a large set of double doors, Vincent blew them open and we all stormed the dimly lit room. Several yards in front of us were the 12 Iron Soldiers we were warned about, as well as something much larger behind them. A gargantuan version of the Iron Soldiers stood motionless in the background where chains were attached to it from the walls and ceiling. Metal walkways stretched out in front of it on several levels where soldiers must've been standing to build it.

"Is…is that it?" my eyes were wide with fear, "That's the Iron Sentinel?!"

"It must be," Keith said, "It puts the Iron Soldiers to shame!"

"No kidding," Vincent said, "How was building something like that even possible??"

"I don't know," I stepped forward, "But right now, I don't really care. Let's get started destroying these things before-"

"Look out!" Zephyros shoved me out of the way to parry the strike from a black rapier.

"Quick as ever!" Lancer jumped away from Zephyros.

"Damn!" I sat up from the floor, "It looks like he escaped Felix's trap."

"Give up Lancer!" Zephyros commanded, "It's all over!"

"Don't think you've won yet!" Lancer stood his ground, "The end result will be the same!"

"You're outnumbered!" I stood up, "You can't win against us now!"

"Is that a fact?" Alfonso appeared from behind a metal pillar.

"Alfonso," I glanced my eyes to the right.

"Gotta give you kids credit for coming this far," Alfonso raised two blades.

"You will not escape your death this time," Jabari walked in front of me to confront him.

"I think it's time for you to see exactly what you're all up against," Alfonso snapped his finger.

Suddenly the sound of metal grinding against each other echoed loudly throughout the entire room. All of a sudden, dust began to slide off the Iron Soldiers as they slowly began to come to life.

"This is bad," Keith jumped back, "They were ready to go this whole time!"

"Get ready!" I raised my sword.

Suddenly a larger sound shook the very foundations of the room. The sound of grinding metal rang throughout the entire room, and I looked up to realize the cause. The arms of the Iron Sentinel suddenly slammed themselves into the walls as if it were trying to make room for itself. Its very movements began to disrupt the entire base and caused it to begin crumbling around itself from the force of the Sentinel's power. What left me stunned with fear was when it let out the sound of a metallic roar.

"No…" Vincent's eyes were wide with shock, "NO!!"

"It's moving!!" Keith took a step back.

"We were too late!" Robert yelled.

"Behold the absolute strength of OSC!!" Lancer flew up to the top of the Iron Sentinel, "Everyone and everything that stand in our way shall be crushed by our power!!"

"You've been defeated!" Alfonso began to step back into a dark vortex as debris began to fall, "You all shall be buried within the ruins of the base, and we'll be free to accomplish our goal!"

"Stop you coward!" Jabari swung his blade at a disappearing Alfonso and missed.

"Alex!" Selena grabbed my arm, "Alex, snap out of it! We have to get out of here!!"

"R-right!" I snapped out of my trance, "Zephyros! Come on!!"

In the previous room, the battle with the OSC soldiers and our allies came to a halt when the entire base began to rumble and collapse on itself. Wasting no time, the surviving OSC soldiers fell back and disappeared into a cloud of darkness.

"What's happening?!" Karen looked around frantically.

"It feels like the base is collapsing!" Eleanore sheathed her blade, "All units evacuate immediately!!"

Our soldiers began scrambling for the nearest exits as fast as possible. Rachel, with the help of Eleanore and Karen, lifted those who were unable to run up through the collapsed ceiling with a strong whirlwind to safety.

"We have to find the prince immediately!" Rachel descended to the ground.

"Here they come!" Karen pointed to us emerging from the collapsing hallway.

"Help me get them all out!" Zephyros lifted off the ground while holding onto me and Jabari.

We made it out of the collapsing base just as the ground outside fully caved in. Zephryos, Jabari, and I scanned the area to do a quick headcount and make sure that no one was missing.

"Is everyone ok?" I asked.

"Somewhat," Vincent was holding his bleeding head, "I think a rock hit me on the way out."

"I'm a bit grazed by the debris, but otherwise ok," Keith stood up.

"Same here," Selena and the others said.

"Hold still," Lan began to heal Vincent's injury.

“Uh oh,” I felt a series of loud thuds, “We’re not through yet!”

Back behind us, the tremors began to get louder and louder as we all prepared to fight for our lives. Suddenly, I caught sight of a faint dark aura that appeared near the area where the Iron Soldiers and Sentinel should’ve been and suddenly disappeared. The entire ridge was suddenly eerily silent.

“Wait…” Vincent looked around, “What happened?”

“Aren’t they coming for us?” Keith asked.

“Don’t tell me…” I paused before running to the pile or rubble.

“Wait Alex!” Jabari and Zephyros followed me.

When we got to the site where the Iron Soldiers and Sentinel were, there was nothing there but twisted metal and broken glass. It was possible that the Iron Soldiers got buried, but the Sentinel was way too large. Only one thought came to mind, and it made me fall to my knees.

“No…” the Twilight Star revered back to its medallion form, “They got away…and they’re headed for Valsoria!!!”

At a small outpost that stood in the northwest and barely in sight of Valsoria, several knights kept watch over the area. It was a quiet morning, and the knight there were just finishing up their watch shift when they heard something from the northeastern direction.

“What the hell was that?” one knight looked and noticed a dark ominous looking fog, “What the hell IS that?!”

“Soldiers are gathering from the fog!” another knight looked through a telescope, “Are we under attack?!”

“Let me see!” Commander Tobias looked through and caught sight of the Iron Soldiers described to him, “Damn…that’s OSC alright!”

“How did they show up so quickly and so fast?!” one of the knights asked.

“Quick!” Tobias yelled throughout the outpost, “Someone launch a signal flare! All units prepare for battle! This is NOT a drill!”

Balls of fire shot from the top of the outpost seconds after Tobias’s order. Back in Valsoria, some patrolling knights on the city walls caught sight of the signal and immediately sounded the horns for battle. General Isaac was the first Vanguard in Valsoria to arrive at the northern gate from where he was able to get a view of the OSC army gathering in the hills further north.

“That dark cloud in the distance,” he took flight with fire in the form of wings on his back, “It’s definitely the enemy, but if they’re here, then…what happened to the prince?”

“General Isaac!” one of the knights on the gate began to inform him on the situation, “It appears that Commander Tobias in the northwest and General Bruce in the northeast are already preparing to intercept the enemy with their troops!”

“Orders sir?!” another knight asked.

“Seal and secure all points of entry to Valsoria!! I want all cavalry units mounted and ready to reinforce Commander Tobias and General Bruce on the double!!”

“SIR!!” the knights began to proceed with their orders.

Back in the palace, Lady Claire called out for my mother as she raced through the hallways. She finally found her on the north balcony where she stood in a light armor similar to what the valkyries wear while watching the situation unfold towards the north.

"Your highness!" Claire paused to catch her breath, "It's them…! It's OSC!"

"I was afraid of this," the queen said.

"General Isaac has already taken command in securing the city," she said.

"Very well," she said, "Come with me Claire. We must prepare ourselves to aid the knights at once."

"Yes your highness," she said, "But I can't help but worry about their sudden arrival. Wasn't the prince suppose to be going after them at their base?"

"He was…" she suddenly stopped.

"You don't think that they were too late in getting there…or…?" Claire was scared to finish her question.

"I don't know what happened…" the queen closed her eyes for a moment, "But my son is ok."

"Really?" she asked, "How do you know?"

"I'm not sure," she answered, "But I know he's alright. Let's hurry!"

Atop the hills, Alfonso stood at the front of the line of OSC soldiers ready to attack. The Iron Sentinel stood motionless in the back while the Iron Soldiers began their slow march towards the capital. Three each went to the two outposts to intercept the incoming knights.

"I was hoping we would appear a lot closer than this," Alfonso said, "It will take a while before the Iron Soldiers, let alone the Sentinel, can reach Valsoria."

"It can't be helped," Lancer said, "We exhausted the last of our dark crystals' energy just trying to get everyone here."

"How long do you think before the prince can catch up to us?" Alfonso asked.

"By the time he gets here, all that will await him are dead bodies and ruins of his home," Lancer laughed, "Soldiers! This is our day! March forward and march strong! Make Valsoria an example of what our power is capable of! Move out!!"

My friends had gathered where Jabari, Zephyros, and I stood where we explained to them that OSC had gotten away. We were almost at a loss to what to do.

"I am at a loss at what we can do," Jabari said.

"Even with the valkyrie's help, there's no way we could fly everyone there," Zephyros said.

"And even if we could," Eleanore said, "There's no way we could possibly fly fast enough with all of you."

"Wait!" I suddenly got an idea, "Felix! Where are you?!"

"Up here!" He stood at the top of a large rock.

"Is there any way you could use your power to take us all the way to Valsoria?!" I asked.

"ALL of you?!" Felix looked to the entire squad of soldiers, "I can get there, but I couldn't get all of you close enough. I could only take a few of you, and even then I'm going to be pushing it!"

"Damn!" I said to myself.

"If all of us can't go, then getting some of us there will be better than nothing," Zephyros said.

"But who should go?!" Jabari asked.

"Hmm," I thought for a moment, "I know! Felix! Grab Zaalek and get down here!"

"Alright!" Felix jumped down the other side of the rock and ran around with Zaalek in tow, "Here he is!"

"Ah!" Zaalek almost fell, "What's going on? Why do you need me?"

"We need your help," I said, "Some of us are going to Valsoria, but we need you to help us stop that Iron Sentinel! Is there any way?!"

"Well…" Zaalek thought for a moment, "Perhaps if we could get inside, we could get to its power source and stop it that way."

"I'm assuming the power source must be the Roc Soul Crystal?" Zephyros asked.

"Yes" Zaalek confirmed.

"Alright," I said, "Then we still have a chance! Felix! Take Jabari, Zephyros, Zaalek, and myself as close to Valsoria as you can get!"

"Just you five?!" Vincent protested, "Are you sure you can't squeeze in a few more Felix?!"

"Going that far with five might be too much," Felix said.

"Rachel! Fly to Miliga quickly and inform Lady Caliandra of the situation!" Zephyros ordered.

"At once!" she took of into the sky.

"Is everyone ready?" Felix stood with us.

"Yes," Jabari said.

"Of course," Zephyros said.

"Let's go!" I said.

"Here we go!" Felix began to focus his dark powers around us.

The dark aura that began to surround us began to blur my vision of everything around me. Everyone and everything around me seemed to be disappearing into darkness as they waved us off. As the aura disappeared, we disappeared with it and were on our way to Valsoria.

Episode 39

Valsoria's Desperate Stand! A Beacon of Hope!

All of the Valsorian Knights at the northern outposts had begun to engage the enemy in combat, but they were forced back by the march of the Iron Soldiers. Because of this, Valsoria's first line of defense had been broken and the bulk of the enemy soldiers made their way straight for the capital. The incoming reinforcements were able to intercept them halfway through and halt their charge almost completely, but they were constantly under pressure from the threat of the Iron Soldiers that would soon be upon them, let alone the Iron Sentinel that had just began its march towards Valsoria. At the northeast outpost, General Bruce stepped out into the battle in his heavily plated blue and silver armor wielding his large two handed axe called the Boreas Axe. Many of his troops were still holding off the invading soldiers when he slammed his axe into the ground and raised forth large spears of ice that shot in a straight line into the bulk of the invading soldiers and killed off 11 soldiers at once. The large wall of ice cut off a large wave of enemy soldiers that were coming in from their rear.

"General Bruce!" a Valsorian knight looked relieved, "You're here!"

"Bwa ha ha!" General Bruce raised his axe from the ground, "These enemy warriors are no threat to us! It's the Iron Soldiers that will be a challenge!"

"How can we stop them?" another knight asked.

"Those of you who are well armored are to follow me!" he ordered, "We must get closer to Commander Tobias's side to provide support! The rest of you keep the outpost secure and support the incoming cavalry from the capital. As for the Iron Soldiers, leave them to me! We shall not allow them to pass!"

"Sir!" 14 heavily armored knights with tall shields and axes formed up with General Bruce.

"Now then…" General Bruce brought his axe to his side.

Ice crystals began to spread all over the plates of General Bruce's armor until his entire suit of armor was frozen over with plates of ice that thickly layered his armor plating. His helmet then froze over most of his head and face until his eyes disappeared into the shadow of his Ice Armor. Each breath he took came out in the form of chilled condensing air.

"Prepare to meet the Frozen Sentinel…" his voice almost sounded sinister from his ice helm.

General Bruce lead the march towards the closest three Iron Soldiers with his most heavily armored knights providing him cover against most of the enemy soldiers. The few soldiers that did manage to get close to him found their weapons snapping like twigs against his armor. He continued to march as if he wasn't feeling a single blow land on him until he raised his axe and let loose a wide swing that cleared the immediate area around him and left nothing but several fallen enemy soldiers covered in ice shards and blood. The first Iron Soldier had then reached General Bruce and struck its large right arm on top of him which nearly dropped him to one knee.

"General!" one of the Valsorian Knights yelled.

"These things possess quite some strength," he tightened the grip on his axe, "It's not enough to stop me."

With one mighty swing, General Bruce stepped up and struck his axe all the way through the left side of the Iron Soldier. With its pilot dead on the inside, the Iron Soldier fell over to its right side with some assistance from General Bruce.

"Hold tight Tobias," he faced the remaining two Iron Soldiers coming his way, "We'll be there as soon as we can."

Commander Tobias's troops were completely forced back into the outpost from where they barricaded the door in a desperate attempt to keep the outpost from being broken into by the Iron Soldiers that had reached it. The door was reinforced by two large steel beams which easily kept the soldiers from breaking through, but it was slowly loosing strength against the Iron Soldier that continued to push against it. Tobias flew into the sky with two large packs of arrows on his back that he released in mid-air and carried within a whirlwind around him. From there, he shot them all down in a massive shower of arrows that impaled well over 50 soldiers, but only landed killing blows on about half of them.

"I thought I could take out more than that with my Upper Sky Air Raid!" Tobias began pulling arrows from his side quiver.

"Commander!" one of the knights yelled, "The doors are weakening!"

"Come on Bruce! Isaac! Someone!" Tobias began firing arrows into the crowd, "We can't hold them off at this rate!"

Lancer and Alfonso observed the battle from the very back of their lines with confident expressions on their faces. With each step the Iron Sentinel took, they grew more and more confident in their plan to succeed.

"It looks like the outpost to our right is about to fall," Alfonso said, "But it appears the one to our left is still holding its own somehow."

"It looks like one of the Vanguards has powered his way through two of the Iron Soldiers," Lancer said from above, "He must be the Frozen Sentinel I've heard about."

"Frozen Sentinel?" Alfonso laughed, "I'd like to see him go against the IRON Sentinel!"

"You may not get the chance," Lancer said, "Vanguard or not, he'll be worn down soon."

"You think we should jump in yet?" Alfonso asked.

"There's no need at this point," Lancer said, "They will do all the hard work for us."

General Isaac led the fight at the front lines against the soldiers that had broken past the outpost defenses. The best they were able to do was keep the enemy soldiers from advancing any further. The few knights with an earth affinity were able to raise pillars of earth to assist the knights with tall shields that were holding the front line steady. The Iron Soldiers hadn't reached them yet, but with each pressing moment, time was running out.

"Sir! We can't get through to aid commander Tobias!" a sub-commander yelled, "We're barely able to hold our own line!"

"Muster all the power you can to fight through!" General Isaac ordered, "I shall do what I can to the Iron Soldiers!"

General Isaac's body was suddenly cloaked in a whirlwind of fire that flowed to his back and split outward into a set of wings which allowed him to take flight above the fighting. From there, he held his two handed Phoenix Sword upward and began focusing his power into it. It steadily grew brighter and brighter in the sky as the fires that surrounded it burned more intensely with each passing second. His strongest attack was ready, and he set his sights on the Iron Soldiers in the distance.

“Those who would bring harm to Valsoria shall be burned to ashes!” he suspended his sword above his head in a cloak of fire, “May your sins be cleansed in fire! Burning Blade Strike!!”

General Isaac hurled his flaming sword straight into the thick of the invading army and scored a direct hit on the lead Iron Soldier. The resulting explosion shook the entire land and completely obliterated the targeted Iron Soldier, along with a large number of enemy soldiers that were scorched to death.

“General Isaac landed a direct hit!” Claire watched the battle with my mom on top of the city wall.

“Excellent!” my mom gripped her blue edged rapier tightly, “This is an example of the power Valsoria uses to defend itself from its enemies.”

“If he can keep that up, he won’t have any trouble destroying the rest of them!” Claire said.

“That Iron Sentinel is too large for him to face alone,” my mom looked at the Iron Sentinel as if it were staring back at her, “And it’s about to pass the outpost line.”

“Everyone’s fighting as hard as they can,” Claire said, “But they can’t get through to assist General Bruce and Commander Tobias. How can we even stop something that big?”

“I’m not sure if even my mom would have the power to stop something like that,” she said, “Maybe if Lady Lydia were here and we had some powerful earth mages we could possibly try to bog it down. There must be something else I can do though. If only I had the Twilight Star with me…”

While praise for General Isaac’s attack was well earned, it clearly wasn’t cause for celebration just yet. The remaining five Iron Soldiers that survived the explosion continued to march through the fire. They had barely taken noticeable damage from Isaac’s distance. He stayed suspended in the air while trying to catch his breath from the last attack. With each step the Iron Sentinel took from behind the lead Iron Soldiers, he grew more and more concerned at how they would be able to stop such a thing.

“If only it were as strong as my dad’s,” he said to himself, “Then I would feel better about trying to attack that Sentinel…”

Tobias continued to provide as much support from the air as he could, but his arrow supply was quickly diminishing. As if that weren’t bad enough, enemy soldiers began targeting him with flamethrowers and arrows of their own to get him out of the sky. He was finally forced back to the safety of the outpost where his knights struggled to hold the door together.

“Bruce! Isaac!” Tobias thought to himself as he stood with his troops, “We need your help now!”

“Commander!” one of the knights at the door yelled, “We can’t hold it back any more!”

“Get ready guys,” Tobias readied two arrows into his bow, “This may be our last fight. When that door falls, we will make them remember the name of the Valsorian Knights!”

“C-commander?” one of the knights sounded scared.

“It’s been an honor to serve with all of you,” Tobias said, “Will you see this battle till the end with me?”

“Y-yes sir!” several knights readied their weapons alongside Tobias.

Nearly overcome with anticipation, all other noises from the battle became deaf to them except for the pounding the steel doors continued to take. Each pounding the doors took made the knights hearts rise further and further up their throats until all pounding suddenly stopped. The knights remained unflinching as they awaited the doors to finally be broken through, but nothing happened after a few moments of waiting. Tobias tilted his head slowly to peek through the cracks of the door, but was temporarily blinded by a sudden flash of light. The knight’s eyes were wide with shock when they heard the sounds of screaming soldiers and metal being cut apart and ripped to shreds. A sudden explosion blew the doors down completely which threw all the knights off their feet and caught the attention of my mother, General Isaac, General Bruce Lancer, and Alfonso.

“No!” Claire nearly dropped her staff, “Tobias’s outpost!”

“This can’t be happening…” my mom took a step back.

“TOBIAS!!!” General Isaac yelled.

“No!” General Bruce downed four soldiers with a violent swing, “I couldn’t make it…!”

"Ha!" Alfonso laughed, "That's one down!"

"Hmm," Lancer grinned.

Tobias and his knights were stunned, but quickly rose to their feet to do battle with the enemy soldiers. However, none appeared from the cloud of dust, and left them all wondering what just happened.

"Is everyone ok?" A slim figure wielding a rapier asked.

"I believe we have made it with no time to spare," a muscular figure wielding dual blades said.

"W-who the hell…?" Tobias began to ask.

"Commander Tobias!" a light began to glow on a figure standing between the other two, "I need the help of you and all others that are still able to fight right now!"

"Y-…your highness?!" Tobias almost couldn't believe his eyes.

"Can you still fly?" I asked.

"Y-yes!" Tobias said, "What do you need?"

"Listen everyone!" I said, "If we don't act soon, the Iron Sentinel will reach Valsoria before we can stop it! We need help getting up and inside it so we can take it down!"

"I can carry both of them with a current of air, but we need cover to get close enough," Zephyros said.

"You all go without me…" Felix said, "I need to rest for a bit…"

"Thank you for getting us this far," Jabari said, "Thanks to you, we now have a chance to win this day!"

"Is everyone ready?" I asked.

"On your word!" Tobias and the other knights stood straight up.

"Then prepare yourselves!" I ran to the outside.

I took the Twilight Star and raised it upward and it quickly took the form of a sword. The pulse of light it emitted as its energies flowed through my body could be seen throughout the entire battlefield.

"That light…" Claire couldn't believe what she was seeing, "You're highness!"

"No way!" my mom quickly recognized the light.

"The Twilight Star…?!" General Isaac was motionless in the air.

"Could it be…?!" General Bruce stood motionless as soldiers aimlessly broke their weapons against his armor.

"There's no way!" Alfonso said.

"You've got to be kidding me!" Lancer unsheathed his rapier, "Come on!"

"Valsoria will not fall to evil!" I held my sword up high, "Fight on so we may continue to see the rise of a new day! CHARGE!!"

With a restored valor, Tobias and the Valsorian Knights fought twice as hard with us as we pushed our way directly to the Iron Sentinel. My eyes were focused on reaching the Iron Sentinel and nothing else going on around me. At about 50 yards away from it, Alfonso appeared directly in my path to hold us off. Jabari dashed in front of me to intercept him and locked him into close combat to allow us through.

"Why?!" Alfonso found himself being pushed back, "It's not even your country! Why are you fighting so hard against us?!"

"I have said it before," Jabari parried his attacks, "An enemy of my friends is an enemy of mine!!

We were about 20 yards away when Zephyros and Tobias pulled me and Zaalek into the air on a wind current. As we flew upward, Lancer descended swiftly directly at us with the intent to kill in his eyes. Zephyros dashed in front of us and intercepted him with such an aggressive nature that it nearly caught Lancer off guard.

"Damn you all!!" Lancer fought desperately to parry Zephyros's attacks, "Why can't you all just surrender to our might?!"

"My uncle would never forgive me for one!" Zephyros continued to attack, "And I'll never surrender when my friends need me!"

Tobias circled Zaalek and I around the back side of the Iron Sentinel where we found what looked like a doorway inside. Using the Twilight Star, I slashed away at it several times until it was loose enough for us to pull open.

"Alright!" I stepped inside with Zaalek, "Thank you Tobias!"

"Good luck your highness!" he flew off to rejoin the battle.

"Ok," I turned to Zaalek, "Lead the way to its power source!"

"Of course," he said, "Follow me."

Episode 40
Everything on the Line!

Zaalek and I navigated our way through the dark, noisy, and hot interior of the Iron Sentinel as fast as we could. With each stomp it took, we fought for balance as we climbed one of the main steel beams that gave it support as if it were a giant metal spine.

"And the Roc Soul Crystal is all the way at the-woah!" I was nearly thrown off balance by a sudden shock, "…top?"

"Yes," Zaalek said below me, "But it's not the only crystal powering the Iron Sentinel. There are several throughout the Iron Sentinel that help provide and regulate power."

"Do we have to get them all?" I pulled myself up on a platform.

"No," he climbed up with me, "If we can remove the Roc Soul Crystal from where it's implanted, the Iron Sentinel will begin to loose power quickly and stop altogether. But it's being controlled by several soldiers, and you'll have to get past them to get to the crystal."

"How many are there?" I asked.

"At least five altogether," he said, "Three should be in the main control area, while the other two are elsewhere to make sure things run smoothly."

"Hey!" a soldier yelled from behind, "How'd you two get in here?!"

Without answering or giving it a second thought, I struck him with a Solar Shockwave that bounced him into the metal walls of the Iron Sentinel before he fell to his death in a lower part of the Sentinel.

"Well," I took a deep breath, "That's one down."

“Woah…!” Zaalek’s eyes were wide with shock.

“If we weren’t pressed for time, I’d like to hear how all this was possible,” I said, “But right now I just want to destroy this thing so I can get down and help with the rest of the Iron Soldiers.”

“You shouldn’t have to worry about them,” Zaalek said, “They shouldn’t be a threat much longer.”

“What are you talking about?” I asked.

“In the Iron Soldiers…actually, in just about everything they forced me to build them,” Zaalek began to explain, “I purposely built a flaw in their weapons.”

“How-” I was interrupted by a sudden rumble, “Actually, just explain it on the way!”

Outside, Valsoria continued to battle against the enemy soldiers by holding a defensive line. General Bruce and Commander Tobias’s forces had managed to join up just before the Iron Sentinel passed by both outposts and marched directly for Valsoria. To prevent the second wave of soldiers from reaching the main force, General Bruce slammed the head of his axe into the ground and raised a wall of ice spires to completely cut them off. From there, General Bruce and Commander Tobias’s forces were able to completely wall the incoming reinforcements.

“So Prince Alexander has entered the Iron Sentinel to stop it from the inside you say?” General Bruce cut down two more soldiers in one swing.

“Yeah!” Tobias fired off arrows into the crowd of soldiers.

"Then we shall do what we can here by routing as many enemy soldiers as possible," General Bruce rested his axe on the ground, "And we shall trust the prince to stop the Sentinel in time."

"There still are a lot for us to face with the numbers we have," Tobias turned around to fire arrows into soldiers breaking away from the main force to help the second wave, "Not to mention that some of the other soldiers are coming back this way!"

A sudden wind blew from the north with an icy chill that made the hairs on their neck stand straight up. Out of nowhere, a long spear of ice in the shape of an arrow suddenly struck the ground in front of the reinforcements coming from the main army which was soon followed by several more that began striking many of the incoming soldiers from both sides of General Bruce and Tobias.

"Ahh! Where are these ice spikes coming from?" Tobias looked to the sky and saw a blue armored valkyrie flying overhead with a glowing short spear in her hands, "G-general…? I think an angel just came to save us."

"That's not an angel," General Bruce recognized her armor, "That's a Zylphan Valkyrie!"

"A Valkyrie huh?" Tobias flew upward to meet her, "Thanks for the save, but what's a beauty like you doing on the battlefield?"

"And you are?" Rachel asked.

"I'm none other than Tobias," he bowed in mid-air, "Valsoria's 'Silver Sniper'! And who might you be?"

"I am Rachel," she said, "Valkyrie of the Northern Wind. I'm here to provide whatever assistance I can to our allies."

"Then you're just in time to assist me," he tried smooth talk her with his eyes shut, "And perhaps after the battle we can get together for dinner and-" he stopped when he realized she had disappeared from his sight, "H-hey! Where'd ya go?"

Among all the chaos, Jabari and Alfonso's duel was quickly coming to an end. Even after his armor was repaired, Alfonso was quickly being worn down and torn apart by Jabari's unyielding assault. With a double rising slash, Jabari tore into the side of his armor which lifted him off the ground and threw him several yards away.

"This…can't be…" Alfonso coughed up blood as he laid face up on the ground, "…happening!"

"Say a final prayer quickly," Jabari closed in on him, "Your time is up."

"Commander Alfonso!" seven enemy soldiers suddenly surrounded Jabari, "We'll get him for you!"

"Are you going to be so cowardly as to gang up against me?" Jabari readied himself.

"You're the one…who should say…a final prayer…" Alfonso stood on one knee and tried to heal himself.

As the soldiers prepared to pounce on Jabari, a whirlwind of fire descended from the sky and caught four of the soldiers immediately as it passed through them. A second burning wind descended down like a bending spear and struck the remaining three at once which left Jabari clear to attack.

"W-what…?!" Alfonso couldn't believe what he just saw.

"Where did that come from?" Jabari looked to find a red armored valkyrie in the sky.

"I didn't mean to interrupt anything," Karen descended down, "But you looked like you might've needed some help."

"It was much appreciated!" Jabari bowed his head, "Many thanks to you!"

"You're welcome your highness," she gave a cheery smile, "But where are Prince Zephyros and Prince Alex?"

"Zephyros is battling against Lancer as we speak, and Alex has entered the Iron Sentinel to stop it from the inside."

"Alright!" she sounded excited, "Then I'm off to rejoin Lady Eleanore. Good luck to you!"

"And to you as well," Jabari said and then turned to Alfonso, "Now I trust you are done with that final prayer?"

Alfonso stood motionless with fear when Jabari faced him. It was as if something greater than Jabari was staring into his soul which made him hesitate to attack. After summoning all the strength he had left, he went into a blind rage and attacked Jabari with everything he had. Jabari blocked and dodged each swing and thrust effortlessly until he decided it was time to put him out of his misery. Jabari swung around his final swing and threw him into the ground where he struck him with his Tomb Blade Strike with such force that it buried him almost completely on the spot. All that was above the surface was his hand that twitched weakly before it finally came to rest.

"May your soul be judged with mercy," Jabari turned his back on Alfonso's grave, "For real this time."

"Wow," Karen watched the events from high in the sky, "He's so powerful it's almost scary."

"Karen!" Rachel found her, "Where is Eleanore?"

"She's gone to find the prince," she answered, "I was just about to go catch up with her."

"We should do what we can for Valsoria first," Rachel said, "Between their abilities, they should be fine without us for a little while."

Throughout most of Lancer's fight against Zephyros, he struggled to keep an advantage over him with each clash they made in the sky. Lancer's power seemed to be weakening much faster than before, whereas Zephyros managed to keep a steady pace throughout the duel.

"You're not so tough without the Roc Soul Crystal aiding your power," Zephyros held his guard up.

"I don't need it to bring you down!" Lancer's arm was bleeding, "You could never defeat me before, and you won't defeat me now! That much won't change!"

"Is that right?" Zephyros asked.

"That's right!" Lancer's anger was growing, "Before I kill you, I'll make you watch as the Iron Sentinel destroys Valsoria. Even if he does have the Twilight Star, Alex won't stop it in time!"

"You're about to lose this fight, and here are two reasons why;" Zephyros calmly sheathed his rapier, "Your arrogance has blinded you to the point where you can't see what Alexander has done."

"He's done nothing but get in the way!!" Lancer dove straight at Zephyros with his rapier ready to strike.

"The other reason you're loosing this fight is…" Zephyros closed his eyes.

In an instant that went almost unseen, Lancer was intercepted by a dark blur that struck him hard and left a large gash on his back. Zephyros casually moved out of the way as he fell to the ground with a loud thud and remained there with barely any movement at all. When he slowly regained consciousness, he noticed several black feathers floating down from the air.

"You let your guard down," Zephyros descended down to Lancer.

"That…was for Count Jaques," Eleanore stood above Lancer.

"Thanks Eleanore," Zephyros landed beside her.

"It was nothing," Eleanore said, "But the blow wasn't leathal."

"That's alright," Zephyros said, "There are some questions I have for him, and he won't be dieing until they're answered."

"It doesn't…matter if I…tell you anything…" Lancer said, "The Iron Sentinel and Soldiers…have nearly made it…to the city. I may be down…but Valsoria is doomed…"

"It's up to you Alex," Zephyros watched the Iron Sentinel march closer to Valsoria, "You can do it."

Zaalek and I finally made it to the control room of the Iron Sentinel where I quickly took care of the three soldiers within. The one soldier we missed tried to sneak up on us and Zaalek barely avoided the swing of a large blade. When it got stuck into the side of the door, I quickly rushed him with a thrust to the chest and kicked him down into the deeper parts of the Sentinel. When we looked around in the center of the room, I found what we came looking for. The Roc Soul Crystal was sitting in a strange metal system where strips of metal and wires ran from the crystal and ran out from the control room to the rest of the Sentinel.

"This is the system you were talking about?" I asked.

"The general idea of it, yes," he answered, "My idea was to create a way for people without an affinity to use any nature element within a crystal. I promise you I didn't intend for it to be used like this."

"I believe you," I said, "But I hope you don't mind that I have to destroy this thing."

"Not at all," he said, "I was hoping these things would destroy themselves after the flaw I built into all their weapons."

"You said that's why the Gale Force Amplifier blew up on Francis's arm right?" I asked.

"Yes," he looked out the window of the control room, "And as to why the Iron Soldiers are about to reach their limit."

When some of the Iron Soldiers reached General Isaac's forces, OSC's main force began to gain momentum as Isaac's forces were being forced back closer to the city walls. General Isaac had managed to down a second Iron Soldier with his attack, but was forced to come to the ground when his power began to weaken.

"General Isaac!" a knight rushed to his aid.

"I'm fine," he held his hand out.

"The enemy forces are pushing through!" he said, "We can't hold the line at this rate!"

"All units fall back and regroup near the castle!" General Isaac ordered.

As the Valsorian Knights began to break away from combat to regroup, they all stopped and turned back around when they heard a loud cracking sound. One of the Iron

Soldiers had ceased all movement and was sparking from the joints of its shoulders. Its left arm soon blew apart from the body and the entire thing collapsed to the ground in an explosion.

"What the hell?" General Isaac was confused, "Did someone do that?"

"No sir!" a knight answered, "It sparked and exploded on its own!"

"Did you see that your highness?!" Claire asked.

"I did!" my mom answered, "But what exactly just happened?!"

A second Iron Soldier suddenly began smoking which forced the soldier inside to evacuate before its interior caught on fire.

"What the hell is going on?!" an OSC commander yelled, "Why are the Iron Soldiers falling apart?!"

I watched the events unfold from the window of the Iron Sentinel. The remaining two Iron Soldiers suddenly collapsed in a similar fashion to the others. The sudden loss of power suddenly shifted the tide in Valsoria's favor, and they were able to launch a counter attack against the soldiers.

"That's what you were talking about!" I said, "Then why didn't that happen in Gravadale and Miliga?"

"My guess is that they weren't put under as much stress there as they were here," Zaalek answered, "Basically, the way the flaw works is by redirecting a small portion of the energy back to the crystals which would cause too much power to build up for the system to handle, and the result would be what you just saw."

"So why didn't that happen up here?" I asked.

“My guess is that the Roc Soul Crystal is able to handle the excess energy being directed to it, Zaalek explained, “Unlike normal crystals, the Roc Soul Crystal seems limitless in the amount of energy it can handle.”

“Well we’re here now, so we can stop it manually,” I said.

I gave two quick slashes at the control system to loosen the Roc Soul Crystal from its set and pulled it out as hard as I could. Once free, it radiated a bright light that filled the entire room and could be seen from outside the window. After a few rumbles and loud noises of metal grinding to a halt, the Iron Sentinel slowly and finally came to a stop just outside the capital. With the Iron Sentinel standing motionless, the fight quickly came to an end when OSC saw their final trump card stand lifeless, which left the remaining enemy soldiers no choice but to surrender where they stood.

“We made it?” I looked out the window.

The Iron Sentinel stood less than 20 yards from the northern gate. All of Valsoria was in an uproar of cheer and excitement that I could hear from here. Many of the knights were throwing their helms in the air celebrate our victory.

“This battle is over,” the ice on General Bruce’s armor began cracking and falling off, “Valsoria is saved! Bwa ha ha ha!”

“That was WAY too close, but the prince pulled through!” Tobias crossed his arms.

“Well done my friend,” Jabari held one blade over his shoulder.

“Excellent Alex,” Zephyros shielded his eyes from the sun, “With this final act, OSC is finished.”

“Queen Adelyne! Victory is ours!” General Isaac held his sword high.

"It's over…" my mom fell to her knees, "Oh thank the Twilight Star's spirit it's all over…!"

"Finally it's all over," I collapsed to the floor, "I almost wasn't sure when this day would come."

"I know how you feel," Zaalek said, "I was beginning to give up hope that I would ever be free again. I wasn't sure this day would come either."

"Well…" I watched the Roc Soul Crystal react to the Twilight Star, "I guess there's nothing left to do now but clean things up here and return the crystal to Zephyros. He and his family will be glad to have it back in safe keeping, and to be honest, I will to."

A sudden shake inside the Iron Sentinel forced the both of us to our feet. Outside, sparks could be seen flying from its joints and smoke began to vent out of the right shoulder.

"Wait! What's happening?!" I fought for balance, "Didn't we stop it?!"

"Oh no!" Zaalek seemed to realize something.

"Why'd you just say 'oh no'?!" I was almost scared to hear his answer.

"R-r-remember w-w-when I s-s-said the Roc Soul Crystal was r-r-resisting the built in f-f-flaw?!" Zaalek began to explain, "The excess energy m-m-must've build up in the other c-c-crystals!"

"W-w-what are you s-s-saying?!" I held onto something as the Sentinel's weight shifted back and forth.

Outside, the knights began running for their lives in fear that the Iron Sentinel could collapse on top of them at any moment. The left elbow of the Iron Sentinel suddenly exploded which left part of its left arm to fall to the ground.

"All units retreat and take cover!" General Isaac ordered.

"General Isaac!!!" my mother yelled out to him, "I never saw my son escape the Sentinel!! He's still inside!!"

"What?!" he turned back to the Sentinel with a look of horror on his face.

"We have to get him out of there before it's too late!!" Zephyros flew at top speed with Eleanore.

"Hurry Zephyros!" Jabari called out to him.

From the inside, I cut open a new way out that put us right onto the right shoulder of the Sentinel. The supports in the knees began to blow and the Sentinel began to shift and fall under its own weight.

"Alex!!" Zephyros called from the air, "Jump!!"

"C'mon Zaalek! We have to jump!" I tried to pull him off with me.

"Are you kidding me?!" Zaalek was fighting against me.

"NO!!" I answered back.

With one final pull, I jumped out and away from the Sentinel with Zaalek as hard as I could. Just as the arm began to blow off completely, Zephyros and Eleanore caught both of us in an air current that pulled us away from the flying debris and took us straight behind the northern wall where my mother, Jabari, and many of the knights had taken cover. One final explosion rocked the entire city with a shockwave that shattered glass in nearby houses and caused severe damage to parts of the north wall. Everything finally calmed down when the last pieces of debris fell to the ground and everything was silence around us. Now…it was over.

Episode 41
The Light of a New Day

"Is…is that it?" I was one of the first to rise to my feet, "Are we finally done?"

"It looks that way," Zephyros said, "Is everyone alright?!"

"Yes," Jabari sheathed his blades, "It seems that we are finally done."

"Well mom…" I stepped to her side.

"Son…?" she responded.

"I know I put you through a scare," I smiled, "But it's finally over. We won."

Without saying a word, my mom gave me the tightest hug I could ever remember getting from anyone, and everyone in Valsoria responded with cheers and praise the echoed throughout the city.

"Wee!!" Karen shot upwards in a burst of fire, "We won! We won! We WON!!"

"K-karen!" Eleanore called out, "I know you're excited, but try to control yourself!"

"Oh let her be," Rachel put her hand on Eleanore's shoulder, "She's done really well today."

"THIS…IS…OUR DAY!!!" Jabari let out a jackal sounding war cry.

"Damn Jabari!" Zephyros jumped back, "What was that?!"

"It is the war cry of Rac' Sagadam!" he answered, "Try it!"

"I think I'll pass…" Zephyros politely refused.

Many of the knights spent much of the day clearing the battlefield of wreckage and bodies while others helped the wounded get back to the city for Claire to begin mending their wounds with help from my mom and other healers. Other knights checked over much of the northern part of the city to survey the damage and help any civilians that were caught by any flying debris. A great chunk of the northern wall was destroyed as well as several of the houses that were built close to it. Other buildings further away had holes torn in their roofs and walls broken down from the falling scrap metal of the Iron Sentinel.

"How's the overall damage?" General Isaac asked Tobias.

"Well the good news is that none of the citizens were seriously hurt," he answered, "But the structural damage is pretty bad. Aside that big hole in the northern wall, a lot of houses either need serious repairs, or need to be rebuilt altogether. It's going to be a while before everything is fixed up."

"I see," General Isaac turned to General Bruce, "Are all knights accounted for?"

"It gives me deep sorrow to tell you no," he solemnly answered, "As of now, seven of our finest have given their lives for us, and depending on the seriousness of some of the survivors' injuries, that number may rise."

"Even if it were only one, I feel like that would be one too many," General Isaac took a deep breath, "Get their names so that I may inform their families. I'll inform the queen and we will arrange a proper funeral."

"Right," General Bruce nodded his head and left.

"Damn…!" Tobias punched a half broken tree, "If I were just a little quicker, I may have been able to save at least some of them!"

"Don't blame yourself Tobias," General Isaac put his hand on his shoulder for comfort, "When they were sworn in as knights, they took on the full responsibilities and consequences that come with being in service."

"I just wish I could have done a little more, you know?" Tobias turned to Isaac, "I know a Vanguard probably shouldn't act like this, but I feel like I let them down when the pressure was on."

"These men died with honor," he said, "They gave their lives for the sake that Valsoria will live to see another day. There's nothing you can do about what's happened, but if you really don't want to let them down, then we all must work harder to make sure their deaths are not in vain. We must continue to carry on their will, their courage, and strength to make a better tomorrow. Do you understand?"

"Yes..." Tobias paused for a moment, "I understand, sir."

"Good," he said, "Then let's continue with the rebuild and recovery operation."

"Right," Tobias nodded.

The injured were gathered together in the northern street where my mother stood in the middle as she used her Soothing Mist Wave to begin treating everyone's wounds around her. A faint blue mist poured from her staff like a fog that surrounded everyone within a 15 yard radius of her. Claire assisted the other doctors by patching them up with bandages and giving medicines for their aches and pains.

"Knights of Valsoria," my mother addressed them as she healed, "I cannot even begin to thank you enough for all the hard work and sacrifices you make for our kingdom. This day could not have been won without a single one of you."

"It's my honor to serve you..." a knight tried to sit up, "Gah!"

"Careful!" Claire warned him, "You'll tear your wounds open!"

"I can take it," he said, "It's just a flesh wound."

"I'm starting to feel better all ready," a knight with his left arm wrapped up in cloth stood up, "I'll be fine after a day's rest or two."

"Provided you don't get yourself plastered tonight," another knight laughed.

"Depends on how much you're buyin'!" he laughed with him.

"There will be plenty of time for celebration when you're able to walk on your own two feet," my mom said, "For now, focus on recovering."

"Yes your highness," he paused, "It's a shame that Sir Damien couldn't make it here with the prince. We may have had a slightly easier time with The Mad Lance raging across the battlefield."

"Maybe," Claire sat on her knees, "He and Lydia would have been a great help. I hope they, the princess, and Lady Caliandra are fine."

"I'm sure they are," my mother said, "But I'll feel a lot better when they return."

"How long before they get here?" a knight asked.

"They were in Miliga the last I heard from them," my mother answered, "So I don't see them getting here until a day's time at the least."

"Then how did the prince get here so fast?" a knight asked.

"From what I understand, he, Prince Jabari, and Prince Zephyros were all brought here by an ally using a power similar to what we saw bring OSC here," Claire answered.

"It's strange," another knight began to speak, "But once I saw them appear and charge the battlefield, it was like I was able to push myself to fight twice as hard."

"It was inspiring to see royals from different nations fighting together for a common cause," a knight sat up.

"I think it may have inspired me a bit too," my mother thought to herself.

Several hours had passed after all the injured were taken home. Up on parts of the northern wall that still stood, I found Zaalek sitting and staring out into the battlefield as if he were in a deep meditative trance.

"Here you are," I stood over him.

"All of this…" Zaalek stared at what was left of the Iron Sentinel, "All of this because of one revolutionary idea I wanted to start."

"To make it possible for anyone to use a nature element," I said "And it resulted into everything that's happened."

"Yes," Zaalek held his head down, "I had no idea that something like this would happen. I came up with the idea and invention almost a year ago, when I was living within Volternia's borders. I tried to publish the paper I wrote on it there, but the Volternian royals wouldn't allow it. They confiscated the paper and everything I had worked on and locked it away. They even went so far as to have guards inspect my house almost everyday to make sure I never began work on it again."

"They wanted to silence the very thought of such a thing," I said, "Given Volternia's history, I'm surprised they didn't execute you."

"They warned that I would be if I ever began research again," he said.

"So how did OSC find out about it?" I asked, "And how did they find out about you?"

"As far as I could tell, someone found and stole it from Volternia's vault," he said, "Then they kidnapped me and I was forced to build weapons based on the research I had done. Whoever found it must've really saw potential in my idea, only it was the wrong kind of potential. They made me design everything from the flamethrowers you faced in the forest to the Iron Soldiers and Sentinel, and other weapons that luckily got destroyed by your group before they had a chance to be used."

"Were you responsible for those artificial crystals I found embedded in those monsters we fought in the desert?" I asked.

"Yes," he said, "I was doing research in growing artificial crystals that were void of any power and that could be infused with any element, including the divine elements of light and darkness. They worked well enough with nature elements, but only one element could be in a crystal at a time, and it could only hold so much. It was the one bit of research that I was allowed to do under Volternia's watch because they deemed it worthless because the abilities that one could do with an artificial crystal were limited."

"Then…" I thought for a moment, "That's why Alfonso was able to absorb Vincent's fire attack."

"That's right," he said, "But it didn't work as well with light and darkness, though I can only remember working with darkness for the time I was with them. Anyway, they proved to be much more unstable in small sizes, and the few that were able to hold its shape and power would deplete itself after so long. The ones planted in the monsters you fought were a result of their failed experiments. They wanted to be able to control a beast at will with its power, but the dark energies warped their minds and bodies to the point where they were uncontrollable. When they went to cast them out, they saw an opportunity to kill two birds with one stone. I heard the leaders talk about keeping Rac' Sagadam from being able to help Valsoria in order for their plan to succeed, so they released the monsters all around there in hopes that they would cause so much destruction that they would be unable to even leave the desert, let alone assist another kingdom under attack."

"That's exactly what happened for a while," I said.

"So…what's going to happen to me?" Zaalek asked.

"What do you mean?" I asked.

"It was my research and desire for a revolution that ended up causing so much pain for you and countless others," he said, "I feel greatly responsible for what's happened."

"Well…" I paused for a while to think about everything that's happened, "Your fate isn't up to me at this point. You're at the mercy of Valsoria's queen. That actually brings me to why I've come out here. She requests your audience in order to speak with you about your role in OSC."

"Oh…" Zaalek sounded scared, "Is she…?"

"Just speak truthfully and clearly to her," I said, "I can't guess what she will say. I'll be taking you to her now."

"Very well," Zaalek stood up to walk with me.

"You know…" I turned back around to look at all the damage.

"Huh?" he stopped.

"I'm not a fan of Volternia in any way, nor do I like how they do things there," I gave a serious look to Zaalek, "But despite their ways, I think they may have been right in censoring your research."

"Wait, what?" Zaalek sounded stunned.

"Before I met you, I met someone else that did something similar to what you were doing, but on a much smaller scale. It wasn't anything with growing crystals, just creating new ways to use real ones. I didn't think much of the idea at first because nothing he did had any big effect, but after everything that's happened, making it easier for anyone to wield an element may not be such a great idea at all. The easier it is to obtain power, the easier it would be for that kind of power to fall into the wrong hands."

"But why??" Zaalek asked, "Where I was from, people felt so powerless because they weren't born with an affinity. Anyone else that had one could just walk right over us and do what they wanted! You can't possibly understand how that feels!"

"I can understand more than you think," I calmly said, "There aren't many people that try to walk over me because I'm a prince, but I was born without an affinity too."

"Y-...you?" Zaalek couldn't believe it, "But you have the-"

"Twilight Star?" I cut him off, "I wasn't able to use it till a few years ago, and even then, I really didn't know much of what I could do with it until after this adventure. I admit prior to me receiving it from my mom that there were times I felt weak, especially when I was on my own in the academy in Miliga. Jabari, Zephyros, Lancer, Elaine- everyone there were able to do things I could never do. Being at the low end of the class made me feel terrible, and almost worthless as a prince at times."

"But," Zaalek paused, "Social status aside, are you saying that without the Twilight Star that you're powerless?"

"Well..." I looked to the sky, "If you asked me that a year ago I would have said yes, but now, I don't think so. I've learned a lot since receiving the Twilight Star, and much of it was probably during my fight against OSC. There were times I used it, and there were times I didn't, and even though the situations were different, I managed to do just as well without it, so I guess the short answer to your question is that I would be weaker, but not completely powerless. Besides, even with the Twilight Star, it's not like I could have done any of this alone. The friends and allies I've made throughout everything are who really made the difference in my success today, and I believe-no, I know they will make a big difference in my future."

"I…I didn't know that you…" Zaalek tried to speak.

"Come on," I suddenly started walking, "We shouldn't keep the queen waiting much longer."

"Alright," he followed me.

My mother and the Vanguards were all assembled in the courtroom when Zaalek and I arrived. I felt like we walked into a heated discussion because as soon as I opened the doors to the courtroom, everything suddenly grew silent and all eyes were on Zaalek.

"Is he the one?" my mom asked me.

"Yes," I answered.

"Step forward," she ordered Zaalek.

Without a word, he slowly walked to the middle of the room where he was ordered to stop. I felt an unusual tension in the room when no one said anything after a few moments.

"Should I stay?" I asked, "Or is there anything else I should do?"

"No son," she smiled, "You've done far more than I could ask you to do today. Go get some rest. I'll call for you if something comes up."

"Alright," I nodded and left the room.

I've never been happier to return to my room and plop down face first on my bed. After everything had settled down, I found myself to be a lot more exhausted than I realized. Just before my eyes completely shut from fatigue, a small chickadee flew into my room and landed right beside my face.

"Huh…?" I was too exhausted to move, "Wait…Aiyana must have sent you to check on us…?"

As if it understood what I was saying, it sung a short melody as it flapped its short wings around.

"Well…I don't know if you can understand me…" I spoke to it, "But…just tell Aiyana…that we're all fine…and that…I…"

My body simply wouldn't allow me to finish my message. I passed out in mid sentence and remained asleep until very early the next morning. After cleaning myself up, I met Jabari and Zephyros in the main hallway of the palace from where we left to await the arrival of my grandmother and everyone else at the north gate with my mother, Lady Claire, General Isaac, General Bruce, Felix, Zaalek, and the valkyries. Aiyana was the first to rise over the horizon on a large hawk, followed by Sir Damien who scaled over the horizon on horseback with my grandmother riding with him, and Lady Lydia riding with Alyssa.

"There they are!" Karen waved from the air.

Damien, my grandma, Lydia, and Alyssa were the first to make it to us and dismount just as everyone else were running down the hill.

"Adelyne! Alex!" my grandmother ran to give us both a hug.

"Mommy!" Alyssa jumped into the family group hug.

"Mom! Alyssa! I'm so glad to have you both home!" my mom was in tears of joy.

"Well done!" grandma praised me and my mom, "I'm so proud of both of you!"

"Welcome back home," General Isaac addressed Sir Damien and Lady Lydia, "I'm glad to see your safe return."

"Sir!" they both stood at attention.

"After you both get some rest, we will need your help in keeping Valsoria secure while we repair all the damage caused by OSC," General Bruce said.

"I apologize for not being able to assist in the battle to defend Valsoria," Sir Damien said.

"It couldn't be helped, so don't give it a second thought," he said.

"Very well," he took Lady Claire's hand and knelt, "And I apologize to you if I have caused you any worry."

"Damien…" her cheeks were flushed with red.

"Prince Jabari!" Fukayna and several of Jabari's warriors rode in on chariot.

"Warriors of Rac' Sagadam! Are you all accounted for?" Jabari asked.

"A few of us sustained injuries that prevented all of us from arriving, but we are all well," Fukayna answered.

"It was nothing we could not handle…" a Sagadam warrior wielding katars said.

"Alex!" Vincent and Selena jumped off one of the chariots.

"We did it!" the three of us gave each other a hug.

"Oh, why did I have to miss it?! Vincent threw his arms in the air.

"I'm sorry, but OSC didn't want to wait around to see your wrath," I laughed.

“Aiyana told us that you were passing out by the time her messenger got to you,” Selena said.

“That little chickadee!” I turned to Aiyana, “I knew you must have sent it!”

“Uh huh! You can really snore when you’re tired!” Aiyana laughed.

“Well it looks like everything will be back to normal soon,” Keith said to Felix.

“Yeah,” he nodded, “Our mission is over.”

“Can we stay in Valsoria for a little while?” Lyn asked, “It’s been so long since we’ve had a chance to visit!”

“And I want a chance to check out Valsoria’s library!” Lan said.

“I guess we can hang out for a few days,” Keith said.

“And I would like permission to rest here before returning to Gravadale,” Robert said.

“None of you are going anywhere until we all celebrate our victory!” I said.

“All right! Party in Valsoria!” Vincent was the first to march into the city.

With Vincent leading the way, we all marched into Valsoria singing random melodies and telling each other about the final battle. Zaalek lagged behind and stopped to think to himself for a moment.

“So…what could I do here?” Zaalek said to himself.

“Hey Zaalek!” I ran back to him, “Aren’t you coming? You’re invited too!”

“Oh!” he broke away from his thoughts, “Of course!”

“So what did my mom say to you?” I asked.

"Basically the same thing you said," he answered, "She's not against advancing our technology and knowledge, but she doesn't want anything being created that could potentially fall into the wrong hands and be used for war, but there is good news for me."

"And what's that?" I asked.

"Queen Adelyne will allow me to take up residence in Valsoria and allow my research to continue to a certain extent. She said as long as I don't create anything even remotely close to something that would give someone too easy access to power, she is fine with me trying to create something to make our lives better."

"That's great! In that case, you should get along fine with a family of alchemists that live here. Welcome to Valsoria!" I held my hand out to him.

"Prince Alexander…" he paused before shaking my hand, "I never knew royals could be so kind before meeting you. Thank you, and everyone, for everything!"

While we ran to rejoin the group, Eleanore had pulled Zephyros off to the side to speak with him in private about some troubling information they got out of interrogating Lancer.

"Do you believe we should inform the queen about what we found out?" she asked.

"Well, we don't know for sure," he said, "So I'd rather not raise an alarm over a rumor. Still, the idea that Lancer was actually taking orders from someone else worries me."

"Then how shall we proceed with this information," she asked.

"Have you told the other valkyries?" he asked.

"No," she said, "Not even Rachel."

“Keep it that way for now,” he said, “If more information surfaces, we’ll inform them immediately and begin an investigation, but for now, let’s just join the party.”

“Very well your highness,” she walked with him to rejoin us.

Elsewhere, in a small town, a man walked through the streets covered in a black cloak that completely covered him all over and held his face in a permanent shadow from the hood. As he casually walked through the market place to blend in, he began to think to himself:

“So that’s Valsoria’s current strength. And more importantly, that’s the current strength of the carrier of the Twilight Star...”

To Be Continued…

www.ingramcontent.com/pod-product-compliance
Lightning Source LLC
Chambersburg PA
CBHW070642310726
48982CB00001B/380
* 9 7 8 0 9 8 3 4 1 5 2 1 3 *